DEATH ON THE MOUNTAIN ROAD

William Simpson

DEDICATION

I dedicate this story to Cathy, my wife of fifty-eight years. We met when she was fifteen and I started going out with her when she was sixteen and I was just twenty. I dedicate it to her, because she didn't knock me back when she knew I couldn't read properly and was hopeless at spelling.

JOAN MEETS STEVE

Joan Kenwright was from a wealthy family. There was her dad, John, and her younger sister, Emma. Her mother died when she was four and her sister was two. Also living with them was a lady named Sandra. She came to look after the girls a couple of weeks after their mother's death, when they were still babies. She moved in with them and had a room in the large, detached house.

Their father was struggling to keep his firm going because he was struggling with the girls, who he said were more important than his business. When a close friend saw that he wasn't managing the firm or the girls too well, he had a word with him and said he should hire the nanny, named Sandra, who used to look after his children up to last year. He told John that he was still in touch with her, and she was thinking of leaving the nanny job she was in currently because they treated her like a slave and had no respect for her as a nanny. He gave her a great reference, took her to meet John and left them to it.

When John interviewed Sandra, he took a liking to her right away. He hired her on the spot and asked her to act like a mother would, but to also let the children know their mother was in heaven and was looking down on them.

Sandra was still single. She was thirty-two and a lovely-looking woman. In her younger days she had had her fair share of handsome men, but she had never wanted to spend the rest of her life with any of them. She loved being with children, and when she left college at eighteen her parents wanted her to go to university, but instead she spent three years getting the qualifications to become an excellent nanny.

When Sandra met the girls, she fell in love with them straight away and after a short time she thought of them as her own. The girls were a little unsure of her at first, but she knew all the nursery rhymes, children's stories, and the games to play with them, and it wasn't long before she won them round. They grew to love her. Joan started calling her 'San', and Emma just copied her. As they got older, they both hoped their dad would marry San. However, through the years, though their dad and Sandra thought a lot of each other, their relationship was just platonic - though all the family's friends thought San and their dad acted like an old married couple, because when it came to a disagreement about the girls it was their dad who lost most of the time.

When they were born their dad gave them shares in his business and the dividend went into a trust till they were twenty-five, because he didn't want them to have any worries about money till they were old enough to use it wisely. He also tried to explain to them how business worked, he would let them look at the books and even sit in on meetings he had with some of the directors.

Both the girls did well in school and their dad wanted them both to go to university. While Emma was clever, she didn't want to go to university. She was interested in cooking and wanted to become a chef. She left school at sixteen and went to train in a restaurant with a famous chef her father was friends with. Joan was the cleverer of the two and she wanted to go to university. She got her wish and now she was in her first year.

When Joan bumped into Steve Thomson, she was at a party on the university grounds. As she was passing him, carrying her drink and one for her newfound friend named Patricia - who Joan shared a room with, she tripped. As she tried to save herself, she knocked into Steve and the drink she was carrying spilt over his arm. Her face went red and she apologised right away, saying, 'Sorry! If you take your jacket off, I'll get it cleaned tomorrow for you.'

He just laughed and said, 'You didn't need to baptise me. If you want to get to know me, just ask my name.'

He put his drink down on a small table that he and some students were standing round, talking.

Then he held out his hand saying, 'I'm Steve Thomson. We haven't met, have we?'

She shook his hand, saying, 'I'm awful sorry and I *will* get it cleaned for you.'

'Don't bother. It's an old jacket,' he answered. 'I was going to get rid of it anyway, but now I will keep it because it helped me bump into you - or should I say, you bump into me. And may I say, it's my pleasure. It's not often that I get a beautiful lady to fall for me.'

Then he pointed to a couple of chairs in the corner of the room. Still holding her hand gently, he led her to the chairs.

He said, as he gestured with his now-free hand for her to sit on a chair, 'Well, you know my name and I would love to know yours because you've just captured my heart.' With a big grin, he sat down beside her.

She shyly acknowledged, with her face burning, 'I'm Joan Kenwright. I've only been here three weeks. I'm in my first year and I really only know my roommate Patricia, because I was ill during Freshers week.'

Steve smiled at her and said, 'I was wondering why I hadn't seen such a lovely girl like you before now. I'm in my final year. What are you here to study?'

Joan, getting over her embarrassment, answered, 'I've come to study a joint degree in Business and Spanish. What are you studying?'

Steve spoke to her in Spanish. 'I'm studying Business and Spanish too! I am pretty good at it, even if I do say so myself. If you want, we can meet in the library and study Spanish. I'll help you with it.'

Joan was particularly good at Spanish, as she had been learning it since she was only five, so answered him in perfect Spanish. 'Yes. That will be great. What time can you make it? And afterwards, could you show me round the university, as I'm still not sure where everything is?'

He was so surprised at how well she spoke the language that he said, in English, 'My God, you could give me lessons - I think you could even give the professor who takes us for it a run for his money... and he's Spanish!' Then he grinned and continued, 'It will be my pleasure to show you round the old buildings and we mustn't forget the great pubs where we can study the different spirits.'

Joan's face went red, and she looked down at the floor as she was pleased but a little bit embarrassed at what he had said about her Spanish.

Then he said in Spanish, 'I can make it at three o'clock. Will that be alright with you?'

She nodded and they both carried on speaking in Spanish the rest of the evening.

Steve asked, 'Have you got a part-time job? It helps to keep body and soul together.'

She didn't tell him about her dad's business, instead saying, 'I sometimes work in an office near where I live. Have you got one?'

He frowned and said, 'I had a part-time job I loved in an old people's home, but they fired me.

They said it was my fault an old man off the second floor died; I thought I was helping him and his wife. He asked me if I could get him some Viagra, so I got him some and gave it to him just outside their room. He took it straight away and then I opened the door for him, and he said it's working and rushed in. I left them to it; later that day the boss called me to the office and said I caused his death.'

Steve had a sad look on his face and went quiet. He took his handkerchief out of his coat pocket, wiped his eyes and then put it away

Joan could see tears in his eyes and didn't know what to say at first. Then she summoned up the courage and said, 'If he had a heart attack, it wasn't your fault.'

Steve looked at her, and in a serious tone, he said, 'He didn't have a heart attack.'

Joan looked puzzled and asked, 'Well, what happened if he didn't have a heart attack? And how can it be your fault?'

Steve, still looking serious, claimed, 'When I opened the door for him, he rushed in and tripped on a rug that was just in front of an open window and did a pole vault out the window.' Then he started laughing.

Joan was taken aback at first; then she joined in the laughing.

She said, 'I really thought you were serious! You had tears in your eyes. You would make a great actor!'

Steve laughed and replied, 'It's my weak spot. If anything touches my eyelids, my eyes start watering.'

During the rest of their conversation, Joan told him who was in her family, but she didn't tell him her dad owned his own business.

She said, 'There's Dad - he's great, and my sister Emma - she likes to cook, and San - her real name is Sandra. We love her, she moved in with us when my mother died.'

Steve said he didn't have any family. He was an only child who had lived with his mother, but she had died three years ago. He didn't know his dad and he didn't want to because he was a - 'pardon the language' - nasty bastard.

He explained, 'My mother said he had a silver tongue and a bad temper. He would blame her when his silly money-making schemes went wrong. He would get drunk and beat my mother up. She said the last day she was with him the police came to the house and said he had conned an old lady out of her life savings. Her son had found out and had reported it to them. The bastard waited till the police left and sneaked in the back door and started to blame my mother. He belted her and knocked her across the room, and then he grabbed me out of my pram and started to belt me across the face, saying it was my fault he needed money, and he never wanted me.'

While Steve was telling Joan this, she felt sorry for him and thought how different her dad was. He was loving and thoughtful.

Steve continued, 'My mother said when he did that to me, she picked up the nearest heavy thing to hand and hit him on the head with it. She said she couldn't remember what it was. Then she grabbed me and left - she went into a women's refuge. My mother was a wonderful mother. She worked two jobs to put me through college. I loved her and worked hard to get into university, and one thing I'm happy about is that she lived to see me get here.'

Joan went quiet for a moment. She was thinking how she would have liked to have known her own mother. Sometimes she could remember her mother singing to her.

Steve said, 'Oh, sorry. Let's talk about nicer subjects.'

They started again, in Spanish, about their futures. Steve laughed and said, 'I think you're great, and I'm going to marry you when you graduate from here.'

Joan smiled at the same time as she blushed, and said, 'You don't even know me.'

He grinned as he answered, 'But I know what I like and want, and I like you and want you. In time, I hope you will want me.'

When the party started to break up, her friend Patricia came over to her.

Joan stood up and said, 'Steve, this is Patricia - my roommate. Patricia, meet Steve. He is in his final year here and is going to show me round the university.'

Steve stood up and said, 'Hello, Patricia. Any friend of Joan's is a friend of mine.'

She smiled and replied, 'Call me Pat, everyone does.' She winked and smiled at Joan as she said, 'Still waiting for the drink you were getting me. It's a bit late now, but I don't blame you! I see you have found a new friend in Steve.

I'm on my way to our room, so if you are staying a little bit longer with Steve, I'm just letting you know so you aren't looking for me later.' Then she laughed and said, 'This might sound like your mother, but don't stay too late - we have an early lecture in the morning.'

She waved, turned and started toward the door. Just as she was about to leave the room, Joan jumped up off the chair and shouted, 'Pat! Wait for me. I'll be with you in a minute.'

As she walked towards Pat, she looked back at Steve and said, 'I don't know where the night went. I really enjoyed tonight. See you tomorrow at three pm. Don't forget.'

Steve stood up, blew Joan a kiss and said, 'Don't worry. I'll be there on the dot.'

As the girls strolled back to their room, they linked each other's arms.

Pat said to Joan, 'You couldn't pick a better one. He's got a lovely body on him - talk about tall, dark and handsome! He's got it all and brains as well. You want to hold onto him if you can.'

Joan, with a grin on her face, agreed, 'He is lovely to talk to and I felt great when I was with him, but I've only just met him and who knows what he is really like... Don't get any ideas, though, because I intend to find out for myself. He said he's going to marry me and, the way I feel right now, I might keep him to that promise.'

They were giggling as they walked along, then they both burst out laughing. Some students who were nearby thought they were drunk.

Joan and Steve saw a lot of each other that year. When their friends met just one of them, they knew the other would be busy studying and would turn up later.

JOAN BRINGS STEVE HOME

At the end of that year, when everyone was going home, Joan knew Steve would have to leave the student halls, so she asked Steve if he would come home with her and meet her family.

Steve answered, 'I would love to, but I've got to find somewhere to live and employment as soon as possible so I can pay off all my student debt. I hate it hanging over my head. You understand, don't you?'

Joan said, 'I know, but everyone is entitled to a holiday, and I want my family to meet you. You got a 2:1 in your degree and I'm sure you could find employment near where I live. Lots of firms would take you on.'

Steve smiled at her. He pulled her into him and, as they hugged, he said, 'Okay, you win. I'll take a week's holiday to meet your clan but I want employment near the university so I will be able to visit you. Of course, if you'd rather I didn't...?'

Joan laughed and gave him a friendly slap, saying, 'Alright, big-head! You know I'd love that, but for now you can stay in my home and meet my family.'

Steve was lost for words when he met her family and realised how wealthy they were, but once he got over the shock, he got on well with her dad and Sandra, although Emma didn't seem to take to him even though it was the first time they had met. They were in the same house but, despite the fact Steve ended up staying a month, he hardly saw Emma.

Though Emma didn't say anything to Joan, she told Sandra in confidence, 'There's something about Steve I don't like, and I don't know what it is. So if I go missing now and then, could you please make up an excuse for me?'

Sandra smiled and said, 'Of course I will, but you've got to get to know him. That feeling you have got is just your love for your sister and because you are worried about her.'

So, Emma made herself scarce whenever Steve came to the house, and Sandra made excuses for Emma so Joan wouldn't get upset at her sister.

Steve said to Joan, 'The vibes I get off Emma... I don't think she likes me.'

Joan replied, 'Emma likes you really, she is just quiet and shy. Next time we come home, just look up some gourmet recipes and talk to her about them and see her become your best friend. She's mad about cooking.'

BACK AT UNIVERSITY

When Joan went back to university, Steve went with her and was taken on as a salesperson by a small car sales business near the campus. Steve took to the job like a duck to water and became good friends with another salesman, named Fred Saunders, who showed Steve the ropes. They went out for a drink now and then.

One evening when Steve suggested going for a drink, Fred replied, 'No, I'm going to the shooting range. I want to know about firearms for when I get into the police force. Do you want to come?'

'Too right I'll come! I've never held a gun and I'd love to have a go with a real pistol and shoot at the targets,' Steve replied, as he went for a make-believe gun and drew it, like a cowboy.

At the gun range, Fred explained, 'Steve, don't pull or jerk the trigger - squeeze it.'

Steve laughed and said, 'You've seen that in the westerns.'

After a few shots with the pistol, Steve hit the bullseye every time.

Fred was amazed and said, 'You're a natural.'

Steve visited the range quite a few times after that. The last time Steve was at the shooting range, Fred said, 'They want you to join the club team and enter the competitions.'

Steve answered, 'Sorry - I would like to, but I want to spend my time building a future in the business world. I know what it's like to be the poor kid in the school, and I am determined to be rich, come what may. They say you have to be ruthless in business and I'm that kind of guy.'

Fred laughed and said, 'We all want to be rich… but I'm sure you will make a lot of money, and I hope you won't forget your friends when you do.'

When the owner of the car company found out that Steve was from university, he was asked to take a job in the office, and he looked after the paperwork and kept the books. He was promised that, if things worked out well, he would get his own showroom to manage.

He told Fred what he was promised because they were good friends. He reported to Fred exactly what the owner of the car showrooms had promised him and said, 'I know you are a good salesman and have been here longer than me, so I wouldn't like to go behind your back. What do you think?'

Fred just laughed. He was standing facing Steve, and patted him on the top of his arm, saying, 'I don't intend to stay here; I have other plans. As you know, I've been a special in the police for the last six months, but what I can say is you better watch out for the boss' two head-working nephews… He thinks they can do no wrong.'

Steve even talked to Fred about Joan and Emma. He looked at Steve and said, 'You don't seem too keen on her sister, what's wrong with her?'

Steve said, 'I don't think she likes me and she's one of those people, you know, who gets under your skin. I can honestly say there is no love lost between us, and if she hates me… well, there's still none lost. She'd better not try to change Joan's mind about me. I think I would kill her if she did.'

Fred smiled as he answered, 'Don't talk like that, Steve, or I might have to arrest you! Just use that smooth tongue of yours, that you use when you're with a customer, and I'm sure you will soon win her round.'

The showrooms were doing great with Steve's help. He kept on top of the books well and was a good salesman, but Fred's heart wasn't in the job. He wanted to be a policeman.

One day he came into the showrooms and said, 'Steve, I'll see you round. I've got the job I've always wanted in the police force. I've got to spend a short time as a cadet, so in three weeks' time, I will be leaving this place, and then I'm going on my holidays to Cyprus for two weeks before starting training.

I've got the job I want. I hope you get the job you want here, you've earned it. Anyway, good luck.'

They shook hands and Steve said. 'I know I will, and I'm sure you will be running the police force before you're finished.'

STEVE HAS A MEETING WITH JOAN'S DAD

Though Steve had done a good job for the company, over time the two nephews of the boss got promoted to the car showrooms he was promised. Still, he stuck with the job till Joan finished her degree. When Joan left the university, it was with a First.

When she arrived home, that morning her dad gave her a key and said, 'I knew you would do well and that office next to mine, that I have kept as a stock room, it's always been meant for you. It is now all set for the new director and that is my girl.'

Joan took the key with a slight smile on her face. Her dad frowned and said, 'I thought you would be made up, but that's not the kind of smile my girl usually gives me. Is there something you are not happy about? You know you can tell me anything, no matter what. I'm your dad and I love you.'

She told him how Steve had been treated. Joan's dad said, 'If he's as good as you say, well, that's just not right! He can come and manage a business we have just acquired. It's a garage with a small showroom; the cars are second hand. He will have to pull his weight, though, because, you know, business is business, Joan.'

She answered, 'You won't regret it, Dad. He's a good businessman and puts a hundred percent into everything he does… and another thing, Dad, I'm going to marry him one of these days.'

Her dad looked surprised and said, 'Well, I'd better give him the job then. Tell him to come and see me in my office this afternoon at one, for an interview.'

Steve was there on the dot. As he walked through the door, Joan's dad was standing behind his desk, talking to an unfamiliar, well-dressed, young man. Steve recognised Joan's dad, but he wondered what the young man, who only looked a few years older than himself, was doing there.

Joan's dad, his hand outstretched, said, 'Well, Steve, you can now call me John, seeing as you will soon be part of the family. And this is my friend and solicitor Doug Thomas. I'm sure he will be a good friend to you in the coming years as you get to know one another.'

Doug put his hand out to Steve. Steve shook Doug's hand and, as he did so, he replied, 'Thank you, John. I've got the engagement ring, but I haven't asked her yet, so how did you know I was going to ask Joan to marry me? I thought I was coming to talk about a job in a car showroom.'

John put his hand out to Steve once more and they shook hands again while they were talking. John said, 'My girl said she loves you and knows you love her; she also said that you said that one day you will marry her. So, being her dad, I would like to make sure things go well for her and I have some contracts that Doug has set out for you to sign.'

Steve was surprised as he went through the contracts and signed them, but he said, 'I'll sign anything you want as long as I can marry Joan. I don't believe in divorce anyway, so I have no intention of ever leaving Joan, and I've even signed the non-disclosure one saying I can't tell her about the prenuptial contract.'

John said, 'I'm sorry, Steve, but I love my daughter and, being honest, I don't really know you that well.

You've got the job and also my daughter's hand. I hope we can still be friends, Steve, and I'm happy you're joining my family.'

Steve stuck out his hand once more and, as John shook it, Steve said, 'Don't worry, when we have children, I'll do the same thing for them.'

STARTING THEIR MARRIED LIFE

Twelve months later, Joan and Steve were married. Joan's dad had had a heart attack a month earlier and it left him in poor health. He had to go to the wedding in a wheelchair. When Joan and her dad got to the church in the wedding car, Emma and Doug Thomas, her dad's solicitor and best friend, were outside the church waiting for them. Doug helped Joan's dad out of the car and into the wheelchair, while Emma fussed round Joan making sure that her dress and veil looked perfect. Doug pushed her dad to the church entrance and helped him to stand up out of the chair, so he could walk Joan down the aisle. He took the wheelchair down a side aisle to the front and, when Joan and her dad reached where Steve was standing at the altar rail, Doug helped her dad back into the wheelchair and sat just behind him on the front pew.

After the wedding, Joan took on all her dad's work with the help of Cathy, her dad's secretary. Cathy had been going to take early retirement, but Joan asked her to stay on and help her to sort out all the firm's files, so taking over the firm would go smoothly. All the people in the firm did their best to help because they all knew Joan was pregnant. Joan and Steve's daughter, Ann, was born ten months from the day they were married, on the sixteenth of August. A few weeks after that, Joan's dad died.

The firm was doing great and now, despite deeply mourning the loss of her dad, Joan had to formally take over the business. She had been a director in the firm from the day she left university, but now she was the managing director. With Cathy's help, Joan put all the ideas she had for the business into practice.

Within a year and six months, her ideas were paying off - business was booming. Joan, Steve and Ann were living in a luxury apartment above the firm's offices on the fifteenth floor, but Joan and Steve wanted to move to the country. Two years after Ann was born, they decided to buy some land - settling on a large run-down farm. Their son, John, was born four years after Ann.

Over the years they turned the farm into a large mansion with lots of rooms, two double garages and stables at the back of it. It was now standing in a well-managed estate with a wide driveway leading down through the garden, which had rose bushes and other plants in it. At the bottom, the driveway went over a bridge, which crossed a small flowing river, to reach the big iron gates.

Living in the big house now was Steve, who was fifty-one, and his son, John, who was twenty-one. Steve's wife, Joan, had died ten years earlier; after that his daughter Ann, who was sixteen at the time, had left home and went to live with her Aunt Emma. Ann was now twenty-five. She hadn't spoken to her dad for years.

ANN STOPPED VISITING JOHN

Billy asked John, 'Have you seen Ann lately? I know she doesn't call in often, but I haven't seen her for yonks.'

John looked a bit sad and said, 'Ann would call in to see me, when she knew Dad wasn't at home. She would only come when she knew Dad was away on business.'

Billy, with a questioning look on his face, said, 'I know she wouldn't speak to your dad, and when I mentioned your dad she would get a bit upset and change the subject - I think it was something to do with the holiday in Spain - but why has she stopped coming to see you? You were so close to one another. Have you and Ann argued over something? I know it is none of my business, but I know you miss her…'

John said, 'We've not argued. Well, I suppose we have… You know about the accident in Spain - well, Ann would go on about the accident every time she came to see me.

She said she could, and would, remember the face of the driver that nearly ran into our mother on that mountain road for the rest of her life, because she was looking straight into her face, as she drove the car at us.

Ann claims she had a plaster just below her hairline, above the left eyebrow, and that she was wearing thick, dark-rimmed glasses and a black wig. Ann said she could see fair hair under it; that the woman's fringe had parted with the wind.

I always said to Ann that she couldn't possibly see all that in the few moments before Tommy pulled her out of the way of the car… It's just impossible.'

Then he said, 'I remember the way Ann would glare at me and go red in the face. Then she would start on about Dad; about how he could have saved Mum if he wanted to. She would paint Dad as this bad, horrible man who just let go and dropped our mum, his *wife*, over a cliff and left her to die.

I suppose we did argue about it a lot, and in the end we stopped speaking because of it. I haven't seen Ann for about two years.

I'm sorry for her really, because she loved Dad and thought he was Mr. Wonderful till that terrible day. Going to live with Aunt Emma only made things worse. Aunt Emma hates Dad. When Ann told her that she thought Dad had deliberately dropped Mum, Aunt Emma's hate really came out and, after a while, she started to agree that what Ann said had happened might be true. At the funeral Aunt Emma tried to push Dad into the grave screaming, *'You should be down there, not my sister, Joan.'*

I tried to tell Ann she was mistaken, and not to listen to Aunt Emma, because she has always loathed Dad.'

Billy said to John, 'You look upset. I didn't think... I'm sorry - I should mind my own business. I do hope you two will get friendly again.'

John wiped his eyes and said, 'No, it helps to talk about it with you, and...keep this to yourself... I heard Dad and Lilly talking about getting married in a few months' time!'

STEVE IS GOING TO MARRY LILLY

A few weeks later, John and Billy were trying on their tuxedos. John was hoping Ann and Tommy, her boyfriend, would come to their father's wedding, but he had his doubts because of what she believed about their mother's death. Before that day Ann had loved her dad; she claimed he was the best dad in the world and would do anything she could to please him. Now she hated him and wouldn't even speak to him.

John couldn't help going over it in his mind again. They had only been in Spain two days when it happened - a car accident that took their mum's life. Ann would never forget her sixteenth birthday, because it was the day their mum died in that terrible accident. John's thoughts turned back to Ann. She was never the same after that day. Ann had never forgiven their dad for the accident and blamed him for their mum's death. John had argued with Ann about it and gone over it in his own mind hundreds of times, and their dad always came out a hero in his eyes. He thought of how, when he was younger, he didn't want anyone to think he was a mummy's boy, but, at twenty-one, he wouldn't mind being one now and tears came to his eyes.

John's friend, Billy, patted him on the back and said, 'It's four months to the wedding. It's a bit early to be trying on the wedding gear... and it's the women who are supposed to cry at weddings, not us.'

John smiled and said to his best friend, 'You know, Dad. He likes to plan for things well ahead, so nothing will go wrong.' As he wiped his eyes, he said, 'I was just thinking of my mum and how I miss her.'

Billy said, 'Oh?' with a worried look on his face and then said, 'Are you all right then?'

John smiled and said, 'Yes, don't worry.'

Still, he knew Billy would be worried about him, because they had been friends since they were three years of age and started kindergarten together. Billy stayed at John's house many times and, after John's mum had died, Billy was there when John had broken down crying. Sometimes, when Billy had stayed overnight, John had woken up in the night, screaming from a nightmare about the accident. Billy would sit up in bed and talk to him, but John wouldn't talk about the accident and, when John's dad was home, he would come in and hug John to calm him down.

John wiped his eyes again, and smiled at Billy and said to him, 'Don't worry. I'm not going back to the bad old days, when I was a kid. Like I said, I was just thinking about Mum and Ann, and hoping we will see Ann at the wedding.

I hope you don't mind, but I asked Tommy to give Ann a message from 'you' about the wedding. If it's from 'you', Tommy won't get in an argument with Ann when he mentions Dad. Is that alright?'

Billy smiled and said, 'Of course it is. You know I'm anything for a quiet life, and it would be great if you and Ann start speaking again.'

THE HOTEL

A few weeks before the terrible accident on Ann's sixteenth birthday, Joan had taken Ann and John on a business trip with her to buy an old, but beautifully kept, hotel. It was called *The Lake Hotel*. While they were there, Joan and the children were met by the owners - twins, Jerry and Mary, and their father, Lawrence. Ann and John both thought the old man must be nearly a hundred years old and the twins were a lot older than their mother.

The old man said to Joan, 'You do know that one of the conditions is that I live here till I die, and I will be treated like a guest?'

Joan replied, with a smile on her face, 'I can live with that, now let's see what we can work out.'

The old man said, 'I'll leave you to work the rest of the deal out between the three of you. I want to show your children my favourite place in this house.

Come with me... I'm sorry! How rude of me - I haven't even asked you your names.'

John shouted, 'I'm John and my sister is Ann. What's yours?'

The old man said, smiling, 'I can't remember. I haven't heard it for such a long time. All I hear is people say 'the old fella'... but if I remember I'll let you know, okay?'

Joan, with a worried look on her face, whispered to the twins, 'Is your dad alright with my children?'

The old man smiled and said, 'I'm not senile - just joking around - and my hearing is in marvellous condition.'

Joan blushed, then smiled, as the old man winked at her and the twins laughed.

Jerry said, 'Dad loves telling the old story he told us when we were kids. Are your children alright with horror stories? It has a happy ending.'

Joan said, 'Yes, I've caught them a couple of times watching horror movies.'

Ann looked at her mother and asked, 'Is it alright if we go with him?'

Joan said, 'I want you and John to look over the hotel. Let me know if you like it as much as I do and tell me what your dad would think of it.'

The old man got hold of Ann's hand and put his other hand round John's shoulder. For an old man, he moved quite quickly as he led them to a large oak door. He took a large key out of his pocket and unlocked the door and opened it, and, as he did, the door made an eerie, crying sound. Ann shivered and tightened her grip on the old man's hand.

He looked at her and smiled as John said, 'I think the door hinges need oiling.'

The old man laughed and said, 'See the big hinges? Just touch one.'

John frowned as he touched the hinge; then he pulled his hand away and said, 'Yak! It's covered in oil. Why is it making that noise?'

The old man replied, 'The door likes to give you a fright, but it means you no harm.'

Ann and John looked at each other. The old man smiled at them and said, 'You think I'm making it up, don't you? Well, shut the door and open it again, and I bet it doesn't make a sound.'

John closed the door and opened it again, and it swung open like a well-oiled door would.

John laughed and said, 'It's some sort of trick, isn't it?'

The old man smiled and replied, 'If you say so. Anyway, let's get on with our adventure. It's four steps along this panelled corridor.'

He took four large steps and pressed on a panel, and it opened like a door. He walked into the dark room, while Ann and John stayed where they were. A light came on and the old man was standing just inside the doorway, at the top of some steps leading down to a well-lit room with a roundish swimming pool that went right up to the wall.

When they got down to the pool, it seemed to go under the wall of the building.

Ann said, 'For a swimming pool the water isn't very clean, is it?'

The old man said, 'I know. That's because it's the water from the pond.'

Then the children followed him past two doors that had '*changing rooms*' written on them, to what looked like a kitchen. Round the walls, there were cupboards, a sink and a fridge. He opened the cupboard, took out a tray and put a box full of different sweets and three glasses on it. Then he went to the fridge and got three cans of Coke, placing them on a small table which was in front of four comfortable chairs.

He waved to Ann and John to sit down as he said, 'Come and help yourselves while I tell you how I got this wonderful house.'

He stood in front of the middle chair by the table and poured the three Cokes out. As Ann and John went to the chairs either side of him, he put a handful of sweets in front of them. Then he picked up his Coke, took a drink and said, 'Cheers! Are you comfortable?'

Ann and John nodded as they ate the sweets.

The old man said, 'I know you two know what a business venture is. Well, when I was younger than your mother is now - you've got to try to imagine that, I know it will be hard for you to think of me as a young man - this was to be our new house.

Well, when I say 'new house', I mean new to my wife and I. Really, it's about four or five hundred years old and, as you've seen, stands in its own grounds, surrounded by trees. There's a large pond at the back of the house; in fact, at one place, it is only six feet away from the house.

When we first came to view the house, the pond had about a dozen ducks on it and lots of different coloured water lilies growing in the middle. The pond was one of the reasons we bought the mansion.

Eve, my wife, liked the story the estate agent told us about it. It was about a young girl who lived in the house with her mother and father. She was about eighteen when her mother died… on a year to the day that her father had also died.

A monk told the villagers she was a witch and had killed her parents in sacrifice to the devil and that next year it would be one of them. The villagers believed him. They told stories about how when she was a child, if anyone went to the great house they would have to go round to the doors at the back, and she would always suddenly appear from nowhere in the middle of the pond, laughing at them.

The monk led the villagers to the house and dragged her out saying, "From the evil you came, to the evil pond you will return."

Then he tied her to a large boulder, and told four of the men to carry her to the deep part of the pond by the house and throw her in.

The monk threw a dagger at her as she sank into the black water, saying, "May this holy cross lock you in that evil place."

Then he made a wreath out of a branch of a bush, placed it on the water and said "May this wreath help all the souls you've touched rest in peace."

In time, the monk went to live in the house and the villagers turned against *him*. They said she had 'taken him over' and when they went to the house to see him, they would run away, saying he had her face. They boarded him up in the house to die.

Eve and I laughed when we heard the story. We didn't believe in ghosts, but what a great story to tell at the business parties we planned to hold at the house. We would be holding lots of parties for different companies in the house… That's the main reason we bought it. Eve and I thought it would be a good business move.

It was summer when we first saw the house. It looked proud and inviting as the sun shone down on all its greenery, and that of its grounds. The ivy that grew all over the house was green and red, with a touch of yellow. As you approached from the top of the hill and looked down on it, it appeared to be on fire - with little flames that seemed to dance all over it, even on the roof and on parts of the chimney. It looked wonderful.

But it was winter before we got into the house, and all the green leaves on the trees and bushes in the ground had died away... and you couldn't even see any green on the grass because of the rotting leaves. The ivy on the house had shed its leaves as well, and the house looked like it was entrapped in a large net that seemed to be pulling it down into the mud and rotting leaves that surrounded it.

We had only been in it two days, so we were living in one room at the back of the house till we could get things sorted out, when, at night, there was a knock on the main doors. When I say 'a knock' on the front door... by the time the sound reverberated along the large hallway, it was like someone was banging a drum in the foyer and, at the same time, an old clock in the hallway clanged twelve o clock.

I looked at Eve and she looked at me.

As I got up I said, "I wonder who that could be at this hour."

Eve, with a worried look on her face answered me, but I couldn't hear because of the noise the room door made as I opened it to go into the hall, to answer the front door. As I went into the hall, I called back "Pardon?"

It seemed to echo back at me.

Eve's voice sounded strange and the words I heard sent a cold shiver all over my body, the skin on my head seeming to shrink onto my skull.

Eve seemed to say, "A good wreath, a terrible knife to catch your death."

I looked back at Eve as I unlocked the door, but she just smiled back at me and I thought I must have misheard her. I turned and opened the door and, pinned onto it with a long, wicked-looking knife, was a wreath.

I slammed the door shut, and the house shuddered, and the lights went out and Eve screamed...

Then the lights came back on and Eve was standing beside me. I asked, "What happened?"

Eve said, in a trembling voice, "I don't know. When you opened the door, the lights went out and I felt icy cold fingers around my throat; then I thought you were fighting with them and dragged me over here!"

I was in shock, and it showed in my voice when I answered Eve. "Well, I didn't have time to move when you screamed; I couldn't see a thing when the lights went out. It was so dark; I've never seen anything so black in my life. How did you know about the wreath and the large knife outside the door? And what did you mean 'catch my death'?"

Eve was shaking. She started crying and said, "I don't know anything about a wreath or a knife. The only thing I said was, "Good grief, it's a terrible night - they'll catch their death."

I didn't scream... I couldn't - I was too afraid. I was just frozen to the spot. Let's get out of here."

I was only too happy to agree. I turned and opened the door, but there was no wreath or knife on it. Then, as we went outside, we found we were standing in a pool of blood and, at that moment, a large figure dressed as a monk appeared about two yards in front of us. As he lifted his head, his hood revealed his eyes, looking at us. They were evil. They seemed to burn into our very souls. Then his arms opened out towards us, and in one bony hand he had a wreath and in the other he had a long dagger, dripping with blood. We ran back in and I slammed the door.

We held onto one another in shock, as I said, "It will be alright."

Eve answered, "What do you mean 'it will be alright'? You're as frightened as me... You've wet yourself!"

I looked down at the pool of water I was standing in and, as my eyes followed the water, I don't know if I was glad at what I saw or if I nearly did wet myself. There was a small, young woman standing there, dripping wet. Eve was looking at my face and when she saw the puzzled expression on it, she looked to where I was looking and saw the lady.

The lady beckoned us, and then turned and walked into one of the rooms without opening the door. I looked at Eve and she looked at me; I don't know who was shaking the most.

Then a gentle voice seemed to whisper all round us, "Come on. We have got to help one another. It's my last chance and it may be yours!"

I said, "Eve, she must be the witch. What shall we do?"

Eve seemed to pull herself together and said, "I think I like the look of her more than I do of him... And someone helped me before

- it must have been her. But don't you let go of me when we go in that room! Promise me."

I half led and was half pushed into the room, where the lady pointed to a desk, which moved to reveal a trap door when I pushed against it. I opened the trapdoor with Eve hanging onto my arm. We looked down to see some steps leading down to a cellar, full of water.

Eve screamed, "I'm not going down there."

The spirit came toward Eve and I stepped in front of her to try to protect her, but the spirit just drifted through me and for a moment I simply froze. The spirit put her arms around Eve and led her to one of the panels on the wall; as I ran over to Eve, the spirit touched the panel and it just crumbled to dust. Behind the panel was a small oak door with two big metal bolts on it, which were rusted up.

I said to Eve, "It's a priest hole!"

Eve, backed away pulling me with her, saying, "Lawrence, the monk's in there."

The lady's spirit whispered, "No, I'm in there. Please open it. I cannot."

I looked at the bolts and thought "I'll never move them" but, with a little effort, the bolts slid back and we pulled the door open.

The spirit made a sobbing noise and backed away. We turned and looked at her, and she beckoned us to open the door wider. We did and she looked past us, into the tiny room, and we could see tears running down her face. She moved past us and into the room. Our eyes followed her, and we could see through her, to a small skeleton lying on the floor.

The spirit pointed to a brick in the wall, and it moved to reveal a book and a dagger.

She whispered, "Put the dagger in the bolt, standing up as a cross, and he won't be able to come near."

I did this and the spirit told Eve to get the book and read it.

Eve looked at the book and said, "It's her diary. Her name is Eliza."

I said, "Well, read it to me. Let's hope it will help us get out of here."

Eve read it out, *"I'm in heaven when I'm in the pond swimming. Today, for my tenth birthday, my father showed me a secret priest hole and a cellar, full of water. Under the water is a passageway to the pond. It's wonderful. Whenever anyone comes to the house, I go through the passageway and swim underwater to the middle of the* pond, and then I pop up, laughing and waving to them. They wonder where I've come from. It's fun to see their faces."

Eve read out the pages she thought were important to us. She turned the pages carefully and read on.

"Today Father died, and I'm so upset, but I'm worried about Mother. She said she can't go on without him."

"It's now six months since father died and mother is no better. I'm worried, she won't eat and is getting weaker."

"Today it's the anniversary of Father's death. Mother died. I think she died of a broken heart … and if she did it herself, please, God, forgive her and let her be with my father."

"It's been four weeks since my mother died; the servants are all leaving. They're afraid of a monk in the village. He's saying I'm a witch, and they are afraid he will say they are too. They want me to leave with them, but this is my home, and my mother and father are buried in the grounds, and I will never leave them."

Eve had trouble getting the next few pages open - they had dried blood on them. Once she had sorted the pages out, she carried on reading.

"An evil man came here, with the villagers, to the house; he said I was the witch from the pond. He held up a dagger like a cross and said to the villagers, "Take the witch and tie her feet and hands." I tried to fight them off but I couldn't, and they tied my wrists and ankles. My ankles were tied to a boulder, and he told them to throw me into the deep end of the pond. As they threw me into the pond, he said something about the cross and threw the dagger at me as the boulder pulled me down. The dagger went into my leg. I pulled it out and cut the rope on my ankles. Then I swam up the passageway to the house and hid in the priest hole.

No one came into the house except the monk. The villagers were afraid and wanted to burn the house down. He told them if they burnt the house down the evil would move into the village. He said he would go into the house and bless it and drive the evil back to hell. After a few hours of drinking and ransacking the house, the evil monk left. I dressed the gash in my leg."

"It's been a week since they threw me into the pond and the monk has been back every day with his things. I think he is moving in. It's hard to stay in hiding - my leg is festering… but I have to stay in the priest hole when he's here."

"The evil monk has moved into the house and I can't come out of hiding at all now. My leg is swollen and turning green. I can't stop myself from crying out in pain."

Eve stopped and looked at me. She had tears in her eyes. We looked at the spirit. She was kneeling and looked as if she was praying. I put my arm around Eve, and she carried on reading.

"I cried out in pain and the evil man heard me. He tore the panel down and opened the door.

He stood there laughing and said, "So, my little witch got out of the pond after all."

I said, "I'm not a witch and the authorities will hang you for this. They haven't believed in witches for years."

He laughed and said, "I know. I don't believe in witches either, the nearest thing to a witch round here is me. I just like your house and now it's mine... but I'll let you have this little room all to yourself to hide from the villagers. And, just to make sure the villagers don't bother you, I'll bolt the door. As he closed the door he laughed and said, "The only authority round this lonely, sleepy village was your father and he's dead. So now it's me."

Eve looked up and said, 'The evil bastard. He left her here to die."

I asked, "Is that the end of the diary?"

Eve shook her head and started reading again. *"I'm locked in the priest hole and I'm dying. My prayer is that my spirit doesn't leave this house, and may the villagers see my spirit whenever they see him, please God."*

Eve closed the book, and I said, "So now we know the stories are true, but no one said the house was still haunted now. We need help."

The spirit moved to Eve and touched her hand. I heard a whispering sound and Eve turned to the spirit, smiled and nodded her head. The spirit stepped into Eve's body; sometimes I was looking at Eve and sometimes I was looking at the spirit.

Then I heard Eve's voice, "Don't worry. It's alright and this way she can tell us things she wants us to know. She is weak from fighting that evil bastard - that's why she is whispering. It was her who screamed, to summon all her strength to drive him out of the house, but he will be back soon. I'll let Eliza tell you the rest."

Then Eve's voice changed to that of a young woman. "You know I took his body over by force when he was alive and then, when the villagers came, they thought he was a witch, and he died because they boarded him up in my house. He was an evil man, not a monk at all, and when he died, he cursed the house and all who would live in it."

I butted in, "Well, if he has been haunting the house all this time, how come no one knows?"

Eliza answered, her voice seeming a bit stronger, "He possessed anyone who came to the house, and we would fight for their souls. If they were good, I would win sometimes, but if they were bad, he would win every time."

I butted in again, "You mean we could die and lose our spirit to the devil? Why can't you do what you did the last time you got rid of him for years?"

Eliza replied, "*I* didn't get rid of him. A real priest came and exorcised my house. The priest drove him back to the grave where they had buried him and placed a large stone cross on it. Over the years the cross has broken, and parts have been moved. Then last year, some foolish people who lived here held a séance. I frightened them away, but it was too late - they had let the evil back into my house. He can't enter this holy room. It would cast him down to hell for all eternity."

I said, "Yes, he can't enter but we can't leave, and if we stay here, we will die like you did and if we go it's us who will end up in hell for all eternity. So, what do we do?"

Eliza said, "Take the dagger and hold it like a cross. You *must* believe it to be a token of the holy cross, then if you touch him with it, he won't be able to move away from it. He committed blasphemy calling the dagger a holy cross then trying to kill with it. If you touch him with it he will make a lot of noise and try to hurt you, but as long as you don't take the cross away from him, he can't hurt you. As soon as you touch him, push it into him. The cross will go into him, but don't let go and he will become just a mist floating round the cross."

I said, "It sounds too easy, so why am I shaking?"

Then Eve spoke, "Eliza said it's not easy. He will try to get the cross away from you and, if he does, God help us. So be careful."

The minute I left the small room, holding the cross, the outer room seemed to be full of unnatural things. I sank into the floor which had turned into dead, rotting flesh and the walls ran with blood.

The monk was screaming and spitting clots of blood at me. Then he said in a quiet and stern voice, "You're going to hell."

I was afraid before but now I was petrified; then I heard Eve's voice behind me. "You're winning, he's backing away."

I felt a bit braver and started moving forward towards the monk. He roared and things started to fly all around the room and, as the things hit my hand, the blade part of the cross cut my fingers. My hold got weaker and, in desperation, I launched towards the monk, but at that moment a large chair flew at me. It knocked the cross out of my hand and across the room.

In a blink of an eye the monk was on me. He had his icy cold hands around my throat; he was pushing me down into the rotting flesh and maggots. I could hardly see and I couldn't breathe. The rotting flesh, bad blood and maggots were in my mouth and up my nose. I could just see his distorted face and his evil eyes; then blood ran out of his eyes and into mine. As I sank into that vile-smelling mess, I felt thousands of worms and maggots sliding over me. They were starting to eat me. I was in agony. I said, "God help me." Then I blacked out.

I heard a noise and opened my eyes to see Eve, with Eliza still inside her, standing over me, holding the cross... or dagger - at that moment I didn't know what to call it, till I saw the mist around it; then, to me, it was a cross.

Eliza said, "Come on, Lawrence. We'll put this evil thing in the priest hole and send it to hell forever."

As she said this, she parted from Eve and asked me to move her remains out before Eve put the evil monk in there. I did, and when Eve put the cross on the floor of the priest hole, the floor opened up and the cross floated there as the mist was sucked down into the doorway to hell. As we closed the small door, we could hear screaming.

Eve said to Eliza, "Where shall we put your remains to rest before we leave?"

Eliza said, "Please don't leave my house. I and no other spirit will bother you here. Please put my remains in the water in the cellar. If you stay, it's a good story to tell at your parties. No one will believe you anyway, and when your two children swim in the pond, you know I will be looking after them."

I said, "We haven't got any children."

Eliza turned to Eve and, smiling, said, "You will have. Goodbye."

Then she walked down the steps into the water.

I looked at Eve, and she laughed and said, "I'm pregnant, with twins. I found out last week. I was going to tell you when we got the house sorted out."

Eve and I have lived here ever since… I bet you don't believe me, do you?' asked the old man, continuing, 'But do you know what my name is?'

John shook his head, but Ann said, 'It's Lawrence.'

Then Lawrence said, 'You're a clever child. You're right.'

Ann, in an annoyed tone said, 'I'm not a child. In a couple of weeks I'll be sixteen.'

Lawrence said, 'I apologise. Can a young lady like you forgive an old man?'

Ann smiled and nodded, and with that he continued, 'Now you know my name and you know this house is blessed with love. That is why I don't want to ever leave it and, if you spend the night here, in the morning you can swim from here into the pond.'

When they saw their mother, they both went on about the story Lawrence had told them and how they would be able to swim in the pond. However, Joan said they had to go home as she had a business meeting in the morning.

They were upset and so Joan promised, 'We will come back when I complete the deal for the hotel, which will be in four weeks' time.'

Then they headed home. That night, Ann and John told their dad all about the hotel and how they would love to swim from the cellar to the pond. The next morning John was still going on to his dad about how it would be a great birthday present for Ann to swim in the hotel.

His dad smiled and put his arm round John, saying, 'I agree, but I've already planned Ann's birthday present. I can't tell you because I haven't spoken to your mother about it yet, so mum's the word… or should I say mum's not to hear a word?'

John asked, 'Can you tell me what it is, Dad? I promise not to say anything.'

His dad replied, 'I know you would keep your promise, but it's a surprise for the whole family, so I can't tell you yet.'

THE HOLIDAY

A little under two weeks later, Steve said to his wife, 'We are all off to Spain tomorrow.'

With that Joan looked at Steve with a frown on her face, and said, 'Steve, you know I'm busy. I've got a couple meetings and Emma's restaurants to sort out.'

Steve said, with a smile on his face, 'Come on, honey. I know you are the wealthiest and cleverest lady in these parts, so I'm sure you haven't forgotten what is happening in three days' time.'

Joan said, 'Of course I wouldn't forget Ann's birthday, but I have two board meetings to chair. Emma's restaurants are due to be signed over to her. The loan was paid off last month. I was going to take Ann's birthday off and have arranged for a limo to take Ann and all her friends to see her favourite band and meet them in person, then go on to a party with a disco.'

Steve went over to Joan, put his arms round her and said, 'The business won't miss you and me at the board meetings this once, honey. The business will still be there after next week, but I don't want us to miss our lovely daughter's sixteenth birthday.'

With that, he got down on one knee, held Joan's hand and with a sad look on his face and in a silly voice said, 'Please, honey? We haven't been on a holiday, all of us together, for a couple of years.'

Joan couldn't help herself laughing at the daft faces Steve was making. She said, 'Get that silly look off your face - one of these days it's going to stick like that.'

Then she said, 'Okay, you win. I'll postpone the board meeting for two weeks. I'm sure Emma won't mind waiting a little while longer. I will speak to Emma myself and ask my secretary to get in touch with our beach hotel in Spain and request they get the villa ready for us tomorrow.'

Steve got up off his knee and grinned as he said, 'Good girl, you know it makes sense, because you can still do all that with Ann when we get back off holiday, and I've told the pilot to get the firm's jet ready for ten tomorrow.'

Then Joan's face changed. She looked a bit angry but before she could say anything he put his arms round her and kissed her on the lips, saying in a sort of a whisper to her, 'Don't be angry, love. I know you have a big heart and so I knew you would go to Spain for Ann's sixteenth birthday.'

Joan calmed down and turned and went into the games room, where she saw John and asked him to go and tell Ann they were going to Spain, as Steve sang 'We're all off to sunny Spain - A Viva Espana!'

John and Ann came back into the room where their mum and dad were. Their dad had a big smile on his face. With his arm round their mum, he waved his hand to beckon them to come to him, as he said, 'Come here, you two. We all have to make a promise that this holiday won't be interrupted, so we will leave our phones at home.'

They all started protesting at once and their mum was the loudest of the three. Their dad said, 'Your mum has the floor, so be quiet, you two.'

Joan, with an angry look on her face, answered him in a low tone, 'You know I need my phone to keep in touch with the board, and you should do the same.'

Steve replied, 'Yes, Joan but we delegate to them all the time. If the board can't phone us, they will deal with it themselves... and if it's a real emergency that they *can't* deal with, then there are lots of other ways that they can contact us, love.'

Joan looked at Steve and as he spoke the look on her face softened.

She placed her phone on the table that they were standing by and said, 'Alright, Steve, but I am taking my old pager with me. They will only use that if it's an emergency and they can't reach me by phone.'

Ann and John weren't too pleased about giving up their phones but, when they saw their mum had given her phone up, they both knew they stood no chance of keeping theirs. Each of them pulled a face.

Their dad said, 'Well, you two, let's have them. Put them with mine and your mums on the table.'

As they reluctantly did as they were told, they looked at their mum, who just shrugged and said, 'What will be, will be.'

Their dad moved a large frame that had a painting of the family in it. The painting opened like a door and behind it was a safe. He opened the safe and put the phones into it.

As he closed it, he turned back to look at the family and said, 'Now we know our holiday won't be interrupted.' Then he started singing again. 'We're all off to sunny Spain - A Viva Espana!'

They spent the rest of the day packing with their dad. Every now and then he would break into 'We're all off to sunny Spain - A Viva Espana'.

Their mum said, 'We will all have an early night.'

Even though they all went to bed early, John couldn't get to sleep, because this would only be the second time he would have been on their jet and last time the captain asked the co-pilot to let John sit in his seat.

John was in the co-pilot's seat for about twenty minutes, with the co-pilot standing behind him, telling John what the controls did while the captain flew the plane. He was so excited about sitting in the cockpit of the plane that he couldn't get to sleep, and it was two o'clock before he eventually dozed off.

Their mum was always up early, but that morning she had them all up at six thirty. Ann came down in a nice-looking tracksuit, but then after breakfast she said, 'I think I'll change these clothes for a dress.'

John said, 'You look alright to me.'

Ann stared at him and said, 'I don't dress to please you, I do it for myself.'

It was about seven fifteen when the doorbell rang and the maid answered the door.

Their chauffeur was standing there and just behind him in the driveway was their limousine. It was parked just outside the door. The maid smiled at the chauffeur. He nodded and smiled back at her as he pointed to the luggage in the hallway. There was a large trunk and three suitcases.

He said, 'Are they for me?'

The maid nodded and said, 'Yes, I'll let the family know you are here.'

With that she turned, but before she was halfway across the hallway the family came out of the dining room into the hallway. The chauffeur was about to pick up the trunk; he waved and smiled at them as they entered the hall. They all said 'Hi' to him, then he lifted the trunk, and turned and carried it out to the boot of the limousine.

Their dad picked up the big case and said, 'Well, come on, you two. Get a case each - we can't let the man do all the work while you are just standing round watching him.'

They both picked up a case and Ann followed their dad out, but John just stood there, holding the case and yawning.

Their mum was talking to the housekeeper and two maids. She said, 'We will be gone for a week. If you have any heavy jobs to do, get Joe the gardener to do it, and if there are any problems, phone my office. I'm sure they will handle it. The phone number is on the table by the phone.'

They all wished Joan to have a good holiday.

Joan smiled and said, 'I'm sure we will.' As she walked towards the door, she put her hand on John's back and said, 'Come on, get a move on or we will miss our slot for the plane.'

John went out with his mum. He put the case down and sat on it. The housekeeper and the maids followed them and stopped at the door.

Steve opened the limousine door for Joan to get in. Then Steve turned to Ann and gave her a hand into it. He looked at Joan and Ann and said, 'Just look at him.'

They both glared at John as Steve said, 'John, stop sitting on the case, yawning. Wake yourself up and give it to the man to put in the boot of the car.'

John did as their dad had told him. He would usually ask the chauffeur if he could sit in the front with him, but because he was awake half the night and his mum had got them up early, he decided to have a rest in the back, where he fell asleep almost straight away. As they drove down the driveway, the housekeeper and the maids waved them off. They waved back as the limousine drove away and down the driveway. It crossed the bridge and approached the big iron gates, which opened, then closed immediately after they went through them, out onto the road.

When John opened his eyes they were at the airport and the limousine was just pulling into the hanger where the jet was.

When they stopped their dad said, 'Let's get out and give the men a hand to load our luggage onto the plane.'

When they got out and went to help, one of the men said, 'We thank you for your willingness to help, but we must refuse because if you got hurt the management would have our jobs.'

Their dad smiled and said to the men, 'You are quite right, I should have known better. I will get them out of your way.'

Then he said to the family, 'Come on, we'll go aboard. The men want to be left to it.'

As he walked to get on the plane, Joan was close behind, with Ann by her side. John was still watching the men work. He was in a world of his own when his mum shouted to him, 'John! Will you *please* get on the plane!'

When Steve saw John was just standing there, he laughed and shouted, 'Leave him. We will go without him - it will serve him right.' Then he said, 'Come on, John, you are lagging behind. Move yourself and get on the plane.'

John ran to the steps, bounding up them two at a time and, as he went into the plane, he shouted, 'Well, I'm here, let's go!'

When the plane left the runway and levelled off, John asked his dad to have a word with the captain, to see if he would let him sit in the co-pilot's seat again.

Steve knocked at the door, opened it and popped his head in. The captain who was sitting in his seat turned to look at him. John stood alongside their dad so he could hear what was said.

His dad asked the captain, 'Is there any chance that John could sit in the cockpit, in the co-pilot seat, like he did last time?',

The captain said, 'I'm sorry, sir, but I've never flown with this young co-pilot before and so I would like to keep an eye on him. Tell John I'm sorry. It's likely when we are flying you home, he will get a chance then.'

Steve smiled and said, 'I understand - safety first. I'll explain it to John.'

The captain nodded and turned back to his controls. Steve closed the door and looked at John, but John had heard the conversation. He was now looking down and his smile had turned to a frown.

His dad said, 'Come on, John, it's not that bad. He said you can do it on the way home and, let's face it, it's better to be safe than sorry. We'll play a few games of cards and we'll soon be in Spain.'

Before his dad could finish the sentence, John butted in, 'You're alright, Dad. I'll play a game on one of the firm's laptops, if you will let me use it?'

Steve gave him some keys, pointed to a locked cupboard and said, 'They're in there, but only use the laptop that's labelled 'miscellaneous'. That has a few games on it that you can play.'

John opened the cupboard, took out the laptop that had the label 'miscellaneous' on it, then sat down and opened it on a small table. He looked around the plane. His mum was sitting on a seat, with the back in a resting position. She had her eyes closed as if she was asleep. Their dad sat down beside her and put his seat in a resting position too. Ann had her earphones on and was sitting on one seat with her feet up on another, and John thought, 'They will all be asleep soon.'

He was soon engrossed in his game and it didn't seem long before the captain was announcing, 'We will be landing in 25 minutes. Will you please put on your seat belts? We hope you had a good flight. Have a great week's holiday. See you then, and, John, you can be my co-pilot for a little while on the way home.'

The plane taxied into a hangar and stopped near a limousine, which drove up close to the steps as they were lowered down for the family to leave the plane. Steve was in the front, followed by John, Ann and then Joan. As usual Steve opened the limousine door, helped their mum into it and held out his hand to Ann for her to step in and sit next to her mum. Then he had to shout to John to get in the car. By this time, he was on the other side of the plane, looking round the hangar.

As he walked back toward them his dad said, 'Oh, come on, John! You're always the same! Will you move yourself? At the rate you are going it will be time for bed.'

John got in the car, then their dad followed him in and closed the door.

The driver asked, 'Do you want to call in at the hotel first, sir, before you go to your villa, as the management and staff have arranged a meal for you in your private rooms?'

Their mum said, 'We didn't order a meal. I only requested the limousine to take us to the villa.'

The driver said, 'I hope we didn't upset you, and this might sound daft, but the staff - and that includes myself - are always pleased to see you at the hotel.'

Joan smiled and said, 'I just didn't think of it. It's a great idea - we will be pleased to eat at the hotel, and thank you and the staff for being so thoughtful.'

As they approached the hotel, John looked at it and said to Ann, 'It's massive, it looks bigger than last time we came.'

When they drove into the hotel grounds, as the car stopped just in front of the large doorway, the manager came out and opened the door of the car. As the family stepped out, two of the concierges, who were in smart uniforms, came down the steps and asked if there was anything they could do for them.

Joan and Steve shook hands with all three of them. The manager, as he shook Steve's hand, handed him a small package, saying to him, 'Security found your watch that you left in the villa four months ago. I would have forwarded it on to you but, as you said you would be back soon, I put it in the safe till now.'

Steve smiled and thanked him, glancing at Joan as he put the watch away.

Joan looked at him with a frown on her face and said in a questioning voice, 'Steve, why were you here four months ago?'

Steve looked back at Joan and answered, 'It was just business. I thought I had told you about it, Joan, but let's forget about it now and I'll tell you about it after the holiday. I'm sure you will be pleased about the work I've put into it.' He then said to the manager, 'Please don't make a fuss of us - just treat us like you would normal guests and go about your business.'

The manager led them up some steps and the two concierges held the large glass doors open for them to go through and enter the reception area. As they went in the first thing they saw was a great crystal chandelier and, facing them, was a long oak counter with a jet-black marble top. Standing behind the counter was a well-dressed man about fifty. As Joan and Steve approached him, he looked up from the paperwork he was doing and a broad smile came on his face.

He put his hand out and said, 'It's been a long time. It's good to see the family again.'

They both shook his hand and Joan said, 'It's good to see you and the rest of the staff again.'

Ann and John looked round. On one side of the lobby was a large, beautiful staircase that went up to a balcony. On the other side stood two good-sized lifts, and around the reception room were statues holding different shaped lights. Also there were four chesterfields in the reception area. The manager beckoned Ann and John to follow him and, as they went through the door by the staircase, their mum and dad tagged on behind.

They were in the hotel restaurant where there were quite a few people dining. It was a large room. It was decorated mainly in white with a golden moulding round the edge of the ceiling, which had three good-sized crystal chandeliers hanging from it, lighting the restaurant. There were lots of round tables of different sizes. All the tables were covered with white damask tablecloths and on every table was a pretty, small glass dish with a lit candle in it. Also on each table was a small crystal bud vase containing two roses. On three of the walls were plush booths with royal purple seating that was set round the tables; they also had large purple drapes for the people who wanted to eat in private. In the centre of the restaurant was a marble fountain with statues of four women, standing back-to-back pouring water out of large jugs and, sitting at the feet of them, four children holding bowls to catch the water, which overflowed into the base of the fountain.

They followed the manager past a glass wall, where you could see the chefs cooking the meals, and past the doors where the waiters brought the food out to the guests. He opened a door that had a sign saying 'private' that led to a small room which had a door with a sign above it which said 'private exit'. Also there were lift doors and a staircase at the side of the door.

The family entered the lift and the manager said, 'Once you have settled in, just press the bell when you want your meal and the waiters will bring it into your room. I hope to see you before you go.'

Joan smiled at him, and Steve shook his hand. The lift doors closed, then their dad asked Ann, 'Hit the button that will take us to the penthouse.'

Ann looked for it and pressed the only button that was there. She turned to her dad, saying, as the lift started to move, 'There is only one I could push and that had 'VIP floor' on it.'

Their mum hugged Ann to her as she smiled and whispered to her, 'Our suite is on that floor, so your dad likes to call it the penthouse.'

Just as she finished speaking, the lift stopped moving and the doors opened. They stepped out onto a long corridor. Steve walked across the corridor to a door that was almost facing the lift, took a card out of his wallet and pushed it into a slot in the door. It opened and they all walked in, behind him, to a hallway with four doors in it. Joan held a door open and they entered into a well-decorated apartment.

As they did so, Joan said to Ann and John, 'All the apartments on this floor are as large, and are similar as ours.'

The apartment had lots of paintings hanging round the walls and a large window that reached from the floor to the ceiling, with brightly coloured drapes on both sides of it. It led onto a good-sized balcony. Back in the room were some small tables with ornaments on them, two large sofas and the dining table, all set for the four of them to dine.

As they sat at the table, their dad brought with him one of the remotes from where the TV was and, as he pressed it, he said, 'Let's have some Spanish air in here.' The large glass window split in the middle and both sides disappeared into the walls.

Joan said, 'Will you two stop scrutinising everything, sit down at the table properly and keep still! We have to eat, get to the villa and unpack today.'

As soon as they had settled down round the table, Steve pressed a button on the wall. Then he sat down with them and said, 'This hotel has the best chefs in Spain, so we are in for a treat.'

Then two waitresses brought the food in and placed the tureens on the table. When Joan lifted the top off one of the tureens, the aroma of the food made them all feel hungry. A waiter brought some wine and Joan chose one. The waiter poured out two glasses and placed the bottle on a small stand beside Steve, and then he left.

While they were eating, Joan asked in a hard tone, 'Steve, what business were you involved in that I didn't know about at the villa?'

Steve answered in an angry voice, 'Look, Joan, I admit I didn't tell you about it... I wanted to prove to you - but especially to those stuck-up directors - that I'm a good businessman and I'm not just on the board because I'm your husband.'

Joan said, in a tone that matched Steve's, '*I'm* a bloody good businesswoman and I wouldn't have given you the job if you weren't up to it, even though you are my husband.'

At that, Steve spoke more softly, saying 'I've got a full report about it in my office desk, now let's forget about it till after our holiday, please, hun?'

Joan smiled and picked up her glass of wine, and said, 'Cheers.'

Steve did the same and smiled as he clinked his glass with Joan's, and said, 'Here's to a great holiday for Ann's sixteenth birthday.'

Ann and John clinked their glasses of lemonade and laughed.

John, when he finished his meal, said to one of the waitresses, 'Get me a glass of water.'

His mum, with an angry look on her face and a stern voice, said to John, 'She certainly will not! Now get it yourself - it's just behind you... and don't you ever talk like that to anyone again. Haven't you got any manners?'

Then Ann said to him, 'You should apologise.'

John exclaimed, 'I'm awful sorry, miss, I didn't mean it the way it came out. I hope you will forgive me.'

The waitress smiled at him and nodded, then she looked at Joan and asked, 'Is there anything else you want, madam?'

Joan answered with a smile, 'No, thank you. Everything was perfect.'

When they had finished the meal, Joan went to a sideboard, opened a drawer and took out a pottery dish which had *'Thank you'* on it.

Then she said, 'Come on, Steve. Dig deep! Put some money in it. The staff has done us proud and the meal was like a banquet for a king.'

Steve took out his wallet and placed a small bundle of notes on the dish.

John got up from the table and, while everyone was busy, he wandered out of the apartment, into the corridor. He walked along, looking at the fancy lights and the paintings hanging on the walls. John stopped at a portrait of a man he recognised from the portrait hanging in his home.

A tall, well-built, smartly dressed man approached him and said in Spanish, 'Hello, young man, you must be John.'

John recognised a few words and answered, 'I can't speak Spanish properly yet, can you speak English? Who are you?'

The man answered, in English, 'I'm part of the security team. There are two of us working out of the office on this floor and one working from the office on the ground floor. My name is Mister Diaz and yours is John... And do you know who is in the picture you are looking at?'

John said, 'That's my grandad, I was named after him.'

'Yes, I suppose you were,' the man answered.

Just then Ann popped her head out the door and shouted, 'John! We're getting ready to go.'

He smiled at the security man and said, 'Got to go now, see you.'

He turned and went back into the apartment.

The waitresses cleared everything off the table into a dumbwaiter and, as they left the apartment, Steve handed the plate with the money on it to the head waiter. Then they went across the hallway to the private lift. When it got to the ground floor, the manager was there to meet them. He walked with them but, as they approached the large glass front doors, his phone went off.

He quickly took it out of his pocket, looked at it and said, 'Sorry, I'll have to take this and leave you.'

As he put the phone to his ear, he put out his other hand. Joan and Steve each shook it, as they both nodded and Joan whispered, 'Okay.'

Then the manager turned and walked off smartly towards the restaurant.

As they left the hotel, the concierges held the doors open and one of them said, 'Madam, the food supplies that you requested for the week are in the villa, and the staff hope you have a great week.'

THE VILLA

The limousine chauffeur was waiting with the door open; when they got in, he closed it behind them. It was a short drive of about half an hour to the villa. It was now getting dark and, as the limousine approached the large iron gates, the lights round them came on and lit them up. The grounds around the villa were dimly lit by the road lights.

John asked his dad, 'What is the number to get the gates to work?'

His dad laughed and said, 'it's twenty-ten, but it's a secret, so don't tell anyone.'

John jumped out and went to the security pad. He put the number in and the gates swung open and, as John walked to the car, it went in, causing the lights in the villa grounds to come on. The car didn't stop to pick John up, instead it drove along the driveway to the villa. As he ran after the car, John took a shortcut past the Olympic-size swimming pool, jumped over a flower bed and a small line of bushes and nearly fell into a small nature pond that they had for the wildlife that lived in the grounds.

When the car stopped, John came up the driveway shouting, 'Dad, I knew you would do that to me!'

While they unpacked, John went from one room to another. He looked in the games room, where there was a full-size snooker table and all kinds of games. Then he popped into the gym, where their dad had his weights, a rowing machine and another machine for running on. From where he was standing, he could see the shower room. As he was leaving the gym, he pushed a big punch bag that was hanging from the ceiling and, as he passed it, the bag swung back and nearly knocked him over.

He turned back to it and said out loud, 'Who are you hitting? Just because I'm small… Well, I'll show you.'

With that he started punching it as hard as he could but, after a little while, he got tired and, as he left, he looked back at the punch bag and said, 'That will teach you.' Then he went into the music room and turned some music on. He sat down in one of the large, comfy seats and almost fell asleep. He was in a world of his own.

Ann came in and said, 'You can come in now, sleepy head. We've finished unpacking. We are all ready for bed, so you better go and say good night to Mum and Dad.'

John went into the living room to his mum and dad and yawned, ''Night, I'm off to bed.'

His dad just answered, "Night' back to him, but his mum tried to kiss him good night.

He stood back and muttered, 'I'm not a baby, I wish you wouldn't treat me like one. I'm nearly twelve. 'Night.'

Then he turned and walked up the stairs to his room.

The next morning, his mum shouted several times for him to get up, saying, 'Come on, lazy bones, get up! It's your big sister's birthday! If you're not up in five minutes, I'll be up with a bucket of cold water.'

He shivered at the thought, as he knew she would do it, but he had five minutes yet...

His mother didn't wait five minutes, though, she was in his room in two, throwing the bedclothes off him and covering him from head to foot in a bucket of iced water. He screamed as he jumped up, dripping wet, then he grabbed a handful of ice off the bed.

His mother said, 'Don't you dare.'

Then she turned and ran down the stairs shouting, 'Steve, tell him not to put that ice down my back!' but their dad and Ann were too busy laughing.

Joan ran down the stairs with John in hot pursuit, looking like a drowned rat with his boxer shorts dripping wet. Just as he was about to grab his mother at the bottom of the stairs, his wet feet slid on the tiled floor and he went down with a bang on his bottom. The other three all doubled up with laughter.

His dad, still laughing, helped him up saying, 'It's not funny, he could have damaged his brain.'

After he got over the shock and pain of landing on his bottom John joined in with the laughing, while still rubbing his backside.

They had their breakfast and Joan said, 'Well, Ann, you're the birthday girl, so what do you want to do today?'

Ann replied, 'I want us all to go to the beach...'

'I've a surprise for you. Before we came on holiday, I told my PA to order a champagne picnic for you on that picnic area halfway up the mountain road. The view from up there is breathtaking. Then, after the picnic, we'll stroll down to the beach,' their dad butted in, with a smile on his face.

As he was speaking, their mother complained, 'It's ten miles up to the picnic area and four miles from there down to the beach.'

When Ann and John heard that, they started shouting about the distance too. John repeated what his mum had said, 'It's ten miles from here up to the picnic area and from there it's four miles down to the beach!'

'Yes,' Steve replied laughing, 'But it's alright, we don't have to walk up the mountain. She has ordered a car to pick us up and drop us off at the picnic area. So we'll be in no hurry. We'll have all day to stroll down... and that view! You couldn't get an artist who could portray it and do it justice. From the mountain road, it's beautiful.'

Joan said, 'I'm not going near the edge, everyone knows that I've got vertigo and it terrifies me just the thought of going near it.'

Steve laughed and said, 'I know the rules, hun. You walk on the inside and I'll walk by the edge, but don't you push me over, will you?'

Joan shuddered and said, 'Don't say things like that, Steve, the thought makes me go sick inside.'

Their dad went over and cuddled their mum, and with a big squeeze said, 'Don't worry, love. I know you wouldn't do that to me - we're the original Darby and Joan. I wouldn't go anywhere without you with me.' Then he kissed her and said, 'Come on, let's get ready. This is going to be a day to remember.'

A TRIP TO THE PICNIC AREA

A short while later, a big, black stretch limousine pulled up outside the villa. The chauffeur got out, walked up the footpath to the door and rang the bell.

Joan answered the door and the chauffeur said, 'Excuse me, madam, would you care to check the list of ordered items before we set off?'

Joan gave the chauffeur a big grin and said, 'That's his job.' Then she turned and shouted, 'Steve, come out here, there's a gentleman to see you.'

When their dad came back in after checking the picnic basket, John said, 'Come on, Ann, I'll race you to the car and the winner can sit in the front with the driver.'

Ann replied, 'I'm sixteen, not five. I don't want to play childish games.'

Their dad and mum butted in, 'We'll race you' and, as they ran, their dad said, 'Come on, Ann, you're never too old to race.'

As their dad passed Ann, he put his arm around her waist and swept her off her feet, carrying her out to the car.

John shouted as he got to the car, 'I win, so I'm in the front with the chauffeur.'

Their dad, still holding Ann in his arms, swung her round and said, 'I don't know... What about the birthday girl? I think if you were a gentleman, you would offer your favourite sister the choice. It's her birthday, my dear chap.'

John replied, 'My favourite sister? She's my only sister. Oh, I suppose that *makes* her my favourite sister. Well, okay, you can have the front seat if you want it.'

Then their dad kissed Ann and said, 'Come on, let's get going. This is going to be a great day, one for the family album.'

Ann laughed as her dad put her down and said, 'Let the young boy sit with the driver, the child always likes to be in the front seat.'

John grinned as he got in the car. He knew Ann would let him in the front. She always did; even if she had won the race to the car, she would give in to him if he pleaded with her. Ann always let him have things his way, unless it was something she was serious about and then she wouldn't budge. John always knew when she was determined because of the tone in her voice - which sounded like his mother's voice when she was annoyed with him - and an angry look

Ann would get on her face, and then he would just give up and forget it.

While John was talking to the driver, he could hear their dad teasing Ann about her age and to leave the boys alone.

Their mum joined in for a while but then said, 'Come on, Steve, I think Ann is getting a bit annoyed. We'd better stop it now. We don't want to spoil Ann's birthday.'

In no time at all they were at the picnic location. The chauffeur stopped by a table and benches that John had chosen near the middle of the picnic area.

John got on well with the chauffeur and told him, 'I want to be a racing car driver when I'm old enough.'

He asked the chauffeur if he could be allowed to sit in the driving seat. The chauffeur said, 'Yes,' as he put the handbrake on and turned the engine off. Then he put the car in first gear and said to John, 'I bet you don't know why I put it in first gear, do you?'

John shouted, 'Oh yes, I do! If the brakes fail, the gears act like a sort of brake. I've seen my dad. He always puts the handbrake on and then he puts the car into first gear, and he told me why.'

The chauffeur said, 'I will take the keys and, John, don't touch the handbrake or the gears.' Then the chauffeur added, 'If you do, I'll have to break both your arms and legs,' as he grinned at John.

Then he got out and held open the driver's door for John and helped John to get into the driver's seat, saying, 'Make yourself comfortable, driver, while I set the picnic up.'

While the chauffeur was unloading the car, John was in the driver's seat for about ten minutes, making loud skidding noises as if he was driving a racing car around a racing track and pulling the steering wheel one way, then pulling it the other way. He stopped for a moment when the chauffeur reached for a leather box in the passenger area of the car, opened it and took out a large white paper tablecloth with pink writing on it that said 'Happy birthday, Ann!' The chauffeur laid the tablecloth onto the picnic table and unloaded the picnic basket out of the boot of the car. He placed it on the bench that was attached to the table and then he proceeded to take the food, champagne and soft drinks out of the basket and lay the food all around the tabletop, with a big cut-glass bowl of caviar in the centre.

The people in the picnic area stopped and stared in disbelief at the food and drink the chauffeur placed on the table. When he finished unloading Steve signed the chauffeur's paperwork and gave him a big tip.

The chauffeur said, 'Thank you, sir, the staff will be here in four hours' time, like you requested. They will do anything you want them to do and they will collect the picnic basket, utensils and glassware when you are finished with them, and clean the picnic area.'

Then he gave John a hand to climb out of the driver's seat and got into it himself. He started the car, smiled and said to John, 'I'll see you, driver, on the racing circuit in the future - that I'm sure of.' Then with that he waved and drove off down the winding mountain road.

They had a great time at the picnic and John was amazed at how their dad went over to an empty table next to the food and climbed onto the bench, waving his arms in the air to beckon the people to him. When some people started to move toward him, he stepped down and stood by the table of food.

As they gathered round him, he invited everyone in the picnic area to join them and then he proudly announced, 'It is my beautiful daughter's sixteenth birthday and you are all welcome to celebrate with us on this great day.' Then he repeated it all over again in perfect Spanish.

The picnic was more like an outdoor banquet with all the people who joined in with them and, as usual, their dad was the life and soul of the party. He went round the picnic area to the people who stood back and were unsure about joining in with them. Their dad would go to each family that were just standing there looking in amazement at them. John didn't hear all what their dad said, he just watched as their dad walked up to the man in each family and offered his hand to him. As the man shook it, John's dad pulled the man toward him and gave him a hug, as if they were old friends, and laughing he'd say something like, 'We're just a family like you. Come and enjoy the party.' Then he'd offer his hand to the woman and when a woman offered her hand, their dad would bend and kiss it, and in no time at all they would be laughing and walking to the table.

Their mum said to John, 'Look at your dad. He has still got the gift of the gab in English and Spanish - he has them all eating out of his hand. Well, if not his hand, off the table anyway.'

John replied, 'Mum, your jokes are crap.'

His mum gave him a serious look, and he corrected himself, saying, 'Sorry, Mum, I mean your jokes are last.'

Steve never missed a chance to embarrass Ann about it being her birthday. Everybody was round by the table laughing and talking and one part of the picnic area was empty. When five boys on motorbikes drove into the picnic area, they stopped about twenty yards from the party. They got off their bikes and walked over to one of the picnic benches. They sat down and were having a conversation and now and then were looking over at the party. Steve waved and called them to come over, but they just looked and none of the boys made a move.

ANN MEETS HER BOYFRIEND

So Joan went to the boys, put her head between the two of them who were sitting on the side of the table with their backs to the party and put her arms on both boys shoulders. She looked at the three boys sitting on the other side facing her, smiled and said, 'My husband was talking to you lads, so come and join us. You're welcome.'

Joan took them to the food, gave each boy a plate and told them to get something to eat. She left them to it and went over to speak to the women, who were in a couple of groups talking. She went to the English-speaking women and joined in the conversation for a little while, and then she strolled over to the Spanish women and joined in with them. The other women who were in the picnic area that could also speak both languages went to both groups to talk to them.

Steve did the same. He went round the area to the men who were in two different groups, chatting, and made sure everyone was having a good time. If he saw anyone who looked out of place, he would go up to them and start a conversation with them, and then he would call a couple of people over to join them in the conversation. When it was going well, he would move on and leave them talking.

John and Ann were with some boys and girls about their own ages. The five boys soon found their way over to Ann and John and asked them what names they went by.

John announced, 'I'm John, and this is my sister, Ann - the birthday girl.'

Ann blushed and said, 'Be quiet, John, you are embarrassing me.'

They all surrounded her. With her long black hair and a pretty face, anyone could see she was a beautiful young woman. She was small for her sixteen years. She was only four foot eleven, but she wasn't worried because Joan had said she was small like Ann when she was sixteen, but now her mother was five foot seven and had promised Ann that she would grow as tall as her, or even taller because her dad was six foot five.

Tommy's heart was pounding as he stood back, behind his friends. But she still saw him because he was taller than all of them and, as the boys spoke to her and she answered them, every now and then she would look up at him and smile.

Tommy blushed when Terry, who was one of Tommy's friends, said, 'All right, gentlemen, let's not waste our time... She only has eyes for TT.'

Ann blushed too, looked down at the ground and asked, 'Who's TT?'

Two of the boys who were standing in front of Tommy stood aside to make an opening between them. As they did so, they both bowed and touched their heads, one with his left hand and the other with his right hand; then they both brought their hands down and swung them towards Tommy, as they turned their heads to face him. The boys could hardly stand for laughing and pointing at Ann's and Tommy's crimson faces.

When Ann got over her embarrassment, she carried on talking to the boys for a while, then said, 'Well, you know our names, so what are all your names?'

Jammer answered, pointing at each boy as he said, 'That's Paul, Dave, Terry, and that's Tommy and I'm Jammer.'

Ann smiled at each boy as his name was said, but she blushed again when Tommy's name was mentioned.

Terry repeated, 'Well, lads, it looks like Ann's only got eyes for TT.'

John started to laugh and Ann just looked at him, and with that John asked if he could look at their bikes.

Dave said, 'You can look, but don't touch because the bikes don't belong to us, we got them from the motor hire place.'

As John walked toward the bikes, Paul said, 'We might as well come with you. I don't think these two want us around anyway, so you can sit on the pillion seat if you want.'

John grinned and said, 'It would be great to ride on it with you..?'

Jammer explained, 'We can't give you a ride. We are only learners ourselves and we're a bit nervous on these winding mountain roads. Your parents wouldn't be too happy with us if we did take you on a bike.'

John carried on talking to the lads about their bikes. Ann had her own conversation going on with Tommy, but it wasn't about his bike.

Ann asked Tommy, 'Why do they call you TT? Are you mad about motorbikes? And is that why you hire them?'

He answered, 'No, we only got the bikes because we thought they were the easiest way to get around. My friends call me TT because my first name is Thomas and my second name is Tenant. So Paul started calling me TT and the rest of them joined in. Mind you, I do like motorbikes and after this holiday I'm saving up to get one. I'll give you a ride on it when I get it.'

Ann said, 'You've got a date, but my parents would kill me if I went on your bike and you haven't passed your test. Come to think of it, my dad would kill you as well!'

Tommy was made up and said the first thing that came into his head, 'Now *you* would ride on it, I'm even more determined to get a motor bike and it will be one of the best you can buy... and I will pass my test! I'll make sure of that, just so I can take you for a nice long ride on it. You would get on it with me, wouldn't you?'

Ann laughed and said, 'You don't even know where I live, so how can you give me a ride on this great bike, even if I would go on it with you?'

He smiled and said, 'I know I don't, but you're going to tell me, aren't you? Or you won't be able to get a ride on my bike.'

She replied, 'I live by Delamere but I'm only telling you that. It's up to you to find my home, that's if you want to...'

Tommy said, 'That's not fair. I know where Delamere is, it's not that far from where I live, but I wouldn't have a clue how to find your home. You'll have to give me a better clue than that.'

Ann said, 'I'll give you another easy clue. Look for a Catholic school.'

Tommy frowned and replied in a surprised tone, 'A Catholic school? There must be loads of Catholic schools near Delamere. I take it you don't really want to see me again, do you?'

Ann smiled at him and got hold of his hand as she answered, 'Of course I do. I'm hoping to see you again before we go home, and I live in a house called The Farm, off Goose Green Lane, Delamere.' She then gave him her mobile number but warned him that he would not be able to call her until she got back home, as the family had left their phones behind when they came on vacation.

Tommy was made up at her answer. He grinned and started laughing, and Ann joined in.

When Ann's dad saw her talking and laughing with Tommy, he said, 'Joan, look, I think our young daughter has a date. Do you think she will introduce us to him?'

Her mum was laughing and replied, as they walked over, hand-in-hand, to the young couple, 'I hope so, I wouldn't like her to go out with someone who we didn't know.'

Ann, with a red face, glared at them. Tommy, whose face was just as red as Ann's, stammered, 'My name is Tommy, Mr Thomson.'

Her dad, with a grin, said, 'You know my family name, yours is Tommy what?'

Tommy answered, his face going even redder, 'My name is Tommy Tenant, sir.'

Ann said in an angry voice, as she turned her back on her parents and started to walk away, 'Take no notice of them, Tommy, they think they are funny.'

As she left, she beckoned Tommy to walk with her. Tommy looked at her parents and nervously got his bike, then he caught up with Ann and they walked to an empty picnic table. Ann sat on the bench as Tommy leaned his motorbike against the picnic table, then he sat next to Ann.

Ann asked him, 'Where are you from? And what are you going to do after the holidays?'

Tommy answered, 'I live in Frodsham. It's not too far from where you live and when the holiday ends I've got a bit of a problem. My mother wants me to go to university, but I don't fancy it. I want to do some sort of apprenticeship.

All the other boys are going to university, but if we lose contact with each other we've promised to meet each year for a two-week holiday.' Tommy smiled and then said, 'Now it's your turn. What are you going to do after the hols?'

Ann replied, 'I'm hoping to go to the university where my mum and dad met and fell in love, but I have two more years to study before I can do that.'

Tommy went red, as he said in a quiet voice, 'This might sound bad but don't take it the wrong way. I hope *you* don't meet the love of your life there. I really like you and I've never felt like this about anyone else before.'

Ann blushed, and got hold of his hand and replied, 'I know what you mean. I felt like that the moment I saw you with the boys.'

Tommy gently squeezed her hand and stammered, 'I hope this is not just a holiday romance. I want to see you from now on; I hope you feel the same way.'

Ann's smile seemed to glow as she nodded and squeezed his hand. They talked for a while. They didn't realise they had been sitting there talking for two hours till they heard Ann's dad, as he looked at his watch and announced to everyone, 'We will be going now, but just help yourselves to the food that is left. Some people are coming soon to pick up the dishes and clean up the area. We thank you for your company.'

The people waved and some clapped. Their dad and mum waved back.

As he got hold of Joan's hand and led her away from the picnic, he shouted back to Ann and John, 'Come on, you two, we've a great walk ahead of us.'

Ann asked Tommy, 'Would you come with me to the beach? I'd like you to.' Tommy replied, 'I'd love to, but you better ask your mum and dad if it's alright.'

Ann left Tommy sitting on the bench, caught up to her parents and said to her mum, 'Can Tommy come with us?'

THE WALK DOWN TO THE BEACH

Their parents had stopped just off the picnic area. Her dad said, 'I don't think so young lady,' but her mum said, 'Oh, come on, Steve, don't be an old fuddy-duddy. You were young once!'

Her dad said, 'Okay, but don't get on the back of his bike and make sure you walk on the pavement, not on the road.'

Ann replied, 'Don't worry, Dad, I wouldn't go on his bike - he's just a learner.'

She walked a little way ahead of her parents and waved for Tommy to catch her up as Steve and Joan walked slowly down the road.

Tommy waved to his friends, shouting, 'See you later.'

As his friends laughed and waved back, he got on his bike and in two seconds he had caught up to Ann. He stopped, got off it and walked alongside her.

Her dad looked at them and in a serious voice he said, 'Go ahead, but make sure you walk on the pavement, not the road. It's got some bad bends on it. We will catch you up.' Then he glanced at his watch and sighed, 'We'll have to wait for John as usual.' With that he shouted, 'Come on, John!'

Tommy walked beside Ann while he pushed his bike on the road, as the pavement was too narrow for it and was in poor condition. It was so bad in places that Tommy had to walk on the road with the bike between them. While walking and talking, Ann tripped a couple of times.

The third time she said, 'I think it's safer to be on the road with you.'

He had a worried look on his face and asked, 'What will your parents say about that?'

She answered, 'If I stay on this so-called sidewalk - you couldn't call it a pavement - I'll be black and blue by the time we get down to the beach.'

Ann looked back at her parents and Tommy did the same as she continued talking. 'So, I'll just have to put up with being told off, when and if they catch up with us. That might sound like I will be in trouble, but it's my birthday and I'm sure I'll get away with it. If you push the bike on the so-called footpath we could walk together, and we wouldn't be too far out on the road.'

Tommy did as she said and Ann went round the bike to walk beside him.

Steve looked at his watch a few times while they were walking very slowly, waiting for John to catch up to them. The last time he looked at it, he puffed and, in a sharp tone, shouted, 'John! Get a move on!'

Joan got hold of Steve's hand and said, 'We've got all day to get to the beach.' Steve looked at his watch again and answered in the same sharp tone, 'If he doesn't come now the tide will be in by the time we get down there... Oh look, he's finally making a move now, but he still is in a world of his own.'

'Come on, John, get a move on,' Joan shouted. Then she turned to Steve and said, 'You know, if we get on our way, he will follow and as long as we can see he's safe, just let him tag on behind us as usual.'

John ran after his mum and dad, not to catch up but to keep an eye on them so he wouldn't get lost as they walked down the mountain road. His dad walked by the edge, where there was a small wall on the narrow sidewalk, with their mum walking on the road as far away as their arms would stretch. As John had nearly reached them, he slowed down as he didn't want anyone to think he was a mummy's boy.

As John caught up to them, his dad looked at his watch again. He smiled as he looked up and said, 'You're right, Joan. I'm sorry. It's just that I wanted us all to be at the beach before the tide comes in.'

With that he used his free hand to get hold of a lamppost and, with his other hand still holding on to Joan, he laughed and said, 'It's quite safe. I've got hold of the lamp. If we fall that will have to give way, so you can come on to the side and look over the edge to the sea far below. It's a lovely blue and green with the sun bouncing off it.'

Joan was angry and said nervously, as she pulled her hand out of his, 'Steve, you know I can't, so please stop asking me to try. I just can't do it. I just go sick inside.'

Steve said, 'I'm sorry. I hope you will accept my apology. You know I love you and I would like you to be able to see the beautiful scenery, but it's more important that you enjoy your daughter's birthday.'

With that he let go of the lamp and looked at his watch, then smiled and rested his hand back on the lamp, and held out his other hand to Joan. She got hold and, as they stood there smiling at each other, he said, 'It's three-thirty. You were right, Joan, we'll get to the beach in plenty of...'

He didn't finish the sentence. Just then a small, old sports car came round the bend and, even though the road was wide at this point, it was on their side of the road - heading straight towards Ann and Tommy.

Ann just froze and stood there, staring at the car, as it came speeding towards them. Tommy let go of the bike and, as it fell against the small wall, he grabbed hold of Ann's dress and, with all his might, pulled her to him. As the dress tore, he fell on top of the bike and Ann landed on top of him. The car just missed their feet as it carried on past them and it didn't change course as it headed toward Joan, who was still on the road.

John, who was on the footpath about ten yards behind his mum and dad, screamed to his mum when he saw what had happened to Ann and that now the car was going to hit his mum.

Steve stepped back, pulling Joan as hard as he could towards him onto the small side, but the force sent her past him and over the small wall, with Steve still holding on to her with one hand, as he nearly went over the wall as well. Their dad hit the wall with such force that blood was coming from his legs and his arms, and his hands were covered in blood.

But he still held on to Joan as he shouted, 'Ann, John, help me - I can't hold on to your mum!'

Tommy and Ann struggled to get up off the bike and ran to her dad's side. Ann leaned over the wall and stretched her arms down as far as she could, but she was too small to reach her mum.

Her mum was crying and shouting, 'Pull me up, Steve. Don't let me go.'

Tommy climbed over the wall and, hanging on to it, he edged his way along it by moving one hand then the other, just to where he thought he could get hold of Joan's free hand.

He heard her screaming, 'Don't let go, I'm slipping!'

With one hand clinging to the wall, Tommy reached for her; just as his fingertips touched her hand, he heard Ann's dad shout, 'My God! She's slipped!'

Tommy nearly fell as well, as he made a grab for Joan as she plummeted, screaming, down the mountain to the road far below. He managed to jam his foot in a crack in the rock and hold tight with the hand on the wall. He then grabbed hold of the wall with his other hand but was exhausted from his efforts and with shock at what had happened. He couldn't pull himself back up and over the wall. Tommy was now in trouble, with his hands all cut on the rough bricks. He knew he would have to save himself and struggled to get back over the wall.

Steve just stood there, looking down with his arms still over the wall and crying as he kept muttering, 'She slipped. I couldn't hold her.'

John was crying, as he slumped down with his back against the wall in a foetal position, and Ann was screaming, 'You let go of mum!'

A car stopped when the driver saw what was happening. A Spanish man who was in the picnic area and had also been going round the men there talking in Spanish and English, got out of his car.

As he ran to help Tommy, he said, 'My wife is phoning the police and ambulance.'

Then he pulled Tommy up and over the wall, onto the narrow walkway. Tommy, being exhausted, just dropped onto the ground.

John was still curled up in a ball, crying and Steve was still muttering, 'She slipped... It was my fault. I couldn't hold her.'

Then he bent down and helped John to stand, pulling him close to hug him with one arm as, with tears in his eyes, he reached out to Ann with the other.

But Ann pushed his hand away and just kept screaming at him, 'You let go of Mum!'

Steve replied, in a sobbing voice, 'Mum slipped. I know it's my fault I couldn't hold on to her. I'm sorry, Ann.'

Tommy was hurt and it was difficult for him to get to his feet, so he could go over to Ann. It was then he realised that he had to limp because he had hurt his ankle and couldn't walk properly on it.

As he got to her, she was hysterical; he struggled with her as he led her to where his bike lay on its side, and all the time she was sobbing, looking back at her dad and crying, saying, 'He let go of my mum.'

Tommy left the bike lying on the ground but, whilst still holding onto Ann's wrist and even though his hands were bleeding and he was in pain from his ankle, he got it into a position so Ann could sit on part of the seat. It took him some time to calm Ann down enough to sit down.

Then he sat down on the ground beside her and tried to comfort her till the police and ambulance got there, but she just kept crying and muttering, 'He let my mum drop.'

The Spanish man's wife got out of the car and went straight to John and put her arms round him. As she did, the man got hold of Steve's arm and put his other hand across Steve's back and on to his shoulder, to turn him away from the wall. As Steve was turned, he took his arm from around John.

Steve kept looking back as he was half pushed and half guided to the couple's car by the Spanish man, who opened the back passenger door as he said to Steve, 'Get in the car and we will drive you to your wife.'

Steve put both hands up to cover his face. He was in a daze and muttering. He was helped in and the man put the seat belt around him while he sat with his hands on his face and just kept muttering, 'It's my fault... She didn't even want to be near the mountain. I brought Joan here. It's my fault.'

The woman had to struggle to get John to the car. He was in shock and couldn't move. She had to lift him into it and almost force him to sit on the seat so she could get the seat belt on him.

The man and his wife got in the car. They drove about ten yards, down to Ann and Tommy and stopped. The woman wound down the car window and spoke broken English to them.

With tears in her eyes and a hanky in her hand, she said to Tommy, 'Can you take care of Ann till an ambulance comes?'

Tommy, still holding onto Ann, nodded and replied in a low voice, 'I won't let her out of my sight.'

Then the woman looked at Ann and said, 'We are taking your dad and brother down the mountain. I've told them on the phone to send two ambulances. They will be here in a moment - I can hear the sirens now.'

Then they drove off down the mountain to meet the police and ambulance at the place where the police had parked, as near as they could to Joan's body. As the car with Steve and John in it arrived at the scene, another police car and ambulance drove past them, up the mountain road, with their sirens on.

The police had got to where Joan's body was just before the Spanish man pulled up, and were standing round directing the traffic so nobody could see the tragic accident. While the ambulance men looked after Joan, a police officer came to the car to wave it on.

The lady had the window down and, as the officer approached the car, she said to him in Spanish, 'The woman's husband and son are in the back. I'm the one who phoned you, and their daughter and a young boy are further up the mountain.'

The officer answered, 'There are a couple of vehicles on their way up there now.' Then he turned around and called the two policewomen over to help Steve get out of the car. When they got to it, one of them opened the car door for Steve as the other one started to go round the car to get John, but the first officer called her back to help her get Steve out because he didn't move; he just sat there with his hands over his eyes and muttering. She leaned over him to undo the seat belt, but he didn't move or stop muttering. Then the two officers half helped and half pulled him out of the car.

As he stood there, his hands finally moved away from his face. He looked at them with bloodshot eyes and tears rolling down his face. as he said, 'I just couldn't hold onto Joan. She slipped out of my hands. How is she? I want to see her.'

They helped lean him against a police car to steady him and a police sergeant rushed over to help support him when he saw Steve's legs give way as one of the policewomen said softly to him, 'I'm afraid you won't be able to see her just now. I'm sorry but the paramedics have said your wife's fall was fatal.'

Steve started to sob even louder, and in between sobbing, he muttered from behind his hands, which were once again covering his face, 'It's my fault, she didn't even want to come to Spain, it's my fault. I should have pulled her to safety.'

The sergeant held onto Steve and waited a moment while he pulled himself together. Initially he told the two policewomen to take Steve to the ambulance.

Then, as he went round the car to get John and saw the state John was in, the sergeant quickly said, 'No, put him in that police car and I'll bring the child to it.'

The policewomen walked either side of Steve and helped him to the car, and all the time he had his hands covering his face and was muttering to himself. They got him into the car and put the seat belt on him while the sergeant went back to get John. He opened the door and took the seat belt off John, who just sat there and didn't make a sound, even when the officer picked him up. The sergeant, carrying John, rushed over to the car where his dad was.

He got in the back with John on his knee and said, 'This child is in shock, get to the hospital as fast as you can go.'

One of the policewomen who had put Steve in the car got into at the same time and sat next to the driver.

She said, 'You haven't got your seat belt on, Sergeant.'

He answered in a sharp tone, 'Don't worry about that now, just get going.'

With that the driver put his siren on and his foot to the floor.

TAKEN TO THE HOSPITAL

The sergeant turned his head to look at Steve and said to him in English, 'I'm Sergeant Torres. Will you tell me your name and the child's? We can radio ahead to the hospital, so they know we are on our way. With your names, they'll book you in at the reception desk and can get set up for when we arrive.'

Steve answered in a shaky voice, 'I'm Steve Thomson and my son is John. Will they bring Joan and Ann to this hospital?'

The sergeant answered, 'Yes, they are right behind us.'

The policewoman in the passenger seat was on the radio to the hospital and, as soon as Steve had said their names, she told the hospital who they should be expecting.

Then she turned round to look at them in the back and said, 'The hospital will be ready for us.'

Tommy looked down the road as he heard the siren and saw the police car coming round the bend with the ambulance in hot pursuit. As they approached, Tommy struggled to get to his feet and just managed to as the ambulance stopped by them. The police car went past them and stopped just by the blood that was on the wall. Two of the police officers walked back to them and arrived at almost the same time as the paramedics, while the third officer who got out of the car stayed at the scene, looking at the blood and over the small wall, down to Joan's body.

Tommy was trying to help Ann to get up. One of the paramedics had got two wheelchairs for them out of the ambulance and the other one went to Ann and Tommy to check them over.

Then he said in broken English to Tommy, 'You can leave your friend to us now.'

After that Tommy didn't understand another word, as they all spoke in Spanish. One paramedic helped Tommy into one of the chairs, while the other one picked Ann up from where she was still sitting on the seat of the motorbike, with her head in her hands as she cried. She was still in the same sitting position when he placed her in the wheelchair.

All the time she kept saying, 'He killed my mum, he let go of my mum.'

The two policemen who could speak English looked at one another, and one said in Spanish, 'Do you think we should question them?'

The other officer answered, 'Look at the state of them... and they are only kids. I think the sergeant will have our jobs if we do.'

The first officer, looking a bit worried, replied back, 'I think he will give us a kick up the backside if we don't question them.'

While one paramedic was holding on to the two wheelchairs, the other lowered the ramp on the ambulance, so they could push the chairs on to it.

The paramedic holding the chairs heard what the police officers were saying and butted in, 'If I were you, I wouldn't worry about it because they are in our care, and we won't let you near them. When we get to the hospital, you can talk to the doctors and see what they say.'

The police officers didn't like what the paramedic had said and it showed on their faces.

One of the police officers said, 'Okay, you can follow us down to the hospital.' Then they turned round and walked back to their car, complaining to one another about the paramedic. They were still complaining when they got back in the car.

The third policeman was now sitting in the driving seat.

He asked, 'What are you two going on about now?'

One of them replied, 'Those paramedics telling us we can't question the kids, like they are in charge. Who do they think they are?'

The driver shook his head and said, 'How long have you two been in the job? You should know by now the paramedics are right not to let you near them till the doctor has seen them.'

The driver looked in his rear-view mirror and saw the paramedic getting into the ambulance to drive it. With that he drove up to the picnic area to turn around, with the ambulance following him. They turned and both headed down the mountain road to the hospital.

The police car with John and his dad in it arrived at the hospital's accident and emergency building. As the car pulled in and stopped, a nurse opened the door where the police sergeant was holding John. The nurse helped him out, while the driver and the female officer got out and helped Steve out of the car.

Two porters approached them, one had a wheelchair for Steve and the other porter had a stretcher on wheels for John.

When they went through the hospital doors, the sergeant said to a doctor, 'I think the child should be seen first. He hasn't moved or said a word since he saw what happened to his mother.'

The doctor and a nurse took the stretcher with John on it and pushed it into a cubicle. The nurse pulled the curtains around it. As another nurse showed Steve into another cubicle, the sergeant made his way back to the accident and emergency entry as quickly as he could, to meet the ambulance that had Tommy and Ann in it.

The nurse looked at Steve's arms and legs to check him over. Then she handed him a large dressing and said, 'Hold this on the deep cut on your arm. It's stopped bleeding now but that, and all your other injuries, are large scrapes that will need to be cleaned. As we are so busy, I'm afraid you will have to wait to see the doctor. Could you take a seat in reception?'

The other police officers were waiting in the doorway for the second ambulance to get there when the sergeant arrived to wait with them.

The policewoman said, 'I don't think he knows she's dead, Sergeant.'

He replied, 'He knows. He just finds it hard to accept it.'

While the police were waiting for the ambulance with Ann and Tommy in it to arrive, Steve put the dressing to the cut on his arm, then he put his cut arm against his chest to hold the dressing in place while he struggled to get his wallet out of his back pocket with his other hand. He didn't sit down; instead, he went to the desk to speak to the receptionist. He put his wallet on the desk in front of her as he slid a card out of it.

He said to her in Spanish, 'Would you please phone the doctor on this card and tell him my family needs his help?'

The receptionist looked at the card, then back at Steve as if she was about to say something, but before she could Steve said, 'He's my private doctor and a friend, so you won't get in trouble if you phone him.'

The receptionist smiled and nodded as she picked the phone up and dialled the number. She spoke for a few minutes on it, then she put the phone back on its receiver as she looked at him and said, 'Mr Alonso will be here in a few moments. He's only in the ward next to here.'

When Mr Alonso walked into the waiting room twenty minutes later Steve got up and went to meet him. Mr Alonso, or Mateo as he was known to Steve, had been a friend of the family for years. They had met when he came from Spain to study medicine at the same university that Steve and Joan attended. After he got his degree, he became a doctor in England with his own practice; Joan and Steve became his patients. Within a few years he was one of the youngest consultants in his field. He was happy in England, but he had to leave to go home to Spain because his parents were in poor health. So he set up a private practice there.

Once his practice was established, he had left other doctors in charge and went into the local hospital as a consultant and, after a few years, he was the top consultant there. Joan and Steve kept his practice in Spain on a retainer for the hotel's VIPs.

As Steve started to tell him in a trembling, sobbing voice what had happened. Mateo put his arm round Steve. He couldn't make out what Steve was saying because of his sobbing, but he already knew about the accident.

Mateo spoke in perfect English, saying, 'Come in here, Steve,' as he opened a door and partly pulled him and partly led him into a treatment room.

Mateo sat Steve down on one of the chairs. Steve was still muttering with his head in his hands, looking down. Then he suddenly went quiet, his hands dropped down to his lap and he just sat there not moving. Mateo spoke to him, but Steve didn't answer - Mateo thought he was in shock.

So he placed another chair close, facing Steve, which he sat on and he kept talking to him as he dressed the cut on Steve's arm. It took quite a while for Mateo to get through to him and, while he was taking care of Steve's arm, his phone rang. He got up, took it out of the pocket of his white coat and walked a little way from Steve and answered it.

Once the call was done, he said to Steve, 'I know about the accident. I'm sorry for you and the children, Joan was a lovely person.'

He sat back down and leaned forward so their heads were nearly touching, then put his hand on Steve's shoulder and said in a quiet voice, 'Steve, I've had a word with the doctor who's seen John. He's been given a sedative to help him relax. He will be asleep by now. He will be kept here overnight, and I've requested that they let me know how Ann is doing when she's brought in.'

At that moment Mateo's phone rang again. He got up and walked a few steps away from Steve as he took it out of the pocket and answered it, saying, 'Yes' a couple of times, before adding, 'I have her father here. Oh, I see. Thank you.'

He returned to sit facing Steve and said, 'I'm sorry, Steve, but Ann said she doesn't want to see you. She wants her Aunt Emma -

and she was getting hysterical, so they have given Ann a sedative also.'

'I've asked the doctor to put Ann and John in the same room. They will sleep for a good eight to nine hours, so we will keep both of them in overnight. You should get some rest yourself; you've had a terrible shock.'

Steve was still sitting on the chair with his head buried in his hands and, sobbing, he said, 'I've lost Joan, and my children think it's my fault, and maybe it was. I should have kept hold.'

Mateo put his arm round Steve and tried to comfort him saying, 'I know it wasn't your fault. You did what you could to save Joan and, in a little while, Ann and John will come to realise you did everything you could to save their mother.'

Steve stood up, taking his hands from his red eye and, with tears rolling down his face, said in an angry, sobbing voice, 'I couldn't hold her. She slipped out of my hand. If I catch the bastard who was driving that car, I'll kill him. I want to see Joan.'

Mateo stood, facing Steve, and put his hands on Steve's shoulders.

Looking in Steve's face he answered, 'I'm sorry, Steve, but you won't be able to see Joan till tomorrow afternoon. If you want a couple of sleeping pills for tonight, I can write you a prescription?'

Steve cried out, 'I don't want any bloody sleeping tablets. I just want Joan back with me.'

Mateo said, 'Okay, Steve, I understand. Just sit down and rest. I think a policeman is waiting to take you to where you want to stay the night.'

As he was speaking, with his hands still on Steve's shoulders, he gently pushed Steve down to sit back down in the chair that he had just stood up from.

Just then a buzzer went off in his pocket. He took it out, looked at it and then he said, 'I'm sorry, Steve, but I've got to go. There has been an emergency. Just stay where you are and I'll send the police officer in to you.'

Then he went to the door. As he opened it, he looked back at Steve who was just sitting there, hands resting on his lap with his back bent forward and his head down. Steve looked in a sad state.

Mateo stepped out of the treatment room and, as he did, he looked and caught the eye of the sergeant. He beckoned to him.

Since they had first arrived at the hospital, and the sergeant had left Steve and John with the doctors, the ambulance had arrived with Ann and Tommy. It reached the hospital just as Steve was taken into the private treatment room by Mateo. The porters lowered the ramp and the paramedics brought the wheelchairs down it backwards. They handed Ann and Tommy over to the porters. As they were rolled into the hospital, two of the police officers followed them.

As the porters pushed Ann and Tommy through the large doors into the hospital, the sergeant stopped the policemen and said, 'You can make your full report when you get back to the station. Just tell me now what you saw and heard when you were up there.'

One of them answered, 'The young girl just kept crying and saying her dad killed her mum! That he let her fall.'

The sergeant asked him, 'Was she talking in English? And are you sure you could understand what she was saying?'

The other policeman said, 'He's right, Sergeant. I heard her saying it as well.'

'Okay,' the sergeant replied, 'You all head back to the station and I'll ask Mr Thomson to call into the station to make a statement tomorrow.'

As the policewoman went to go with them, he told her, 'You stay with the young girl as long as the doctor will let you.' Then he added, 'Just listen to what she says, but don't question her because she will be in shock.'

As the officers went to their cars, he stood there watching them for a moment with a puzzled look on his face, thinking about what the young girl had said. Then he turned and walked back into the hospital.

He looked for Steve in the seating area, but Steve wasn't there, so he approached the receptionist and asked, 'Where is Mr Thomson, the man I brought in, being treated?'

The receptionist answered with a question, 'Is he a VIP? His doctor is one of the top specialists in this hospital and he's being treated in a private room. It's that door over there in the corner.' She pointed to a door as she spoke.

He smiled at her and replied, 'I don't know. I've never seen him before today but if he has the top man looking after him, he must be rich.

Anyway, I'll take a seat in the waiting area but tell the nurses I'm not a patient. It's been a long day and, if I nod off, I don't want to wake up in theatre with a limb missing.'

Then he winked, and went and found a seat while he waited for Steve.

When Mr Alonso came out of the treatment room and waved to the sergeant to come to the room, he was writing in his notebook and didn't notice at first. When the doctor did manage to catch the sergeant's eye, he got up off his seat and walked towards him.

As he reached him, Mr Alonso said to him in Spanish, 'Steve is in a sorry state. I've known the family for years; they were so close; I think this could break him. He's sitting in there. He *is* in a sorry state, but I've got to go - it's an emergency. Will you look after him?'

The police sergeant nodded and replied, 'Don't worry, I can speak English and most of my officers can as well. We have a car waiting and I will see that he gets to wherever he wants to go from here.'

The sergeant went into the treatment room and sat on the chair that was facing Steve. After a few minutes of silence, Steve lifted his head and looked at the police sergeant with eyes that were red and watery.

The sergeant spoke in English and said in a quiet voice, 'I'm sorry for you and your family, sir. We have a car for you, it's waiting outside. Where do you want to be taken to? Is it a hotel or are you staying in a villa?'

The sergeant then stood up and, as he opened the door, gestured with his hands for Steve to move. Steve just sat there for a moment, then he got up slowly from the chair and said, 'The villa.'

The sergeant waited for a while for Steve to say the address, but he didn't say anything else. He just stood there, with his head down, shoulders slumped forward and his arms just hanging. His stance was that of a man of eighty.

So the sergeant asked, 'What is the address?'

Steve took a while to answer, then he said, 'I can't think of it… Look under 'villa' in my mobile phone,' as he fumbled in his pocket to get it out. When he did manage to get it out, he gave it to the sergeant, who asked him for the pass numbers to open the phone.

Steve thought for a moment, then said, 'Oh, it's 2, 3, 2, 3,' as he followed the sergeant out of the room.

The sergeant put the number in the phone, then he pressed 'villa' on it. He looked at the address, then, as he put Steve's phone in his pocket, he said, 'Steve, I'll hold onto your phone, so the driver will know where we are going.'

The policewoman approached them as they came out of the treatment room and said to the sergeant, 'The driver has the car just outside the main doors.'

He nodded and when he spoke to his colleagues he did so in Spanish, swapping back to English when he needed to talk to Steve.

He asked her to lead the way to the car. She said, 'Okay,' as she turned round and walked past some chairs in the waiting area. When she got to the receptionist, she turned right and went up a passageway between the chairs in the waiting area, which led to the big main doors. The two men followed her.

The sergeant had his arm round Steve's back, with his hand on Steve's shoulder. He was more or less leading him, because Steve had his head looking down. The policewoman held the door open as the two of them went through and out to the car. The driver got out of the car when he saw them coming and opened the back door for them to get in.

The sergeant helped Steve into the back, then he got in himself and said to Steve, who was in a world of his own, 'Steve, put your seat belt on... You don't mind me calling you Steve, do you? Or would you like me to call you Mr Thomson?'

Steve answered as he put his seat belt on, saying in a quiet voice, 'Steve will do.'

The driver got in and closed his door just as the policewoman got in the front with him.

The sergeant said to the driver, 'Head for that big hotel on the main road facing the beach. It's called The Grandee; then take the first left after it, stay on that road for about half an hour and it's a big villa on the right. I'll tell you when we see it.'

Then the sergeant took Steve's phone out of his pocket. He handed it to the policewoman and said, 'I don't know what I was thinking, just put the address that is on this phone in the satnav.'

She took the phone, put the address in and clicked it into a holder on the dashboard in front of the driver.

The police car stopped forty-five minutes later outside the large villa, and the policewoman got out and opened the back door for Steve, giving him a helping hand to get out. Then the sergeant stepped out of the car. He walked Steve to the gate and, as they got near, two lights either side of the gates came on, shining down on them.

Steve now looked a little bit better; he put the numbers in the pad on the wall for the gates to open.

As they did, the sergeant told Steve, 'We have been in touch with your sister-in-law, Emma, for your daughter. Will you be alright? Is there anyone you would like us to contact for you?'

Steve replied, 'No, thank you - and thank you for all your help. I don't know where I would be without it. Oh, your driver has still got my phone. I will need it to contact the rest of the family.'

At that moment the driver came over to Steve, handed him the phone and went back to the car.

The sergeant said, 'I'm afraid we will need a statement from everyone who saw the accident. I will send a car for you tomorrow. What time would you like to make your statement?'

Steve looked at him and asked, 'Will it be alright if I make my own way to the station tomorrow? I just don't know what will be happening, and how I will feel in the morning. I'll get my own chauffeur to take me there.'

'Yes, there will be an officer there to take your statement,' the sergeant answered.

Steve went into the estate. He walked up the driveway that was only dimly lit by the lights on the road until the gate started to close, and then the lights along the driveway came on and lit up all the grounds around the villa. As he approached the villa, a bright security light came on and another two lamps came on, lighting up the doorway, but the villa itself was in darkness. Before he had even reached the door, the police car left. As he opened the door, he stood for a few moments under the lights of the doorway, looking into the dark, silent hallway. He wiped the tears off his face and went in and the light came on. He went straight to the closest bathroom, headed for the wash basin and washed his face.

In the car the police sergeant asked the policewoman, 'What did the young girl have to say?'

She answered, 'I don't understand it. I think she was hysterical. She kept saying her dad killed her mum. It's hard to believe that he deliberately let her go - just looking at the state that her dad is in, he must have done his best to save her.'

The sergeant nodded and replied, 'It looks that way to me too,' and then he said to the driver, 'Did you get a quick look at who he's been talking to on his phone?'

He replied, 'I tried but there weren't any names on the phone, just numbers - it looked like he had about eight contacts. While it was in my hand it vibrated so it must be set on silent. I looked to see who was calling him, but it just said unknown. I didn't have enough time to look at his texts. Sorry about that, Sarge.'

The sergeant said, 'No need to apologise - you've done well; just remember, this conversation didn't happen.

Well, the only one who is making any sense today is the young man. I've told the officer with him to take him back to the hotel he is staying at and tell him to come to the station to make a statement tomorrow.'

The policewoman said, 'The young man will be kept in the hospital overnight. So the officer who was with him when the doctor told him he would have to stay said he would pick him up in the morning to take him to the station.'

The sergeant answered, 'Okay.' As the car pulled into the station's car park, the sergeant said, 'I'm glad this shift is at an end. It's been a long heart-breaking day. So go home and get a good night's sleep, I think we will have a hard day again tomorrow.

EMMA FLEW TO SPAIN

As soon as Emma Kenwright had the phone call from the Spanish police, she hired a private plane to take her over to Spain. When it landed, she had a taxi waiting.

She told the driver, in broken Spanish, 'It's an emergency. Get me to the hospital as soon as possible.'

She arrived at the hospital around two in the morning. She said to the nurse in the reception area in broken Spanish, 'I am Emma Kenwright, Joan Thomson's sister and Ann and John's aunt.'

The nurse on the reception didn't quite understand Emma at first and asked her to repeat what she had said again. Emma spoke more slowly, and this time the nurse understood and confirmed that Ann and John were in the hospital.

Then she added, 'I'm sorry, but your sister has had a fatal accident.'

Emma did her best to hold back the tears. As she thought that Ann was in one room and John was in another, Emma asked in poor Spanish to see the doctor who had treated Ann and John as she would like a word with them.

The receptionist looked surprised and explained, 'The doctor who treated the children has gone off duty.'

Emma interrupted, saying, 'Sorry, I'm a bit confused… Of course the doctor has gone off duty. Can I see the doctor who is on duty now, please?'

The receptionist again asked Emma to repeat herself, more slowly. Emma did, and the receptionist nodded, picked up the phone and put a call out for the doctor. When he arrived, the receptionist explained who Emma was.

Emma said, in poor Spanish, 'My Spanish is not very good. Can you speak in English?'

The doctor smiled and said, in a strong Spanish accent, 'Yes, how can I help?'

She asked the doctor, 'What has happened to my family? The police only told me that my sister was in a fatal accident and the children were here, in the hospital. How are the children? Please, God, don't let it be bad…'

The doctor said, as quickly as he could, 'The children are in good health, but are in a state of shock and that is the reason we have kept them here. They both have drips in their arms, so don't get a shock when you see them... and I'm afraid all I know is that a vehicle was involved in the accident.'

Emma asked, 'Was their father hurt?'

The doctor replied, 'No...'

Emma interrupted, 'Is their father with the children?'

The doctor said, 'No. Mr Alonso gave their father some sleeping pills and told him to go back to the villa. As the father was angry and upset, we thought if he spent the night with the children... Well, seeing their dad in that state after what happened to their mother - it wouldn't be good for them.

Like I've explained to you, the children are suffering from shock and have been given a sedative to help them sleep. I'm sorry for your loss.'

Emma asked the doctor if he would arrange for Ann and John to be put in the same room, so she could spend the rest of the night with them.

The doctor explained to Emma the children had been put in the same room already. His pager went off in his pocket, he took it out, looked at it and said, 'I'm sorry I have to go.'

He called a nurse who was passing and told her where to take Emma.

When she entered the room and saw Ann and John, she quickly put her hanky to her mouth to stop any sound coming out while she got over the shock of seeing both of them lying there asleep, with drips in their arms. She did her best to pull herself together but the tears just poured down her cheeks and her nose started dripping. She wiped her face and nose, then she put a chair in between the two beds, so she could reach both children. She sat in the chair in-between the beds all night, with a terrible sickly feeling, and she would wipe the tears away when they ran down her face.

NO INTEREST IN THE FAMILY BUSINESS

When their father died, the sisters were to take over the business together, but Emma wasn't interested in it. At the age of eleven she had started reading and studying books about cooking and baking. When she was sixteen her dad wanted her to stay on at school and study, so she could go to university to get a degree. She insisted on leaving school to go to work in a restaurant instead. Her dad knew she loved cooking because from the age of twelve she helped San in the kitchen. When she was fourteen she insisted on making all their birthday dinners on her own.

She was determined to become a chef and, three months before her sixteenth birthday, she started writing to restaurants all around the country. Her dad didn't want her to leave home at sixteen, and so he got her a job with a chef he knew, so that she would be home at night.

The chef told her dad, 'It's hard work and I can't treat her any differently than any of the other trainees.'

Her dad agreed with him and said, 'I will explain this to Emma, and I know she will be made up to train in your restaurant.'

When he got home, Emma's dad put his arm round her and said to her, 'Let's go into the living room. I would like a word with you.'

They went in and sat down, and Emma, with a worried look on her face, asked, 'What's wrong, Dad? Am I in trouble?'

He smiled and said, 'Sorry, love, I didn't mean to worry you. It's something I know you'll like.'

Emma was now excited and butted in, 'What is it, Dad?'

Her dad laughed, and said, 'I've taught you and Joan all I know about business, but I know nothing about cooking. I can't boil an egg without burning it, so I won't be able to help you in what you want as a career.

I was only kidding - I can boil an egg... but that's the best I can do, so I've got you a trainee position with a chef I know. You'll have to really study. It's hard work, and the chef will shout at you and treat you like the other people who work under him. He is a perfectionist and he expects the same from his staff, and if you listen to what he teaches you and you learn half of what he knows, you will leave his employment as a great chef.

Well, I love you, and it's all up to you now.'

Emma jumped up, hugged her dad as tight as she could around his neck and promised, 'I'll make you proud of me, Dad. I love you.'

He went red in the face and choked out, 'If you don't let go, your love will kill me!'

She let go, kissed him on the cheek and said, 'Sorry, Dad.'

He laughed and gave her a hug.

When she started work in the restaurant kitchen, she bought all her whites out of the pocket money she had saved up. When she got to the restaurant she was told by the head waiter, 'The chef will see you just before you start your apprenticeship. Till then you will work with this young man, his name is Sam Webster.'

Sam said, 'Come with me.'

They walked through the large kitchen, filled with huge, hot ovens and the noise of the chefs and waitresses. They passed the walk-in fridges and rows of fruit and vegetables, and she was surprised when he walked up to the sinks that were full of dishes.

He said, 'This is our job till we hear differently. I'll be with you for a couple of days to show you what to do, and then they'll move me onto another horrible job, something like cleaning out the fridges. Happy days, hey?'

Emma asked, 'Hasn't the kitchen in a restaurant like this got a dishwasher?'

'Yes - that's me and you,' Sam replied with a grin. Then he added, 'We wash the dishes first to get the hard, sticky food off and then the dishes go into the dishwasher to clean and to warm them, so when the food is on them the plates will keep the food warm. Let's face it, no one likes to eat cold food.'

Once they started washing, they didn't have time to talk and they didn't even get a full hour for their dinner.

Two days later, Sam said, 'The head waiter has given me another job to do. He said, now that you know the job, you are on your own till he gives you another one.'

Emma wasn't pleased but she remembered what her dad had told her; she stuck with it even though sometimes she didn't even have time for dinner and the only time people spoke to her was to say, 'We want more plates.'

Then, after three weeks, Sam came over to where the sinks were with a man about fifty years of age, and said, 'This is Ted. He has been on sick leave; he will do the dishes from now on.'

Emma wiped her hands and went to offer Ted her hand.

Sam said, 'No time for the niceties, the chef wants to see you right away in his office.'

As Sam showed her to the office, she thought, 'Any job is better than the sinks.'

Sam showed her the door and knocked on it; then he turned and left her, as a deep, hard voice called out, 'Come in.'

Emma was a bit nervous and hesitated, with her hand on the door handle and her other hand twirling her hair around her finger.

Then the voice shouted, 'Are you deaf? I said come in.'

Emma opened the door, stepped just inside the doorway and stood there nervously.

The chef said, 'Come all the way in, you will have to get used to me and the working of the kitchen environment. Now, sit down, because I'm going to tell you the rules in my kitchen and what I expect of you.'

Emma sat there as the chef walked up and down behind his desk, telling her what he expected of her. Emma thought that she had seen him sometimes watching her working at the sinks in the kitchen.

When she started her apprenticeship, she was surprised to see that Sam was one of the students. Another was a boy named Keith. As time went by, Emma became convinced that the chef was picking on her more than the other trainee chefs; she didn't understand why he picked on her.

She was always top when he gave them a test and Emma wouldn't tell her dad that she was being picked on. However, after two years, she did tell Joan.

Joan said, 'You can't give up now. You've always wanted to be a chef, so, like Dad always said when we were little and cried off something we found hard to do, just suck it up. You know you can do it, and when you started there, you told Dad you would make him proud of you. The meals you cook now are fantastic.'

Emma replied, 'I have no intention of leaving. I wouldn't give the chef the pleasure of forcing me out, I just wanted to tell you and get it out of my system.'

Another year went by, the course ended, and she was surprised when the chef said to her, 'You are a good chef. One day you will be a great chef. I would like you to stay here as my assistant. I intend to retire in another ten years, and you will be the top chef when I do.'

Emma thanked him and told him she wanted to be her own boss. From the day she had started to earn her own money, all she had done was work and save every penny she got.

When she left the restaurant, Emma said to her dad, 'I'm going to have a four-week holiday and do a bit of travelling around the British isles, and then I'm going into the restaurant business.'

Her dad replied, 'You have earned it. The chef said you were the best pupil he has ever had and one day will own your own restaurant. Take my credit card and have a good holiday, on me.'

Emma wasn't really going on holiday, she was looking for premises for her restaurant; on the second week she saw a small café for sale. She enquired about it only to find she was two thousand short.

She phoned her dad and asked, 'Could I take some money out of my trust? I want to buy a small café. I think it is in the perfect place to be a small restaurant.'

Her dad answered, 'I'm sorry, love, I'm afraid you won't be able to touch it till you're twenty-five, the way the trust is set up... but don't stress, I will give you the money. I know you wouldn't waste your hard-earned cash on a pig in a poke.'

She bought the café and, in six months, she had turned it into a restaurant. Her father was pleased to see her doing so well but, not long after she started making a name for the restaurant he died.

A few years later, Emma's small restaurant was getting very well-known and she wanted to build her own restaurant chain. Emma wanted to ask Joan if she would buy her shares in the family business off her, with the money that was in Joan's trust.

On the day she planned to tell Joan her plan, Emma was nervous about asking Joan to buy her out of the family business, so she just stood outside Joan's office for a few minutes. Then she took a deep breath and knocked on the door.

Joan's voice sang out, 'Come.'

As soon as Emma walked into the office, Joan looked up from her desk and laughed, saying 'What are you up to now, Emma?'

Emma answered, with a frown on her face, 'What makes you think I'm up to anything?'

Joan, laughing and pointing, said, 'Just look in that mirror! Your hair is in a bit of a mess... You've been twisting it round your fingers. You always used to do that when you had something on your mind - but you haven't done it since we were children so, whatever it is, it must be important to you.' She smiled and carried on, 'Don't worry. You and I can sort anything out when we put our heads together.'

Emma was looking in the mirror, laughing at her hair, as Joan was talking and when she had finished, Emma turned to face her with a smile on her face and said to Joan, 'I'm not that worried, really... Maybe a little bit though.'

Then she explained her plans and what she would like Joan to do to help her get the restaurants.

Joan didn't want to buy Emma's shares in the family business, but she said, 'I'll do it but my trust will only be enough to buy one third, and, anyway, I want you to stay in the firm. So I'll buy one third of your shares.'

Emma frowned and said, 'With that and my trust, it still won't get me what I want. I'm after a small chain of cafés and I will need a lot more money. Can the business back me up with a loan? You know I'll pay it back with interest.'

Joan thought for a moment, then said, 'Money's a bit tight at the present time, but if we approach the bank with the restaurants in the firm's portfolio, we should get the money you want without any problems.'

Emma didn't look pleased, and said, 'You don't understand. I don't want to manage them, I want to own the restaurants and run them the way I like to.'

Joan laughed as she explained, 'You *will* own them. I'll just get the contracts drawn up with the restaurant chain in my name, with the backing of the firm, so the bank will give us the loan, and with your money we can buy the restaurants. You get a contract drawn up by your own solicitors - not the firm's - for me to sign, saying the restaurants are yours when you have paid the loan off; then they will be officially yours. Well, what do you say to that?'

Emma, still with a worried look on her face, said, 'What will the board say about the loan? And Steve mightn't like the idea.'

Joan replied, 'The directors on the board aren't shareholders - we own all the shares, so they won't be a problem... and, as for Steve, he is a good businessman. I'm making him a director. He knows business is business... but he also knows I will always put my family first, before the business.'

Emma grinned, stepped forward to Joan and hugged her and kissed her saying, 'I knew you would work something out for me.'

Joan laughed as they hugged one another. Then she stepped back, at arm's length with her hands on Emma's shoulders, and looked at her with a serious look on her face, as she said, 'There is one condition.'

Then she paused, as Emma's face changed from a grin to a frown.

Joan just smiled and said, 'Don't look so worried - I just want you to use my office for your business, as I will move into Dad's office. I don't want us to drift apart because we're too busy. This way, even if we are too busy to see one another often, we will still bump into one another all the time and we can have a coffee break when we're in the office at the same time.'

Emma laughed and shouted at Joan, 'You cow! I went sick inside then. You know I will be made up to get my big sister's office. Let's have a drink on it.'

Joan grabbed a bottle of wine from the mini fridge in the corner of her office and two glasses from the nearby cabinet.

As she poured the wine, Joan said, 'Say when.'

Just as Emma was about to answer, Steve walked into Joan's office and asked her to pour him a drink as well.

Then he asked them, 'What are we celebrating?'

Joan picked up another glass and poured the wine with her back to Steve. Emma turned to look at him, but the smile had faded off her face.

Joan laughed as she poured the extra drink for Steve and said, 'You will be pleased to hear you are now a director.'

Steve smiled and Joan continued with, 'And we are backing Emma's restaurants with a loan.'

As she finished speaking, she turned around with the drinks on a small tray. It took Steve all his willpower to keep the smile on his face when the loan for Emma was mentioned. Emma, who was looking straight at him, saw the change in Steve's smile to a fake smile.

Joan handed a wine to Emma and one to Steve. Then Joan said, 'Let's drink to the three of us. May all our dreams come true.'

She touched Steve's glass with her glass and smiled; he did the same and smiled back. She did the same with Emma, but Emma had tears in her eyes.

Joan put her arm round Emma and said, 'I hope those are tears of happiness. Now let's finish the toast with two of the people I love most in the world.'

Joan clinked Steve's glass and then Emma's. Steve, still with a smile on his face, turned his glass towards Emma's. Emma smiled as the glasses touched and, as they clinked, Emma thought, 'I can fake a smile as good as you. Who are you to begrudge me a loan from a firm I half own?'

Now Emma was getting a bit angry, though she didn't show it. Instead, she smiled because she knew what she was about to say would upset Steve. Then Emma turned to Joan and, as she spoke to her, walked past her to Joan's desk.

She ran her hand along it and, in a happy voice, she said, 'I will get my PA to move all my paperwork into your office tomorrow morning.' Then she giggled and put her hands to her mouth as if to stop herself and said, 'I'm so happy, I'm getting ahead of myself! You will have to move into dad's office first. I'm so excited.'

All the time Emma was talking she was watching Steve out of the corner of her eye.

Steve couldn't hold the smile any longer, it turned into a frown and he said, 'I thought when you moved out of here, I would get your office. Emma will be running her own business and has nothing to do with this firm. So why have you given her your office?'

Joan turned to face Steve, with her back to Emma. She knew Steve didn't care much for Emma and she knew, though Emma tried to hide it, she felt much the same for Steve as he did for her. At that moment, if she could have seen Emma's face, Joan would have realised that Emma had no love for Steve and a lot of hate.

Joan smiled at Steve and said, 'Come with me down the hall.'

If looks could kill, Emma would have been a dead woman from the one Steve sent in her direction as he walked past her. With one stride he was alongside Joan as she went out the office into the hallway and, as he looked into her face, his face had changed to a bit of a smile and had a questioning look on it. They walked along the hallway to where some workmen were working on a storeroom. It had large dust sheets hanging all along it.

Joan beckoned to one of the men.

When he came towards her, she said, 'Joe, would you ask the men to have a tea break for an hour in the cafeteria? We want to see if there is anything else we would like to do in the office.'

Steve looked at Joan, with a frown on his face, and said, 'That's not an office, it's the big, dark room they put the stores in, when your dad turned the old storeroom into your office. Before that room was your office, it was a large office with a great view that your dad *used* as a storeroom. Whereas this is an actual storeroom that you are trying to turn into an office… but it will still be a storeroom.'

Joan laughed and could hardly get her words out, 'You've been busy and haven't been near this office building for three months. Well, just to show you what a good businessman we think you are, this will be your new office when the work is finished, and I just know you will like it.'

Steve, still with a frown on his face said, 'You can make it look like an office on the inside, but anyone I do business with will see it for what it is - an office without a view, for a clerk that just works in this firm, not a director. It will shake their confidence in me when we're doing business. They will think I can't make decisions without getting the okay from someone higher up the firm.'

Joan just took Steve by the hand and led him through the large dust curtains. Just inside them was a large oak door, with a protective coating on it, under which you could just make out a plaque which read 'Director Steve Thomson'. On both sides of the door were large windows, which were also covered with a protective coating that you couldn't see through. In big writing it said, 'pull from here to remove'.

Joan looked at Steve, smiled and said, 'Well, what do you think now you've seen the front of your office?'

Steve half smiled and answered, 'It's got an impressive front to it, but inside it will still just be a glorified storeroom without windows. Any decent office in a building like this would have a great view.'

Joan opened the door a little, then she stopped and turned to look at Steve with a smile on her face.

Steve didn't look at all pleased as he pointed to the gap in the doorway and muttered, 'Look how dark it is. The lighting it will need will make it look like a Christmas grotto, and who'll take me seriously as a director then?'

Joan put her hand through the gap in the doorway, turned on the lights and, with that, she pushed the door wide open, laughing out loud.

Steve just stood there, staring, with his mouth open at what he saw. The room, though still large, seemed a bit smaller than it had been and there wasn't a wall in sight, just windows with two impressive pillars one at each end of the office. The windows had a dark protective coating on them. Joan tugged on Steve's hand and, with him behind her, walked across the beautiful marble floor to the windows. She touched a spot on the frame and two of the windows slid back, behind the other windows, to reveal a small veranda with a fantastic view of the city.

Joan, still smiling, looked Steve in his face and said, 'Well, when you pick the furniture for *this* storeroom, will your clients still think you are a glorified clerk or will they know you're a director who should be taken seriously..?'

When they came out of the office, from behind the dust curtains, Emma had been talking to Joan's PA and was just passing by on her way out.

Steve said to her, with a grin on his face, 'Sorry about what I said, but understand I thought I was getting a storeroom as an office... But, you want to see it - it must be the best office in the building. I can't wait to get the furniture in there.'

Emma walked towards Joan, saying, 'I'll see you tomorrow.' As she hugged and kissed her sister, she looked over Joan's shoulder with eyes that could kill and said, 'I'm made up for you, Steve.'

Then, she waved, with her back to them, as she walked into the lift. Emma didn't turn to face them as the lift doors closed.

TOMMY MET EMMA IN THE HOSPITAL

Tommy, who had also been kept overnight at the hospital, had spent the night tossing and turning, partly with the pain in his ankle and partly from thinking about the accident and how Ann was doing. He was up at six o'clock, wandering around the hospital on a crutch, with his ankle strapped up, looking for Ann. He saw lots of nurses, but some didn't understand him because he couldn't speak Spanish and the nurses who *could* speak English didn't know who he was asking about.

One of the nurses who could speak English took him to the reception. At first the woman on reception wouldn't tell him what room or floor Ann was in, but when he told her they were admitted together, she looked it up on the computer and gave him the floor and room number. The nurse who helped him find reception was still standing by him and offered to take him to the room.

As he hobbled along, the nurse saw the pain on his face and said to him, 'Stay there. I'll be back in a minute.'

When she came back, she had a wheelchair with her. When she told him to sit in it, he didn't want to but, seeing she had gone to the trouble of getting it, he thought it would be bad manners not to. So he did as she had instructed and sat in the wheelchair.

The nurse pushed him into the lift and they went to the fourth floor. Once there, she stopped at room ten. Tommy thanked her as she left, with the wheelchair. Then he knocked gently on the room door and was surprised when a woman's voice said in English, 'Come in.'

He opened the door and went in. Both John and Ann were still asleep; Emma stood up and turned to face Tommy.

She said, 'I'm Emma, their aunt and their mother's sister. Who are you and what do you want in here?'

'I'm Tommy Tenant,' he answered nervously, keeping hold of the door handle to support him by taking the pressure off his leg.

Emma asked, 'Well, why have you come here?'

Tommy, still feeling a bit nervous, stammered with tears in his eyes, 'I was with Ann when the accident happened. Me and Mr Tompson tried to save your sister. I am so sorry for you, and Ann and John.'

While Tommy was talking Emma moved her chair back into the main part of the room, by a table and another chair, which she then turned so the two chairs were facing.

With tears in her own eyes, she replied, 'Come and sit here... And will you please tell me what happened?'

Tommy was still standing by the closed door, with one hand holding the handle and his other hand holding onto the crutch. He let go of the door and hobbled over to where the chairs were. Just as he sat down next to Emma, there was a knock on the room door, but the person didn't open it.

Emma looked surprised and asked, 'Who is it? What do you want?'

A man's voice, with a Spanish accent, said in English, 'I'm sorry to disturb you. I'm a police officer and I was told that a young man named Tommy Tenant has just come into this room.'

Tommy answered, 'Yes, I will be right out.'

He looked at Emma. As he was about to speak, he got up and he felt a pain shoot up his leg from his ankle. The pain showed on his face, so Emma stood up to help him. Tommy, with one hand on the crutch, gestured for her to sit back down with his other hand, then he turned and hobbled to the door.

As he opened it, he looked back at Emma and said, 'Sorry, but I've got to go with the officer to make a statement. Will you tell Ann I was here and I will be back as soon as I can get out of the police station?'

Emma just nodded, using her hanky to wipe the tears from her eyes as they started to run down her cheeks. When Tommy went through the doorway, Emma went to the washbasin, washed her face and tried to stop the tears, but she couldn't hold them back. She dried her face with the towel that hung by the sink, pulled herself together the best she could and placed her chair back between the beds, so she would be in reach of Ann and John when they woke up.

ANN AND JOHN WAKE UP

Just at the moment Emma sat down, Ann opened her eyes. She lay there, looking at the ceiling in a daze and, as her head cleared, turned over in the bed and started to cry. When she saw her Aunt Emma, the full horror of what had happened to her mother came flooding back to her.

With the picture of her mother in her mind, she started to sit up in bed, hysterical and screaming, 'Oh, Aunt Emma...' but before Ann was in a sitting position; before she had even finished her sentence, her aunt was up and out of her chair - which fell backward, with a bang against the bedside cabinet - and leaning over the bed, hugging her.

With the noise, John woke and started crying, as he sat up with his hands over his eyes, saying, 'I want my mum. I want my mum.'

Emma, still holding onto Ann, couldn't help pulling her to the edge of the bed while reaching for John. When John felt Emma's hand on him, he took his hands from his eyes and looked at Emma, then started crying even louder. Eventually, he went a bit quieter, as he climbed out of the bed and hugged Emma, still muttering, 'I want my mum.'

Ann got off her bed too and all three stood there, hugging and crying.

Emma tried to pull herself together for the sake of the children. She wiped her eyes and said to them, 'I'll take you to the villa to see your dad.'

With that Ann screamed at Emma, 'I don't want to see him, he let my mum fall.'

John, still crying, shouted at his sister, 'No! He didn't! He tried to save her.'

Both of them went hysterical for a few moments, shouting at each other,

Emma didn't know what to do. She was crying as she pulled them into her and sobbed, 'Don't be arguing, your mother wouldn't like it,' but they both pulled away from her, still shouting.

Emma was out of her mind with worry. She no longer looked like that good-looking, smart, confident woman who ran a restaurant chain. Now her hair was in a mess with her constantly touching it and her eyes were red; her face was wet with tears and her nose kept running. She wiped it with the tissues off the bedside table, picked up the buzzer and pressed it to get the nurse.

As the nurse entered the room, she asked in English, 'Can I help?' just as the children both stopped shouting and sat on one of the beds, crying.

Ann put her arm round John and pulled him in close to her.

When Emma saw they had calmed down and were trying to comfort each other, she wiped her eyes and said to the nurse, in a quiet, upset voice, 'It's alright now. I thought I would need help with the children, but they are a bit calmer now.

I'll ring for a car. When it comes, the driver will come to the reception desk. Will you ask the person on the desk to tell him we are in this room, please?'

The nurse said, 'Of course I will. I'll tell the desk right now,' as she left the room.

Emma was going to tell Ann and John that she would phone their dad to let him know where they were, but then thought better of it. She would let him know without telling them, because she was concerned about what had happened - if they got that upset again, she wouldn't know what to do. Instead, she braced herself and just said to them, 'I'm sorry, but first we'll have to stay at the hotel - till you tell the police about the accident.'

Steve arrived with the driver from the hotel half an hour after Emma had phoned. Steve's eyes were red and watery as he and the driver entered the room.

When John saw his dad, he ran to him, crying, 'Dad, I want my mum.'

Steve knelt down and wrapped his arms round John.

He looked at Ann and said, in a distressed voice, 'Come here to me, Ann,' but the moment he had entered the room, Ann had backed away as far as she could, into a corner of the room, pulling her Aunt Emma with her as she did so.

She screamed at him, 'You let my mum fall. I saw you let go of my mum.'

Steve, with an agitated tone in his voice and a pleading look on his face, said, 'You know I loved your mum, and I tried my best to pull her to safety out of the way of the car - you saw me.'

Ann just kept shouting, 'You let my mum go. I saw you do it.'

At the same time, John was crying and asking for his mum. Steve got up from his kneeling position, lifting John in his arms. As he stood up, a doctor and nurse entered the room.

The doctor said to Steve, 'I will give the children a sedative. It will calm them down while you take them home.'

Steve was holding John as the nurse pushed John's pyjama sleeve up for the doctor to inject the sedative. Just from the shock of getting the injection, John stopped shouting for his mum and started sobbing.

Then the doctor and nurse went towards Ann.

She said in a quiet voice, crying as she pointed at Steve, 'I'm alright now, but I'm not going anywhere with him.' Then she hugged Emma and cried, 'Take me with you.'

Emma looked at Steve and everyone in the room could see the hate in her face. When she spoke to him, her tone was furious as she muttered, 'You take John to the villa and I'll take Ann to the hotel.'

While she was talking, Steve's face changed from a sad look to a wicked one. He was angry to think she was telling him what to do with his children. She was the last person he would take that off, but he thought better of making that clear to her while Ann and John were in distress, and they were all at the hospital. So he just looked at Emma with a face that showed his hate for her.

He didn't answer, he just turned and, as the driver opened the room door, Steve said in a sharp angry voice, 'Take us to the villa.'

As Steve, John and the driver left the room, the doctor and nurse followed them out.

As the nurse and doctor walked along the corridor, the nurse looked back, to make sure Steve wasn't in earshot, then said to the doctor in their own language, 'I don't understand it. When there's a death like this one in a family, they usually all come together to comfort one another but with this family not only could you see the hate in their faces, you could feel it in the room. I think, by looking at his face, that man would and could have killed her, if we weren't there.'

The doctor nodded and replied, 'I think she felt the same way about him, the way she looked and spoke to him. It proves, with all the money they have, you really can't buy love.'

The nurse laughed and said, 'Give me the money they've got and I'll have a damn good try.'

The doctor just smiled.

Back in the hospital room, Emma pulled Ann close as she phoned for a taxi to take them to the hotel.

TOMMY GOES TO THE POLICE STATION

When Tommy left Emma and came out of the room where Ann and John were sleeping, the police officer was standing there with a hospital porter, who had a wheelchair for him. The porter pointed for Tommy to sit in it.

Tommy said to the porter, 'Thank you, but I'll walk.'

The porter didn't speak English, he just kept pointing to the wheelchair. The police officer put his hand on Tommy's shoulder, smiled and said to him, 'He doesn't understand you and he would lose his job if he let you walk to the entrance and you got hurt, so please sit in the chair and keep him happy.'

As the officer winked at him, Tommy smiled back, nodding to the porter as he sat in the chair. He was pushed to a lift, with the officer following just behind them.

The three of them entered the lift and the porter pressed the button for the ground floor. When the lift stopped, Tommy was pushed out, and along past the reception desk. They turned right, up the path between the seats in the waiting area to the big main doors. The officer held the door open for the porter to push Tommy through it and out to the driveway, where a police car was waiting with a driver in it.

The police officer and porter helped Tommy out of the wheelchair and into the car. While they were helping him, they could see by his face that he was in a great deal of pain. Both officer and porter apologised for hurting him as they helped him into the back of the car. Tommy tried to smile and thanked them for their help.

Then the officer thanked the porter for his help to get Tommy in the car and got in the front next to the driver, saying in Spanish, in an angry tone, 'You're an arsehole. You could have got off your arse and helped get the lad into the car. You could see he was in pain. If you had got in the back and pulled him in we wouldn't have hurt him as much.'

The driver just laughed and answered in Spanish, 'A little hurt never killed anyone.' Then, as he started the car, he called to Tommy in broken English, 'You're alright, aren't you, lad?'

Tommy answered in a pained grunt, 'I think I will live.'

The officer sitting by the driver turned his head to look at Tommy and could see the pain he was in. He turned back to face the driver and said out loud, in English so that Tommy could hear him, 'You're a fucking arsehole.'

On the way to the police station, the policeman sitting next to the driver radioed to the station in Spanish, 'We've picked the young man up from the hospital.'

A woman's voice answered back, also in Spanish, 'Take him round the back of the station. The sergeant will meet you there. Some newspaper reporters are gathering at the front, they want to know about the accident.'

'Okay,' the policeman replied.

As they passed the front of the station, they could see people with cameras milling around the steps that led up to the station doors. The car drove into the yard at the back of the station. It was a large yard with lots of police cars parked there. They drove past some of the cars and then pulled up, just outside two big metal doors.

TOMMY'S STATEMENT

One of the doors opened and out walked the sergeant who was at the accident. He smiled and waved to Tommy. As the car stopped, he opened the back door. The officer who helped Tommy get into the car got out of the passenger seat and climbed in the back beside Tommy, to help him.

The sergeant said to a passing officer in Spanish, 'Help us get this brave young man out of the car. He has a badly damaged ankle.'

The three of them were as careful as they could be, but Tommy couldn't stop from crying out in pain a couple of times as they tried to ease his leg out of the car. Once they had got his legs out and he was in a sitting position, they each got hold of one of his arms and the officer behind him helped move him along the seat. The sergeant and the officer pulled him out of the car and helped him to stand up. The sergeant supported Tommy while the officer who was in the back of the car got Tommy's crutch and gave it to him.

Then the sergeant angrily said to the driver in Spanish, 'Are you stuck to that seat? You could see we needed help with the lad. I will want a word with you later.'

Then he said to Tommy in English, 'Sorry, we don't have a wheelchair here. Would you like me to help you into the building?'

Tommy replied, 'No, thank you. I would rather manage myself, but thank you anyway.'

The sergeant led him slowly up the steps, through the doors and into a long corridor.

As they walked along it the sergeant asked Tommy, 'Do you speak Spanish at all?'

'No,' he replied. Then, with a smile on his face, he added, 'I don't even think I speak English as good as you.'

The sergeant laughed and said, 'Thank you, kind sir. Don't worry, I'll speak to you all the time in English. I'm Sergeant Torres.'

Tommy told the sergeant his name and where he was from whilst the two of them walked towards the interview rooms. The two of them went past a few doors, and then the sergeant stopped outside one and said, 'We'll try this one.' Whereupon he opened the door and popped his head in.

Tommy heard the sergeant say something in Spanish, and an angry voice came from the room. With that, the sergeant backed out, shutting the door and saying to Tommy with a smile, 'No luck that time. We'll try next door, but I'll knock first this time, because if I walk in on another senior officer I'll be back on the beat or even directing traffic.'

When they came to the next office door he knocked first and no one answered. As he opened the door, he said, 'It looks like we're in luck. Come on in, Tommy, and take a seat. Would you like a coffee or a tea?' The sergeant pulled a face as he spoke and added, 'The coffee here is terrible, but the tea is just pure poison. Someone should be locked up for it.'

The sergeant placed a seat next to the table and, as he helped Tommy sit down, he smiled. As he stood next to Tommy, with one hand on Tommy's shoulder, he made a gesture with his other hand to show the room in all its glory and said to him, 'Sorry this room is so bare, but it's too good for some of the scum we get in here. As you can see there are only four chairs, a table, a small filing cabinet, and a large mirror on the wall.'

Tommy exclaimed, 'I know! I've seen them on the television, it's a two-way mirror.'

The sergeant laughed and said, 'In that case don't pull any funny faces at it. I bet you know what the red line that goes round the walls of the room is?'

Tommy nodded and said, 'It's an alarm, in case of an emergency.'

The sergeant said, 'You're right, we get some real nut cases in these statement rooms. It's rare to have a young hero like yourself.'

Tommy butted in, as his face went blood red, 'I'm no hero. I just did the only thing anyone would do in that situation.'

The sergeant patted Tommy on the shoulder and said, 'No, you're wrong, son. Lots of people would just stand round and look. Believe me, I know, from doing this job.'

Then he walked round the table, sat facing Tommy and said, 'We would like you to make a statement about the accident. As you don't speak Spanish,' he added, as he picked up the phone, 'I'll get an interpreter to take your statement.'

He spoke into the phone in Spanish. Then, as he put the phone back on the receiver, without pausing his voice went back to English and he said, 'The interpreter will be here in a few moments. She will take your statement and type it up in Spanish, and then type up an English copy, so you know what you are signing off on in the Spanish statement.'

Just as he finished talking, there was a knock on the door. A woman in her early thirties entered. Tommy looked up at her and she smiled at him as she walked past his side of the table.

He smiled back at her, and thought, 'God, she's gorgeous. She doesn't look like she would work in a police station, she looks more like a model!'

She wore a lovely pink and white flowered dress, and her hair was an orangey red with a fringe that came to her eyes. Her hair was tied back in a long, wavy ponytail and her face was beautiful even though she had no makeup on it. It seemed to glow when she smiled at Tommy. The sergeant stood up and gestured to the interpreter to sit next to him, facing Tommy.

They both sat down, and the sergeant said to the interpreter, 'Introduce yourself to my young friend, Tommy.'

The interpreter introduced herself with a smile, saying, 'I'm Pearl Brown, from Chester in England.'

Tommy butted in with surprise on his face and in the tone of his voice. He said, 'You're English?'

She nodded and said, 'You can't get any more English than coming from Chester.' Then she continued with, 'You can call me Pearl. I'll take your statement and type it in Spanish and again in English. Then I will read the Spanish one back to you in English for you to sign.'

As she finished speaking, the sergeant said, 'Tommy, I will stop you now and then and ask you to go over what you have said. It's not that I don't believe what you tell us, it's just, when an accident like this happens, well… sometimes one has to go over things a few times in their mind.'

Tommy went a bit pale and answered, 'I feel sick to my stomach just thinking about the accident. I hope I can be helpful.'

The sergeant picked the phone up and said, 'Would you like something to drink? We are getting our usual, a cup of coffee!'

Tommy shook his head and said, 'No, thank you. I don't drink coffee and I don't fancy your tea after what you said about it.'

'Well, what about a glass of milk? I'm sure the canteen can send one over with our coffee and it might help settle your stomach,' the sergeant suggested.

Tommy replied, 'Yes, please, that would be great.'

The sergeant spoke on the phone in Spanish then, as he put the phone back on the receiver, carried on in English, 'We'll settle down and wait for the drinks. They will be here in about five minutes.

You can take your time drinking the milk and think about what you need to tell us about the accident. When you feel you are ready to make your statement, just let me know.'

While they were waiting the interpreter got up and went to the filing cabinet in the corner of the room. On top of it was a laptop but she didn't touch it. She took a key out of a small pocket in her dress and unlocked the cabinet drawer. She reached in and brought out an electric typewriter. She plugged the cable in and placed the typewriter on the table facing Tommy. Then she went back to the cabinet and took out some A4 paper.

As she returned to the table, there was a knock on the door. The sergeant got up off his chair and opened it. A young police officer stood there, holding a tray with two mugs of coffee and a glass of milk on it. The sergeant thanked the policeman. Taking the tray off him, he turned to put it on the table. As he did so, the policeman pulled the door shut and left.

The interpreter took the glass of milk and gave it to Tommy. He smiled and thanked her. She lifted the two mugs off the tray and placed one by her typewriter and the other where the sergeant would sit. He put the tray on top of the filing cabinet and returned to the table. With one hand he picked up his mug of coffee and, with the other hand, he got his chair ready to sit on, but instead he stood for a little while, drinking the coffee.

Then he said to the interpreter, 'Why don't you use the computer instead of that old typewriter?'

She replied, 'I just like typing on it, and you can't lose the work. I've used the computer and I've lost a lot of work on it when it went haywire.'

Then she sat down and moved the chair, so she was in a comfortable position. She had a sip of her coffee, pulled a face and looked at Tommy.

Then she said in English, 'Sarge, this so-called coffee is horrible. Can't you use your influence to get decent coffee in the vending machine?'

As he replied, 'What can I do? I'm only a sergeant,' she took the A4 paper and put it in the typewriter, winding it down to where she wanted to start typing.

Just then the sergeant finished his coffee and, as he sat down, he nodded to Tommy, saying as he put the mug on the table, 'Pearl is right. God, it's pure poison, this stuff... but we have to drink it because it's wet and it's like drugs: once you start on the horrible stuff, you're hooked.'

Tommy took a few mouthfuls of the glass of milk and placed it in front of himself on the table.

The sergeant put his hand over his mouth, coughed to clear his throat and then said, 'Shall we get started with your statement? That's if you are ready to?'

Tommy looked the sergeant in the face and said, 'I don't know where to start.'

With that the sergeant replied, 'Don't look so worried. Just take a deep breath and relax. I think it would be best if you started from when you left the picnic area.'

Tommy tried to do like the sergeant said and relax. He sat back in his chair and, after providing Pearl with his full name, and his age and address, he started his statement.

'Ann and her parents were getting ready to leave the picnic area. Ann had gone to ask her parents if I could go with them to the beach. Her dad didn't look too pleased. I thought her parents wouldn't let her see me again because they are moneyed people and I'm working class, but as they got to the edge of the picnic area, Ann called to me to go with them. I jumped on the bike and rode up to them.'

Tommy stopped talking as the sergeant smiled and interrupted, saying, 'It was a motorbike, wasn't it? You see, Tommy, other people will be reading your statement. I know it was a motor bike because I saw it, but they wouldn't know that from what you've said. You need to be as accurate as possible. I hope you understand I'm not trying to bully you?'

While he was talking to Tommy, Pearl leaned toward the typewriter and corrected 'bike' to 'motor bike'.

Tommy said, as he looked at Pearl and then back at the sergeant, 'Sorry about that, and I know you aren't trying to bully me. I have to get it right, what I saw and did.' Then he carried on with his statement. 'I caught up with the family and Ann and her dad sternly said, 'we'll have to wait for John as usual,' and then he told Ann she had to walk on the pavement. Her dad's voice was really serious, and it sounded like he really meant it when he said, 'I want Ann to walk on the pavement, not the road. It's got some bad bends on it.' I thought if I wanted to see Ann again, I'd better do like he said. So, when we crossed over the road, I made sure Ann and I walked on the pavement, and I pushed the motorbike on the road.'

The sergeant interrupted again, to tell Tommy, 'It's alright now to just say 'bike', because you have already said in your statement it's a motorbike.'

Tommy nodded and stopped for a moment and looked at Pearl. Pearl smiled and repeated Tommy's last few words, 'The motorbike on the road.'

'Thank you,' Tommy said, as he smiled back at her. Then he carried on with the statement, 'We had only gone a few yards when the pavement went so narrow and broken up that only one person could walk on it. So Ann walked on it and it was awkward for me to walk next to Ann. So Ann was on the so-called pavement and I walked on the road with the bike between us. Ann tripped quite a few times.'

Tommy paused for a little while and reached for the glass of milk to take a drink. The sergeant said, while Tommy was drinking the milk, 'In the hospital, Tommy, you told one of my colleagues you landed on the bike and Ann landed on top of you, so the bike couldn't have been between you, could it?'

While he was talking, Tommy, with a mouthful of milk, was shaking his head. As he swallowed the milk he placed the empty glass on the table and spluttered, 'Sorry, Sergeant, I haven't finished how it was yet. I'm trying to tell it the way it happened.'

The sergeant put his two hands out in front of himself and, as his hands pointed back towards his chest, he exclaimed in a quiet voice, but with a smile, 'Oh no. I'm sorry, I jumped the gun. I should have waited to see what else you have to say before I put my size twelves in my mouth.'

Tommy nodded to the sergeant, then he looked at the interpreter, who had stopped typing.

Looking a bit embarrassed, as he hadn't called an older woman who he didn't know by her first name before, he said in a quiet voice, 'Pearl, I've lost my thread. Would you please read me the last thing I said?'

Pearl smiled at Tommy. She could see as a young man he was embarrassed using her first name. She leaned toward the typewriter and read out the last sentence Tommy had said, repeating, 'I walked on the road with the bike between us.'

Tommy thanked her and then cleared his throat to continue with his statement, starting with the sentence that Pearl had read back to him, 'I walked on the road with the bike between us. The footpath was really broken up and Ann tripped a few times and nearly fell.

She stopped and as she looked back at her mum and dad she said, 'It would be less dangerous if I walked on the road with you pushing the bike on the sidewalk. If I stay on this so-called pavement, I'll hurt myself.' I was worried what her parents would say and I had a quick look back at them, but they seemed to be concentrating on John, and I couldn't stop Ann doing what she wanted to do anyway, so she walked onto the road and I pushed the bike onto the sidewalk. After that we had only gone about twenty-five yards...'

Tommy stopped suddenly, the colour draining from his face.

Pearl stopped typing, looked at the sergeant and said, in English, 'Sarge, I think he's suffering from shock. He's gone quite pale.'

At the same time Pearl was talking, the sergeant jumped up off his chair. It went flying back with a bang. He was round the table to Tommy in a flash. As he reached Tommy, Tommy put his hands up and shook them to show he was alright, saying to the sergeant in a low, shaky voice, 'I'm alright, but I don't feel too good.'

The sergeant stood behind him with his hands on Tommy's shoulders and told Pearl to call the police doctor. Pearl picked up the phone and spoke in Spanish. She asked for the doctor, saying, 'Could he come right away to statement room four B, as a young man has taken ill. We think he's suffering from shock.'

As she put the phone back on the receiver, she said in English, 'The doctor will be with you in five minutes, Tommy.'

The sergeant, still holding Tommy, said to Pearl, 'Get a drink of water for him from the water fountain.'

Pearl went out of the room and the sergeant, while still holding on to Tommy, carefully moved round him so he was now in front of Tommy.

The sergeant said to him, 'The doctor will be here soon.'

Tommy, whose colour was a bit better, said, 'I feel alright now. I don't think I need the doctor.'

The sergeant replied, 'You still look a bit pale to me. We'll see what the doctor has to say.'

Just then Pearl came back in the room carrying a plastic cup of water, which she handed to Tommy,

His hand was shaking as he took it and said, 'Thank you.'

He took a sip and, at that moment, there was a knock on the door. It opened without the person waiting for a response and the police doctor walked in, carrying his bag. The doctor walked round the sergeant who still had hold of Tommy. He put his bag on the table, opened it and took out a small blood pressure monitor. The sergeant moved out of the way of the doctor, so he could wrap the monitor round Tommy's sun-tanned arm. As he pumped it up, he put a hand on Tommy's forehead, then he picked Tommy's arm up by his wrist to check his pulse.

The doctor said, in broken English, 'It's now one-fifteen and I bet you haven't eaten since the accident.'

Tommy looked up at the doctor and replied, 'I didn't feel like eating anything, but I've drank some milk,' as he pointed at the glass on the table.

The doctor smiled down at Tommy. He was still sitting on the chair, looking a little bit better now, and he was no longer supported by the sergeant.

The doctor said, 'You're suffering from emotional aftershocks. You will be alright in a little while, but you will have to get some decent food inside you. It's not surprising the way you feel, after what happened to you and what you did. It's all around the station that we have a young hero in here.'

Tommy was embarrassed and blushed.

Pearl smiled at him and said, 'Well, that's put some colour back in his face.'

They all smiled, including Tommy, who was feeling a lot better now.

The doctor packed his things back into his bag; he said to Pearl, in Spanish, 'Can you get him some food from the canteen?'

Pearl replied back in Spanish, 'I know just what to get him, Doctor,' as she picked up the tray off the filing cabinet.

Pearl opened the door and the doctor said to her in Spanish, 'I'll walk with you as far as the canteen.' They both left and the doctor pulled the door shut behind them.

The sergeant looked at Tommy and said, 'How do you feel now? You're looking a lot healthier.'

Tommy replied, 'I feel fine now, just a bit hungry, since the doctor mentioned food, and I promise not to fall off the chair, so you can sit down again.'

The sergeant left Tommy's side, walked round the table and lifted his chair back up from where it had fallen.

Then, as he sat down, he said, 'Pearl has gone to get you something to eat from the canteen. It's only down the hallway, so she shouldn't be too long. I wonder what she will bring you.'

Tommy answered, 'I think the way I feel now, I will eat anything put in front of me. Now I really feel hungry.'

Just then an alarm bell rang. Tommy sat back in fright. At the same moment as he turned his head to look at the door, there was a bang in the room. He turned his head back to see what it was. It was the sergeant's chair, as it went flying back again.

He was up and passing Tommy; as he got to the door, he shouted back, 'Sorry, son, but I've got to go, someone is in trouble.'

As he was pulling the door shut, he carried on with, 'Stay there, and don't open this door for any reason. It could be dangerous.'

Tommy wondered what was going on. After five minutes the alarm stopped, but it was a good twenty minutes before there was a knock on the door. Tommy stood up to open it, then remembered what the sergeant had said, so he sat back down, but it was opened by a policeman who stepped aside to allow Pearl to enter the room. She was carrying a tray with a plate of food covered in tinfoil, a glass of milk and two mugs of coffee,

As soon as Pearl placed the tray on the table, Tommy asked her, 'What's going on?'

Pearl said, 'I don't know. I could have been here five minutes ago, but I had to stay in the canteen till it was all over. The only ones who know are the people who were involved, and they won't be allowed to talk about the incident, so I wouldn't bother asking the sergeant when he comes back.'

While she was talking, she picked up the plate and took the tinfoil off the food to reveal two eggs, two sausages, two rashers of bacon and some beans.

Pearl smiled and placed the plate in front of Tommy, saying, 'An English breakfast for an English gentleman.'

Tommy looked at it in surprise, then he looked up at Pearl and smiled back at her, joking, 'What? No black pudding?!'

They both laughed and, as Tommy started to eat the food, Pearl went round the table and picked up the chair that was lying on the floor on the other side of the table from Tommy. Then she sat down on her own chair and adjusted her typewriter so she would be ready to type when they started taking the statement again.

While he was eating the breakfast, they chatted about England and then Tommy asked, 'What is the sergeant like?'

Pearl said, 'He is a marvellous man and colleague. He is well-liked and respected by everyone who works in this station, and the people he has helped over the years. He likes being in uniform. He has been offered promotion quite a few times, but he has always turned it down. He said he is happy working with the public. He has faced some dangerous people and has the citations to prove it, but he won't tell anyone. So don't let on I've told you, because the Sarge is a dear friend and I don't want him to be upset at me.'

Tommy listened, amazed. It slowed him down eating the food and, just as he finished eating, there was a knock on the door. It opened, and the sergeant walked in, wiping some blood off his lip. Tommy and Pearl looked up at him in surprise, with questioning looks on their faces.

The sergeant smiled at them as he put his hanky away and said, 'You want to see what the other fellow looks like.' Then he added, 'Nothing like a bit of exercise to get the blood flowing.'

As he passed by the table, he stopped and picked up the tray with the empty plate and glass on it.

He put it on the top of the filing cabinet, next to the laptop, then he said to Pearl, 'Are you sure you don't want to use the computer?'

Pearl replied, 'I don't, I've already started on my typewriter and I'm sure none of us want to start the statement again.'

He said, 'Of course, you're right. I don't know what I was thinking.' Then he smiled and said, 'I wonder if I got a bang on my head? Maybe that's why I asked such a ridiculous question.'

He went to his chair and moved it so he could sit on it and, as he sat down, he said, 'I hope this chair will take my weight after the way I've been bashing it about. Well, Tommy, are you well enough to carry on with your statement?'

Tommy was relaxed after talking to Pearl and she had told him the sergeant was a great bloke, which made Tommy like him even more.

He grinned and replied, 'After a meal like I've just had I feel fine and I'll do my best to remember everything I can.'

The sergeant asked, 'Pearl, are you ready to start the statement again?'

Pearl nodded, looked at Tommy and said, 'I'll read out your last sentence, and you can pick it up from there.'

She leaned towards the typewriter and read out, 'She walked onto the road, and I pushed the bike onto the sidewalk. After that we had only gone about twenty-five yards…'

Tommy thought for a moment, then he carried on, 'We had only gone about twenty-five yards on the road, then this car came round the bend at a hell of a speed. When it ended up on the wrong side of the road - where we were - it didn't try to get back to where it should be... It had plenty of road to do so, but it just kept coming at us. I remember letting go of the bike and grabbing hold of Ann as we both fell backwards, on top of the bike. The car was just a few millimetres from our feet. I don't know how it missed us.'

The sergeant interrupted, 'Is it alright if I stop you there for now, while I ask you a few questions?'

Tommy had his head down while thinking about what he was saying. He looked up, nodding, and said, 'Yes.'

The sergeant said, 'Let's start with the make of the car, what do you think it was?'

Tommy thought for a moment, then said, 'It was an old black sports car with a soft top. I think it's called a M.J. It had wire wheels. I saw the wheels because they came so close to us... The wheels were like motorbike wheels.'

The sergeant smiled and said, 'I think you mean it was a MG. Now, just think, did you see the driver? Was it a man or a woman?'

Tommy replied, 'I could see the driver. It was a woman.'

The sergeant repeated, 'It was a woman,' then asked, 'How old do you think she was?'

Tommy answered, 'I haven't a clue how old she was. I didn't have time to think about her age, sorry.'

'You're doing fine,' the sergeant assured Tommy. Then he said, 'Take a little while to think about the woman and see if you can remember anything else about her.'

Tommy looked down. He closed his eyes for a few moments, and when he looked up he said, 'I think she had long black hair... but I'm not sure. Being honest, I didn't get a good look. It could even have been a man with a wig on.'

The sergeant said, 'You're doing great. Try and remember, as the car came towards you, did you see the car's number plate... or anything on the car that you thought was different and looked out of place? Like things on the car that may help us find it.'

Tommy answered, 'I couldn't make out the number plate properly. I think I saw six two six. The car had a large crash bar that didn't look right. It was obvious it didn't belong on a small car like that, and it was nearly covering the numbers, but when we fell back onto the bike, I saw red.' Tommy stopped to take a breath.

The sergeant asked, 'You said the car was black and when you fell back you saw red. When you say you 'saw red', did you mean on the car, or did you mean that you were angry at the driver?'

'Sorry to sound confusing,' Tommy apologised, carrying on, 'I saw red on the car somewhere, but I don't know whereabouts on it. It all happened so fast.'

The sergeant said, 'Well, I think they will get rid of the crash bar. The car itself sounds like it's a classic, so someone should have noticed a car like that with a crash bar on it and that may help us to find the driver.' Then he asked Tommy, 'Are you alright to carry on?'

Tommy said, 'Yes, I'll just have a drink,' as he picked up the glass of milk.

With that, the sergeant picked up his mug of coffee and said, 'Cheers' and drank it all in one go.

As he was doing so, Pearl picked up her mug and had a sip of her coffee. She pulled a face and, as she put it down, she said, 'It's gone cold.'

Tommy put the empty glass on the table, took a hanky out of his pocket and wiped round his mouth, asking, 'Shall I start again?'

The sergeant replied, 'Yes. You and Ann fell onto the bike... Start from there.'

Tommy nodded and said, 'We fell onto the bike, Ann was screaming. We watched the car in a sort of a daze as it carried on toward Ann's parents. I thought I heard John shouting.

Their mum was walking on the road. Their dad pulled her out of the way of the car, but it seemed like a dream... I thought they were both going to go over the wall; Ann's mum did go over, with their dad holding onto her with one hand - the other seemed to be pointing at the lamp that was near to them and, when he hit the wall, he reached over with that hand. Her dad shouting for help made us come back to reality. He was shouting out to Ann and John that he couldn't hold her.

We got up as fast as we could, and Ann ran to help her dad. While they were pulling her up, I thought that I could help her if I climbed over the wall, and she could grab one of my hands while I held onto the wall with my other.'

Tommy stopped for a moment, with a sad look on his face, and his eyes filled up with tears.

The sergeant and Pearl looked at him but, before they could respond, he said, 'Don't worry, I'm alright.' Then he wiped his eyes with his hanky and carried on with his statement.

'I got over the wall and edged along it to reach Ann's mum. She was crying and shouting, 'Steve, pull me up! Steve, I'm slipping!' Just as I got there,' Tommy stopped, took a deep breath and continued, 'and my fingers touched hers. I think she screamed, 'don't let go!"

He stopped, and looked at the sergeant and Pearl and, in almost a whisper, he said, 'Our fingers touched... Then she fell, screaming, down the mountain.'

Tommy went a bit pale again, wiping at the tears running down his face as he said, 'Ann was hysterical and was blaming her dad. I did my best to calm Ann down and get her away from where her dad was, so I took her back to where the bike was lying and sat her on its seat. I felt sorry for John. He was sobbing, sitting on the floor, leaning against the wall, but I couldn't help him. I was afraid to leave Ann. I didn't know what she would do.

I'm afraid that's all I can remember,' he finished. Then in an angry tone, with a look on his face to match it, he added, 'Pardon my language, but I hope you get the fucking wicked bitch who was driving that car.'

He went ever paler and said, 'I get this real horrible, sickly feeling inside when I think about it.'

Pearl stopped typing, as the sergeant said to him, 'Are you alright, Tommy?'

He answered, 'Yes,' as the colour came back to his face, and continued, 'Like I said, just thinking about it turns me sick, but I'll be alright in a moment.'

The sergeant got up and walked round the table to Tommy, who stood up with a bit of difficulty as the sergeant got to him.

The sergeant put his hand out to him, Tommy took hold of it and, while they shook hands, the sergeant said, 'You have done a good job on your statement, and it's been a pleasure to meet you. Now, I know this is almost impossible, but you've got to try to put the accident out of your mind for now. When you get back to England, you should get some counselling.'

While the sergeant was talking to Tommy, Pearl was on the phone to the carpool and when she put the handset back on the receiver, she said to Tommy, 'I'll show you out to the car we have waiting for you. It will take you to your hotel.'

The sergeant patted Tommy on the back as he opened the door for him to leave, and said, 'I'll stay in touch with you. Bye for now.'

Tommy replied, 'I hope so. I want you to get that bitch. She has taken a mother from their family. I don't know what I'd do if I lost my mum.'

MANPOWER

The sergeant went over the statement on his way to the chief inspector and he got angry when he thought of Ann and John without their mother. He knocked on the chief inspector's door and just entered; he didn't wait to be called in.

The chief inspector looked up from the work on his desk and was about to tell him off for not waiting to be asked to come in but, when he saw the look on the sergeant's face and the folder he was holding, he just said to the sergeant, 'Sit down. Is that the statement from the English boy?'

The sergeant handed him the folder and said, 'Two children without their mother now. It makes my blood boil.'

When the chief inspector had read the statement, he said, 'I'm leaving you on the case as it seems strange for anyone to fit a large crash bar on an old MG. It's as if it was put on to take this family out, but surely anyone would know they would have to use a heavier and bigger car? If it had hit them, the crash bar wouldn't save the car or the driver.

I have heard of this family. They are rich and know a lot of people that are in the government. It's very important that we catch the people involved who did this. It's also bad publicity for the resort. So I'm placing a lot of confidence in you to do a good job, because I'm sure I'll be hearing from the higher ups.'

The sergeant agreed with him and said, 'It looks like she was out to kill someone and, like you, I think they were just after the parents in this family. Maybe they've done a bad business deal and the driver didn't care what happened to her as long as she took them out. They are one of the richest families in England. They own that big grand hotel by the beach and a few more in other Spanish resorts. God knows what they own in England!

I will need as many men as you can spare to interview the hotel staff, and it will take quite a few men to find the people from the picnic area to interview, which will be a big job in itself.'

The chief inspector, as he sat behind his desk, rubbing his chin and frowning, thought, 'The sergeant isn't going to like the manpower I can give him, I'll tell him when he's a bit more relaxed.'

So instead, he said, 'Let's recap our situation one more time.'

The sergeant thought 'What the hell is he on about? We've just been all through this,' as the chief inspector continued, 'I think you're right, but who would know that they would be at that spot on the road, at that time of day? And she headed for the whole family and, let's face it, a car just wouldn't kill all of them. It would be almost impossible for it to do so... For someone to go to these lengths, they must have made some enemies who really hate them. Well, they say you have to be ruthless in business and they do have a massive business.'

The sergeant nodded and said, 'That's why I think she was after the parents. Like you said, they have a massive business, so they may have some rich enemies. So we'll have to work on finding the car - or what's left of it. I'll send a couple of men out checking the scrap yards right away, in the hope the car hasn't been broken up yet.'

The chief inspector took a deep breath, as he thought, 'I'll just have to take the bull by the horns and tell him.'

He stood up, put his hand up to his mouth, cleared his throat and then said, 'Including yourself, you only have five of you to investigate this case. That is all the men I can spare.'

The sergeant's face changed to a serious look, as if he was about to say something, but the chief inspector didn't give him a chance. He took no notice and carried on talking, 'I, like you, think it might be murder, and we have to do our best to catch the bastard... but if it's a professional job, paid for by some rich businessperson, we stand little chance of getting our hands on them. They could be anywhere in the world. If it's just some nutcase who was looking for anyone to drive over, and the family were unlucky enough to be there when the bastard came round the bend, then we may have a chance at catching them. And we can't rule out at this point that it may have just been an accident caused by someone who shouldn't really have been behind the wheel.'

While he was talking, he picked up the phone and held his other hand up to the sergeant to indicate he was going to make a call.

When he had finished, he put the phone down and said to the sergeant, 'I've told four officers to meet you in the small conference room. Sorry about the manpower, but you know how we need more officers in this station.'

All the time the sergeant was in the office, he hadn't sat down. He had been standing by the side of the chief inspector's desk while they were discussing the case. Now, he nodded and turned to leave, but his face showed that he wasn't pleased about only having four officers to help with the case.

The chief inspector saw the sergeant's face as he left the office and muttered to himself, 'I'm doing the best I can, I just haven't got the manpower.'

When the sergeant got to the conference room, there were four officers already sitting in the front row of seats, talking. As the sergeant walked to the desk in front of them, they went quiet. When he got to the desk, he stood in front of it, picking up some folders from it, and turned to face the officers. He handed each one of them a folder but was left holding five more in his hand.

He said, in an angry voice, 'I told Pearl to make ten copies of the case file, because that's how many officers it will take on this case, but the powers that be have only allowed me you - four officers.'

With his anger subsiding, his tone went back to normal as he carried on talking, 'Well, we all know we're short of officers in this station, so I know you will do your best. I want you to study the so-called accident. That is what the press release we are putting out says happened, but we will be looking at the case as murder. I'll give you a few minutes, get a drink and study the case file. You will see we only have one statement as yet.'

He stopped talking and pointed to the vending machine.

A young officer, who was sitting nearest to it, stood up and said, 'I want a coffee. Do any of you want anything different?'

The three other officers all asked for coffee as well. The young officer picked up a cardboard tray with holes in it from the small table at the side of the vending machine, to put the plastic coffee cups in and pressed the button on the machine.

As the coffee started to pour into the first cup, the officer asked, 'Do you want a cup of coffee, Sarge?'

The sergeant replied, 'Don't talk so soft. Does a duck quack? Of course I do.'

The officer handed each man a cup as he passed them. He reached the sergeant last.

The sergeant, with a smile on his face, said to him, 'I don't think you will go far up the ladder in this job, son.'

While he was talking the young officer looked worried, but the sergeant continued, 'You've got to get things right if you want to get on. You never, ever give the boss his coffee last.'

The other officers started laughing and, as the young officer sat down, he realised it was just a joke.

They drank their coffee as they each read their copy of the file and, after ten minutes, the sergeant said, 'Well, I think it's time to get started.'

He pointed at the young officer and the officer next to him, and said, 'You two can question people working in the local garages, and scrapyards. Oh, and look up the dealers of vintage cars.'

Pointing at the remaining officers, he added, 'And you two can try to trace the people in the picnic area and anyone nearby who might have seen a strange, old, black car. As you see in the file, we only have part of the number plate; it's six two six.

I also want you to interview the staff and guests at the hotel. I know it's a lot of work for the four of you, but don't think I will be sitting back doing nothing. I will have to interview the husband, daughter and the son of the lady who was killed.'

The officers got up to leave the room and as each one of them passed the vending machine they threw their plastic cups in the rubbish bin standing next to it. The officer in the front opened the door for them to file out. As they did so the sergeant could hear them complaining about the work they would have to do but, as the last one left the room, the sergeant heard him say, 'Well, I'm glad I'm doing the legwork. I would rather do this than interview the family. That's one job I don't think I could do.'

After the officers left the conference room, the sergeant went to his office and sat down at the desk to sort out the paperwork on the case.

EMMA AND ANN GO TO THE POLICE STATION

After a short while, there was a knock on the sergeant's door. He stood up as the door opened and a female officer stepped into the room, announcing, 'Sarge, there's an Emma Kenwright, with a young girl, asking for the person in charge of the investigation into her sister's death. They are in the reception area.

I was told you were in charge of this case. So, should I show them to your office? They can speak our language, but they are both in distress and it sounds like they are too upset to concentrate, so should I get them an interpreter who can speak in English?'

The sergeant replied, in Spanish, 'Yes, I'm heading up this case, and we won't need an interpreter. You know I can speak fluent English.

I'll go back with you and you can introduce them to me. I think it will be a bit kinder that way.'

They walked down the hallway. As they went, the sergeant stopped at a door that had a sign on it that read 'Superintendent'. He knocked, opened it to check that no one was inside, and then reached inside to take a tag from the back of the door that read 'engaged' on it. He closed the door and hung it on the handle. As he did so he looked at the officer, who had a questioning look on her face.

He winked, grinned at her and said in a conspiratorial voice, 'I'm sure he won't mind me using his office. He's on leave and I won't tell him if you don't.'

She replied with a smile, 'Not me, Sarge.'

He then said in his normal tone, 'It's more comfortable for them than the interview room.

Oh, could you tell Pearl to bring her typewriter and meet me in this office?'

The officer nodded.

When they got to the reception area, the officer approached Emma and Ann. They both kept wiping their wet eyes, which looked red and sore through crying.

The officer pointed to the sergeant and said, 'This is the officer in charge of the investigation, Sergeant Torres. If you go with him, he will help you all he can... He can speak English.'

Emma asked the policewoman to repeat what she had said.

The sergeant explained in English to Emma what the officer had said, but, as he said, 'I don't want to upset you when I talk to you about the accident. I'm sorry for what has happened to your family, with the loss of your sister...' he looked uncomfortable as he tried to find the right words to say to them.

Before he had time to continue, however, Ann broke down sobbing. Emma put her arm round her and pulled her close, as the tears started to run freely down Emma's face as well. The sergeant stood there for a few moments, not sure what to do, and was relieved when Emma looked up from Ann and asked him to take them somewhere private.

He stood beside Emma, put his hand gently on her arm and said, as he slowly started to walk back along the corridor, 'Come this way, I have a quiet office where we can talk.'

He led them along the hallway, to the door with the tag on it.

He opened the door, stepped aside and said, 'Please go in and sit on the settee, it's the most comfortable seat in here.'

Emma helped Ann in and sat her on the settee. All the time, Ann had a hanky held to her eyes. She was still sobbing, but a lot quieter. Emma sat down beside her and wiped her own eyes as she tried to comfort Ann.

The sergeant took a chair from a corner in the room and placed it by them, but not directly in front of them, as he didn't want to be looking straight at their faces while they were so upset.

He sat down and waited a few minutes for them to compose themselves. Then he took a deep breath and said, 'I know this will be hard on both of you, but I have to take a statement from Ann. If she is up to it?'

Before he could continue, Emma looked at him in anger and almost shouted, 'Ann is in no condition to give you a statement.'

Ann jumped up off the settee and screamed, 'Yes, I am! My dad killed my mum. He let go of her and let my mum fall.'

Then she started crying again. With that Emma stood up, got hold of Ann and sat her down again. As she sat down beside her, there was a knock on the door and it opened.

Pearl walked in and closed the door behind her. As she did so the sergeant said to Emma, 'This is Pearl. She was to take Ann's statement.'

Emma looked from Ann to him; her face was red with anger and she was clearly about to say something but the sergeant put his palms up in front of him, with his fingers outstretched to show he understood and wasn't going to push Ann to give a statement.

He said, 'But I think you're right, Emma. Ann is in no condition to give it.'

Then he said to Pearl, 'I won't need you at the moment.'

Pearl never said anything, she just turned and left the room. When she was outside the office, she had tears in her eyes; as she wiped them, she thought, 'I'm glad I didn't have to take that statement right now.'

Emma hugged Ann as they sat on the settee. The sergeant felt uneasy dealing with the situation, but he did his best not to show it.

He said in a quiet, caring voice, 'Emma, would you and Ann like a drink? We have tea, coffee and Pepsi or lemonade?'

Emma answered, 'No, thank you,' while Ann just shook her head.

The sergeant said, 'I'll go and arrange for a car to take you back to your hotel.'

As he turned to leave the room, Emma said angrily, in a sobbing tone, 'Excuse me, Sergeant, where are you going? We came here to see what is being done and what you know about...' She had to stop for a moment, to wipe the tears away from her eyes and face, before continuing, 'My lovely sister Joan's death.'

Ann stood up, her face red with anger, as she screamed, 'I've told you he did it. He let her fall. He *let go* of my mum, I saw him. Why don't you arrest him?'

With that, Emma stood up and pulled Ann into her. With her hand on Ann's head, she gently pulled it into her shoulder, as Ann's voice became a sob.

Emma nodded to the sergeant and said, in almost a whisper, with tears running down her cheeks, 'On second thought, I will take Ann to the hotel now, if you will get a vehicle for us, Sergeant?'

The sergeant had only once been in a situation like this before. He didn't know how to act then, though he did his best, and he wasn't sure if he was doing the right thing now. He was worried about Ann.

Looking at Emma and Ann, he felt behind him for the door handle; as he opened the door, he said, 'Certainly. Come with me. I'll get you a car right away.'

Emma steered Ann out of the room, following the sergeant into the long corridor. He didn't go back the way they had come. He turned up the hallway instead. He was almost walking sideways, trying to both keep an eye on Emma and Ann and watch where he was going. When he came to two large iron doors, he pulled one open and stepped just outside and when Emma followed, still guiding Ann, the sergeant got hold of Ann's arm as he helped them down the three steps.

He said to them, 'Just wait here a moment and I'll get you a car.'

He walked across the yard, to where the cars were. There was a group of officers standing around talking.

They stopped when they saw the sergeant approaching them and a couple officers asked, at the same time, 'Looking for a driver, Sarge?'

Then one of them asked, 'Are you alright, Sarge? You don't look too good.'

The sergeant answered, 'I'm fine, but I think one of you policewomen who can speak English would be best for this job. I want you to take two very upset people to The Grandee hotel. That's the big one by the beach.'

One of the officers said, 'I've just come on duty, Sarge. I'll take them. Are they relatives of the woman who died on the mountain road?'

The sergeant nodded, as he replied, 'Yes, the woman's name is Emma and the young girl is Ann.

Don't talk to them about the accident, they get too upset. Just listen to what they say to one another and answer if you have to. When you get back, report to me.'

The officer said, 'Okay, Sarge, I'll get the car.' As she started to walk to her car she checked, 'Is it the two people standing by the steps?'

He answered, 'Yes, and I can't emphasise this enough, it is important: I want you to just listen to them. But do concentrate on your driving.'

Then he turned and moved quickly back to Emma and Ann. Just as he got to them, the police car pulled up alongside him, with the back door in line with Emma and Ann. The policewoman got out and opened it and the sergeant helped them get into the car.

The policewoman got back in the driver's seat, as the sergeant said to Emma, 'This officer will take you to your hotel. If I can help in any way, just ring the station and ask for Sergeant Torres.'

Emma nodded and he closed the door and tapped on the driver's window, pointing for her to go. He stood there, feeling sorry for them as he watched the car leave the station's carpark. He shook his head, turned and went up the steps and back into the station.

As they came to the hotel, Emma asked the driver, 'Will you take the road at the side? We don't want to see anyone.'

The driver replied, 'Certainly, madam,' still listening carefully to the muttered conversation in the back seat as she gave her main attention to the road ahead of her.

When the car got to the hotel, they went past the front entrance and saw that the outside of the large glass doors and the bottom of the steps were surrounded by reporters. When the reporters saw the police car passing, they moved towards it, trying to take photos of the people in it. The driver put her foot down to speed past them; when she got to the corner, she turned down the road and drove along it, passing twenty large windows in the hotel's ground floor.

A door came into view, and Emma said, 'Would you stop by the door, please?'

'Of course I will, madam,' came the reply from the driver.

She slowed the car, coming to a stop in front of the door. Then she got out and opened the back door of the car. While she was driving, she had seen Ann in the mirror when checking the traffic behind her, and had felt sorry for her then, but seeing her sitting there now, in the state she was in, the policewoman felt her own eyes filling up. She quickly composed herself and, as Emma was struggling to get Ann out, reached into the car to help. Just as they were both out of the car, the door opened and two maids rushed down the steps to them.

They got hold of Ann to help her, as she was as limp as a rag doll. As the four of them got her up the steps and into the hotel, she never stopped sobbing. Emma thanked the officer for her help and then turned her attention back to Ann.

The officer left the hotel, closed the back door of the car and then got in the driver's seat, wiping the tears from her eyes. She sat there for a moment to compose herself, then she checked her mirror, indicated and drove off back to the station.

When she got back, she parked in the station car park alongside the other police cars, went straight to the sergeant's office and knocked on the door.

He said, 'Come in. Oh, it's you! Were they still upset on the way home? What am I saying? Of course they were... What I meant was, did you drop them at their hotel without any problems?' Upon receiving an affirmative nod to this inquiry, he added, 'Did they say anything that might help us with the case?'

She replied, 'Not really, Sarge, but I don't think the woman likes her brother-in-law, because the young girl was really upset and kept saying her dad let go of her mother deliberately. Surely her aunt should have calmed her down by telling her it was an accident and that her dad didn't do it deliberately. You'd think she'd tell her he did the best he could and that he just couldn't hold on, so her mother slipped out of his grip. I think her aunt could and should have said that he loved her mother, and he wouldn't do what she's saying he did.'

The sergeant remarked, 'They are both upset and don't realise what they are saying. When they calm down, they most likely will be sorry for what they have said. I think the young girl will need a lot of love and, when she gets back to England, a great deal of counselling to try and help her put this tragedy behind her… But, at the same time, no matter how upset she is, it's important we don't discount her statement. We need to look into all leads to do our job properly, so if she's saying that her dad let go of her mother, it's important that we do rule that possibility out.'

A NURSE FOR JOHN

The morning after the accident, once Steve had picked John up from the hospital and taken him to the villa, John was sobbing and sometimes would get hysterical. Steve didn't know what to do; it was all too much for him. He was confused, and in desperation he rang for his doctor and friend Matteo but was told that he was doing an emergency operation and couldn't be disturbed.

The doctor he was put through to instead asked, 'Can I help?'

Steve explained the problem he was having with John and the doctor sent a paramedic to the villa to check him over.

The paramedic settled John down and gave him a sedative. While he was looking after John, Steve rang for a nurse he knew. She was a nurse they had used before in the hotel.

He asked her to come over to help with John and told her, 'I have left the gates to the villa open, so you can drive straight in.'

When Steve put the mobile phone back in his pocket, the paramedic said to him, 'Put John in bed and make sure there is someone with him all the time.'

Steve replied, 'I've employed a nurse we sometimes use in the hotel and she will be with John as long as he needs her.'

Then Steve bent down and picked John up out of the easy chair he was in. John didn't move; he was nearly asleep as his dad carried him to the bedroom. John was muttering something but Steve couldn't make out what he was saying and, by the time Steve had covered him with the bedclothes, he was asleep.

The paramedic was just going out the door when the nurse drove up. They knew one another and he told the nurse what he had been doing there.

Then he opened his medicine case, took out some pills and said, 'When John wakes up it will be late afternoon. Get him to eat some food. Then give him two of these pills and he will sleep till tomorrow morning.'

She took the pills off him and said, 'Thank you. I will spend the night with him.'

As the paramedic left, the door of the villa was still open. The nurse went inside and found she was in a large hallway with five doors off it.

She looked around and called out, 'Mr Thomson, are you there? It's me, the nurse you called.'

Steve answered right away, 'Thank God! I'm in this bedroom with John. Will you come in, please?'

The nurse headed for the door that Steve's voice had come from. She was amazed as she entered into a magnificent bedroom. Steve was standing by a large four poster bed, with his hand on the sleeping John's forehead.

She could see Steve was distressed, as he looked from John to her with tears in his eyes. She quickly walked over to Steve who was looking like he was about to say something.

The nurse put her hand on Steve's shoulder and, before he could say anything, said, 'The paramedic has told me what has happened. Try not to worry about John, I will take good care of your son.' Then she added, 'Mr Thomson, may I offer my condolences? I am so sorry for what has happened to your family. I think you also need to go and lay down for a couple of hours, because your children need you to look after yourself and stay healthy for their sake.'

Steve turned his back on her and made a quiet sobbing sound. He put both his hands to his face, as he replied, 'I can't. I have to go and see Joan.'

As he turned to walk past her, his hands were still covering his face, but he opened his fingers a bit so he could see where he was going. The nurse felt sorry for him as he passed her, because she could see the tears running down his cheeks.

Steve carried on talking, 'Anyway, I want to go to the police station to see if they have got the bastard who destroyed my family.'

He opened the door and turned to look at John as he left the room. She could see his face; his eyes were red and his face was wet with tears. She gently picked up John's hand by the wrist to take his pulse.

Though he was asleep and didn't move, she whispered to him, 'Well, John, your dad is very shaken up. I hope he can pull himself together, for your and your sister's sake.'

When she was sure John was settled, she looked around the room. Directly facing the bed was a large window with blinds on it and on either side of it there were reddish-purple drapes of velvet. On the same wall as the door, there were shelves full of all kinds of books. As she pulled a reclining chair to the side of the bed, she looked around and thought to herself, 'What a beautiful room! How can one family have so much money?'

Then she went to the bookshelves, looked at a few of the books and chose one to read. She went back to the bed and put the book on the arm of the chair. She checked that John was comfortable and tucked him in more securely. Then she went to the kitchen to get a glass of milk and make herself a sandwich.

She was amazed at how lavish the kitchen was. She got the milk and some cheese out of the large fridge and took it to the prominent work counter that was in the middle of the kitchen. When she reached it she found on it: bread, a chopping board with two slices of cheese and a sliced onion.

She said to herself, 'I'm glad to see the man has eaten something. I'll put some of the left-over onion on my sandwich. It will save it from going to waste.'

She made her sandwich, poured out a glass of milk and put it all on a tray. She took the snack back into the bedroom and put it on a small table by her reclining chair. Then, after checking John's pulse and his temperature and making sure he was still comfortable, she settled down on the reclining chair with the milk, sandwich and the book, while she waited for John to wake up. She wondered why Steve had gone out when John needed his dad here with him.

STEVE VISITS ANN

As Steve went to his garage, he pressed the remote so that the two large doors rose to reveal a Rolls Royce and a Mustang. He got in the Rolls Royce and, as he drove out of the garage, the doors closed behind him. He drove down the driveway and, as he got near the gates, he pressed the remote again and the gates opened. He drove out and they closed the moment the car was on the road outside the villa grounds.

Steve was driving to the hotel and on the way there he phoned and asked for Emma's room. The operator put the call through.

Emma answered, 'Hello, who is it?'

Steve said, 'It's me. I would like to speak to Ann.'

Emma paused, then said, 'Ann said this morning that if you phoned, she wouldn't speak to you, but I will try to get her to come to the phone. Hold on a moment.'

Before Steve could say anything, Emma put the phone down and went to Ann's room.

She knocked and waited nervously. Ann answered in a quiet, distressed voice, 'Come in.'

Emma entered, went to the bed that Ann was in and picked up the extension phone from the bedside table by her bed, handing it to her.

Emma said, 'Your father is on the phone.'

While Emma was talking Ann's face went red with anger and she refused to take the phone, screeching, 'I said I don't want to talk to him or see him. He killed my mum.'

Emma put the handset back down on the receiver without thinking, so she could comfort Ann. Steve had heard Ann before the call was ended and right away thought, 'I hate that bitch. She is only too happy to turn Ann against me. Well, she's *my* daughter.'

In his anger he gripped the steering wheel with all his strength, turning his knuckles white, and he put his foot down and drove even faster to the hotel.

He didn't see the police car, as he drove past where it was parked. It chased after him with the siren on and he was ordered to pull over.

As he stopped, he swore, 'This is that fucking cow's fault.'

Two police officers approached the Rolls Royce and the older one asked Steve for his licence and insurance. When Steve got his documents out of the glove compartment and turned to face the officer, the officer saw who he was.

He said in English, 'The way you were driving, sir, someone could get hurt.' Then he checked Steve's documents.

The younger one asked Steve, 'Have you been drinking, sir? And are you willing to take a breathalyser test?'

He started to get a breathalyser out of the police car. The older officer told his younger colleague not to bother, and then said to Steve, 'Thank you, sir, but be sure to drive more carefully from now on. No speeding.'

He handed Steve back his documents.

Steve took the documents and said, 'I'm sorry, officer, I will pay more attention to my driving.'

The officer told Steve to go with a wave of his hand.

Steve nodded and drove off, and as he drove away, he said to himself again, in a whisper so the officers couldn't hear him, 'That's Emma's fault - the fucking bitch.'

The two officers walked back to their car and the young officer said to the older one, in an accusatory tone, 'Why did you let him off? I wanted to book the rich so-and-so. He was speeding and he'd been drinking - you could see by his blood shot eyes. He must have been drinking to be in that state. People with a car like him think that just because they've got a Rolls, they can get away with anything... Well, I would have given the rich so-and-so a ticket. Why didn't you?'

The other officer went red in the face while the young officer was talking and, in an angry voice, he answered, 'You think I let him go because he's in a Rolls Royce, you fucking idiot? I didn't book him because I *know* why he's in that state. He's the husband of the woman who was killed yesterday on the mountain road. His two children saw their mother die. He has enough troubles. As for him drinking, could you smell any alcohol on him...? Well, could you, smart arse? Because I couldn't.

Do you think you're the only one who has the balls to book a rich person, you fucking daft git? So don't you ever accuse me again of being afraid to do my job.'

The young officer stammered, 'Sorry, I didn't mean it like that.'

The angry officer remarked, 'Well, that's the only fucking thing you could mean.' They both got in the car in silence. The older one was driving, and the tyres screeched as the police car moved off.

Taking things a little more carefully, Steve drove to the hotel's private entrance. He went in and the staff in the lobby made as if to come over to him, but he ushered them away with a wave of his hand and a shake of his head and instead went straight to the VIP lift. When he got out, Steve went to Emma's apartment, where he knew Emma and Ann would be. He took the master key card out of his pocket, put it in the slot and opened the door.

He walked into the large living-cum-dining room, but no one was there so he shouted, 'Emma? Ann?'

Steve went sick when he heard Ann screech, 'Don't let him in here, Aunt Emma. I hate him.'

She carried on screaming as Emma came out of the room she was in, and when she saw Steve was in her apartment, she spat at him, 'I have just calmed her down after your phone call. Now get out of here, you have no rights coming in here without my permission.'

Steve was angry and red in the face as he roared, 'Ann is my daughter and you shouldn't keep her from me. You have always hated me and now you are turning Ann against me.'

Emma screamed back at him, 'You're right! I never did like you... but it wasn't me who turned her against you. You did that when Ann saw what you did to Joan.'

There was a loud knock on the open door and the hotel manager stood there with two security personnel. As soon as Emma and Steve saw them, they both went quiet, but Ann was still screaming in the other room.

Emma said to the manager, 'Get him out of here, he is upsetting Ann,' then she turned and went back into the bedroom to try to calm Ann down.

Steve turned to face the three men who looked a bit unsure of what to do. Steve walked towards the door and the three men moved back into the corridor.

When he got to the corridor, he paused for a moment and said to the manager and the security men, as he wiped his eyes with his handkerchief, 'I'm sorry I have put you in this situation. It won't happen again.'

Before they could say anything, he got in the lift and turned to face them as the doors closed. The three men walked back to the office at the end of the corridor.

The manager said, 'Mr Thomson is in a bad way. Did you see his eyes? And he was wiping tears from his face... It's no time for the family to fight. They will need to help one another.'

The two security men nodded and went into their office, while the manager headed for the lift.

When Steve disembarked from the lift into the hotel lobby, the staff all looked at him. They had never seen him like this before. He was always smiling and pleasant but now he was muttering, and his face was red and distorted with anger. As he strode past them, he didn't seem to see them at all.

Steve hurried out of the hotel and got in his Rolls. He sat there for a little while, cursing and belting the steering wheel. Just when he had calmed down a bit and stopped lashing out, some reporters came running up to the Rolls with their cameras flashing. He drove off, cursing at them and nearly knocking two of them down as they tried to get a photo of him. As he headed from the hotel to the police station, his anger showed in his driving again but as he got to the same spot where he had been pulled over earlier in the day, he remembered and told himself to calm down and drive more carefully.

When he got to the police station, he parked a few yards up the road from the building. As he got out of the car, some paparazzi came running towards him with cameras, taking photos and shouting questions at him.

He shouted, 'Get away from me, you fuckin' bastard leeches.' Then he grabbed a camera off one of them and threw it into the road, shouting, 'Now fuck off, you fucking bastards.'

He angrily shoved his way through them. He pushed out at two blocking his way, and they both fell. Steve didn't even look at them as he went up the steps; four police officers came down to help him and ordered the newspaper reporters to move away. They did, but only to the other side of the road, where they had parked their cars facing the station entrance. Some of them sat in their cars watching for when Steve came out.

One of the others, leaning against a car, shouted across to the police 'We're only doing our jobs in trying to interview him' causing one of the officers to call back, as they went back up the steps, 'Well, that's just what we're doing when we move you lot out of the way!'

Steve went into the station and looked around, as he stood just inside the entrance. There was a bench on his left with three people sitting on it; on his right the bench was empty and about five yards away, in front of him, was a large counter. On the other side of it there were two policemen, talking, and a sergeant who was working on some paperwork which was on the counter.

Steve took his handkerchief out of his pocket and wiped his face. As he walked up to the counter, he put it back in his pocket.

He approached the sergeant and said in English, as tears started to run down his cheeks, 'Excuse me, I'm Steve Thomson and I have been asked to come and make a statement.'

Just as the sergeant looked up from the paperwork, he saw Steve probing his pocket for his handkerchief, which he took it out and wiped his face with again.

The sergeant answered back in English, 'We are sorry for your loss, Mr Thomson. I will get someone to see you right away.'

He picked the phone up and he spoke in his own language, saying into it, 'Sergeant Torres, I have Mr Thomson here. I'll get an officer to take him to your office.'

Steve understood what he had said and didn't wait for the sergeant to finish speaking. In an annoyed voice, he said, 'I would like to see the chief inspector. My wife was killed, and I want the top men put on finding the bastard who did it.'

Then he wiped his face with his handkerchief again. While Steve was talking the sergeant put the phone down to listen to what he was saying, then he picked the phone up again and pressed the numbers for the chief inspector, saying in English, 'I'll speak to the chief inspector, and ask him to see you, Mr Thomson.'

The chief inspector had heard what the sergeant was saying to Steve, and said to him in English, 'I'll be right out.'

The sergeant put the phone back on the receiver and said to Steve, 'The chief inspector will be here in a moment, Mr Thomson.'

Just as the sergeant said this, a door opened behind him and the chief inspector came out. He came to the counter, opened the hatch upward, swung open the small door in the counter and said, 'Will you come through to my office, Mr Thomson?'

Steve went through and into the inspector's office. As soon as he entered, the chief inspector shut the door behind them and said, 'Will you take a seat, Mr Thomson, please? We are all sorry for your loss and feel for you and your children.'

Steve sat on one of the two easy chairs this side of the large desk and said, 'It doesn't look that way to me. Why was I only going to be interviewed by a sergeant?'

I want someone with detective service, who knows what they are doing… and if I don't get a senior detective looking into the death of my Joan, I will go over your head.'

The chief inspector sat down on the other easy chair, so that he was facing Steve and said, 'I'm sorry, I can see you are upset.'

Steve stood up saying, in a loud angry voice, 'You can see I'm fuckin' upset?'

The chief inspector said in a calm voice, 'Please sit down, Mr Thomson, and let me explain what we are doing.'

Steve slowly sat back down.

The inspector continued when Steve was back in his seat. 'You think that Sergeant Torres is just someone we have picked at random... Well, let me assure you, he is the best man we have got in this station. He is still a sergeant because he has said he doesn't want promotion. He really cares about people, and he wants to stay in uniform until he retires. I will be in ultimate charge of everything, and I can assure you we will be doing our best for you and your family.'

Steve wiped his face and said, 'I'm sorry I went off the deep end, but Joan is part of me and I'm lost without her. I hope you can understand that. Clearly you know what you're doing, so I'll leave you to do whatever you think will get the bastard who killed my Joan and ruined my family,'

With that, the chief inspector went to his desk, picked up the phone and said in Spanish, 'Put me through to Sergeant Torres.'

He waited a moment, then he said in English, 'Sergeant Torres, I have Mr Thomson in my office. He has come to give you a statement.'

He put the phone down on the receiver and said, 'The sergeant will be with us in a moment. If you will go with him to his office, he will take your statement there.'

As Steve got up from the chair, the chief inspector went to him and, as they both walked towards the door, the chief inspector put a friendly hand on Steve's shoulder. He opened the door to find the sergeant standing there, about to knock.

The inspector said to Steve, 'This is Sergeant Torres. You go with him.' Then he offered Steve his hand and shook it, as he said again, 'You can be sure we are doing everything possible to get the person who did this terrible thing.'

Sergeant Torres also offered Steve his hand, who shook it, remarking, 'You're the officer who took John and I to the hospital, and then you dropped me off at the villa.'

The sergeant nodded and said, 'Yes. I wish we had met in different circumstances.

Now, Mr Thomson, if you will come this way, it is just a few doors up this corridor.'

They walked along till they came to the door with the sign 'Superintendent'. The sergeant opened it and invited Steve in. Steve wiped his face and looked at the sign.

Then he asked the sergeant, 'Is this your office?'

The sergeant answered, 'No, I'm just borrowing it while he's on holiday. The seats in here are more comfortable, so take a seat.'

Then he closed the door, as Steve sat down in one of the armchairs. The sergeant went to the desk and picked up the phone.

He pressed a couple of numbers and said, 'Is that you, Pearl? Will you bring your typewriter to the superintendent's office? I would like you to take down a statement.'

Then he put the phone down and asked Steve, 'Would you like a coffee or tea? We have a vending machine in the corridor. It doesn't taste very nice, but it's wet.'

Steve still had his handkerchief in his hand. He wiped his eyes and, as he put it back in his pocket, he answered, 'No, thanks.'

Then he bent his head down as if he was looking at his lap. The sergeant felt a bit uncomfortable, seeing the state of Steve. He moved the other armchair to sit on, so he would be able to talk to Steve, but he wouldn't be face to face with him. As he sat down there was a knock on the door.

He said, 'Come in.'

The door opened and Pearl walked into the office, carrying a small electric typewriter. She shut the door behind her.

The sergeant said, 'This is Pearl, she will type your statement.'

Steve looked up, nodded at Pearl and put his head down again. Pearl was about to say 'hello' but was taken a bit aback when she saw Steve's face, with his bloodshot, watery eyes.

She didn't know what to say, so she just said, 'Hi.'

She went up to the desk and put her typewriter on it. As she plugged the electric cable into the socket, the sergeant said, 'This is Mr Stephen Thomson.'

Pearl walked round the desk to the big executive office chair and sat in it as she set her typewriter up in front of her. The sergeant waited till Pearl was ready, then asked Steve for his personal details, so they could note down his name, age and address accurately for the beginning of the statement.

Then he said, 'Mr Thomson, could you tell us everything that happened from the time you left the picnic area? I might interrupt you with questions and ask you to go over something again; it's just to help you remember anything small that might not have seemed important at the time, but just might help us catch the driver of the car.'

Steve, without looking up, put his hands up to his face and sobbed, 'Oh my God.'

Then he seemed to pull himself together and said, 'We wanted to go down to the beach before the tide came in so...' He stopped, took his handkerchief out and wiped his eyes and then carried on, 'Well, that's not really right. What I should say is it was *my* idea. *I* wanted my family to go down to the beach before the tide came in, so I said to Joan, 'We will have to go now if we want to get to the beach before the tide comes in.' Then I told the people there to help themselves to what was left of the picnic, and that some of my staff would come and clean up the picnic area.

Then Joan and I shouted for Ann and John to come with us as we left the picnic tables. John was hanging back as usual. Ann asked if a boy could come with us. I didn't want him to come because I thought she was too young to get mixed up with boys, but Joan...' He sighed and stopped to wipe his face, and when he continued it was in a low tearful tone.

Pearl looked at the sergeant because she couldn't hear what Steve was saying, so the sergeant asked, 'Sorry, Mr Thomson, but could you speak up, as Pearl can't hear you. Would you start again from 'I didn't want him to come because I thought she was too young to get mixed up with boys, but Joan...''

Steve nodded and said, 'I didn't want him to come but Joan just laughed and said something like 'don't be a fuddy-duddy' and told me to let him. So Ann went ahead with the boy... I think his name was Tommy. He had a motorbike. I told Ann she wasn't to get on it and that she was to stay on the footpath. When Joan and I saw John was finally following us we started along the road down to the beach.'

Steve made a bit of a sobbing noise, then he continued, 'Joan wouldn't walk on the sidewalk. She wanted to walk on the road, because she was frightened of going near the edge... Joan had had acrophobia for years.'

He stopped again for a moment and sighed. Then he took a deep breath and said, 'It's my fault. We should have stayed at the picnic area.'

The sergeant interrupted, 'Mr Thomson, you can't think like that. What happened was the fault of the person who was driving the car, so please just try to remember what took place, and we will get the driver.'

Steve wiped his eyes and said, 'I'm sorry, I'll try not to get emotional and I'll try to remember everything I can.'

As he was talking, he looked up at the sergeant. Pearl had stopped typing and wiped her own eyes when she saw the look on Steve's face.

The sergeant said, 'Mr Thomson, take a moment and try to relax. We know this is very upsetting for you. When you feel ready to carry on, just let us know. Would you like a glass of water or a hot drink?'

Steve sat up in the chair, leaned forward a bit and said, 'No, thank you and I promise I won't get too upset again. Please just call me Steve.' He took a deep breath and continued, 'I was a bit annoyed with John because he goes into a world of his own and never keeps up with us and I'm afraid I got a bit angry. We had to call him quite a few times for him to catch up with us. I shouted for him to get a move on, and Joan said something like, 'Just leave him to follow us, as long as we can see that he is safe. Don't worry he won't lag too far behind us, he will keep us in his sights.'

Ann and the boy with the motorbike were about fifteen or twenty yards ahead of Joan and I. We stopped by a lamp and, like the idiot I am, I went into my usual daft tricks and I started joking with Joan. I should have known better.'

He stopped for a moment and wiped the tears off his face, and then he carried on, 'I got hold of the lamp. I had hold of Joan with my other hand.'

He stopped again, wiping his eyes and the tears off his face, and said, 'I asked Joan to come to the wall, like the bloody daft idiot that I am, and I said to her, 'You can't fall because I've got hold of the lamp, and you can look over at the great scenery below.' Joan was really angry and backed away further out into the road, but we were still holding hands when the car came round the corner. Joan and I froze when we saw it heading for Ann.'

He sobbed as he paused again, and asked, 'Can I have that glass of water now?'

Pearl stopped typing and said, 'Yes, I'll get you some from the water fountain, it's just in the corridor.'

She got up and left the office. When she got outside, she was glad of the small break away from typing Steve's statement, and took the opportunity to wipe her eyes again.

While she was out the sergeant asked Steve 'Was the car black and red?'

Steve answered, 'No, I'm sure it was black all over, including the black shabby soft top.'

The sergeant then inquired, 'Besides it being an old model, was there anything else you might have noticed about it?'

'No, it all happened too fast,' Steve replied, continuing, 'Like I said, Joan and I froze. I was watching Ann and then I tried to save Joan.' Then he wiped his eyes.

The sergeant said, 'When you continue your statement, tell Pearl what you saw of the car.'

Pearl was back in just a few minutes, carrying a plastic cup of water. She handed it to Steve as he finished wiping his eyes again. He put his handkerchief in his pocket and took the cup of water off her with a shaking hand, saying, 'Thank you.'

He looked down into the cup for a moment, and then he drank it all at once. The sergeant suggested to Steve 'Would you like a break?'

He answered in an angry tone, 'No, I don't need a break. I want you to get the fucking bastard who did this to my Joan and my children. God, they saw her fall...'

Pearl went back to the desk and sat down in front of her typewriter.

The sergeant said, as she sat down, 'Pearl, will you read back the last sentence?'

She looked at the typewriter and read out, 'We froze when we saw the it heading for Ann.'

The sergeant said, 'You can continue when you are ready, Steve.'

He took a deep breath and said, 'Like I said, we froze when we saw the old, black, shabby sports car heading for Ann and the boy. It was an old MG and, I've just remembered, it had a big crash bar on it that didn't belong on a car like that. Thank God the boy pulled Ann out of the way of it. They both fell on top of the motorbike, and the car still didn't change course. I don't understand - it had plenty of time to change, even before it reached Ann, and then it came at Joan and I.' He made a small noise but carried on, 'I pulled Joan to me with all my might, but she went flying past me.'

He put his head in his hands and stopped for a moment.

Pearl looked at the sergeant. He put his hand on Steve's shoulder and was about to say something to Steve, but Steve pushed his hand away and carried on talking. 'Joan went past me, and I kept hold of Joan's hand but the force pulling her towards me made me let go of the lamp and Joan went over that fuckin' bit of wall and almost took me with her.' He stopped again, then, almost crying, he continued, 'I hit the wall, but I was determined to hang on to Joan the best I could. I think I called out for Ann and John to help me.'

Then he shouted in anger, 'Fucking hell! I'm as strong as an ox; I should have been able to pull Joan up to safety. I just don't know why I couldn't save her.' Then he went quieter as he said, 'It's all my fault. I couldn't hold on to Joan's hand, it slipped out of my grip.'

He wiped his eyes and face, as he said, 'You know the rest. I just can't remember anything more. I have to get out of here.'

Steve stood up and the sergeant did as well, and held his hand out to him.

Steve shook it and the sergeant said, 'Steve, we know how upsetting this is for you, but if you do remember anything else, like the number plate or *any* small thing, it might be of importance. Just call in and ask for me, or phone. You know I'm Sergeant Torres.

I'll show you the way out. It can be a bit difficult to find your way if you haven't been here before.'

Steve, as he went to the door and opened it, said, 'No, thank you. I would like to be alone to think.'

The sergeant replied, 'I understand. I'll phone and tell the officers to keep the reporters away from you as you leave the building.'

Steve nodded and turned and shut the door behind him as he left the office.

The sergeant picked up the phone and dialled a number. Once it was answered, he said, 'Is that the front desk? Send some officers to move those reporters from the front of the station, so Mr Thomson won't be hassled.'

As he put the phone back down, Pearl stood up and wiped her eyes and the sergeant said, 'You big softy.'

She looked at him and replied, 'When I see someone's eyes watering it makes my eyes water and, anyway, look who's talking! I saw your face when he was making his statement.'

He nodded to Pearl and said, 'I guess I'm human after all.'

She said, 'But what I don't understand, if he is as strong as he said, why *couldn't* he pull his wife to safety?'

The sergeant replied, 'Have you heard of Houdini?'

She answered, 'Yes, he was a magician years ago. Well before my time... Did you go and see him on the stage?'

He said, 'Hey, don't be cheeky. I'm not that old - I read about him in an article. Well, anyway, one of his tricks was to ask a strong man from the audience to punch him in the stomach.

Houdini was a very fit man and had very firm stomach muscles, and just as he was about to be punched, he would tense all his stomach muscles, so he was ready to be hit. Then one day he was dining out and one of his fans saw him and told the people he was with 'that's Houdini.' He told them about Houdini's trick where he gets hit and doesn't flinch. Then he said 'I'll show you'. He went up to Houdini and said 'I'm a fan'; Houdini stood up and offered him his hand. The man punched him in the stomach; Houdini wasn't expecting the punch. He dropped to the ground and was dead in a couple of days.

Well, it's the same with Mr Thomson, he wasn't ready for what happened and as he hit the wall, he had the wind knocked out of him.'

Pearl replied, 'Oh, I understand.'

They both left the office, and the sergeant went back to his own, to read the reports from the four officers he had working on the case with him. In all the reports no one had seen the accident, except the couple in the car who had phoned the police. Lots of people had seen the car as it had sped past the picnic area, but no one knew where it had come from or where it had gone.

Finally, he came across one report from a police officer with some more positive news. The police officer had asked a woman who had been in the picnic area with her young son if she had seen an old, black car. Although she had not, her son had been collecting number plates of cars at the time. She had called him to come over to them and the officer asked, 'Did you see an old black car?'

The son had replied, 'I think I did. I've never seen a car like that before. It was black, with wire wheels like a motorbike and a big iron thing on the front... Is that the car you're talking about?'

The officer had confirmed it was.

The lad then said, 'I have got its number in my book.' He opened his notebook and read, 'It's 626 7KB.'

The officer had thanked the mother and son, and submitted his report as soon as he could.

When the sergeant was checking the paperwork and saw the report with the car registration of 6267KB in it, he got on the phone right away, exclaiming, 'I want someone in administration to trace a car with the number plate, 6267KB. It's urgent. I want to know the minute you have traced it. It could be a big help in this case.'

Then he picked up the phone and let the inspector know the progress his team had made.

GOING HOME

When Emma and Ann had left the police station, in the car organised by the sergeant, Ann was sobbing. They went straight to the hotel and when they arrived there, with the help of the policewoman and two maids Emma got Ann to her apartment. She tried to calm Ann down, even though she was silently crying herself.

Emma wiped her own eyes, and then she wiped Ann's eyes and face. She hugged her for a little while and, when she thought that Ann had calmed a bit, she said quietly, 'Ann, you know your dad loved…'

Before she could finish what she was going to say, Ann pushed Emma's arms off her, sobbing, 'I hate him!'

She left the room and went into a bedroom. She climbed into the bed, and pulled the duvet over her head as Emma followed her into the room. Emma sat on a chair beside the bed and pleaded with her, but Ann didn't take her head from under the duvet.

Emma wiped the tears off her face and continued, 'Please, love, listen. You may have got it wrong. When you think of it, if your dad hadn't tried to save your mum…' Emma paused as the tears ran down her face again.

She wiped them away and carried on, '…she would have been hit by the car and died on the road. You know he loved your mum, and her falling was an accident. He did his best to save your mum, but he just couldn't hold on.'

Ann screeched from under the duvet, 'I know you don't even like him, so why are you saying he didn't do it? I was there. You *weren't*. I know he let go of my mum. I know what I *saw*. Now, leave me alone.'

Emma was taken back that Ann knew she didn't like Steve. She thought she had hidden it from her and John.

She replied, 'You're right. I don't like your dad but just because I don't like him, it doesn't mean I think he would do something to my sister, your mum.'

By now Emma was almost crying out loud herself and she had to leave Ann's bedroom because Ann was sobbing inconsolably. Emma went to her own bedroom and told herself, 'I've got to get some self-control, for Ann's sake.'

She had a shower and, later that afternoon, went back into Ann's room. Ann was still sobbing, with her head under the duvet. Emma was worried. She moved the small chair from the side of

Ann's bed and put a reclining chair there instead. She sat there, holding Ann's hand, which seemed to calm her down.

In the morning, while Ann was asleep, Emma crept out of the room, had a shower and got dressed. The rest of the day she was in and out of Ann's room, visiting her whenever she heard her crying. Emma also spent the next couple of nights in Ann's room, sleeping on the reclining chair, because of the nightmares Ann was having. Steve's visit made things worse, after that Ann sobbed and stayed in bed all day.

Emma tried to talk to Ann, but the only thing Ann would say was, 'You won't leave me, will you, Aunt Emma?' Then she would carry on crying.

Emma was worried about Ann. She wouldn't come out of her bedroom; she just stayed in bed, crying and muttering about her dad. She hadn't eaten properly for the last three days. So Emma asked a nurse hired by the hotel, who had been looking in on Ann for a couple of days, to call a doctor. When he arrived, Emma started to explain to him about the accident, but she got too upset.

The nurse gave Emma some tissues to dry her eyes, put her arm round her and sat her down on one of the armchairs.

As she did so, she said to Emma, 'Try to relax. I'll explain everything to the doctor, don't you upset yourself.'

Then the nurse showed the doctor into Ann's room. Ann was curled up on the bed, now and then making a sobbing noise. The nurse pointed to Ann and whispered to him what had happened to her mum, telling him the state she had been in since the accident.

The nurse looked back to check on Emma, but she was walking just behind them, wiping the tears off her face.

Emma said, 'I have to know how Ann is.'

The doctor said, 'I quite understand. I will give your niece a good examination.'

When he had finished examining her, he set up a drip and gave her a sedative, saying to Emma, 'Your niece will sleep till tomorrow. She is suffering from shock. May I suggest you take her home to England as soon as possible; away from here. It may help her get over the shock and come to terms with what has happened to your family.'

Then he handed Emma two tablets and said, 'You're exhausted. I would like you to take these two tablets. They will help you to sleep. You need rest if you want to look after your niece. I'm sure your hotel will help supply a nurse for the night, so you can get some sleep. You need it, if you don't want to end up in poor health.'

The nurse brought Emma a glass of water, and said, 'The doctor is right. Now, please take them.'

Emma explained, 'I can't leave Ann all night. She is having nightmares.'

The nurse looked at her watch and said, 'I will be here another one and half hours, and I will arrange for another nurse to take over from me - she will stay all night with Ann.'

Emma nodded and took the two tablets the doctor had given her. Then she put the tissues she was using to wipe her tears in her pocket.

The doctor said, 'I think you will feel a little better in the morning, because your niece will be a lot calmer once she has had a good sleep and with the tablets you have just taken, you will also get a good night's sleep.'

As he packed his bag and was leaving the apartment, he said to Emma, 'If you need me, the nurse will let me know.'

Emma was exhausted and the tablets started working on her right away. The nurse could see this and suggested that she went to bed.

Emma just said, 'Yes.'

She went back into Ann's room and tucked her in, and then she went to her own room.

The next morning, Emma got up and went straight into Ann's room. The replacement nurse was sitting by her bed; Ann was asleep. The nurse looked up at Emma and put a finger up against her lips, as a sign to be quiet, as Emma walked towards Ann's bed.

The nurse stood up and whispered, 'Ann had a glass of milk and some soup when she woke up at about eight o'clock. I ordered it earlier, while she was asleep, and she was quite keen to eat it.

Now she has gone back to sleep, would you like me to send for some breakfast for you?'

Emma answered, 'No, thank you. I don't eat in the morning. What time is it?'

'Ten-fifteen' replied the nurse.

Emma said, 'I've never slept this late in my life!'

Then she got hold of Ann's hand, which was outside the duvet, and bent down and kissed it. Ann made a small, tired sound and turned over onto her side. Emma was just glad Ann sounded a bit more normal.

She asked the nurse, 'Have you been here all night?'

'No,' the nurse replied, 'I took over at six o clock.'

Then Emma asked, 'I will have to leave Ann with you for a while if that's alright with you. Will you stay with her while I make some arrangements to get her home?'

'Of course, I will stay with her as long as you want me to,' the nurse replied.

Emma said, 'Thank you. Help yourself to room service or anything else you might need, because I might be gone for a while.'

Then she went back over to Ann, and bent over and kissed her on the forehead. Ann didn't wake, she just moved her head a little further into the pillow and settled down.

Emma thanked the nurse again. She left Ann's room and went to her own room to shower in the ensuite but, before she got fully dressed, she phoned the airfield and made arrangements for her and Ann to go home to England on the plane. Then she spoke to the hotel's receptionist, asking her, 'Is that you, Sara?'

The receptionist replied, 'Yes, how can I help you, Emma?'

Emma said, 'Will you have one of the hotel's cars pick Ann and I up at twelve-thirty? It's to come around to the private entrance at the side of the hotel and, if there are any reporters there, will you ask the security to move them as far away from the door as they possibly can? Also, ask security to let me know, as I don't want them anywhere near Ann. She is far too fragile and upset for them to be bothering her.'

The receptionist, who knew Emma well, replied, 'I'll do that right away, Emma... and we are all sorry about the accident. We thought the world of Joan, and we'll miss her. She was a lovely person.'

Emma held back the tears and tried to keep the emotion out of her voice as she said, 'Thank you, Sara. You all have been a great help, and I can't thank the staff enough.'

Then Emma finished getting dressed, putting her makeup on a bit thicker than usual to try to hide the way she really felt. She was determined not to break down again in front of Ann. When she thought she looked confident, she went straight to Ann's room. Ann was sitting up in the bed and the nurse was washing her down.

When she saw Emma, she started crying and held her arms out to her, sobbing, 'Aunt Emma, my mum's dead.'

Emma rushed over to Ann, gave her a hug and kissed her. Then said, 'You have been through a lot, and I know how you feel, so cry all you want to... but you mustn't just stay in bed. Your mum would be upset to see you so distraught, so try to pull yourself together. I have been arranging for us to fly home on the private jet tomorrow.'

Ann stopped crying and asked, 'Is John coming with us? I don't want my dad to come with us. I hate him.'

Then the tears started running down her face again. The nurse wiped Ann's cheeks and helped her get into a sitting position on the edge of the bed.

Emma replied, 'I will ask your dad whether he wants John to come home with us or if he will bring him home himself, but listen, Ann, it's important that you pull yourself together and put on a brave face for the airport... or they mightn't let us fly.'

Ann pulled away from the nurse and wiped her own face, then she claimed, 'I will Aunt Emma, I promise. Don't worry about me.'

Emma looked at her. Ann was sitting up a lot straighter on the bed, and her face looked more normal, apart from her eyes being red and swollen.

Emma said, 'I'll leave you with the nurse while I make some phone calls.'

She left the bedroom and went into the living room. Once there, she phoned the villa to ask Steve about John.

The phone rang for a while before the nurse answered, 'Hello, this is the Thomson villa. Will you hold on a moment, Mr Thomson will be with you in a minute.' She called out, 'Mr Thomson, you're wanted on the phone.'

Steve came out of John's room, and she handed the phone to him. He took it, saying, 'Steve Thomson here.'

The moment he heard Emma's voice, he slammed the phone down, saying, 'You can fuck off, you cow.'

Emma put her phone down, thinking to herself, 'Will John be alright? I hope he's being looked after by a nurse.'

Then she picked the phone up again and called the police station, asking in English to speak to Sergeant Torres. The officer didn't understand what she was saying at first, but when he heard the word 'Torres', he understood who she wanted.

While she was waiting, she wiped her eyes.

After a few minutes the sergeant answered the phone and said, 'Hello, I'm Sergeant Torres. How can I help you?'

Emma answered, 'I'm Emma Kenwright, and I'm phoning to explain to you, Sergeant, that the doctor said I should take my niece Ann Thomson home to England as soon as possible. So we are flying home tomorrow. I am just letting you know because I don't want to waste your time looking for Ann, when it's more important that you use your time to find the villain that caused the death of my lovely sister.'

The sergeant said, 'I can understand that, but we would like a statement of what Ann saw.'

Emma, in an angry tone, interrupted, 'I've just told you, Sergeant, that she is under the doctor, and he has told me it's important that I take her home to England. Ann is having nightmares, and she isn't well enough to give you a statement. So, I am taking her home to England tomorrow like the doctor advised me to do, so, please, don't you dare try to stop us - or you will be dealing with my solicitor.'

The sergeant didn't say anything while Emma was talking, he knew how upset she was.

He just waited until she had finished, then he said in a quiet tone, 'I am sorry, Miss Kenwright, all I meant was, when Ann is well enough at home, would you get Ann to give a statement of what she can remember to the English police?

They will send it to me, because we will need all the information we can get to help us catch the person who drove the car at your family and caused the death of your sister.'

He heard her sniffing over the phone and thought, 'She is trying to hold back the tears.'

Emma wiped her eyes and replied, 'Sergeant, I'm sorry. I don't mean to be aggressive. I'm just upset, and I think I should tell you - before you hear it from other people - that I don't like my brother-in-law. In fact, I can't stand to be in the same room as him. I will admit, I have no reason. It's just something I've felt from the first time I laid eyes on him; he hates me also. I know my sister, Joan, loved the bones of him and only had good things to say about him, and I also know Joan would tell me if he ever did anything to upset her... But the things that Ann is saying, I promise, have nothing to do with me.

I have even tried to explain to her how much they loved one another, but Ann just sticks to the same story all the time... So now *I'm* starting to believe that what she is saying is the truth. Though I hope she is wrong; that it's not right what she is thinking about her dad, for her and John's sake. Because, if what Ann is saying is true, it will take a great deal of time for them to get over it. I hope they will be able to put this behind them in time, and that will be easier if their dad had nothing to do with it.'

The sergeant replied, 'I have a good idea what Ann has been saying, right from the day of the accident, so I know you have nothing to do with her accusations, and may I say again, I am sorry for you and the children.' He understood when Emma didn't answer and instead just put the phone down.

Emma left Ann in her room and went down in the lift to wait for the car. It was twelve-thirty exactly when a small four-door, chauffeured car pulled up at the side of the hotel. It stopped by the private door.

Just before it arrived, one of the security team came in the private entrance and said to Emma, 'We've told the reporters to move back from the front entrance and not to bother our guests when they come out.'

Emma butted in, 'We're not going out the front.'

He put his hands up to show he wanted to say something.

Emma looked at him and asked, 'What's going on?'

He answered, 'There were two reporters just outside the door that you *will* be going out of, and if the other reporters at the front saw their cameras flashing, they would all come round here to bother you. So we 'let it slip' that you're going out the front way to the reporters there. We also had one of the hotel's limousines park at the front. With all that, the reporters started making a bit of a commotion, and the two reporters that were at this door have run round to the front.

We have a four-door Ford Focus that will be stopping at this door in just a few minutes, with the driver ready to leave the second you ladies are in it, so that you can go out, get in the car and be away before the reporters realise what is going on.'

Emma thanked him and went and got Ann with the help of the nurse. As they left the hotel, Emma had her arm round Ann.

The staff tried to help as much as they could: one of them opened the door of the car and another asked, 'What about your luggage, Madam?'

Emma answered, 'You can send it on later, thank you.'

Emma thanked everyone and got in the car and, just as the car drove away, the reporters came running down the road, flashing their cameras.

When they got to the airport, they didn't have to speak to anyone. Emma had made all the arrangements over the phone. The car just went into the hangar and up to their plane.

When they got to the plane, the stewardess helped Emma get Ann settled.

Emma asked the staff who were fussing over them, 'Please, don't come into the cabin on the way home, unless I request you to.'

They all understood and didn't bother Emma and Ann till they landed in England.

It was a miserable, wet and murky day when Emma and Ann left the passenger cabin of the plane. The driver of the limousine was at the bottom of the steps with a large umbrella, and he covered them till they got into the limousine.

They were in Emma's house within four and a half hours of leaving the hotel. Emma took Ann to one of the guest rooms and said, 'This is your room, from now on till you go home. I hope you like it, but if you don't, you can change anything you like. If you don't like the decor, you can pick out something more to your taste.'

Ann said, 'I want to stay with you and make this my home from now on, Aunt Emma, if you will let me.'

JOHN GOES HOME TO ANN

Steve was confused about what to do about John because he kept saying, 'I want my mum' and crying, and when Steve wanted to go out, John would start sobbing. He would say, 'Don't leave me by myself, Dad. I want Ann to come and be with me, and I want my mum with us.'

Steve tried to explain to John that he wanted to help the police find the person who drove the car at them, but this just made John even more upset. He became hysterical, continuously sobbing, so it sounded like he couldn't get his breath, and repeating, 'I want to be with Ann.'

Steve said to the nurse, 'I want you to stay in the villa, so John will get the care he needs, because I don't know how to calm him down. Of course, that's if you are willing to do so? You can use one of the bedrooms.'

She replied, 'I'll stay as long as John needs me.'

When she got settled in, Steve asked her in a quiet tone and with an embarrassed look on his face, 'Will you look after John? I have to go out.'

The nurse replied, 'Yes, if it's that important to you, but don't leave John too long. He is mourning for his mother and needs the love and support of his family right now.'

Steve wiped his eyes and replied, 'I love my family, but I can't rest till I find the bastard who ran that car at us.'

She answered, 'I can understand that, but John needs you close.'

Steve said, 'I've left my mobile number on the small table in the hall by the phone. If you need me, just call.'

He left the nurse and went into John's room. He kissed him on the head as John, in a sobbing voice pleaded, 'Please, Dad, I don't want to be on my own. Don't go - stay here with me.'

Steve said, 'You're not alone, the nurse is here with you, and I've got to go.'

John sobbed and grabbed hold of his dad. Steve, with a pleading look, turned to the nurse for help. She got hold of John as Steve pulled away, still looking at John who was crying and struggling with the nurse, trying to get to his dad.

Steve moved out of John's reach and, as he turned away, he wiped his eyes. He went out and got into his Rolls Royce, running the gauntlet of the paparazzi as he drove out the gates of the villa.

John was in bed, asleep, when Steve got back to the villa.

He said to the nurse, 'I can't face John. When he looks at me, he's so distressed. I feel like I've let him down and that it's my fault what happened to his mum - she didn't want to come to Spain. It was all my idea.'

She felt sorry for Steve, who looked in a bad state, but she was worried about John; she was about to say something about it, but Steve just left her standing there and went into his bedroom.

Over the next few days, he would be up and go out before John was awake. He would stay out all day and would only see John in the morning and again in the night when he was asleep in bed. The nurse phoned Steve at five o'clock on the evening of the fourth day and asked him to come back to the villa.

'John needs you,' she said.

Steve was back in half an hour. John was lying on his bed, sobbing, and when he saw his dad, he jumped off his bed and ran to him, crying, 'You left me, Dad. I'm sorry if it was my fault my mum is dead, because I didn't come when you called me and I held back instead. I want my mum.'

Steve picked him up and tried to comfort him, saying, 'It wasn't your fault, it was the mad driver of the car, and I didn't leave you. I was trying to get the bastard whose fault it really was, and I will always love you. Don't you ever forget that.'

John carried on sobbing and the nurse said, 'Mr Thomson, I can see by the tears in your eyes that you are grieving, but John can't go on like this. He will have a nervous breakdown.

You will have to stay with him a lot more or let him go to his sister. He needs someone he loves to be with him. He is grieving for his mother and if he goes on this way, who knows what harm it may do to him when he's older.'

Steve answered, in a desperate tone, 'You don't understand - I can't stay in the villa with John. I have to find the bastard who caused the death of my Joan.

I couldn't stand it if anything happened to John or Ann. I don't know what to do! I want John with me, but I just can't face him right now.'

As Steve sat down, he was still holding John in his arms. John was sobbing and holding tightly onto his dad.

The nurse said, 'I'm so sorry for you, but I have told you what you need to do. Let John go to your daughter.'

Steve wiped his eyes, as tears ran down his face, and nodded as he said in a tearful voice, 'You're right, of course.

I found out this afternoon that Ann went home to England a couple of days ago. If I arrange everything for John to get home to his aunt and Ann, would you go with him? My plane will take you to England and a car will meet you at the airport; the driver will take you to the address where Ann is staying. You should get there at about eleven, if you leave soon.

You can have a holiday and stay there for two weeks in one of my hotels of your choice, with all expenses paid. The hotel will inform Ann you are coming.'

The nurse didn't know what to say at first and just stood there looking at him.

Steve handed her a card and explained, 'When you want to come home, just phone the number and my office will arrange for you to be picked up and flown back in my jet.'

She replied, 'Yes - I can take John, but I will have to go home and pack some things and make some arrangements with my mum and dad. I will be back in about an hour, but I must emphasise that it's important that you mustn't leave John alone while I'm away. I am really worried about him.'

The nurse phoned for a taxi. On her way home, she phoned her parents and explained to them that she was going to England. When she got home, she asked the taxi driver to wait and was back in the taxi just ten minutes later, with a small suitcase. She got back to the villa just as the car arrived to take them to the airport.

She had to help Steve to get John off him, as John had his arms round Steve's neck and was clinging to him, sobbing and saying through his tears, 'I'm sorry, Dad. I'll come when you call. I'll be good. Don't leave me, please.'

He only started to let go when Steve said, 'I'm not leaving you, and you don't have to be sorry. You have done nothing wrong and I love you, but, John, you did say you wanted to be with Ann, so I am getting the nurse to take you to her in England. I will be with you as soon as I can.'

When Steve mentioned Ann, John calmed down a bit more and let go of Steve.

Once they had got John into the limousine, everything went well. They drove into the airport, and on a narrow road that ran along the airport fence and into the plane's hanger. The limousine went up to the plane, stopping at the stairs that led up to the plane's door.

The pilot was waiting at the bottom of the stairs and the nurse asked him to carry John into the plane. She went ahead into the plane first and asked the pilot to put John on one of the reclining seats. John just lay there and didn't make a move or a sound during the whole flight. The nurse was worried and kept checking his temperature and pulse every half hour.

On arrival in England, the plane was allowed to taxi into the hangar. A limousine was waiting there and, as the pilot carried John out of the plane, the driver of the limousine held the back door open for the pilot to put John in the car. The nurse thanked the pilot and got in the car with John, who looked a little better and was sitting up and looking around.

They arrived at Emma's house just on eleven in the evening. Emma was expecting them. She had had a phone call from the manager of the hotel in Spain, and when they arrived Emma had got two rooms ready - one for John and one for the nurse. She insisted that the nurse stay the night and, in the morning, Emma arranged for a car to take her to a hotel and gave her a list of her restaurants. Emma told the nurse she could eat in any of them as her guest.

The nurse said, 'I'm so sorry for you and the children.'

Then she thanked Emma for the list, as she got in the limousine that had stopped outside of the house. Emma told the driver to take the nurse to a Kenwright hotel of her choice, no matter where it was in Britain.

The driver looked in surprise at Emma, and she smiled at him and said, 'Don't look so worried, you can claim all your expenses from the Kenwright Company.'

The driver said, 'I'm sorry to ask but would you give me that in writing, please?'

She smiled, and gave him an envelope, saying, 'It's all written down in there and you will have no problem getting your expenses. If your firm complains, tell them to get in touch with Steve Thomson. This is for you,' as she gave him a fifty-pound note.

He smiled and thanked Emma. She waved as the limousine drove away.

When the nurse and John had neared Emma's house, and he saw Ann, he had tried to open the door of the limousine before it had stopped, and the nurse had had to grab him and hold on to him. When it did stop, she had let him go and he had opened the door and jumped out and ran to Ann, crying. They had hugged one another; then Ann couldn't hold back the tears as John kept crying, 'Ann, I want my mum.'

Ann had tried to act like a big sister, attempting to stop crying though the tears kept running down her cheeks, as she said, 'I want our mum too, but she is in heaven and looking down on us, so don't cry. I love you, and Emma and I will take care of you from now on.'

The rest of the night John wouldn't let Ann out of his sight - he wouldn't go to sleep in the room Emma had for him, he wanted to stay with Ann in her room.

He had cried as he promised, 'I will move into the other room tomorrow night, but let me stay with you now.'

Ann had hugged him and taken him into her bedroom. She put him in bed next to her. Emma came in and kissed both of them as she tucked them in and said, 'Goodnight and God bless.'

As she closed the bedroom door, she said to herself, 'Joan, I miss you. Please help me look after Ann and John.'

ANN'S STATEMENT

When they had been home for a week, a police officer called at Emma's home and asked, 'Does a Miss Ann Thomson live here?'

Emma answered, 'Yes, come in. Have you come for a statement from Ann?'

The officer replied, 'Yes, we have had a request from the Spanish police for it. May I offer my condolences? I know it's about the death of her mother, and it will be very upsetting for her, so could you stay with her while she makes the statement, please?'

Emma answered, 'Yes, I will have to, because she gets so upset all the time about it. Will you take a seat while I go and get Ann?'

Emma left the officer and, as she went and knocked on the door of Ann's room, she said a little prayer to Joan. Ann opened the door and Emma told her the police officer had come for the statement.

Ann said, as her eyes filled up with tears, 'I have written it all down over the last few days, I couldn't say it all out loud. The words would make me sick. I would just start crying, Aunt Emma... I just can't say anything about it.'

When Emma saw Ann was getting upset, she didn't wait for her to finish what she was saying; she gave Ann a hug and said, 'It's okay. Go and get what you've written and we'll give it to him together.'

Ann got her statement out of her dressing table drawer and they both went into the sitting room where the officer was but, when Ann saw the officer, she gave the statement to Emma and went back into the bedroom.

Emma, with tears in her own eyes, explained, 'Ann has written down what she saw. It's in this envelope, so you will be able to send it to Spain.'

The officer took the statement and said, 'Thank you, Miss Thomson.'

Emma wasn't pleased, and it showed on her face as she corrected him with a sharp voice, 'I'm Miss Emma Kenwright.'

'I'm sorry, I didn't mean to upset you. I thought you had the same name as the young girl,' was his embarrassed reply, as he was leaving the house.

Emma felt bad about her tone and said, 'I'm sorry about the way I spoke to you. I had no right to, but Ann's mother is my sister, and I miss her.'

He nodded and said, 'I understand,' and, with a slight smile on his face to show he grasped her situation, he turned and walked to his police car.

Sergeant Torres received Ann's statement the next day. He sent for Pearl, to type it in Spanish.

As she set up her electric typewriter, he said, 'I've read it a few times, but I will read it to you, so if I want to add a comment you can put it in brackets at the right spot. Like where she's said she's changing her name to Ann Kenwright.'

Pearl got set up and announced, 'Well, I'm ready when you are, Sarge.'

The sergeant started with, 'Pearl, will you put in today's date, and that this is a copy of a statement, by Miss Ann Thomson, age sixteen? Note her name is now Ann Kenwright. The statement starts from here:

My family were at a picnic area in Spain, having a sixteenth birthday party for me. My mum, brother John and my dad were there. I met a boy named Tommy and when my dad said we were going down to the beach before the tide came in, I asked my parents if Tommy could come with me. They joked around a bit and said 'yes'.

My father said I wasn't to ride on Tommy's motorbike and that I was to walk on the sidewalk, not on the road. I did for a while, but I kept tripping on the uneven sidewalk. So, I suggested that Tommy push his bike on the side, and that Tommy and I should walk on the road. Tommy was worried about what my parents might say, but I said they are about twenty yards behind us and by the time they catch us up, we will be at the beach. I thought then it was more dangerous walking on the uneven sidewalk.

I was wrong because a funny-looking car came round a bend in the road; it headed straight at us. I couldn't move. I just stood there looking at this black car with a big bar across the front of it, and the face of a woman with a black wig on - I could see her blond hair underneath it. She had large sunglasses on and a plaster on her forehead. Tommy pulled me out of the way of the car, and I think I saw red on the side of it.'

The sergeant said, 'Stop typing there, Pearl, and make a side note. Tommy also said he saw red on it somewhere.

Ann must have stopped here and started again with a different pen; the ink is a different colour. I think she saw a lot in that short time. She was terrified. I wonder if she is getting her nightmares mixed up with what really happened? Pearl, also add that she's been having nightmares onto that note, just in case someone wants to question it, when it goes to court. Her aunt told me about them when we spoke on the phone before they went back to England.'

Pearl nodded; he waited a few moments for her to make the note and then he continued dictating the statement.

'I landed on top of Tommy and the bike, I didn't know what was happening for a little while, then I heard my father shout and John was screaming. I got up and ran to help my mum.'

The sergeant stopped reading, and looked at Pearl and said, 'The writing is hard to read from this point. I think the more she remembered, the more she got upset and the worse her writing got. I think she was crying when she wrote this. Some parts of the paper look like it's been wet and some of the writing is smudged, so I'm afraid I will be reading it a lot slower.'

Pearl replied, 'That's okay. I can type slow as well as fast. You can carry on now.'

So he did, reading, *'My father had hold of my mum, who had fallen over the wall, and my mum was screaming 'Don't let go of me, Steve!'*

I tried to help, but I couldn't reach my mum - my arms weren't long enough. Tommy had climbed over the wall and was about to get hold of my mum's hand, when I heard my mum scream 'You're letting...'

I saw my father's hand letting go of my mum's, and my mum fell to her death. I know when my mum screamed, 'You're letting...', she was going to say 'letting go.' And I know that my father killed my mum.

I know he did. I saw him let my mother fall. He is my father; the killer, he's no longer my dad. I hate him, and I'm changing my name to my mother's maiden name: Kenwright. If you want me as a witness, please address me as Ann Kenwright from now on.'

The sergeant finished reading and said, 'Ann has put 'my father killed my mum' in black, bold capital letters.'

Pearl looked at him and asked, 'What do you think? Is it possible?'

With a frown on his face, the sergeant answered, 'I suppose it is possible... but it would be impossible to *prove* that he let go of his wife deliberately. He would have had to have really hated her to do that and, if he wanted her dead, he didn't have to pull her out of the way of the car. Also, everyone who knows them said they think the world of each other - even his sister in-law who claims she hates him said he was a good, loving husband. The reports from the police in England say the same.

I hope the young girl is wrong. He would have to be a right bastard to do kill his wife in front of his children and, if he did, he's a good actor. I'd swear those tears he cried were real.'

Pearl said, 'I don't think he could do that to his wife. I think he loved his wife and blames himself because he couldn't hold on to her.'

'Yes,' replied the sergeant, 'That was my reading of the situation too. And in one of the statements, the man who helped them said that Steve was saying, 'It's my fault, I let Joan fall'. Ann was in shock when she heard her dad saying that. Maybe it's got stuck in her mind, and now she thinks she saw him let go of her mum. Like I said, her aunt said she was having nightmares; I think she might have gotten them mixed up with her memory of what really happened. If so, she will need a lot of counselling. Maybe in time, with help, she will realise her dad did his best to save her mother.'

TWO WEEKS AND THEN HOME

Steve spent days going round the scrap yards and garages asking about the car, but he got nowhere. So, on the third morning, he called into the police station. He had to fight his way through a crowd of reporters to get into the building. When he was inside, he asked to see Sergeant Torres.

He was told by the officer behind the counter, 'The sergeant is on his day off and won't be in till the day after tomorrow.'

Steve demanded in an angry tone, 'I want to see the chief inspector.'

The officer knew who Steve was. He picked up the phone and asked, 'Will you put me through to the chief inspector?'

Steve was pacing up and down while he was waiting, and the officer behind the counter could see Steve was getting more annoyed with each step.

The inspector came out ten minutes later and asked Steve to come with him to his office.

They entered the room and, as the chief inspector walked round his desk, he said, 'Mr Thomson, I'm sorry I had to keep you waiting, will you take a seat?'

Steve did as the inspector requested and, as soon as he sat down, he blurted out in an angry voice, 'What are you doing about my wife's murder? I've been all over this area asking questions and I can't find anything out about it. I also didn't come across any of your officers asking questions about my wife's murder.

It *was* murder - the bastard who drove the car at us meant to kill my family. What I want to know is, is there anyone doing anything about my wife's death, besides me? This great Sergeant Torres you told me about isn't even in the station - he's on holiday, so how can he be investigating my Joan's death? Tell me that.'

The chief inspector sat down slowly while Steve was talking, allowing him to say his full piece to help him get over being annoyed.

As Steve calmed down a bit, he answered, 'Mr Thomson, Sergeant Torres isn't on holiday. He is on his days off and, as you know, we all need a rest, or we don't do the job properly.

Sergeant Torres and I have our men out twenty-four hours a day, picking up anyone who might know anything about the criminals in this area. They are checking all the garages, the car showrooms, and even vintage car clubs and the scrapyards. Just because you didn't see or hear any of my officers, don't think we are doing nothing.

I'm glad you came in to see us because I was going to send an officer to have a talk with you. We knew you were trying to investigate on your own. My officers have been told of a man who can speak Spanish very well, but with an English accent, who is asking questions about what happened on the mountain road and the car that drove at the family there.

I would advise you to leave such questions to my officers, going forward. You most likely didn't see the officers because they are not in uniform - when the criminals see a uniform, they disappear. Asking these kinds of questions is safer for my officers than for yourself because they travel in pairs, and they can take care of themselves. They can deal with any problems they come across. So, please leave the investigation to my officers.

If, as we suspect, this was a deliberate attempt to harm you and your family, the people you are trying to find could hurt or even kill you and if, God forbid, that happens, your children will have lost the both of you. They need you now that their mother has gone.'

Steve was drying his eyes while the chief inspector was talking and, when he stopped, Steve said, in a quieter tone than before, 'You don't understand. I can't go home yet, not without knowing the bastard who drove that fucking car at my family. I will try not to interfere, but I want to be kept informed about anything you find out.'

The chief inspector nodded and agreed, 'We will keep you up to date with any developments but, I must ask, your firm is a family one and over the last ten years it has taken over a lot of family businesses, and some other big firms. Can you think of anyone from these businesses that might be holding a grudge? The kind that might build up into hate?'

Steve was angry at what the chief inspector had asked, exclaiming, 'Every firm we negotiated with and took over was happy with the deal they got. The people who wanted to stay with us were offered a job in our firm, with a chance to end up on the board. We never went in for hostile takeovers because we run our business as a family firm and we think it's the best way to get on.'

The chief inspector was writing while Steve was talking. Then he put down his pen, stood up and offered Steve his hand.

Steve stood up and shook it and, on the way out, as the chief inspector opened the door, he said to Steve, 'If we get any information, I will let you know right away.'

Steve nodded and wiped his eyes again. He left the station and had to push his way back through a crowd of reporters, cursing at them as he made his way to his car. He was surrounded by flashing cameras as he got in his vehicle and the press ran after the Rolls as he drove away. When he got back to the villa, he had a shower and made himself some cheese and onion sandwiches, then he had a look around the house to see what jobs he could do while he was waiting to hear what information the police had for him.

Steve didn't call in to the station over the next few days. He just stayed in the villa and made himself busy with the jobs he had found. He also spent time phoning his office, so he knew what was happening there.

One morning, he was so engrossed in cleaning his Rolls, he was surprised when someone pressed the intercom at the villa gates and a voice spoke through it, saying 'Mr Thomson, are you there? It's Sergeant Torres. Can you let me in? I would like to speak to you.'

As he pressed the button to open the gates, Steve replied, 'Yes I'm here, I've been waiting to hear from you.'

The sergeant drove up the long driveway to the villa. Steve was waiting by the door for him and, when he got out of his car, Steve invited him into the villa and said, 'Will you sit down? And would you like a drink of coffee or iced water?'

Sergeant Torres answered, 'No, thank you. I can't stop. I'm on my way to check on a couple of scrapyards. I just wanted to give you this information personally. We have the number plate that was on the car. It's 626 7KB but, as we suspected, it doesn't belong to the car. We have traced the number and it's from a Ford Anglia. The last time it was registered was to a person named Simpson in Liverpool, England; that was in 1971.

So, the switched-out number plates on the car suggests this definitely wasn't an accident. Someone was out to harm your family. We think it may be the driver themselves, because if they had succeeded in knocking your family over, the damage to the car would have meant the driver would likely be dead or too injured to get away, which makes it less likely they were paid to do the job.

We think that whoever wants to harm your family will try again when you are back in England. I would advise you to get more security for you and your children. If the boy with the motorbike hadn't been with Ann, the car could have mounted the walkway.

Thank God the bike was at the front and the car couldn't afford to hit that.

We also think the car was waiting - parked in a small parking place just before the bend, with someone watching you at the picnic area who phoned when you left to walk down to the beach.'

Steve wiped his eyes and, in a loud angry tone, said 'I will get the best security I can find for my children, but I don't want any myself. Just let them fucking try and get me. I'll kill the bastards with my bare hands... and I'll make them suffer.'

The sergeant didn't look too pleased, but he put his hand out to Steve.

Steve shook it and, as he did so, the sergeant looked him in the eyes and said, 'I can see in your face how upset you are, and I understand you being angry, but it's not advisable to take chances.

Please get some security for yourself as well as the children. If you did kill someone, it's you who would end up in prison and you would miss your children growing up. If you get killed, your children will have lost both mother and father. You would be safer at home in England with good security around you and your children, till we catch the driver of the car.'

Steve explained, 'Don't you think I want to go home to my children? I'm desperate to go home to them, but Ann doesn't understand that I couldn't hold onto Joan. So I want to be sure the bastard who caused her mother's death is caught, so Ann will know I did my best to save Joan.'

While he was talking, he was wiping the tears off his face. The sergeant shook his head, and said, 'Look, I'll be honest, Steve. It could take months or even years to catch who did this.

Please go home and be with your children. They need you right now, and I can see you need your children too.'

As the sergeant was getting into his car, Steve promised, 'I will go home, but I'll wait till the end of the week, to see if you get the bastard who drove the car.'

The sergeant nodded, waving to Steve as he turned his car around and headed down the driveway and out the gates. They closed behind him and after he checked the places he'd told Steve he was going to, it was late, so he went back to the police station.

At the end of the week, Steve called into the police station, and asked, 'Can I speak to Sergeant Torres?'

The officer at the counter picked up the phone to request Sergeant Torres but, as he did, he looked past Steve and put the phone back down.

At just that moment Steve heard a voice behind him say, 'Hello, Steve.'

He turned to see the sergeant coming into the station with a young man, who he was holding by the top of his arm.

The sergeant said to the officer in Spanish, 'Stick this fellow in a cell. I've just caught him breaking into a car just outside our door! How hard-faced can he be? Or he hasn't the sense a baby is born with! I'll charge him later.'

He carried on without stopping, as he looked at Steve and changed to English, 'I was just about to get in my car to go to your villa when I saw what he was up to, Steve. Will you please come with me to my office? It's more private there.'

When they entered the sergeant asked, 'Will you take a seat, Steve? I was just going to see you with some information that we think may have some bearing on the driver of the car.'

Steve went a bit pale, wiped his eyes, and said, 'Will you get the bastard who drove the car?'

The sergeant explained, 'Not yet, but a couple of criminals we know who deal in stolen cars... Well, one of them was shot last night. We were watching them, but one gave my officers the run around and they lost him - the one who was shot. He must have gone to meet his killer. We think he was killed because he didn't do what the people wanted.'

Steve butted in, 'So you think he was the driver and the others killed him?'

The sergeant explained, 'No, this gang wouldn't drive a stolen car, they are too clever to do that. We know that they supply stolen cars to others and then scrap them when the criminals are finished with them.'

Steve, in a questioning voice, asked, 'Why don't you pick up his partner and the drivers? You seem to know what he and his drivers are doing and one of them might be the driver of the car that came at us.'

'We did,' replied the sergeant, 'and the drivers are all small-timers. None of them would get involved in violence like that, it would cause too much trouble for them... and none of the drivers would risk their lives, no matter how much money they were offered.

We think it was someone they brought in, which either means a lot of money was involved or the driver is the person who wants to harm your family. We also think the driver wanted to make sure he or she couldn't be caught. He or she shot the dealer once in the chest from a short distance, and then walked up to him and shot him in the head. It looked like it was a professional killing.'

Steve stroked his chin in thought and asked, 'What do you mean 'he or she', do you think it could have been a woman driving the car?'

The sergeant replied, 'We don't know. We have to keep an open mind.'

Steve, with a worried look on his face, said, 'It looks like my firm *has* made someone angry, but I can't think who, because our policy is not to take over firms unless they want us to.'

The sergeant said, in a serious tone, 'Look, Steve, I really think you should go home and get some security around you and your children, because I think they will try again.'

Steve replied, 'I've called in today to tell you I'm taking Joan home tomorrow, and I'll get the best security I can find.'

He stood up and offered the sergeant his hand. The sergeant shook it, and said, 'You know it makes sense, Steve. Your children need you now more than ever before. I'll walk you out of the station and move the bloody paparazzi out of your way.'

When the reporters saw Steve with Sergeant Torres, they all backed away but their cameras were still flashing and they were shouting questions at Steve, who put his hand up to cover part of his face, looking through his fingers to see where he was going. The sergeant walked Steve to his Rolls and opened the door for him to get in. He watched as Steve drove away, with the paparazzi chasing after the Rolls. He shook his head as he walked back into the station to make his report to the chief inspector.

STEVE TAKES JOAN HOME AND CALLS AT EMMA'S

When Steve left the police station, he went and finalised the arrangements to get Joan's body home. The next day Steve had to run the gauntlet of the paparazzi again on his way to the airport. Once at the hangar, the pilot met Steve at the door of the jet, reassured him that Joan's coffin was already on the plane and offered his condolences, asking, 'Is there anything we can do for you while you are in the cabin?'

Steve just shook his head, looking down as he replied, 'No, thank you. I just want to be alone with my thoughts and Joan.'

He settled down in the cabin and the plane flew him home with Joan to England.

When the plane landed it was met by the funeral director, who was waiting at the airport. As they got Joan's coffin off the plane, Steve had a worried look on his face and was saying to the pallbearers, 'Please, be careful with her.'

They placed the coffin in the hearse and, as they did so Steve wiped his eyes and put his hand on the coffin, saying, 'Joan, you are my soulmate. I will always love you and I'll never forget you. I feel as if part of me is missing, and that part is you.'

The funeral director could see he was getting upset and tried to comfort him saying, 'Mr Thomson, you can leave everything to us. We will look after Joan, so you can go and see your children.'

Steve nodded and left.

As soon as he got home, he drove round to Emma's house and knocked hard on the door.

Emma opened it and said, 'You've no need to knock like that. You know where the bell is. Come in.'

Steve stepped back and, in an angry tone, he said, 'I've come for Ann and John. Please send them out now.'

Emma gave him a look that could kill, as she turned and went back into the house. She was in there for about ten minutes; when she came back out, she was with John.

He was looking back into the house, calling, 'Come on, Ann, let's go home with Dad.'

Ann shouted from inside the house, 'No. I'm not going with him. I hate him.'

Steve snarled at Emma, 'You evil bitch, this is your doing. You've never liked me and now you are trying to turn Ann against me. Well, you will pay for that, you cow.'

Emma replied, in an angry voice, 'You're right - I didn't like you from the minute I saw you... But I swear on my life, I didn't, and I wouldn't, come between you and Ann, because I loved Joan and it would upset her.'

Steve put his arm round John to take him to the car, glaring at Emma with a wicked look on his face. Hardly moving his lips, he said through gritted teeth, 'I'm the boss now and you will get no favours from the firm.'

He took John to his car and drove off without looking back, the tyres on the Rolls screeching. Emma slammed the door shut as the car pulled away.

She thought, 'He's one hard-faced bastard, half the firm belonged to me at one time, and I've still got two-thirds of my shares!'

Still, worried about what he had said, she got out her mobile phone and called her office as soon as she had closed the door.

Her PA answered, 'Emma Kenwright's offi....' but Emma interrupted, 'Pam, it's me.'

With that Pam said, 'I'm so sorry about Joan.'

Emma cut in again, 'Thank you. This will sound bad, what I want to ask of you. I love my sister but I want you to go to Joan's office now. You know I was to get my restaurants back last week? Well, I think my so-called brother in-law is going to say I haven't paid off the loan. You know I have, but my files are just copies. So, if you go now, before Cath goes home, and ask her for the original files, I know she will give you them, because she was Dad's secretary, and his conscience in the business and she knows I was to get them last week.

Make sure she knows I will compensate her if he dismisses her.'

'I'll go right now,' Pam replied, putting the phone down and rushing out of the office and into Joan's office next door.

Emma paced up and down in her living room for three quarters of an hour. When the phone rang, she grabbed hold of it and said, 'Emma here.'

Pam said, 'Sorry to take so long, I've got all the files. Cath made sure that they were all there. She was so upset about Joan; she said she would only be staying long enough to hand over to Mr Thomson's PA, then she would be leaving. She officially retired two years ago, because your dad arranged a private pension for her, so she could retire a few years early. When your dad died even before the pension paid out, she was going to leave. She only stayed on because Joan asked her to help her to take over the firm. So, Cath ended up staying longer than she ever intended, because she knew about all your dad's files and all the firms he was trading with.'

Emma was relieved and asked, 'Pam, will you send a bouquet of roses to Cath's home? And if there is anything you want, please get it for yourself, because it's all I can do to thank you for helping me to keep my restaurants. I'll never forget it because, without your and Cath's help, I know he would never have let me have my restaurants back. Pardon the language, but he is one horrible fucking bastard, and I just hate the thought of him in Joan's office. If there was any way I could keep him out of there, I would.

All I can say now is 'thank you' and that I'll see you in my old office in a couple of days. Bye.'

Pam replied, 'See you soon; I will miss Joan. Bye for now.'

STEVE CALLS IN AT THE POLICE STATION

When Steve left Emma he drove to the police station.

As he got out of his car, he said, 'John, you will be alright if I leave you in the car, won't you?'

John nodded but Steve could see he didn't really want his dad to leave him in the car.

Steve said, 'Good boy. You know I won't be long, listen to your music; I'll be back before you know it.'

He winked at John, closed the car door and went up the steps and into the station. He didn't look around; he just went straight up to the counter.

As he approached the desk, the duty officer looked up from what he was doing and said, 'How can I help you, sir?'

Steve replied, 'I would like to see someone in authority.'

The duty officer answered, 'Certainly, sir, but I will have to tell them your name and what you want to speak to them about. So, what do you want me to tell the inspector? So that he will come to speak to you.'

Steve said angrily, 'I'm Steve Thomson and I want to see an inspector because my wife is dead. Some bastard killed her.'

The officer said as he picked the phone up, 'I'll get you someone right away, sir.'

Then he spoke on the phone and, when he put it down, he said, 'An inspector will be with you as soon as he can. I'm afraid we are busy at the moment. Will you take a seat?'

He pointed to the bench against the wall that was behind Steve. Steve walked over to the bench, but didn't sit down. He just walked up and down alongside the bench for about fifteen minutes; with an expression that showed he was annoyed.

Then an inspector appeared at a door at the end of the counter and said, 'I'm Inspector Tytherington, sorry to keep you waiting. Will you come with me, Mr Thomson?'

Steve went with him into his office.

The inspector motioned with his hand for Steve to sit down, asking, 'Are you alright? I can see you're distressed.'

Steve told him what had happened in Spain.

The inspector said, 'Yes, we know about the case. We have a report about the accident from the Spanish police and, I can assure you, Mr Thomson, here in England we will be doing all we can to help. But, at this moment, we have nothing to go on.

If the Spanish police find some information that we can help with, my men will be right on it. That I can promise you - and I will keep you informed.'

Steve didn't wait for him to stop speaking, he was getting angry and red in the face while the inspector was talking.

He stood up and almost shouted, 'It was no fuckin' accident! It was murder. They tried to kill my family.'

The inspector put his hands out, with his fingers open wide to show he wanted to say something.

Steve went quiet for a moment, then he said in an angry tone, 'What?'

The inspector said, 'I'm sorry, Mr Thomson. I can see you are upset and I didn't want to mention the death of your wife. We all agree it was murder; it was foolish of me to say what I said, and I want to reassure you that we will do everything we can to help the Spanish police to solve the murder of your wife.'

Steve just glared at him and turned around; as he went out the door, he slammed it behind him.

It was about half an hour later that Steve got back in his car. John's music was still playing but he was fast asleep in the back seat, so Steve drove home, carried John into the house and put him in bed. He tucked John in and kissed him on the forehead. He closed the door as he left the room and went into the kitchen. He made himself a cheese and onion sandwich; from there he went into the living room, picked a book off the bookshelves and settled down in a large reclining chair to eat his sandwich and read his book. After an hour he drifted off to sleep.

JOAN'S FUNERAL

On the day of the funeral, Emma and Ann left Emma's house early to go to the church, because Ann didn't want to see or talk to her dad. As they got in their limousine they were upset. As they entered the church grounds, Emma told the driver to stop a few yards from the church. They got out of the limousine and stayed outside the church; both were crying. The people going into the church were starting to stop and stare at them, because they looked like they were arguing.

Ann was saying, 'I'm not going near him. I hate him. We wouldn't be here now if he hadn't let my mum fall.'

Emma was pleading with her, 'You will have to go in. Your mother would want you to be there. You can be next to John - your dad will be on the other side of him. John will need you with him to comfort him and hold his hand.'

The priest saw the people starting to gather by the entrance of the church, looking down the church steps to where Emma and Ann were standing. He went to see what they were looking at.

When he saw it was Emma and Ann, he invited them into the vestibule, and said, 'I will leave you alone to compose yourselves.'

He left and as he closed the door behind him, Emma hugged Ann for a moment before pushing her out to arm's length.

She looked at Ann's face, wet with tears, and said, 'Your mother will be here soon, and she will be looking down on us. She would be upset to think that you wouldn't hold John's hand at her funeral and that her family aren't here all together to say goodbye to her.'

Ann dried her eyes and face, as she said in a croaky, sobbing voice, 'All right, Aunt Emma, I'll sit next to John and you, but don't let my dad near me, please.'

Emma tried to smile and said, 'I will be with you all the time, so don't worry,' but she knew she couldn't really intervene if Steve spoke to Ann.

Just before they went into the church, Ann held onto Emma's hand and squeezed it, saying, 'I don't want to sit by my dad, and I don't want his name. I want my name officially changed to Kenwright... And I wish my mum would have married someone else.'

The church was full and there was a large crowd outside. In the front pew were Steve, John and some of the family's close friends, with a couple of places saved for Ann and Emma.

San was now eighty-four and couldn't walk very far, so she was in a wheelchair at the end of the front pew.

John was crying, and asked Steve 'Why aren't Ann and Aunt Emma here? Where are they?'

Steve was wiping his eyes. He bent down and kissed John on the head, whispering, 'Don't worry, Ann is upset. She will be here soon.'

When Emma and Ann entered the church, Emma half-helped, and half-pushed Ann into the pew next to John.

He hugged Ann as soon as she arrived, sobbing, 'Ann, I've lost my mum. You don't think it was my fault, do you? Please, Ann, I miss you, please come home.'

She put her arms round him and replied, with tears running down her cheeks, 'No, it wasn't your fault and no one thinks it was. I love you, but I can't come home.'

All the time she was talking, she was glaring at her dad. Emma tapped her on the shoulder and said, 'Sit down, Ann and face the altar. Your mother will be here soon.'

Just before she did what she was told, Ann took her handkerchief out of her coat pocket and dried John's eyes and face; then she wiped her own face. She sat there, looking towards the front of the church, with her arm round John's back and her hand on his shoulder, pulling him into her and away from Steve. Emma got hold of Ann's other hand.

There were a lot of people crying when Joan's coffin was carried into the church, and up to the altar.

The priest carried out the service and, at the end, asked the congregation, 'Would you please give Joan's family privacy at the graveside? But before we move there, Steve will give a eulogy for Joan.'

When Steve stood up and went to the podium, Ann, who had taken hold of John's hand during the service, let it go.

She pushed past Emma, ran round San's wheelchair and up the middle aisle, crying and saying, 'Not him. I hate him.' All the people in the church watched, as she ran out of the building, crying.

Emma went after her and John followed them. When Ann passed San and she saw what was happening, she struggled to get out of the wheelchair, as Emma walked out, with John running after her.

Cath came out of the pew she was in, walked over to San and said, 'Sandra, sit down and I'll push you out to Emma and the children.'

Cath pushed the wheelchair out the church and down the ramp to where the three had stopped. Emma had her hands full, trying to calm the children down. San thanked Cath, as she helped her get up out of the wheelchair. Cath left them there and went back into the church. San helped Emma with the children. She was like a mother to Emma and a grandmother to Ann and John. San got them all calmed down, including Emma. They walked to the graveside, with Emma pushing San in the wheelchair. The four of them waited for Joan to be brought there, hugging one another, crying silently and drying their eyes.

When Joan's coffin and the rest of the family arrived at the graveside, John and Ann got separated from San and Emma by the mourners moving around the grave. Steve went and stood between John and Ann. He tried to put his hands on each of their shoulders, but as soon as Ann realised it was Steve standing there, she pushed his hand away, glaring at him as she went further down the graveside to Emma, who was still holding on to San's wheelchair.

When the service at the graveside ended, Steve walked down to where Ann was standing and tried again to put his arm round her, but she became hysterical.

She pushed him away, screeching, 'Get away from me. I hate you. You let my mum fall. I *saw* you.'

Steve, in anger, turned on Emma as she was trying to calm Ann down.

He bellowed at her, 'You're an effing bitch. I know you are turning my daughter and the people you know against me - and that you've stolen the files for the restaurants. I *will* find out who the fuck helped you get them from my office.'

Emma let go of Ann and grabbed hold of Steve instead, pushing him back towards the grave screaming, 'It's not your office, it's my sister Joan's office. You should be down there, not Joan, you bastard.'

San struggled to get up out of the wheelchair and tried to go to Emma but, on the uneven ground, she fell back into her wheelchair. As Emma and Steve struggled and neared the edge of the grave, some mourners moved towards them, but Cath and Pam got to them first. They pulled Emma back, and away, from him.

Pam held on to Emma, while Cath let go and turned to face Steve.

She looked him in the eyes and said, 'I took the files from Joan's office and gave them to Pam. Joan told me to get the files for the restaurants ready to give to Emma when she got back...' She stopped for a moment as the tears started to run down her face. She wiped them away and carried on, in a sobbing voice, '...from her holiday, because the restaurant was paid for, and Joan was made up and wanted to give the files to Emma herself.'

Cath stopped and composed herself, finishing, 'So I did it for my best friend, Joan.' Then, in a commanding, angry tone, she said, 'The two of you should be ashamed of yourselves. What would Joan think of the way the two of you are acting?'

Emma went back to Ann. As she put her arm around her, she looked back at San, who was sitting in the wheelchair, crying. Emma led Ann over to her and the three hugged.

Emma whispered to San, 'Please forgive me, San. I'm sorry.'

San kissed Emma on the cheek and asked her, 'Will you take me home now, please?'

Emma looked across to Pam and Cath and said, 'I'm sorry, I'm taking San and Ann, and we are going home now. I will give you a phone call tomorrow.'

As they walked away, Pam and Cath caught up to them and gave them a hug.

When they reached the funeral cars the three of them got in one car; Emma said to the driver to drop San off first.

The people round the grave had watched them in silence while the struggle played out and as the limousine left the church grounds. Then they turned to look at Steve. He had his arm round John, holding him close, but he was still watching the limousine and his face was red with anger and hate. The people just stood there, not knowing what to do or say to him; some of them were walking away, talking among themselves about what Ann had said to her dad at the grave.

Steve calmed down and said to the people still present, 'I apologise for the way I was acting. I know I shouldn't be taking my grief out on the people around me. I hope you will all accept my apology, and you will all join John and I at the reception in my hotel in town.'

Ann never went back to live at the family home after the funeral. At first Steve and John went to visit Joan's grave every Sunday.

Sometimes they would see Emma and Ann, who also visited the grave every Sunday. When John saw Ann, he would go over to her and beg her to come home with him. She would take his hand and walk round the cemetery, away from Steve. They walked and talked, and every now and then he would again ask her to come home; when they were leaving, he would always ask again.

She would kiss him and say, 'I love you, but I can't go with you.'

After about eight months, Emma and Ann never saw Steve and John at the grave again, but there was always a bouquet of flowers on Joan's grave. On one occasion Ann picked the large bouquet of flowers up and read the card.

It was a place called *Rose's florist* and said, 'With all my love from Steve'. Under that was written, 'I'm sorry. Please forgive me. E'

Ann was angry when she read it and went to throw the bouquet of flowers away saying, 'He's 'sorry' - the horrible, sarcastic bastard.'

Emma said, 'Ann, don't do that. They are off John as well.'

Ann put the bouquet back on the grave but was still angry, saying, 'Emma, he's put on the card a capital E, and 'I'm sorry' - when he did it deliberately, the bastard... And why didn't he put John, not just that 'E'? What is it there for?'

Emma calmed Ann down and replied, 'I don't know why he's put that on the card. Just put him out of your mind.' Then they both stood there and said a prayer in silence.

Over the years, Emma and Ann were at the grave every Sunday they could get there, but sometimes they would have to work on a Sunday. Whenever they went, however, there was always a fresh bouquet of flowers and, on it, the card with the same inscription. They both would have liked to know what it meant but neither of them would talk to Steve or could even look at him without hate and disgust in their eyes.

STEVE MOVES INTO JOAN'S OFFICE

Steve took over as Acting Managing Director of the firm. Emma and Ann were angry about him moving into Joan's office and essentially becoming Managing Director, but Emma knew she didn't have enough shares to stop him.

The day after the funeral, Steve went into his own office and sorted out a lot of files and paperwork. He had never really wanted a permanent PA before, but now he was in charge of the company, he knew people would expect him to have someone to manage his appointments. He picked up the phone and got in touch with the person in charge of the flexible secretarial staff department, to tell them to promote one of the temporary secretaries, who usually covered absent PAs, to a permanent position in his office. She was one he had used in the past when he needed additional help with his admin. Her name was Lilly Blake, and she would be his PA going forward. He told her to come to the Managing Director's office.

Then he went from his old office to Joan's office. As he walked into the office, Cath was standing at her desk, putting some files in order.

She greeted him, 'Morning, Mr Thomson. You will find I have everything up to date.'

Steve, in a sarcastic voice, said through gritted teeth, 'You think that will make up for what you did, giving my files to that fuckin' bitch of a cow?' Then his grimace turned to a grin as he snarled, 'Well, you're wrong. You are dismissed for gross misconduct. Which means you will lose your pension.'

Cath just smiled and said, 'You can't fire me, Mister.'

Steve went red with anger, butting in, 'If I said you're fired, you fucking well are. You think, just because you've been here for so long, that you can't be fired? You might have ruled the place when you were with Joan, but I'm the boss now and I have my own PA. So, you *are* fired... And that means get out of *my* office and out of this firm.'

Cath just stood there, looking Steve in the eye, and said, 'You can't fire me because I am already leaving, and my pension is *quite* safe. You can't touch it; no one can stop it.'

Steve clenched his fist and banged it down on her desk, spittle flying out of his mouth as he butted in again, 'I'll have your job and your fuckin' pension, you hard-faced bitch. Now get out of my office.'

Cath walked slowly round the desk to the door.

As she opened it, she stood there for a moment and then turned and looked back at Steve, saying, 'If you would have let me talk without you interrupting me...' Steve had an infuriated look on his face but held his tongue, as Cath carried on, 'I was trying to tell you that I took my frankly fantastic pension two years ago. It can't be stopped by anyone and that includes you. I only carried on as Joan's PA because she asked me to. So you can stick your job, because I was only working as a favour to Joan - and there's no way I'd do that for you anyway.'

Steve just stood there, dumbfounded, as Cath continued, in a tone of authority, 'I will give you this bit of advice as a parting gift. You would be wise to forget about the restaurants. They are legally Emma's, and she has the documents to prove it. I know, because I gave her them.'

As she exited the room, she closed the door behind her. Her face showed she was sad to be leaving the firm she loved and had helped to build.

She had been there when John Kenwright started the business. She was fourteen and still at school when she started working there. She did it in her spare time for pocket money. It was a small warehouse with the boss - John Kenwright, three other men and Cath working there. Even in her holidays, when she didn't go abroad with her parents, she would be in the warehouse working and, when she left school, she started working nearly full time, with two days a week off to learn to be a secretary.

As the firm grew, Cath was the one John Kenwright would discuss all his plans with and he had made sure that she got a pension that showed what she was worth to the firm when she retired.

Though he was only fourteen years her senior when she started working for him, he looked on her like a daughter and, when her dad died, he was there for her. When she was getting married, he walked her up the aisle and gave her away at the wedding, and he was like a grandad to her two girls when they were born. She would turn to him whenever she needed help and she had nearly left the firm when he died, but she stayed to help Joan manage the firm because she knew that's what John would have wanted. It broke her heart to be leaving this way, but she knew she wouldn't like working for Steve, after what he had tried to do to Emma.

THE READING OF THE WILL

Three days after the funeral, Joan's solicitor, Mr Thomas, requested the family convene in his office. He also asked San, Cath and Pam to attend the reading of Joan's will.

Steve and John arrived first. They came in and sat down.

They were early and Mr Thomas asked, 'While we are waiting, would you like a drink?'

Steve and John, at the same time, replied, 'No, thank you.'

A short time later Emma, Ann and San came in. They sat as far away from Steve as they could. San got up from her wheelchair, went over to John and hugged and kissed him. Then she went back to Emma and Ann to sit with them. They were sitting on the other side of the office.

Ann waved to John. He was looking at her with tears in his eyes and the pleading look he had when he wanted something off her. She wanted to go to him and give him a hug, but she didn't want to go near her dad. So, instead, she looked at Mr Thomas, who was sitting at his desk with a file open in front of him.

He looked up and asked, 'Would you ladies like a drink of coffee or tea?'

They all thanked him for the offer but refused.

After a little while, Pam and Cath came in together. They smiled at John and then at Emma, San and Ann, as they sat on the two chairs that were left for them in the middle of the row.

The solicitor said, 'I see you are all here. Before we start, I would like to say Joan wasn't just a client, she was a personal friend of mine. I was at her christening, as my family have been friends of your family for as long as I can remember, and this is a job I hoped I would never have to do.

If it's agreed, I will read out Mrs Joan Thomson's will.'

He stopped for a moment and cleared his throat, and then he read, 'I leave Steve, my husband, 49% of the shares in the firm, with the condition he can't sell them and when he dies, Ann and John get all his shares.

I also leave 20% to Ann and 20% to John, to be kept in trust by the firm's solicitors and Steve, my husband, till they are each eighteen.

I have done it this way so Steve will be able to spend more time with Ann and John now I am no longer with them.

To my lovely sister, Emma, who has 10% already, I leave one percent of shares. I also leave her two hundred thousand pounds, and I leave San a trust that will pay her six hundred pounds a week, index-linked to inflation, so she can keep her home the way she likes it. To Cath, to thank her for all the work she helped me with, I leave one hundred thousand pounds and to Pam I leave ten thousand pounds. What remains of my estate is left to be shared between Steve, Ann and John.

I also ask Steve, if business is good the year I die, to give the staff a bonus.'

Mr Thomas closed the folder he had in front of him and said, 'That concludes the reading of the will.'

Steve wasn't pleased to get conditions on what he would receive in the will, and it showed on his face.

When they all got up to go, John went over to Ann, grabbed hold of her arm and asked, 'Will you come home with me and Dad?'

She hugged him and answered, with tears running down her cheeks, 'I can't. I love you, John, but,' she added, glaring at her dad, 'I couldn't live with him. He let our mum fall.'

John pushed Ann away and, angry, almost shouted, 'Don't say that. Dad did his best to save Mum. I saw him.'

Then his voice changed to a pleading tone, and he asked again, 'Please, Ann, come home?'

'I can't, John. I love you, but I just can't,' Ann replied.

San and Emma were standing just behind Ann and when John, upset, turned to go back to Steve, Emma and San moved toward him.

San stopped Emma and said, 'You look after Ann. I'll see to John.'

San got hold of his hand as he started to go back to Steve and, as he looked up at her, she gently squeezed it. She kissed him on the forehead and pulled him to her.

John said, 'Gran, I want Ann to come home with me. I miss her.'

As she hugged him, San whispered, 'Don't worry, John. We all love you and we will speak to Ann and ask her to come and see you. Just give her a little time to come round, and I'm sure in a few weeks she will be home with you and your dad. Just remember Ann loves you.'

John kissed San and nodded, saying, 'I hope so, Gran.'

San smiled at him and said, 'Well, I'm sure she will.'

She wiped the tears from his eyes but, as he went back to his dad, he kept looking back at Ann.

Steve was talking to the solicitor. He didn't know him personally. Although he had seen him with Joan's dad when he first met John Kenwright in his office and he had seen the solicitor around the firm over the years, he had never had any direct dealings with him.

Steve asked Mr Thomas, in an irritated tone, 'Why did Joan do that to me? I'm supposed to be in charge, and I have my hands tied. If the firm is in trouble and I need to float some shares on the stock market to save it, what power do I have to do that?'

Mr Thomas answered, 'As a representative of the firm's solicitors, I can tell you the firm's portfolio is so financially sound that it would take a significant change in fortunes for things to go so wrong that we would need to make a decision like that. But if it did, and the board agreed with you, we would use Ann and John's shares to vote with you. So you don't have to worry about that. Yes, Joan made all the decisions and yes, you are now the chairman of the board instead… but you will have the firm's solicitor on the board acting for the children to help you, and to take some of the responsibility off your shoulders. That is what Joan was thinking of when she set things up this way and, like she said in the will, it will give you more time with Ann and John.'

Steve was angry and it showed in his voice as he exclaimed, 'I thought Joan would have had more faith in me to run the firm my own way. I just can't believe she would do this to me. Is there any way I can change this, so I have full control of my firm?'

'I'm afraid there is no way. Your wife spent hours with our team of solicitors sorting it all out and you know how good Joan was when she put her mind to anything.

Steve, you know Joan was down to earth and she was determined that if she died young, you and the children would have more time together, because she wouldn't be there with them.'

Steve wasn't pleased with the answer the solicitor gave him. He got hold of John's hand to leave but, as he looked towards the main door of the offices, he could see the women talking, just inside the doorway.

He asked the solicitor, 'Is there another way out of here? I don't want to pass those nagging, clucking hens who are blocking the doorway.'

The solicitor showed Steve and John another way out of the building, to the car park.

Once there, the solicitor offered Steve his hand. Steve shook it but his face showed he wasn't pleased. He got in his Rolls Royce, and the tyres screeched and smoked as he drove out of the car park.

The solicitor watched and thought, 'He was taking Joan's intentions the wrong way.' He also thought, 'The way he's driving, we will have to defend him in court!'

Then he walked over to where Emma's limousine was waiting and stood by it.

When Cath and Pam left the office, they got into the taxi that they had ordered, while Ann and Emma helped San get home.

Ann said to San, in an angry tone, 'I heard what you said to John, Gran, but you are wrong. I won't go back to live with Dad. I hate him.'

San hugged Ann, and kissed her and explained, 'I don't know what you are going to do, darling. I just said what I thought would calm John down, because it really upsets me when you and John are unhappy.'

As Cath and Pam's taxi drove off, Ann kissed San and the three of them went round to the car park, with Emma pushing San in her wheelchair. In the car park, the solicitor was standing next to the open door of the waiting limousine. He helped San get comfortable and loaded her wheelchair into the boot.

As San, Ann and Emma got into the car, he shook their hands, saying, 'I'm sorry for your loss. Joan was a wonderful woman, and we will miss her.'

They thanked him.

Emma was also a friend of Mr Thomas. She got in last, and he hugged her and said, 'Don't you become a stranger. Keep in touch.'

Emma just nodded, with tears in her eyes, as he closed the door. Then she told the driver to drop San home first. After they had, Ann asked the driver to take them to the cemetery and they paid Joan's grave a visit, saying a quiet prayer before they headed home to Emma's house.

TOMMY AND HIS FRIENDS

Tommy and his four pals were the best of friends when they went on their holiday to Spain together, but it wasn't always that way. When they were eleven years of age, Tommy and David happened to move into the school district about the same time.

The school year had started two months earlier, so they were the new boys in the school. They had met the week before, when their parents had brought them to look over the school. It was a massive building - old, but impressive at first sight, with steps leading up to a large arch with great oak doors. There were some smaller arched doorways round the building and large oak windows all around the school. It was four storeys high.

The parents and the boys met in the school's large reception room.

While their parents were in a discussion with the school secretary about registering the boys to enrol, the two boys looked at each other, and then Tommy broke the ice, saying, 'I'm Tommy. Do you go to this school? What is it like?'

David replied, 'No. I've just moved here but I will be going to it after today. My name is Dave.'

They found that they got on well together, so they agreed that when they started in the school - as the new boys - they would be friends and stick up for one another if they got picked on. Dave was particularly glad of this because he was small for his age, though he could and would stand up for himself, whereas Tommy was tall and broad and didn't look like a person anyone would mess with. Tommy had a nice smile. It was hidden below the surface, but it came out every chance he got to show it off, because he had a friendly personality.

They met Paul, Terry and Jammer, on the first day they started there, when the three of them thought it would be a good joke to tease the new, small kid.

Paul said to Dave, 'Have you lost your way? You have to be eleven to be in this school and a little kid like you could get hurt.'

As Paul was standing in front of Dave, Jammer stood behind him and pulled Dave's bag from under his arm. He passed it to Terry, and they laughed as they started to pass it round, teasing him to try to get it.

Dave grabbed for it but they were all taller than him and he couldn't reach it.

Then Jammer, who was a little on the chubby side, held the bag high above Dave's head and said to Dave, 'Come on, Titch. I bet you can't get it, even if you stand on a box and jump for it!'

By now Dave was red with anger and said, 'You will lose that bet, Humpty Dumpty.'

Jammer's smile turned to a frown as he said, 'I don't think so. It's too high for you to reach it.'

Dave shouted, 'We'll see,' and brought his knee up with all his might into Jammer's groin.

As Jammer fell to the ground, Dave grabbed for his bag and tried to run but Paul grabbed him by his black, wavy hair and nearly lifted him off the ground, saying, 'You little bastard. There was no need for that - we were only joking.'

Terry helped Jammer up off the floor.

Jammer was holding his groin and, as he struggled to stand up straight, he said to Paul, 'Hold onto the little git. I'm going to kick the shit out of him.'

Just then Tommy came out of the school building. When he saw Paul holding Dave by the hair, he ran over to them and grabbed Paul by the scruff of his neck. Paul let go of Dave with shock.

Terry and Jammer sprang towards Tommy but, as they came in with their fists flying, he pushed Paul into them and all five of the boys ended up in a pile on the ground.

Within seconds a crowd was around them shouting, 'Fight! Fight! Fight!' which brought the headteacher, who was standing just in front of the large oak doors at the front of the school, running down the steps and over to them.

The crowd dispersed, fading away as soon as he said, in an angry voice, 'All of you boys move. Get away from here now. I said *all* of you… or you will be sent to the detention room!'

As the crowd walked away, two of them stopped and looked back.

The master roared, 'I said move! And I mean *now*,' causing the two boys to scurry away. Then he turned his attention to the five remaining on the ground and, still in an angry voice, said, 'You boys! Stop this fighting at once!'

They all froze at that moment, when they realised it was the headteacher shouting at them. Then the boys stood up and brushed themselves down, looking up at the large male teacher who stood there, out of breath and red faced.

He puffed, 'Get to the detention room now! I'll deal with you later.'

Tommy looked at the headteacher and said, 'Dave and I are new here, Sir, and we don't know where to go. We only started this morning.'

The teacher looked at Tommy and Dave, then glared at the other three and puffed out in short, sharp, angry words, 'New boys? This better not be a case of bullying! I'm sure these newfound friends will show you the way to the detention room... and there better not be any more fighting.'

Jammer picked up Dave's bag with one hand; with the other hand he was still holding his groin.

Then he said, 'This way, mate. Sorry, but it was only supposed to be a joke. I didn't like it when you called me Humpty Dumpty, so I suppose we were bullying you.

So, sorry, but don't worry. Anyone who tries to pick on you two would have to be soft!'

Terry and Paul nodded in agreement with Jammer, as Paul butted in, 'Well, we're in a bit of trouble now. We will be suspended for the week, that's what you get if you're caught bullying... But you two will be all right, we'll admit it was all our fault.'

Terry asked, 'Anyway, what are your names? Because when we get back, we can be friends, if you like? We're not bullies really. It was just a bad joke that wasn't funny, sorry.'

As they walked across the school courtyard, Paul shuddered and said to the others, 'This part of the school has been empty for years. I think they put the detention room in this horrible part of the building as part of the punishment.

My older brother - he's left now, but he and his friends said it's haunted. They hated being sent there, because one time when they were, a strange teacher that they hadn't seen before was just standing there. As each of them went into the room, he didn't speak, he just beckoned them with a pale white bony hand and, as they reached a desk, he would point with a misshaped bony finger to the desk for the boy to sit in it. He moved his lips as if he was talking but no words came out, and he had bloodshot eyes with small thin wire glasses on, and his clothes looked like the ones people wore a hundred years ago. He never made a sound; he just stood there staring at them with his bloodshot eyes that were sunk into a pale bony face.

My brother and his friends were terrified. They had been in the room for about fifteen minutes, when they heard a noise in the corridor outside the room. They turned to look and the door started to open; then there was a noise at the back of the room, so they all turned back to look at that and something disappeared into the wall that looked like the back of the teacher. Then the door at the front of the room, to the left of where the strange teacher had been standing, finished swinging open and a voice of a teacher they knew rang out.

They all looked at him as he shouted, 'I'm away for a few moments and you boys think you can just walk into this empty classroom without a teacher present and make this much noise?'

The teacher said he didn't believe them when they told him what had happened, but my brother reckoned the teacher did, because he seemed uneasy all through the detention and kept looking around.

My brother, he had nightmares about it.'

Paul paused, taking a deep breath as they entered the building, and then he sighed and shrugged his shoulders as he said, 'Well, I don't like it but we'll have to walk down this long, dark corridor to get to the room.'

All the boys looked at him and then they looked down the long dimly lit corridor, and they all stopped.

Paul burst out laughing and said, 'I'm only joking! You should see your faces.'

As they walked down the corridor, Terry looked round and said, 'You could be right. This place looks like it *could* be haunted.'

Jammer looked at Dave and, in a pained voice but with a sort of smile on his face, rubbed his groin and announced, 'I bet that hurt me more than it hurt you, Dave.'

They all laughed, distracted from the gloomy atmosphere of the corridor, and when they reached the classroom, Terry opened the door and said, 'Be my guest, gentleman. After you, to go into the valley of death.'

He bowed and waved his hand for them to pass him and enter the classroom.

Dave was the first to enter and, with that, turned to Tommy and said, 'Detention room? It looks more like a storage room. Look at all them dusty desks and chairs, stacked up on that side of the room.'

Dave stopped talking because as they entered the room the teacher in charge said in a loud voice, 'Be silent. Take a seat at the back of the room, gentlemen, and be quiet as mice, please. I'm sure the master who sent you here will be in soon, to deliver your well-earned punishment.'

The boys sat on the side of the room that had three rows of double desks. Tommy and Dave took the first desk at the back of the room. Paul and Terry took the desk next to them, while Jammer went to the third and had the desk to himself.

When they had sat down, Tommy whispered to the boys, 'How do you know you will get a week's suspension? Have you done it before?'

They all replied with variations of 'God, no!' Their voices went a bit loud and high and, with that, the teacher slammed the book he was reading down on the desk with a loud bang, shouting, 'Be quiet or you will find yourselves spending the rest of the term in this room with me! And it won't be a nice stay, I will make sure of that, believe me.'

All the boys looked up with shock at the teacher when the book hit the desk, including the four boys who had already been sitting in the front desks when they had arrived. None of the boys spoke for a little while but when they thought the teacher was again engrossed in his book, looking at him just to make sure, Paul whispered, 'We know it's a week because every now and then in assembly they tell us that anyone caught bullying will get a week's suspension.'

Then Jammer butted in, 'Yes, and if you get caught a second time you will be told to leave the school all together.'

Tommy looked at the three boys and said with a smile, 'Why are you looking so worried about it? Just look at it as a week's holiday.'

The boys whispered almost as one, 'We have still to face our parents!'

Jammer continued, 'The week off school's alright, but we will have to live with it at home and it will be a lot longer than a week, the punishment there. Our parents won't let us live it down. God, I'm dreading seeing them.'

The other two boys looked as pale as Jammer, as they both slowly nodded their heads in agreement.

Tommy said to Dave, 'I think they're sorry, don't you, Dave?'

Dave smiled and replied, 'Yes. Anyway, I wouldn't call that real bullying. I had a lot worse than that at my old school.'

Just at that moment the headmaster came into the room and clapped his hands with a bang. Everyone in the room looked up, including the teacher and the four boys who were at the front of the room, working on their laptops.

The headmaster nodded to the teacher, and said to the four boys in the front, 'Just carry on doing your work.'

He pointed to the back of the room and said, 'You five boys, come with me to my office.'

The five of them looked at each other as they stood up nervously, then they followed the master out of the room into the corridor.

As they followed him their footsteps echoed along the corridor and Terry whispered to the boys, as he walked from the back to the front of them, 'Look out for the ghosts.'

The master went out of the building and down some steps, with the boys following. They crossed the courtyard to a small house.

Paul tapped Tommy and Dave on the shoulder, pointed to the house and said, 'This was the gamekeeper's house back when a rich family owned the land.'

The master stood aside and waved the boys into the house, saying, 'This is my home, so wipe your feet on the doormat.'

Then, as they wiped their feet, the master went past them and said, 'You boys come with me to my office.'

The boys followed him into the room. They looked around and saw the walls were covered with bookshelves with not a space on them. At the back of the room was a large window and, just by it, was a big, black, leather swivel chair standing behind a large, oak desk.

As soon as they entered the office Tommy said, 'I am sorry, Sir. It's all my fault. I bet the others that Dave and I could beat the three of them in a friendly wrestle, but with neither team wanting to lose, it got a bit out of hand. That's why everyone thought it was a real fight.'

The headmaster looked at each boy in turn and said, 'It looked like a real fight to me.'

The other three boys started to answer all at once but, realising they were talking over one another, Paul and Terry quietened down, leaving it to Jammer to say, 'No, Sir. It wasn't a real fight.'

The master turned to Dave, put his hand on his shoulder and led him out of the room and into the hallway, so the other boys couldn't hear.

He said, 'You are the smallest boy here. If you were being bullied, you needn't be afraid of these boys. You can tell me, and I can promise you there will be no more bullying from these boys or any other pupils in this school.'

Dave replied, 'Tommy is telling the truth, Sir. We were talking about the wrestling on the TV; then Tommy said, 'Dave and I will take you three on in a friendly wrestle' and that's how it looked like we were fighting.'

The master said, 'I will believe you, but if I find out you are lying to me, you will be in even more trouble than the other boys would be for bullying.'

The master called the boys out of his study and told them, 'If I find out you boys are lying to me, it will be God help you! So you boys had better be on your best behaviour from now on. I have all your names, and I will be keeping an eye on every one of you. I don't want to hear any of your names mentioned, unless it's to say how well you are doing in your lessons. Now get along to your classes.'

After that day if you saw any one of them, you could be sure the others would be around somewhere.

Jammer, after a few months of hanging round together, suggested, 'We could call ourselves the hand gang.'

The other boys pulled their faces and Tommy said, 'We're just friends, we're not a gang. Anyway, why the hand gang?'

Jammer replied, 'Well, there are five of us and five fingers on a hand. You're right, it is a bit soft. Just forget I said it.'

Dave laughed and said, 'We can't forget it… Saying that name is a daft idea is the first time we have all agreed with you!'

They all laughed, and they stayed friends all through their school years. On the day they left the college, they planned a holiday in Spain and promised that if they drifted apart that they would meet up every two years, no matter what they were doing.

TOMMY AT THE POLICE STATION

Though Ann and Tommy were just teenagers on the fateful day they met, in a short while they were lovers, and their love stayed strong throughout the years that followed. Ann's nickname for Tommy was 'Smiler' because people said he seemed to always have a smile that was just waiting to light up his face.

They were very close but, for the first few years of their relationship, when Ann and Tommy were talking, she just couldn't help herself and the conversation would nearly always end up about her dad killing her mother. Tommy didn't think her dad had let go on purpose; he thought Steve just couldn't hold on any longer because he must have been exhausted. When Tommy would try to tell Ann this, the conversation would get heated and Ann would go red in the face.

In one of their many arguments about that day, Ann said, 'I was there. I *saw* him. My dad was as strong as an ox, he would spend about two hours a day lifting weights in his gym, and an hour running. To show off sometimes, he would say to Mum and I to stand facing each other and hold John in the middle of us. I would stand on a box so our waists were level, and he would put a hand on my waist and the other on Mum's waist. Then he'd bend his knees till he was almost sitting on the ground and his head was level with mine and Mum's waists, and he would tell Mum and I to lean over towards him. He would take a deep breath, and with a loud shout of 'Who's the daddy?' he'd lift the three of us off the ground as he stood up. So, don't tell me he couldn't hold my mother and save her life.'

Tommy replied, 'It was the driver of the car that caused your mother's death, and I'm determined to find the fucking, bastard driver, because he or she has ruined our bloody lives.'

Ann answered, 'I've told you before - it was a woman driver with a black wig.'

Tommy still thought it might have been a man with a wig on but held his peace.

After a few years, they didn't talk about it anymore, but it still seemed to be there with them, hanging over their heads and both of them knew it. A few times, Tommy suggested to Ann getting some counselling might help her to put it all behind her, but Ann wasn't pleased and always said angrily that she didn't need counselling. So Tommy stopped mentioning it.

He was now a private detective. He had gone into the job about twelve months after they got back from Spain, because of the way Ann had turned against her dad, constantly saying he had killed her mother. The fact that Tommy was nearly killed himself was another reason for going into it.

When the police didn't find the car or driver that caused the death of Ann's mother, Tommy wanted to find the car and driver himself, but he didn't know how to go about it or where to look. So, when he got home, he went to the police station where he lived and started asking questions about the case in Spain.

At first, they didn't listen and, when they did, they just said that if it happened in Spain, then it was a Spanish case and out of their hands. He was angry that they weren't interested in the case; he was determined to find someone to help him. So he would go at least twice a week and in the end they just sent him away with a few choice words in his ear. He had a few more goes at phoning the police in Spain, but often got someone who couldn't speak English. When he did get a person who could speak English, they would say they didn't know anything about the case. So the last time he went to the police station, he was reluctant to leave. One of the police constables there was annoyed with him calling in all the time and going on about the same thing.

The constable said, 'If you come in here again, I will put you in a cell... Like I said last time you came! I mean it this time, it will be for the night, and I'll charge you with wasting police time and creating a nuisance. Now be on your way and don't come back.'

Tommy was angry but he kept calm. He was just heading to the door when a man came out of an office and headed straight over to him in the foyer of the station.

The man said, 'I've heard about you. I am speaking to Tommy Tennant, right?

I'm Detective Sergeant Jackson and I would like a word with you in my office.'

He held his arm out, suggesting to Tommy to go into the office he had just exited. Tommy was a little bit nervous, because even though Tommy was taller than the detective, the man in front of him was well-built and looked like he could handle himself. Tommy definitely didn't want to get into another argument with this police officer, because he thought they weren't far off throwing him into a cell.

As he entered the office, the detective smiled and said, 'Don't be nervous. I know each time you come here they send you away with a flea in your ear, but they had no right to.

It's not my case but seeing you so determined to get someone to listen to you, well, you caught my admiration and attention. So I got in touch with Scotland Yard, and they sent me the files they received from the Spanish police. Oh, by the way, they call me Jacko.

Anyway, I've read the case notes that they have sent. It said that the few witnesses that came forward said you were nearly killed. You are a very brave lad to risk your life to try to save Mrs Thomson.

Now I'll tell you all we know but I'm afraid it's not much. The Spanish police officially think it was just a tragic accident, but in the footnotes Sergeant Torres put in red 'we didn't find the car or driver that nearly hit the Thomson family and Tommy Tenant'.

I think this Sergeant Torres thinks it's murder as well. The Yard has investigated it, but it happened in Spain and the police there couldn't help us. So, as you see we got nowhere. It's an open case in Spain, but as a traffic accident as far as the Spanish police are concerned.'

Tommy went red with anger and almost shouted, 'A traffic case? It should be murder! Mrs Thomson was killed and, but for the grace of God, I would have been as well. That's murder in anyone's book... except the police's, apparently.'

Jacko smiled and said, 'Calm down, son. I'll keep an eye on the case, and I'll let you know if we get any more information from Spain.'

Then Jacko, with a questioning look on his face, said, 'I can see you want to do your bit, and you are in here all the time... You must have a good job with a lot of spare time?'

'No, I haven't got a job at the minute,' Tommy replied, continuing, 'I've had a few, but I just can't concentrate on them. The only thing on my mind is what happened in Spain and I just can't get it out of my mind. It's there all the time. I told my girlfriend to see a counsellor, but I think I might need to see one myself.'

Jacko grinned and said, 'You need a job? Well, I know just the job for you, and you might learn a thing or two to help you in your quest. It's a job with a private detective who is looking for an assistant - but don't tell him I told you about the job. You mightn't get a look in, because he can't stand me.' Jacko laughed and continued, 'I don't know why. I'm a lovable fellow, don't you think? And I've only threatened to arrest him twice. I haven't actually arrested him yet.'

Then Jacko stood up and placed the folder he had been showing to Tommy in a steel basket that was on top of a filing cabinet behind him.

He turned back to face Tommy, with his hand still resting on the folders and said, 'These are the cases I'm determined to solve before I retire, and now your case is one of them.'

With that he walked to the office door and opened it, beckoning to Tommy to follow. As they went through the door, Jacko reached up to put his arm around Tommy's shoulders.

He smiled as he pulled Tommy to his side and spoke, 'You're a big boy for your mother; you must be about six foot seven? So, you should be able to look after yourself?'

Tommy frowned and looked at him, saying, 'Yes, I can, and I'm a black belt in karate… but I don't like fighting, so what did you say that for?'

Jacko laughed as he patted him on the back and said, 'Don't worry. It's just that detective job I told you about. If you get it, well, you will meet some angry people *and* some downright nasty ones… but with your size and your black belt you will be alright, I'm sure.'

Jacko laughed as he showed Tommy back into the foyer of the police station, saying, 'Make sure you don't lose your black belt, your trousers may fall down.'

Tommy just looked at him.

Jacko smiled at him and said, 'Well, I thought it was funny, even if you didn't.'

Tommy smiled as he started to walk towards the front door of the station.

Jacko said, 'Hold your horses, Tommy,' and, as they passed the counter in the waiting area, Jacko leaned on it and wrote the address of the private detective on the back of one of his cards.

He shook Tommy's hand and said, 'Good luck, but don't mention your case to the boss man till you have been there a while. Anyway, give it a go, you might get good at it.'

He handed Tommy the card. As Tommy left the police station, Jacko walked into the building and back to his office.

A policeman walked alongside him and asked, 'What are you giving him the time of day for? He's a bloody nuisance. You're a glutton for punishment.

The kid is here all the time. He was here last week and it took a good while to get rid of him. In the end I threatened to lock him up for the night and, as you see, he's back again. He was going on about a murder and it's just a traffic case that happened in Spain, and nothing to do with us.'

Jacko replied, 'Well, I think he might be right. When you look at it from his point of view, he was nearly killed on that mountain and a woman did die.

The police in Spain and our crowd can't find the driver or the car, the number plates were off a 1.1 Ford Anglia from here in England and the witnesses who saw the car said it was an old small sports job, something like a MG with a large crash bar on it that didn't look right. If you were him, what would you think?'

The police officer said, 'You've got a point, but it happened in Spain. What can we do about it? It's a Spanish police case.'

Jacko said, 'Yes, we know it happened in Spain but if it was a murder, the one or ones who did it will most likely live here, because this is where the victim lived.'

The policeman butted in, 'It might have been someone from Spain that drove the car at them.'

Jacko patted the policeman on the back and said, 'If the driver was from Spain, he or she just happened to have a car with the wrong English plates on it and a large crash bar that would kill anyone it hit *and*, as luck would have it, the family the driver drove at just happen to be billionaires. How likely does that sound?'

Jacko thought he wasn't getting through to the policeman that murder in any country has to be investigated, but he continued anyway, 'I know that murder, apart from the nutters, is for power, love or for the love of money... and there is a bloody lot of money in this family.

So the Spanish police said in their report that it was a traffic case? Well, you and I know why they put it in as a traffic report. To make their crime figures look a little better - just like us.'

The policeman answered, 'That's what I mean. We have nothing to do with it really.'

Jacko put his hands up in the air and exclaimed, 'You just weren't listening to me, were you?

Never mind, I know you like things in black and white.'

The policeman was a bit puzzled and stared as Jacko turned and walked up the hallway, shaking his head as he went into his office. With that the policeman went back to the counter, sat down and got on with his paperwork.

THE JOB

Tommy looked at the card the detective had given him. It was a small card that had Jacko's full name and phone number on it. Tommy turned it over and read what Jacko had written on the back: *Max Jameson, Private Detective Agency - the best in town. HA HA! Three Red Cross Street. Phone no. 0161 223 7990.*

As he read it, he thought, 'Well, all the times I've tried by myself I've got nowhere. Even I know I'm useless at finding things out but, if I get this job, I can learn how to go about looking into things and, in the time I'm not working, I can investigate the bastard who drove that car. I better not give them the card though, if they see what Jacko has written on the card, they might not give me the job!'

So he phoned the number on the back of the card and a woman answered, 'This is the Jameson Detective Agency. How can we help?'

Tommy said, 'I've heard you have a vacancy and I would like to apply for the job.'

She replied, 'I'll put you through to Mr Jameson.'

Tommy could hear her saying, 'Mac, it's for the job,' then a man said, 'Jameson here.'

They talked for ten minutes and he told Tommy to be there the following morning.

After the phone call, Tommy went home and got ready. He was going to meet Ann that afternoon on his motorbike, so he put Ann's helmet and leather jacket in the carrier on the back of the bike. When he met Ann, she was waiting outside one of her and Emma's restaurants on the High Street. She looked lovely standing there, in her dark leather boots, light blue jeans and a white blouse. Her long, black, silky hair hung over her shoulder, quivering in the light breeze.

When Tommy stopped just in front of her, he was still excited about getting the job interview. As he got off his bike the first thing he said to her was about his conversation with Jacko.

Ann responded, with a slight smile, 'Hello, Ann, I've missed you?'

Tommy kissed her, saying, 'Sorry, I just couldn't wait to tell you.'

She smiled, kissed him back and asked, 'Well, do tell what news you bring!'

Tommy's voice went a bit high as he said, 'I've applied for a job he told me about. It's in a private detective agency. The boss is Mr

Jameson, and he said I sound like the right kind of person for this type of job, but he would have to interview me. I will have to start at the bottom, even if I do get the job, but I'm to be at the office at eight o'clock tomorrow morning and we'll go from there.'

Ann looked worried, asking, 'Is it safe? It sounds like you could get hurt if someone gets angry because they don't like what you're doing.'

Tommy laughed and replied, 'They would have to catch me first and you've seen how fast I can run!'

Then he suggested they go for a ride on his motorbike.

Ann said, 'Okay - it's a good job I've got my jeans on. We can take a ride to the Lake District and have a coffee in a little café I know there, and when we get back it will be time for bed.'

Tommy grinned, replying, 'I'm with you. I'm all for that.'

Ann answered, 'Wipe that silly grin off your face, I mean our own beds. I have to be up early in the morning to meet Emma in this restaurant, and you will have to be fresh for your interview.'

While Ann was talking, Tommy was grinning. He put a flat hand on his forehead, drew it down his face, transforming it from happy to sad, and then just stood there.

Ann just smiled. As she walked over to his bike, she said, 'Well, come on, soft lad. Get a move on, or we won't have time to go.'

Tommy took the jacket and helmet out of the carrier and gave the jacket and helmet to Ann. As Ann got ready, he put his helmet on. He got on his bike and Ann got on the back.

As he started the bike up, she squeezed him and whispered, 'I love you.'

Tommy shouted, 'I can't hear you,' over the noise of the engine, and she just squeezed him again.

As they rode away, Ann's long black hair was flowing back from under her white helmet.

Tommy was keen to make a good impression and got to his interview at seven fifteen. A woman of about thirty opened the office and invited him in.

She said, 'I'm Val. Are you Tommy?'

He answered, 'Yes.'

Before he could say anything more, a hefty man of about fifty years of age, walked in behind them, saying, 'Hi, Tommy. I'm the boss, Mr Jameson, but we don't stand on ceremony here, so just call me Mac.'

As he walked past Tommy, he put his hand on Tommy's shoulder and said, 'Come with me to my office. We'll have to fill in a few forms if you get the job.'

As Mac said, 'office,' Val laughed, which caused Mac to give her an angry look.

Tommy watched as Mac squeezed through the half open door. When he followed him, he had to move sideways so the door could be shut.

He thought, 'An office? This is a cupboard!'

The room had one filing cabinet, a table and a chair. Mac sat down behind the small table and asked Tommy the usual questions, filling in the necessary forms as he did.

Then he said to Tommy, 'Are you sure you've never been in trouble with the police?'

Tommy replied, 'No, I've never been in trouble, unless you count getting moved on when I was a kid.'

Mac said, 'That's just the police's pastime, moving kids on.' Then he handed Tommy the forms, continuing, 'Read them and check that everything is correct. There will be a police check on you and if there is anything wrong on the form, you won't get a licence to do the job.'

Tommy was still standing as he signed the forms, because there wasn't any room for a chair.

When he handed them back, Mac smiled and said to him, 'You will fit in well. You can start right away, and I can see you cleaning up all the small jobs around the office by yourself in no time at all.'

Tommy felt good. He was made up to think he was going to start straight away… and then Mac gave Tommy a brush and told him to clean the office up. He was angry at first, but Val knew what Mac was like, so she was listening and opened the door.

She started laughing as Mac squeezed through it, saying to Tommy, 'Don't take it to heart, Mac just thinks he's being funny. You've got the brush - I'll get the shovel and we'll both clean the boss' 'big' office up first. After that we'll do the rest of the office and when we've finished, we'll have a look to see what case we can work on together.'

Tommy smiled when he realised that it was just a bit of fun.

Over the next couple of years Tommy learnt a lot of the tricks of the trade from Val and Mac, and he also kept in touch with Jacko. When Mac was working and he met Jacko they would throw insults at one another, but Tommy knew that they were friends really.

After a few years he left home and got his own terraced house, but he visited his mother and father regularly and if he was away on a job, he would make sure he phoned and let them know where he was. Over time, Tommy got Mac to start looking into the case in Spain with him, as well as Jacko, who had phoned Sergeant Torres on the first day he met Tommy and still kept in touch with him even though he was now retired.

TOMMY IN SPAIN WITH SERGEANT TORRES

Tommy was also in touch with Sergeant Torres. He had invited Tommy over to Spain a couple of times over the years; he would take Tommy round the known crime spots, and the scrap yards and garages which he thought had dodgy owners.

There was one garage that Sergeant Torres had thought from the beginning might be involved, because the same week the car had driven at the family, the owner's partner in crime was shot dead. However, though the police had kept an eye on him, they couldn't prove anything and each time they questioned him all they got was abuse and him saying 'I want my solicitor'.

Sergeant Torres took Tommy there five years after the accident, which was a year before he retired.

As they walked into the garage, Tommy asked who owned the business and the sergeant replied, 'Alonso.'

Tommy said, 'That's the same name as the doctor that looked after Ann and John after the death of their mother. This fellow isn't a relation, is he?'

Torres smiled, replying, 'No way. You've heard of good and bad angels. Well, we have a sublime Mr Alonso and a real evil bastard Alonso. This one I'd give up my pension to put behind bars.'

Just as he finished talking, the owner saw them and came out of his office. He had an angry look on his face and stood there for a while watching them. Then he approached, picking up a metal pipe about two feet long as he walked towards them.

Holding it in his right hand and smacking it against his left, he snarled, 'Have you come to question me again? And have you got a warrant to come in here?'

Sergeant Torres smiled and answered, 'We don't need a warrant, we might be customers.'

The owner said, 'That means you haven't got a warrant, and I wouldn't have you as a customer, so, Batman, why don't you take Robin and fuck off.'

Sergeant Torres kept a smile on his face as he said, 'I'll do that little thing for you for now, but I just want you to know I'm not Batman. I'm more like the terminator because I'll be back... and I'll be watching you.'

The owner put on a false laugh and answered, 'You'll be watching me? That's a good one. You've been watching me for years and you're crap at it! You can't prove anything against me and you haven't got a warrant, so, like I said, fuck off and don't come back without one.'

The sergeant stood there, smiled and winked at the owner answering, 'You know I'll be back, I said so didn't I?' Then he said to Tommy, 'Let's go, Robin.'

As they left Tommy said, in English, 'I've been learning Spanish and I understood most of it. Especially the fuck off words.'

As they walked away the sergeant put his hand on Tommy's shoulder and with a serious look on his face said, 'Tommy, I want you to promise me that you will never go near that man by yourself. He's a dangerous and evil bastard. We suspect him and his so-called business partner were involved in what happened to Joan Thomson. We are pretty certain they supplied the car, but his partner was murdered about the same time and we think he did it… or that the person who was driving the car might have done it, to conceal their identity.

Alonso's alibi at the time was that he was on a month's holiday, and he had all the receipts for the hotels and the tickets for the trains that he was supposed to have travelled on, so we couldn't disprove any of it. Still, like I said, we're sure he had something to do with the car and scrapped it… We just can't prove it.'

Tommy nodded and replied, 'Don't worry, Sarge, I have no intention of going near him. Just looking at him with that pipe in his hand and hearing the nasty tone in his voice frightens me.'

Tommy went back to Spain many times after that and sometimes he stayed with Sergeant Torres and his wife.

JOHN MEETS LILLY'S DAD

One day, when John was twenty-one, he was in his room with his headphones on, playing the latest *Gran Turismo* on his PlayStation, when his dad and Lilly came to see him together. He was so engrossed in the game, he didn't hear when his dad and Lilly knocked at the door. So his dad opened the door a little bit and knocked even harder.

John jumped with fright, pulled his headphones off but, as he got over the shock, he said, 'Come in.'

His dad announced, 'I've got Lilly with me, is it alright if she comes in too?'

John laughed and said, 'It's alright, Dad. I'm fully clothed. I'm just playing a game on my PlayStation, and I've just crashed my car, so you both can come in.'

Steve opened the door properly, standing aside to allow Lilly to enter first and following her in. He and Lilly stood there for a few moments, looking at John.

John became a bit worried and, in an uneasy voice, asked, 'What's wrong? I haven't been out of my room all day, so I know I haven't done anything.'

Steve seemed nervous; he cleared his throat, smiled and replied, 'We know you haven't done anything wrong, son. I'll get to the point. Lilly and I want to do something, and we want to know if it is alright with you.'

John hadn't seen his dad like this before and was puzzled.

He had a sickly feeling, so he butted in, 'What's up, Dad? Is Ann alright?'

Steve, with a grin on his face, put his hands up to show everything was alright and said, 'Ann is fine, as far as I know. What made you ask that?'

John replied, 'I don't know... It's just that you looked worried.'

Steve answered, 'I'm sorry, I should have come out with it right away. Lilly and I have been dating for a good couple of years now and I want to marry her. Are you alright with that? We're hoping so.'

John laughed, got up from sitting on his bed and, as he was shaking his dad's hand, he said, 'You had me worried then! I knew quite a few months ago.'

Steve looked at Lilly, as John kissed her on the cheek, and asked, 'How did you know, John? We haven't told anyone yet, we wanted to tell you first.'

John answered, grinning, 'I heard the two of you talking in the dining room a few months ago.'

As Steve got hold of Lilly's hand, she said to John, 'I love your dad and I don't want to come between him and his children. So, are you sure you don't mind? Because we will do what makes you happy.'

John smiled and said, 'I'm sure you won't be a wicked stepmother! Now let's have a drink to you and dad. He could do with someone in his life to give him some happiness. I know you will make him happy, and if my dad is happy, so am I.

Now we are family, can I meet your family? I've been looking forward to meeting them.'

Lilly explained, 'Well, I don't have much family. There is only my dad. He lives down south and I'm ashamed to say I haven't seen him in the last couple of years, but I always keep in touch with him by phone. He knows I want to marry your dad. They've met a few times, but it was years ago. My dad said he would like to meet you too. I tell him all about you and Ann.'

John, with a worried look on his face, asked, 'What do you tell your dad about Ann?'

'Oh, I only tell him how well she is doing in the restaurant business with your Aunt Emma,' Lilly replied.

John smiled and said, 'Well done, super step-mum. Now, when can I meet your dad?'

Lilly answered, 'We will have to arrange something.'

John grinned and said, 'Great, when do you think it will be likely to happen? Will he come here?'

'No,' Lilly replied. 'He works and will need to use his holidays to come up for the wedding.'

John's smile disappeared as he exclaimed, 'Oh, you mean I won't see him till the wedding?'

Lilly smiled and said, as she winked at John, 'I think my boss will let me have a week's holiday to take you to meet his soon-to-be father-in-law! My dad is a down to earth type of man. I really think you will like him and you will get on well together. He's a very hard-working man with a warm personality.'

John looked straight at his dad and said, 'Well, Dad, it's up to you. You're Lilly's boss.'

Steve replied, 'I've some important contracts to go over and sign. It's a busy time at work.'

John and Lilly looked at each other, and John said, 'Oh, come on, Dad - you can let Lilly off for a week, you have a pool of PAs to pick from.'

Steve was a bit reluctant, but he didn't want to spoil the moment, so he said, 'Okay, I'll arrange it for next week. One of the flexible secretarial staff can take your place, you'll have a week to show her the files and what the procedures are.'

Lilly looked at Steve and smiled archly as she said, 'Not permanently, I hope and just in your office; definitely not in your life, because I'll soon be your wife.' They all laughed.

A week later a limousine drove up to the large gates of the family home. The driver phoned John and asked him to open the gates. Once that was done, he drove up the driveway and stopped outside the door. The driver got out and opened the back door of the limousine and Lilly stepped out, as John came out of the house carrying a large suitcase. He kissed her on the cheek as she hugged him.

The driver took the case and put it in the boot. Then he held the door open as Lilly and John got into the car. He closed the door and got back in the driving seat.

Lilly asked the driver, 'Did they give you the address in London to take us to.'

He answered, 'Yes, madam. The manager himself put it in the satnav. We will arrive there in about four hours. If you want to stop for something to eat, just let me know, but there is also food and drink in the small cupboard in front of you. Help yourselves to anything you want.'

They stopped once for a bathroom break at a motorway service station and arrived at Lilly's dad's house exactly four hours later. The driver opened the door of the limousine for them to get out. John was expecting Lilly's dad's house to be about the same size as the house he lived in, so he was surprised when he saw the house. It was just a small, semi-detached building with a large garage on the side that was nearly as big as the house.

Lilly was pleased to be home and gave the driver a large tip.

He smiled and said, 'Thank you, madam. Is there anything else I can do for you?'

Lilly smiled and said, 'No, thank you.'

He replied, 'In that case, I will head off now and will come back here to pick you up next Sunday at ten o'clock. If you want to change your plans at all, just phone and make new arrangements with the management.'

Lilly smiled and nodded, then turned and took hold of John's hand. She pushed the gate open and led him up the small driveway to the front door.

She put the key in the door but, before she opened it, Lilly put her finger to her lips, whispering, 'I want to surprise my dad. I haven't told him who I'm bringing home with me; he most likely thinks it will be your dad.'

Lilly opened the door and went in, still holding John's hand.

She shouted, 'Dad? Are you here? I'm home, Dad.'

Though she was smaller than John she stood in front of him, trying to hide him.

Her dad called back, 'I'm in the garage and a bit oily now. Give me five minutes and I'll come into the house.'

They waited a few minutes and he came into the small hallway from a door attached to the garage, wiping his hands with an oily cloth. He was made up to see his daughter. Then he saw John standing behind her and his face changed to a puzzled look but, before he could say anything, Lilly turned sideways so her dad and John could see one another properly.

She blurted out, 'This is John, Steve's son, and he will soon be my stepson.'

John smiled and put out his hand, as Lilly said, 'John, this is my wonderful dad.'

Her dad smiled, looking down at John's hand and then his own hands as he pointed to the door facing and said, 'Take John into the living room, while I go and wash my hands. I don't think the lad would appreciate an oily hand.'

Lilly opened the door facing the garage door, and said to him, 'This way, John' as her dad turned right and opened the door to the kitchen.

When John entered the living room, he thought how close together everything was. There were two easy chairs and a small settee, all facing an old fireplace. In the middle of the room, there was a small coffee table and in the corner of the room there was a TV. The largest thing was the front window, which had flowered curtains on either side of it. Though the house was the average size for a semi-detached house, John hadn't been in one before and he sat there wondering, 'How can anyone live in such a tiny house? Dad's *garage* is three times the size of this room.'

Lilly said, 'Sit down, John.'

John nervously sat on the chair nearest to him; he could see Lilly was made up to be home. She opened a door in the living room that went to the kitchen. John could see her dad, wiping his hands and putting the towel on a worktop. When her dad saw John he smiled, then he walked into the living room and the first thing he did was hug and kiss Lilly, saying, 'I've missed you, Flower.'

Lilly answered, with a big smile on her face, 'I've missed you as well, Dad. I'll have to try and visit you more often.'

As they stopped hugging, her dad looked at John and said, 'Lilly's told me all about you, John, when we talk on the phone. I imagined you to be about five eight, but you're a big, broad lad! Like they say, you're a chip off the old block. How tall are you?'

John replied, 'I'm six four, sir.'

Lilly's dad laughed and said, 'Did someone make me a knight and not tell me? Don't call me 'sir'. My friends call me Sam; I hope you will be one of them.'

John stood up as Sam was talking and offered his hand to him. Sam shook it with both his hands.

John thought, 'What a strong grip Sam has for an old man' as Sam carried on talking, saying, 'I'm afraid I'm a teetotaller, so I don't have any alcohol. Would you like a cup of tea or coffee?'

John replied, 'I would love a cup of tea, thank you.'

Sam sat down, facing John, and smiled. He was looking at Lilly and winked as he said, 'Well, Lilly, you know where the pot and tea bags are kept. I'll have one as well.'

Lilly smiled at her dad and answered, 'I'm a guest in this house too, Dad. Oh, alright, I'll make the tea *and* I'll raid the pantry for some of your favourite cakes. While I'm in the kitchen, you and John can get to know one another.'

Sam winked at him and said, 'We feel like old friends already, don't we, John?'

With that John felt more relaxed and said, 'Yes.' He smiled at Lilly, who was standing in the kitchen doorway. She smiled back at him, then turned and went into the kitchen to make the tea.

Sam asked, 'What do you do for a living, John? I know you and your dad work together in the firm, but I don't know what you do.'

John replied, 'I've been on the board as a director since the age of eighteen. When my dad told me that's what I'd be doing in the firm, I thought I would just be sitting around and giving orders, and it sounded like I'd be important... But no one take's any notice of me, yet. My dad said I have to learn about the firm from the bottom up before I can expect to be making decisions.

So, I have been a janitor, a dishwasher and a waiter and before they would let me be a waiter, I had to be the tea boy for the office, and lots of other jobs since I left school. I've worked my way up to training in Accounts now.'

Sam said, 'Lilly told me you were brilliant at school. I thought you would go to university?'

John answered, 'I could have gone to university, but I like to *do* things - and I wanted to learn all about our firm. Mind you, when they gave me some of the first few jobs I had to do, I thought I should have gone to university then!'

Sam asked, 'So, what do you think of your job now?'

John replied, smiling, 'Well, I count myself fortunate that I don't have to do any of those jobs now… but they still don't take much notice of me in directors' meetings!'

Just then Lilly came in, with the teas and cakes on a tray. She placed them on the coffee table and sat down on the settee facing it. As Sam was sat on the easy chair on one side of the table and John on the easy chair on the other side, she gestured for them to help themselves and they chatted together a little more as they ate.

While they were talking. Lilly's phone rang. She got it out of her bag and answered it, saying, 'Hello, Steve.'

She listened for a little while, then she answered, 'Oh no. Don't worry, I've not even unpacked yet. I can be there in about four and half hours. I'll leave right away.'

She hung up and turned back to John and Sam, saying, 'Sorry, Dad, I have to get back to the office. The so-called PA who was to do my job has messed up. She has got some important files mixed up and they are needed tomorrow morning.'

Sam's face showed his disappointment, but he said nothing and just nodded.

John had stood up with a worried look on his face when he heard his dad's name mentioned but Lilly said, 'John, don't look so worried. It's just office work… Would you mind if I leave you here with Dad? He will be made up to have you stay with him. If you want to come with me, you can, but I've got to go straight away.'

John was relieved when she told them what the phone call was about. He smiled as he answered, 'No, it will be great to spend some time with Sam, he can show me around. That's if he wants to, of course.'

Sam smiled at John and put two thumbs up to him as Lilly phoned for a taxi. The taxi arrived twenty minutes later.

Sam asked with a worried look, 'Are you going all the way in a taxi? How much will it cost? You will have to pay for the taxi's return fare back here as well as the journey up!'

Lilly just laughed and explained, 'Don't worry, Dad, I don't have to pay for it myself. I will charge it to the firm.'

While she waited for the taxi, they finished their tea and cakes.

When it arrived, Sam was upset to see her go so soon and, as he hugged and kissed her on the cheek, he said, 'Please, Flower, try and get back here soon, I miss you.'

Lilly kissed him, got into the taxi and said, 'If I get a chance, I will, but if I can't get time, I'll definitely be back to pick John up at the end of the week. Love you, Dad.' She threw John a kiss as the taxi pulled away.

Sam and John got on well from the start. They talked for quite a while that first evening.

John asked, 'My dad is a bit older than Lilly. Do you mind them getting married?'

Sam replied, 'Age is just a number. I was made up when Lilly started going out with your dad, because when she first left school, she was going out with a boy named Eric Lang. He was no good; he went to jail for really hurting a boy who was a lot younger than him.

I was worried that when he came out he might try to get back in touch with her and lead her astray. So you see, to me your dad is the right person for Lilly.'

John said, 'When I was younger, I had a few friends like that myself, but I don't think any of them went to prison. That could be because they had good solicitors though! Anyway, what were you working on when we got here, Sam? I hope I didn't stop you from doing your job?'

'No,' Sam replied, 'I work for myself. I'm a window cleaner. When Lilly told me she was bringing someone special to see me and that they would stay with me for a week, well, I thought it would be your dad... but I'm pleased to meet you, John.

I have met your dad a few times before. The first time was about five years ago when I was visiting Lilly and she showed me where her office was. I've met him a couple more times since then, but your dad has never been here, so I decided to take the week off. I don't really like letting my customers down, but I felt I must, to be a good host.

What I was doing in the garage is my hobby. Come and have a look.'

Sam led John into the garage through the doorway in the hall. John was surprised to see an old red car. He frowned.

Sam looked at him, asking, 'Don't you like my baby?'

'It's not that,' he explained, 'It's just... I've never been here before, but I'm getting a feeling of déjà vu.'

He looked at the car. It was jacked up at the front and the engine didn't have a bonnet on it. He looked round the garage and hanging on the garage walls above a workbench were a lot of tools.

Sam said proudly, 'This car was built just after the war, it's older than me.'

John stood staring in amazement at it, thinking, 'God, it must be old to be older than him!' Then he said, 'It looks brand new, even the engine is spotless.'

Sam, with a big grin on his face, said, 'I rebuilt it myself.'

John asked, 'How did you do the body work and spray it in this garage? It's a bit small to spray the car in, isn't it?'

Sam smiled and said, 'There's no flies on you, John. I must admit, Lilly got me the car body from a scrap yard. I think the chap who was originally going to rebuild it must have run out of cash. Lilly knows the owner of a bailiff business, who also owns a scrap yard. When she was at school, she worked part time for him. He told her that now and then the bailiffs reclaim cars, some go to auction and some get scrapped. Lilly asked him to keep an eye out for, as she put it, a very old car, for me to spend time on.

Then, imagine my surprise, when a trailer turned up with the body of *this* car. I saw one like it when I was about twelve and it was a vintage car then. It has taken half my life savings and some help from Lilly to pay for it. The body was in the condition you see it now, with just a few small scratches, so I just had to respray them.'

John looked puzzled and asked, 'I thought you said you rebuilt the car?'

Sam answered, his voice going a bit high, 'I *did* rebuild the car. When I got it, nine years ago, I only got the body and two wheels because, though the scrap yard had most of the parts, I just couldn't afford to buy them all at once. The scrapyard - don't laugh but it's called *Honest Joe's* - kept all the parts for me. Lilly helps out with the money sometimes, when I'm short, but the chap who owns the scrap yard who sold the car to me was as good as his word and let me buy the parts over five years. There were some of the parts he didn't have, though, so I had to look round the country for them. Others I had to get made, like the red soft top it has now. Originally it had an old, torn, black one on it. What you see here has taken me seven years to put together. Mind you, I had to do my window cleaning job as well.'

John said, 'You've done a great job on it, but why is the front of it jacked up? And where is the bonnet?'

Sam was pleased that John said he'd done a great job on the car and answered, 'The bonnet is in the shed at the back of the garden. I have an oil leak from the sump gasket and, with the bonnet off and it being jacked up, it gives me more light to see what I'm doing while I'm under it. That makes it easier to get the sump off.'

Then he turned, putting his hand on John's shoulder as he looked John in the eyes, and asked, 'Do you fancy working on it with me?'

John was made up, answering, 'Yes, but if we finish working on it, can I take it for a drive? I have a driving licence.'

Sam was a bit nervous about John driving his car, and said, 'Well, you know, I love this motor car more than myself, it's my baby, so you can drive it, but you understand that I will be in the passenger seat with you. I can't let it out of my sight. If anything happened to it, well, it would break my heart.'

John nodded and said, 'I can understand that.' Then he smiled and continued, 'Well, I'm ready when you are. Let's get started... Have you got a spare pair of overalls I can use?'

Sam laughed as he found a pair and said, 'Yes, but they are my size and will be small on you.'

John put them on, and they were short in the arms and legs. Sam started laughing.

John said, with a smile, 'You can laugh, but I would hate any of my friends to see me now! I'm always smartly dressed when they see me and they would really take the - pardon the language - piss.'

Sam was chuckling as he looked in a cupboard and brought out a camera.

John shouted, 'Don't you dare take a...'

Sam, still laughing, butted in, 'I'm only kidding. There's no film in this camera.'

John laughed too and said, 'Thank God for that.'

Sam put the camera back in the cupboard and they started to work on the car.

Sam was glad of John's help and John was made up to learn about the engine they were working on. They got on well together and spent nearly all week in the garage, working on the car.

When they had put the car back together, John asked Sam, 'Do you enter the vintage car shows?'

He replied, 'No. I know she's good enough, but I don't want anyone climbing all over her. Like I said, she's my pride and joy.'

On the last two days of Sam's holiday, Sam and John took turns driving the car up the motorway and around the country roads. On one trip they stopped at a café Sam knew.

While they were there, John handed Sam his phone and asked, 'Will you take a photo of me in the car? I can't wait to show it to everyone when I get home.'

Sam took the photo, looked at it and then he said, 'Sorry, John, your head and some of your body is missing. I'll take a few more, and we should get a good one out of them.'

When he had taken them, he handed the phone back to John.

As he did so, he said, 'I was hoping to take Lilly to the church in my pride and joy for the wedding, but she said she always wanted to arrive at the church on her wedding day in a Rolls-Royce, even when she was a little girl. I can't begrudge her a wish like that. She asked me not to tell your dad about my car, in case he insisted on using it for the wedding. So please don't show the photo to anyone till after the wedding or I will be in trouble with Lilly.'

John promised, 'My dad won't find out about your car from me.'

When Lilly turned up on the Sunday to take John home, he was surprised because he had enjoyed working on and driving the car so much that he had lost track of the days. He told her how fast the week had gone.

JOHN FINDS OUT ABOUT THE SECURITY

When John got home, his dad asked, 'What do you think of Lilly's dad?'

John said, 'He's a great guy. I enjoyed the week with him but the house is so small! The bedroom I was in was so tiny, I felt like I was in a small box. I must admit I missed my room... Even this chair I'm sitting in is nearly as big as Sam's settee.'

His dad laughed and said, 'The trouble with you is that you're spoilt. I lived in a house just like that till I was eighteen and went to university. Then, when I left uni, I lived in a small room and had to share all the facilities with ten other people in the house. Well, John, how would you like to have to do that?'

He looked at his dad and said, 'It must be awful to live with ten people in a small house?'

His dad laughed again and replied, 'It wasn't that bad. Sometimes we had a laugh.' Then his face took on a serious look, and in a hard tone, he continued, 'I didn't mind university, but before that... Well, I have no intention of going back to live like that again.'

John was puzzled and said, 'When you laughed, Dad, I thought you liked it, but you sound like you hated living that way?'

His dad answered, 'The way you felt in that house, well, I felt like that all my life, till I went to university, and you're right, I couldn't stand living that way. And, like I said, I won't live like that again.' Then his voice softened, and he asked, 'How did Sam entertain you while you were there?'

John thought for a moment; then he answered, 'I helped him work on his old banger. It had a leak from the sump and we sealed it. When we got it going, we spent a couple of days driving it, just to make sure it had no oil leaks.'

His dad, with a serious look on his face, walked across the room and stood just in front of John, saying, 'John, can I ask you to do Lilly and I a big favour?'

He replied, 'I'll do anything for you, Dad, you must know that?'

'Yes, son, I know that,' Steve replied, 'I want you to ask Ann to come to the wedding.'

John went to interrupt but his dad put his hand up, to stop him, and carried on, 'I know Ann doesn't visit you anymore, because you argue about me.'

John stood up. He was as tall as his dad now.

He looked his dad in the face and, in a loud angry voice, asked, 'Have you got people spying on me and Ann?'

His dad took a step backwards, putting his hands on John's shoulders, and smiled as he said, 'No, John, please calm down. I love you and Ann, and after what happened to your lovely mum, I don't want anything to happen to either of you. I have security keeping the both of you safe.'

John sat down again and asked, 'Well, why did you ask me how the week went, when you know everything I did while I was there?'

His dad replied, 'I didn't know what you did while you were there, because I knew you would be safe with Sam. No one knows who you are there and the people who live round there would just think you were one of Sam's relatives. So I gave the security that week off. I hope you understand why I have the security on you and Ann?'

John answered, 'Yes, Dad, but you should have told us. We have the right to our privacy. Now I will feel like someone is watching me all the time.'

His dad explained, 'I didn't want you to feel like that, so I told the security never to let you see them. I'm sorry I upset you, I guess it's time for you to make up your own mind, if you want the security or you don't.'

John said, 'I'm big enough to take care of myself... and I think you should let Ann know about it too.'

His dad answered, 'You know I can't go near Ann. She just screams at me to go away. Would you tell her about the security and explain why I did it?'

John jumped up off the chair, his face red with anger, and his dad backed away with his hands out to calm John down.

John blurted out, 'What the fuck, Dad? You know Ann's not speaking to me, and you want me to drop a bombshell like this on her? You've had a person who has been watching her all these years! She will think I knew about it and I doubt if I would get out of that conversation alive. I already miss my sister. If I tell her this, she might never speak to me again.'

As John started to calm down, his dad interrupted, 'I'm sorry, John, you're right. I think I will just cancel Ann's security without telling her, because to Ann, with the way she feels about me, I suppose she will think that I'm spying on her.'

John said, 'Yes, you're right. If I was Ann, that's the way I would look at it. I think it's the best thing to do. What she doesn't know, can't hurt her.'

His dad walked to John, put his arm around him and pulled John to him, with a funny look on his face.

John tried to push him off, but he wouldn't let go, saying in a Yogi Bear voice, 'Are we still friends, Boo-Boo?'

John tried not to laugh but he had a bit of a smile on his face, as he said, 'Get off, Dad, and act your age.'

When his dad let go of him, John said, 'Listen, Dad, I'll ask Tommy to tell Ann about your wedding, but I'm sorry I just can't tell her myself. Like I said, I miss her, and I want to be friends again like we used to be when we were kids.'

His dad nodded and wiped his eyes.

John could see he had tears in them, as he said, 'I hope you and Ann get close again too, and that one day Ann will come back to me. I love and miss her. I would give the world to get her back.'

His dad suddenly turned to leave the room saying in a low voice as he did so, 'I've got to go, John.'

Before he could even answer his dad had shut the door behind him. John felt bad for losing his temper with his dad.

JOHN PHONES TOMMY

The next day, when John woke up, after getting showered and dressed, the first thing he did was to phone Tommy.

The phone rang a few times and, just as he was about to hang up, a voice answered, 'Tommy Tenant speaking. I'm busy at the moment, leave your name and number and, if I like you, I'll get back to you.'

John said, 'It's me, Ann's brother, John. I would like to speak to you, but don't tell Ann just yet, please. I don't want to upset her. You know my mobile number.'

He put the phone in his pocket and went down to the kitchen to make himself some breakfast.

As he was frying a couple of eggs, a maid came in and, when she saw what he was doing, she said, 'Sit down, John, I'll do that.'

John smiled at her and answered, '*You* sit down and have a break. You've been here since six am. How many times have I told you, I'll do my own breakfast? I'm a big boy now, but thank you, anyway.'

The maid smiled back at John and said, 'Alright, I'll leave you to eat your breakfast in peace.'

As she went to leave the kitchen, his phone rang. As he was getting it out of his pocket, he called the maid back and said, 'You can finish cooking this and eat it, if you would like to.'

He put the phone to his ear as he left the room, calling back to the maid, 'I've got to get this and I can pick up something to eat at the office.' Then he answered the phone, 'John Thomson here.'

The voice at the other end said, 'Hello, John. This is Tommy. You called me?'

He replied, 'Yes, but I would like to talk to you in person, if that's possible?'

Tommy was a bit puzzled and asked, 'Is everything alright?'

John explained, 'Don't worry, everything is fine. I'm just about to do a bit of creeping to you. We've been friends for a long time, and there's something I want you to do for me.'

Tommy said, 'I've got a job on at the moment. Can you meet me at that small café, near where I work, at five pm?'

John asked, 'Is it the one in New Road?'

'Yes,' Tommy answered.

With that, John assured him, 'I'll be there on the dot.'

He arrived at the café at four forty-five. When he walked in, Tommy was already sitting there. John sat down on the other side of the table, facing him.

As he did so, Tommy asked, 'Do you want a tea or a coffee?'

He said, 'I'll have a coffee, please,' as Tommy got up and went to the counter.

While he was sitting there, he looked around and only saw five other people in the café.

He thought, 'If this was one of Emma and Ann's cafés, it would be full this time of day.'

Tommy brought the coffee back and gave it to him.

As he sat down, he smiled at John and asked, 'Well, if you're willing to creep to me, when are you going to start? And what's the big secret you can't tell me over the phone?'

John nervously cleared his throat, took a drink of his coffee and said, 'Dad and his PA, Lilly Blake, well, they are getting married.'

He paused for a moment and Tommy, with a puzzled look on his face, asked, 'And you want me to do what about it, John? I can't check up on...'

John butted in, blurting out, 'No, Tommy, I don't want you to check up on anyone! And I don't want you to do anything about the wedding. What I want you to do, if you're willing, is to tell Ann about the wedding and ask her to come with you to it.'

Tommy smiled and said, 'I know why you want me to do it... Because if you told Ann yourself you would end up in another argument with her. Well, John, what do you think will happen if *I* tell Ann about the wedding and ask her to go to it with me? I'll tell you. The same thing. I'll be in an argument the moment I mention your dad.'

John sounded a bit sheepish as he tried to explain, 'I apologise, Tommy, for being such a coward, but Ann and I are not speaking now. Like you said, I'm afraid if I tell Ann I will get in an argument with her, and it might go too far.

I'm hoping that one day Ann and I will be as close as we were when we were kids. I don't want to just send Ann an invitation to the wedding; I want her to know that we love her and she is very special to Dad and I.'

Tommy could see John was getting upset and said, 'John, Ann told me you two have fallen out over your dad and she was nearly crying, so I think she will want to repair the relationship with you one day. I'll tell Ann about the wedding and your invitation to it, but I won't get into an argument about it. And, by that, I mean I won't be asking Ann to go to it with me. I hope you understand that.'

John said, 'I accept that. I know that mentioning my dad to Ann is like waving a red flag to a bull and you don't know how pleased I am that you're willing to do it for me. If you ever want me to do anything, and I mean *anything*, for you, just let me know.'

Tommy smiled and winked as he said, 'Now you're getting the idea. That's what I call creeping… And that's a big promise, John. Let's hope I never need to use it.' He wanted to change the subject, and said, 'Well, I heard you are a bit of a womaniser, these days. Are you getting serious with anyone yet?'

John's worried look changed to a smile, and he replied, 'I've been out with a few women for a few weeks, and some exclusively, but no one really special, like you and Ann are to each other. I enjoyed myself last week and there wasn't a woman in sight.'

Tommy grinned and replied, 'Yes, I saw San last week and she told me you had phoned her and said you were on holiday with a friend called Sam.'

John was embarrassed at the way Tommy grinned and said 'Sam', so he butted in, 'Don't get the wrong idea, Tommy. When I said I was with Sam enjoying myself, we were working on a vintage car, and Sam is Lilly's dad. I told Gran who he was.'

Tommy laughed and replied, 'I'm just kidding, I didn't get the wrong idea. San told me you and Lilly's dad were working on an old car, and you told San you were in your applecart there.'

John smiled with relief and commented, 'I've nothing against gay people. Live and let live, that's what I say, but I don't want anyone thinking I'm batting for the other side, you know what I mean.'

Tommy laughed and said, 'Methinks the laddie does protest too much.'

John laughed and said, 'F-off, Tommy. Do you want to go for a proper drink?'

He answered, 'I can't, I'm back on a job at ten thirty, that's why I suggested meeting in this café. Mind you, I could have murdered a pint right now, but the job comes first. Talking about jobs, did you and Sam do a good job on the car?'

John was really relaxed now and smiled as he replied, 'We did a great job on it, I'm proud to say. We had to make a gasket for the sump and it didn't leak a bit of oil when we put it back together. And when we finished that, we had to put the front wheels and the bonnet on.'

Tommy asked, 'With it being an old banger, did you drive it?'

John, with a big grin on his face, replied, 'I was made up to drive it! It's a bit of a bone shaker but, for a small, old car, it could really move. The way Sam has rebuilt it, even the engine is spotless. You'd think it's just come out of the showroom.

Sam wanted to take Lilly to the wedding in it, but she wants to go in Dad's Rolls-Royce. Sam asked me not to tell anyone about it, especially my dad, till after the wedding, in case he wants Lilly to go to the wedding in it too. So I promised I wouldn't tell anyone. Oh no! I promised, and I've already told Gran and now I've told you too... But I must admit that I really wanted to tell someone about it and the work I did on it - and show the photo of me driving it. You won't tell, will you?'

Tommy said, 'I don't mix with the people you are friends with and I haven't seen your dad in the last eight years. So, no, I won't be telling anyone.

So you still like speed! If I remember right, you wanted to be a racing driver when you were a kid? Let's see the photo of you driving the car.'

John blushed a bit as he found the photo on his phone and said, 'Well, on the photos I wasn't actually driving then, I was parked up in a cafe... But I had done just over a hundred and twenty miles an hour, on an old airfield that Sam knew and directed me to.'

John handed Tommy the phone. He took it and, as he looked at the photo on it, he went sick inside. His mind flashed back ten years to the road in Spain, with the car hurtling towards him and Ann, and for a moment he just sat there.

John saw the look on Tommy's face and asked, 'Are you alright, Tommy? You've gone white.'

Tommy snapped his mind back to the present and replied, 'I'm fine, I think I must have eaten something that didn't agree with me. You look made up to be in the car.

I get the feeling I've seen this car before, has it always been red?

John answered, 'I had that feeling myself, the first time I saw it, but there isn't one around here. It's just one of those feelings they call déjà vu. Sam said it is the original colour but for the soft top. It was black and damaged, so he had one made in red. He thought it would look better that way.'

Tommy said, 'You're most likely right about it being déjà vu. Will you text me a copy of the photo of you in the car?'

John hesitated. He looked at his phone, then he looked at Tommy and, in a nervous tone and with a look on his face that showed he didn't want to give Tommy it, he asked, 'What do you want it for? You can't show it to Ann. It might somehow get back to my dad and Sam won't be pleased with me because I did make him a promise that I wouldn't show it to anyone.'

Tommy answered, 'It's alright John. I won't show it to Ann or anyone who knows you. I am meeting some old school friends. You have seen them but that was ten years ago in Spain. It's a reunion in two weeks; we haven't seen one another for the last two years. I want to ask them if they can remember seeing a car like it when we were kids - it's just really bugging me where I might have seen it.'

John, who was still nervous, asked 'Tommy, are you sure it won't get back to my dad?'

Tommy answered, 'It won't. I'll tell you what, edit the photo and, dare I say, cut your head off it. Then no one will be able to tell who owns the car.'

John seemed a bit more relaxed and said, 'Sam made a mess of one photo half my head is missing. I'll edit the rest out and text you that photo, but you've got to promise me it won't get back to my dad. I know I'm a hypocrite; I didn't keep my promise to Sam. Please don't let me down, Tommy? I'm best man at the wedding.'

As he was talking, he texted Tommy the photo and Tommy showed him that he had received it.

John nodded and carried on, 'Billy and I have to go for a fitting for our suits in the next couple of weeks.'

Tommy promised, 'I won't let you down, so don't worry. Your dad won't find out from me. When is the wedding? Is it soon?'

John smiled and said, 'It's about three months off.'

Tommy asked, 'If it's that long before the wedding, why are you going for a fitting next week... and why are there two best men?'

John replied, 'Only I'm the best man, but you know Billy! He's a friend of the family, my best mate, and so he's coming to help me in case I lose my bottle. As for the fittings being early, my dad likes to plan things well ahead of time. He says, if things go wrong, you always have time to put things right and so it's the best way to get your plans to work out perfectly.'

When they both got up to go, John said, 'I've got an idea that just might stop us getting into an argument with Ann.'

Tommy pulled the door open and, as he did so, he asked, 'What's your idea?'

John walked out of the café as Tommy closed the door behind them, answering, 'I know Billy wouldn't mind if you tell Ann that he asked you if she would be upset if I came round to give her a message about Dad getting married.'

Tommy said, 'I'm willing to try it but, at the moment, I don't think you stand a dog's chance that Ann will say 'yes' to seeing you once your dad has been mentioned.'

John smiled and said, 'Yes, I think you're right. How about you say instead that Billy asked you to tell her that her dad is getting married, and John would love Ann and you to come. This way you haven't told Ann about the wedding straight out, and if she gets upset, she won't argue with you about it because you're just passing a message on from one of her friends. With a bit of luck, she just might get curious about the wedding, and I'm hoping she might phone me about it.'

Tommy exclaimed, 'A bit of luck? You'll need a lot of luck, but I'm game for anything that will keep me out of an argument with Ann.'

John said, 'Great' and put out his hand to him.

Tommy laughed as he shook it, saying, 'Well, I'll see you around... if Ann doesn't kill me first!'

John smiled as he got into his Jaguar, which he had parked just outside the café. Tommy walked down the road a couple of blocks and went into a building with a sign over the door which read 'Licensed Jameson Detective Agency' with 'No job too small or too big' in smaller letters underneath it.

THE CLARK CASE

When Tommy entered Val's office, he asked, 'Is Mac in the cupboard?'

She laughed and replied, 'I wouldn't like to be you, if he heard you calling his office a cupboard!'

Tommy laughed and said, 'I'd just say it was you who started calling it a cupboard.'

Val replied, 'You're safe this time, he's out on a job. Today's Friday on the last weekend in the month... Aren't you supposed to be on that Clark divorce job tonight?

You'd better be careful; he likes to fight when he's been drinking. Mrs Clark wants us to watch him all weekend this time.'

Tommy replied, 'I know, I'm the one who told you about him.'

'Oh, I thought it was Mac,' replied Val, rifling through a drawer in the filing cabinet, with her back to him.

Tommy said, 'What I didn't tell you is that he was sitting down when he picked an argument with a man who accidentally knocked his table. Good enough, the man apologised, but 'angry-head' Clark wasn't happy and went on about it in a threatening tone. The man told him to shut up in the end.

Have you seen in the films the way they break a bottle on the table and go for the person they are fighting with?'

Val replied, 'Yes, did Clark do *that?*'

Tommy smiled and said, 'Well, yes and no. He jumped up, grabbed the bottle on the table and banged it down on the table, going for the man as he did so... But the bottle didn't break - it just bounced out of his hand, so he went for the man with nothing in his hand. The man just put his own hand in Clark's face and pushed him back down in his seat. With that everyone started laughing, so Clark got up and left the pub.' Then Tommy asked in a serious voice, 'Would you do me a favour, Val?'

She turned round and said, 'Of course. You only have to tell me what you want.'

Tommy showed her the photo of Sam's car and said, 'I'm sure this looks like the car that tried to run us down ten years ago.'

Val looked at the photo, and said, 'It may look like the car, but there are still a few vintage cars like it left. Do you want me to look into who owns it?'

Tommy replied, 'No, I know who owns it - a bloke called Sam Blake. What I would like you to do, if you would, is find out his address in London.'

Val said, 'I'll get onto it in the morning,' writing '*Sam Blake, London*' on a notepad on her desk.

Then she looked up at Tommy, and gave him a map, saying, 'Let's get back to the job. This is a map of where the Clarks' boathouse is and the land around it that belongs to them. Mrs Clark said the boundaries aren't marked out well, but upriver the boundary is where three large streams merge together and turn into the river that the boathouse is on. Mind you, she's the one with the money. She said to go to the boathouse, if we lose him this time. Now, you'd better move yourself. Mrs Clark rang just before you came in and said he's gone upstairs to get ready to go out.'

Tommy replied, 'I'll be there in a jiffy on my bike.'

Val in a surprised voice asked, 'You're going on your motorbike?'

As Tommy went out the back door to the building's shared car park, he laughed and said, 'Well, I wouldn't get far following a car on a pushbike, would I?'

Val shouted after him, 'Alright, smart-arse, I'll see you tomorrow.'

Tommy got his crash helmet out of the boot of his car, which was parked next to his motorbike. He put it on, got onto his bike and pressed the starter. The bike kicked into life. He saw Val looking at him through the window, and waved, pressing the horn as he drove off.

Val said to herself, 'Please be careful, Tommy.'

She gave a little shiver as she thought back to when she was young and went round with bikers on her own bike, until the day she got into a bad skid and was hit by a car as she came off her bike. She was in a coma for a week; when she woke, she had a broken leg, a broken arm and a large cut on her thigh, which had left her with an ugly scar.

Her biker friends had visited her in hospital. The ones who had been in crashes, like her, had told her, 'Don't worry, you won't remember anything about the crash.'

When she got out of hospital, they wanted her to get straight on a bike again, but, unlike them, she remembered everything about the accident; now she hated the thought of anyone on a motorbike. As Tommy left the car park on his bike, she sighed and turned from the window to straighten up her desk. Then she went to the coat hook and put her coat on, to go home.

Just as she shrugged into it, Mac arrived. She smiled as she looked up and said to him, 'What time do you call this to come in? It's the end of the working day!'

Mac looked at her, as he walked past to go to his office, and said, 'I've got to relieve Tommy at 5 tomorrow morning, so I've been getting a few hours sleep.'

Just as he was squeezing past his office door to get into the room, he added, 'Anyway, who's the boss here?'

Val laughed and said, 'The one with a cupboard as an office.'

Mac's face showed he wasn't pleased as he shut the door.

He came out with his notebook a few minutes later and said, 'I've got some expenses for the job I was on last night. Will you type them up tomorrow?

I'll strangle Tommy when he comes in. I know he's the one who started calling it a cupboard. I bet you didn't tell him it's really your office and I swapped out the kindness of my heart.'

Val laughed out loud and replied, 'The kindness of your heart? You've got a swinging brick! You swapped because I told you that I *wouldn't* work in there and have all my filing cabinets with my paperwork out here.'

Mac just smiled, because he knew he was on a loser to get in an argument with Val about the office, and claimed, 'Well, it was still out of kindness.

Oh, by the way, Tommy texted me a photo of a car. He thinks it looks like one that tried to run them down.'

Val nodded and replied. 'I know. He showed me the photo and asked me to look into it. I told him there are still a few vintage cars like it about, but said I would, so I'll ring round first thing tomorrow.'

Mac said, 'Well, I hope he is concentrating on the job he's doing now. I texted him to see if he managed to follow the crafty bastard without losing him. Anyone would think he knows we're following him!

His wife said they had an argument this month and he claimed during it he goes to his boat house every weekend. He told her he is fixing up a woodchipper. He said it was the one he found in the woods last year that she helped him to get into the boat house, and now he says the place is covered in oil and she shouldn't go with him.'

Val raised her eyebrows at him and said, 'When Tommy lost him last time, you said Clark must have spotted Tommy's car following him and yet, when you lost him last week,' she laughed as she carried on, 'you said he didn't spot your car because you're too good at blending in - he's a crafty bastard who was just being careful, so he doesn't get caught.'

Mac pulled a face and said, 'Alright, alright. Well, anyway, Tommy shouldn't lose him this time. I gave Mrs Clark a new mobile phone, told her not to let her husband know about it and to let us know when he's going out.'

Val replied, 'Yes, she called in with the map of where the boathouse is and told me you have given her a phone. She said she didn't know why, because she has her own mobile phone and he doesn't know the number to unlock her mobile. She claimed he can't hear her because she only phones us when he is in the bathroom getting ready.

She says she would know if *he* knew she had employed us, because he's a bully. He wouldn't be able to hold his temper if he found out - he would make her life hell. He has threatened to kill her on more than one occasion. She is terrified and believes that one day he will kill her, so she wants him out of her life for good.' Val continued, while she buttoned up her coat, 'He must be the only person who dresses up to go to work on an oily machine. He must really think his wife is daft.'

Mac replied, 'What he thinks is that she's too scared of him to question what he does. Well, anyway, like I was saying, before I mentioned the phone, Tommy shouldn't lose him this time, because I texted him last night, and told him to follow Clark on his bike and, if he does lose him and can't find him again, then to go to the boathouse to see if he is there. You did give him the map?'

Val answered, with a serious tone in her voice, 'Yes, of course I gave Tommy the map, but why the bike? It's safer in the car. You know I hate him riding that bloody motorbike.'

'Don't worry,' Mac reassured her, 'Tommy is as safe on the bike as he is in his car. He's a careful rider. I know, I've been on the back of his bike with him and I felt quite safe.'

THE LADIES OF THE NIGHT

Tommy kept a good distance on his bike from Clark's car; putting a couple of cars in between them. He had been following the car for about forty-five minutes.

Tommy thought, 'He's going around in circles, but he couldn't have seen me. I've been watching him through the windows of the cars that are between us. It's about this time he's given us the slip in the past.'

So Tommy dropped back, putting three cars between them. Now and then he would drift out to the middle of the road, so he could see Clark's car. He was surprised when they ended up in the red-light district. He knew it was the red-light district because of the way the women were dressed and approached any car that slowed down.

Clark's car slowed to a crawl as it passed the women on the pavement and Tommy didn't want to get too close, so he parked his bike around the corner and took his helmet off as he walked to the corner to watch the car from the end of the road. Women swiftly approached almost all the kerb-crawling cars, so Tommy was puzzled that only a few women started to approach Clark's car. When they did so, one or more other women would get hold of their arms and say something to them, and they would back away from the car.

As the car crawled round the next corner, Tommy put his helmet on, running back to his bike. He rode it to the corner the car had turned down and stopped just before he reached it.

When he got off the bike a couple of women approached him.

One of the women, who looked about eighteen, laughed and said, 'I've never done it on a bike, love, but I think you'd have to take your helmet off first?'

The older woman, who was also laughing, said, 'Take no notice, Sonny Jim. She's got no experience and it shows - it's your trousers you have to take off. I don't mind if you leave your helmet on.'

Tommy took his helmet off to hear what they were saying.

The younger woman laughed, as she pointed at his helmet and said, 'See, he knows when he is getting good advice.'

The older woman, with a grin on her face, said, 'Leave the young man alone.'

Tommy tried to speak but the women were on either side of him, got hold of an arm each and he couldn't get away.

The older woman was going on about showing him a few new tricks, and the younger woman was saying, 'I'm young and can get into positions that will blow your mind.'

Tommy pulled his arms away from the women and claimed, 'I'm a police officer.'

The two women let go, both of them saying, 'Sorry' at the same time.

They backed away, as the older woman said, 'We were only joking. You can take a joke, can't you?'

Tommy rushed to the corner and looked along the road, but Clark's car was nowhere in sight. When he turned round to go back to his bike, he saw the two women were moving swiftly back along the street.

As they passed the other women standing there, they would say, 'Hop it. He's a copper,' and a few more women would move down along the road.

Tommy put his helmet on, jumped on his bike, and turned it around to go after the women. As he got near them, they all stopped.

He pulled up next to them, turned the engine off and, as he took his helmet off, shouted to the women, 'You're alright. I'm not a policeman. I just said that because I was in a hurry. I was following a car and I've lost it now.'

Three older women came towards him. As they got nearer two of the women hung back, but the other came right up to him.

As they did so Tommy thought, 'God, they look angry - and like they could handle themselves.'

He said, 'I'm sorry, ladies, but it was important that I didn't lose that car.'

As the two women who had hung back drifted over towards the kerbside, the one who had come right up to Tommy, a woman who was nearly his height, squared up to him. He thought that when she was younger, she must have been a beautiful looking woman. She had long, wavy, red hair, blue eyes and a lovely figure, but her life must have been hard and it showed in her face, which was now nearly as red as her hair.

She said angrily 'You long piece of shit - you nearly gave us girls a heart attack. You've lost a car? Well, we've lost about ten fucking cars, thanks to you. Didn't you see us waving them away as we started to leave?

I'm alright. I do this for myself, but some of these women have pimps. Your fucking boss might bollock you, but some of the fucking bastard pimps will hurt the girls really bad.'

Tommy said, 'I am sorry, but the girls look like they are doing alright now. You can't have lost much in a few minutes. Can I ask you a question?'

The other three women in the group started to walk away, as the woman who was telling Tommy off calmed down a bit, but said sarcastically, 'Oh yes, we'll tell you *all* about our johns and lose even more fucking work.'

He replied, 'The car I want to ask about isn't one of your clients.'

She asked, 'Then what would he be doing round here if he doesn't want a girl and he's not looking for a fuck?'

Tommy answered, 'I don't know. That is why I'm following him, and I know he's not a client because each time he stops by a girl, you women stop the girls who do go towards his car. I'm wondering why?'

Her voice softened as she answered, 'They call me Ginger so, if you are a copper, it's an easy name to spell for a clever fellow like you. If you're really after that car, well, we don't know who he is, but we think he's a pimp and he's looking for young girls who have just started on the game.'

He shook his head and replied, 'I know he's not a pimp. Seeing we're friends now, my name is Tommy. Why do you girls think he's a pimp?'

Ginger laughed and said, 'To be my friend will cost you money, sonny.'

He smiled, put his hand in his leather jacket pocket and pulled out his wallet. As he opened it, Ginger put her hand in it and pulled out three twenty-pound notes.

She looked at them and handed one back to Tommy, laughing as she said, 'Now we're friends, seeing as I've just given you mates rates. The reason we think he's a pimp - and the worst kind - is, like I said, he goes after young girls who are just starting out and when they get in his car, we never see them again. We think he's got a brothel, and he forces them to work in it.'

Tommy asked, 'Well, why don't the pimps the girls work for do anything about it?'

Ginger, with a serious tone in her voice, answered, 'He knows who to pick. He doesn't pick any of us regular girls that might have a pimp. We think he just gets a kick out of scaring us by driving past.

He picks the girls who stand by themselves, the new girls. If they don't know any of us, they will stand a street away from the regular girls and we know he picks those girls up.'

Tommy asked, 'Why don't you girls warn them?'

Ginger answered, 'Just look along the road. Do you see any Mother Teresas among us girls? And do you think if one of us did tell them, they would believe it? They would think we were just trying to get them to move away from a good place to work... And now, Tommy-lad, our friendship has just run out, like your money.'

Tommy smiled at her and, as he put his helmet back on, he said, 'Well, your friendship may cost money but mine doesn't, so you can still be my friend.'

As he started his bike up, he looked at her and waved and, as he drove off, she waved back, shouting, 'I'm here till five in the morning, so if you get lonely, come back and see me.'

Riding away, he only heard 'till five'. He rode round the area looking for the car till it got dark. He was just passing where he had spoken to Ginger, when he saw her being chased by a man holding something in his hand that shined when the lamp light hit it. The other women were running in the opposite direction. Tommy stopped his bike as he saw Ginger go into an alleyway, with the man close behind her.

He jumped off his bike and ran up the alley after them. He saw the man pushing her up against the wall, with one hand round her throat. In his other hand he had a flick knife, which he opened by her face. In the dim light, Tommy saw blood was already coming from Ginger's lip as the blade flashed out, stopping just by her eye. Tommy was moving as fast and quietly as he could behind the man. He grabbed him by the hair with his left hand and, as he pulled the man's head back, Tommy clenched his right fist and punched the man as hard as he could in the back three times, where he thought the kidneys were. The man groaned and dropped the flick knife, falling to his knees.

Ginger managed to pull herself from in front of him and as she did so, she said, 'You fuckin' horrible bastard, you've broke the heel of my best shoes.'

Then, as she kicked him in the side as hard as she could, she said, 'I told you Ricco was still looking after us, and he wouldn't like it if you tried to move in on his business. Fuckin' kill him, Ricco.'

At this the man started struggling to feel round for his knife, as Ginger just turned and ran off down the entry. Tommy still had hold of the man's hair and was stunned for a moment, at what Ginger had done and said. As the man struggled, Tommy realised he was now in real danger, so he banged the man's head into the wall that they were facing twice, as hard as he could. The man slumped to the floor. Tommy was worried in case he had killed him. He bent over the man and felt for a pulse in the man's neck. He was relieved when he found one. Then, having checked, he swiftly walked away.

He took his mobile out, phoned 999, and said, 'I've just seen a man in a bad condition. He looks like he's been beaten up. He's just off Juno Street, in the alleyway there.'

Then he went back to his bike. As he rode away, he hoped the man didn't see who he was and wouldn't recognise him if they met again.

Tommy rode round a bit to see if he could find Ginger, to find out what she meant when she let on he was her pimp. He passed Juno Street a couple of times till he saw an ambulance stop by the alley. In the lamp light, from the bottom of the street, he could see the paramedics helping the man. As they got him to the ambulance the man suddenly pushed them away and ran back into the alley. With that, Tommy knew the man was okay. He drove around looking for Mr Clark's car for a little while longer, but there was no sign of it.

At twelve o'clock he decided it was gone. He stopped to check the map that Val had given him and then he headed for the boathouse. It was in the country and surrounded by woods.

As he drove down some dirt track road he thought, 'Mrs Clark said it was in the woods - this is more like a forest!'

When the road came to the river, it turned and ran along the side of it, till it came to a bend. Tommy stopped again to check the map. When he saw that the map showed the boathouse was a mile further along the river, he carried on driving for a little while but, when he was half a mile away, he got off his bike and pushed it for a quarter of a mile. He then put his helmet in the carrier and hid his bike in the bushes.

He had an app on his phone to find his bike, but he was worried in case his phone lost power, so he took a pen knife out of his leather jacket and, as he walked back to the road, he cut a small mark on each tree he passed. When he got to the road he looked around, picked up four large stones and placed them on the side of the road where his bike was hidden.

He walked the rest of the way to the boathouse; he was surprised at how large it was. The river, which was about ten metres wide, ran through the middle of the house. It had large doors on both sides, so that a boat could enter or sail right through it if the doors were open.

When Tommy first saw the house, he thought no one was in there. It was all closed up; all the windows had metal shutters over them.

He went round the part of the house on his side of the river, making sure he stayed hidden in the bushes. When he came to a small clearing just in front of the house, he saw Mr Clark's car. It was parked there, by the front door, so he started to creep up to one of the windows, causing a security light to come on.

He stepped quickly back into the bushes, because Mrs Clark had told them that the security cameras sent pictures to her husband's laptop. Tommy continued round the house on his side of the river. After the light came on he made sure he stayed well-hidden in the bushes, until he found a spot right on the edge of the river, where the security lights couldn't pick him up as he went to the house.

Once he was there, he made sure he stayed close to the house, so he wouldn't be caught by the security lights and cameras. As he moved from shutter to shutter, trying to see what was going on inside, all he could see through the small gaps was that the lights were on in some of the rooms.

Tommy hung around, watching the door that the car was parked by till two am, and then he texted Mac: *Clark is in there, but I can't see anything. TT*

Mac texted back: *We know he's staying all weekend, so go home. I'll get there at about five in the morning, good night.*

It was now pitch black and Tommy was glad he had remembered to bring his torch, but he couldn't use it yet, in case he was seen, so Tommy had to find his way to the road in the dark. He tripped a couple of times on the way to get his bike. Once he was sure he wouldn't be seen, he took the torch out and turned it on. He walked for about fifteen minutes and, just as the torch lit up the four stones on the side of the road, the app on his phone started to make a low beeping sound. As he got nearer to his bike, the sound from the app went a bit louder and faster. Tommy turned it off, got his bike out of the bushes, put his helmet on and rode home.

When Tommy got home, he took a small, solid chain out of a toolbox on the side of his bike and chained his bike to the large tree that stood in front of his house; he tugged on the chain to make sure it was secure. Then he opened the gate and walked up the small garden path to his terraced house. When he opened the front door, he thought, 'My whole house could fit in a couple of rooms in that boathouse.'

He went straight to the small kitchen and made himself a cup of cocoa, which he took upstairs and drank. He took his phone out of his pocket and sat on his bed for a time, looking at the photo of the red car that John had texted him. After a while he put his mobile phone on charge and had a shower to get the dirt that he had picked up while he was moving around in the bushes off him, and then he got into bed.

He didn't sleep well. He tossed and turned, as he dreamt the red car hit him and Ann. Ann was falling over the edge, screaming at her dad; her dad was laughing as Tommy grabbed for her, and then the both of them were falling. The red car kept changing colour, from red to black and back to red, following them even as they fell - it was going to hit them again. Then he was fighting with the man in the alley and Ginger was lying on the floor covered in blood; he was struggling with the man and could hardly move, and the man punched him in the face.

He banged his head on the headboard and woke up in a fright. When he realised he was in bed, he untangled himself from the bed clothes and sat on the side of the bed, remembering bits of the nightmare as he did so. Then he thought of Ginger and was worried about her, and also what she had said as she ran away. In the end he got up. It was three forty-five; he had only been asleep for forty minutes, but he knew he wouldn't be able to go back asleep. He quickly got dressed, got his bike and drove back to where he had last seen her, though he didn't really think he would see her after the man had attacked her.

GINGER TELLS TOMMY A STORY

After a short while riding round the red-light district, Tommy was surprised to see Ginger getting out of a car. As it moved off, she blew a kiss after it and, when she saw Tommy coming up to her, she grinned at him.

He stopped and turned his bike off, saying in an angry voice, 'I didn't think you would be here. You must have some bottle. Anyway, I would like a word with you. Now, how much will it cost me this time or do I still get 'mate's rates'?'

She knew why he was angry and said, 'I know I shouldn't have let on that you were Ricco, my pimp, but Clancy is a coward who only came after me because Ricco hasn't been seen around here for a while. I shouted Ricco's name because Clancy couldn't see who you were. Ricco quite often dresses in his bike gear. You're quite safe and we are too now, because he won't come near me or Betty or Grace, while he thinks Ricco is back on the scene, because Ricco is known as a nasty, jealous bastard. He's been in prison for GBH.'

Tommy asked, 'Is he in prison now? Is that why he's missing? If he is, this Clancy fellow won't be fooled for long and that could put me and your girls in danger.'

Ginger looked serious and her voice hardened as she answered, 'He's not in prison and you needn't worry about us girls. Ricco won't be back, but Clancy will think he's still around after what you did to him earlier on.'

Tommy was no longer angry and asked, 'Well, where is he? And how do you know he won't be back?'

Ginger replied, 'I told you, Ricco was a nasty bastard, and me and the other three girls used to get beaten up by him all the time. He would always hit us where it wouldn't show - mainly in the stomach - and he would say that it did two jobs, kept us in line and made sure we couldn't have a baby.'

Tommy butted in, 'You said Betty and Grace. That's only three of you. Who's the fourth one?'

Ginger replied, in a softer tone, 'Alice. But, well, Alice is only sixteen now - she was just turned fifteen when she left home and Ricco got his claws into her and from the first month with fucking Ricco, all she wanted to do was to go home. So, when I knew Ricco wouldn't be around anymore, I made sure she did.'

Tommy frowned, because he was still puzzled, and asked, 'You keep saying Ricco won't be back, and he's not in prison. Do you know where he is and why he won't come back?'

She smiled and said, 'I think you were telling the truth about not being a copper. So I will tell you a little story, though of course it's not true. And anyway, even if it were, I can tell the police other stories too - like the one about you committing GBH against Clancy, so just remember that.

Ricco always beat us up when he wasn't happy with the money we brought in. Well, some weeks ago I walked into his room to find him beating up Alice. She is only small and slender; she didn't want to go to a man we call 'the Ripper'.

Ricco knew what he's like - the bastard is a sadist, but he is a rich bastard and paid Ricco a lot of money to do what he wants to us. I've been with him, and I was in hospital for a week after he had finished with me.

Alice was crying and he was punching her in the stomach. I was terrified and angry at what he was doing to her; I was afraid for her and I suddenly heard the words coming from my mouth. I don't know how, but I was shouting, 'Leave her alone, you bastard.'

With that he threw Alice across the room. She banged her head on the wall and was knocked out. Then he turned, picked up his baseball bat and came at me, but his foot caught in the kids' clothes that he wanted Alice to wear. He tripped and fell at my feet.

After that I wasn't going to let him touch any of us girls again, so I put Alice in her room and locked the door. Later on that night I let her out and told her Ricco had left her two hundred pounds to keep her mouth shut about him, and had said she was to go home as she was no good to him. She was too frightened of him to believe me till I gave her the money and a suitcase with her clothes in it. I even had to go with her to the station and see her onto the train.'

Tommy said, in a puzzled voice, 'That doesn't tell me where Ricco is and why he won't be back.'

Ginger smiled and winked at Tommy as she said, 'I'll just tell you this, there was a lovely, large, heavy, brass ornament of the three monkeys. He said it was for us girls. He'd had the words under the monkeys changed to read: 'see nothing, hear nothing, say nothing'. I just thought he would like a closer look at it.

Betty and Grace help me clean the brass ornament and the rest of the… rubbish out of the house. Now you know we're all safe.'

Tommy said, 'Yes - I now have a good idea why he won't be back, but I'd like to be sure that Clancy doesn't know who I am. I don't want him coming up behind me one dark night. I'd like to go somewhere I can casually bump into him, to see if he recognises me.'

Ginger replied, 'He won't recognise you, I'm sure. He will be round tonight at ten, that's when he's always here to make sure his girls are working. You can see him then. I'll be here as well, so don't let on you know me.'

Tommy said, as he put his helmet on and started his bike, 'Thanks. I'll be back if I'm not busy. Good night... or should I say good morning?'

With that he moved off. Ginger just smiled and blew him a kiss.

SAM'S ADDRESS

Tommy didn't get much sleep. When he woke up and looked at the clock on his bedside cabinet, later that same morning, it said eight-fifty. He stood up and did a few stretches, like he did every morning, then he picked up his mobile phone and unplugged it from the cable that was charging it.

He looked at the photo of the red car again, then he texted the photo to Sergeant Torres and wrote: *Sarge, this car is the same as the car that ran us down. I'm sure of it. Could you show this photo to the few people who saw the car on the road that day? Hope to hear from you when you get a chance, best wishes, TT*

He got dressed and had a quick breakfast. He checked the time as he left his house; it was nine thirty. He took the chain off his bike, got on it and rode to the office. He went round the building to their car park, parked his bike next to his car and then took his helmet off and put it in the boot of his car.

When he went into the office, Val was sitting at her desk with the phone to her ear. She nodded to Tommy. He waved back in acknowledgement, as he went up to a cupboard and took out a jar of coffee.

He held it up so Val could see it and mouthed, 'Would you like a cup?'

She nodded again, still speaking on the phone. Tommy made a pot of coffee, and he poured her and himself a mug of it. Just as he put the mug in front of her, she put the phone back on the receiver.

She reached for the mug and, as she went to pick it up, Tommy asked, 'Any news about Sam Blake?'

Val was a bit sharp with her reply. 'At least give me a chance to have a drink. I've been on the phone since I got in this morning and that's all thanks to you.'

She picked the mug up and, as she started drinking it, Tommy said, 'I'm sorry, Val. I was being a bit rude. I should have at least let you get yourself settled before I jumped in with a question, but here's another one anyway, why thanks to me? What did I do?'

Val took a drink and put the mug on her desk, smiling as she said, 'No, Tommy. I'm sorry - it's just been one of those days when nothing goes right and I didn't sleep too well last night.'

Tommy butted in, 'Ditto.'

Val looked at him, gave a knowing smile and carried on, 'I've been all this time on the phone trying to get information about Sam

Blake. He's not a member of any vintage car club. The only thing I could find out was his address. It's 102 Station Road, London. He is a member of Green Flag, the roadside breakdown company. With a vintage car like he has, I thought he'd be in one of the clubs for vintage cars and I've spent this morning up to now ringing every one I could find.'

Tommy looked at Val and said, in a serious tone, 'That's strange. You'd think he would be proud of his car, unless he has a good reason to keep it out of sight.'

Val got up off her chair and went round her desk to Tommy.

Standing facing him, she put her hand on his shoulder and spoke to him as if she was his mother, saying, 'Look, Tommy, we all know you have been looking for a car like this for some years, but don't get your hopes up too soon just because he doesn't show his car in these clubs. It doesn't mean it's the car you're looking for.

Just think - would *you* hold onto the car if you'd committed a serious crime with it? I'm sure there are quite a few old car owners who like to keep their cars to themselves.'

'Yes, I suppose so,' Tommy replied, 'but he might have got it off the person who did it.'

Val shook her head and said, 'Tommy, listen to yourself. You are talking as if you know it's the car. Yes, of course, check it out... but don't convince yourself before you have found out for sure that this *is* the car.'

He replied, 'I know you're right, Val, but I've just got this weird feeling in my gut that it is the one - still, I'll take your advice. I know you always put me right. Anyway, what time does Mac want me to relieve him?'

Val answered, 'He said he would stay there for a twelve-hour shift, so you won't be needed till five this afternoon. He took a one-man tent but said to tell you to take some rations to last you till five in the morning.'

Tommy looked thoughtful and, as he put his mug down on the small worktop where the kettle was, he said, 'It's about 230 miles to London. I wonder if I could make it there and back on my bike in time to relieve Mac?'

Val was annoyed and said, 'No, you can't make it in time - and to try it on your bike is far too dangerous!

Like I said, we know how you feel about it and we are willing to help you, but this job comes first - it's our bread and butter. So I don't think Mac would be too pleased if you go off to London chasing a nightmare by yourself.

You know Mac, Jacko and Sergeant Torres have been checking things out for you when they have any free time.'

Tommy could see she was annoyed and the stress in her voice told him she was worried about him going on his bike.

He said, 'You're right, Val. It is a nightmare and to sort it out it will take a little more time. And, no, I don't think Mac would forgive me if I let him and the Sarge down after all they have done for me. Instead of going to London, I'll go home and try to catch up on my sleep.'

Val, who was still standing facing him, smiled, saying, 'That's a great idea, Tommy.'

He leaned forward, putting his hand on her shoulders as he kissed her on the cheek and whispered in her ear, 'You're like a mother to me. See you later, Mum!'

Then he turned and quickly walked out the office, as Val called after him, 'You what? I'm not old enough to be your mother!' but with a big smile on her face.

She went to the window to see if he took his bike. When he reached the parking lot, Tommy looked up at the window because he knew, if he mentioned his bike to her, she would be watching him get on it with a disapproving look on her face. He waved to her and pointed to his car as he walked toward it. She nodded and smiled as he got in it, watching him as he drove out of the car park and headed home.

When he got into the house, he made himself a hot drink and sat in his living room to have it, while studying the photo of the red car on his phone. He finished his drink and sat there for about fifteen minutes more, looking at the red car.

Just as he put the phone in his pocket and got up to wash his mug, his phone vibrated and beeped. He got it out to see what the text said.

It read: *Hi, Tommy. I'm in France at the moment, on a week's holiday. I get home on Tuesday. I will ask around as soon as I get home, but it's been nearly ten years, I doubt if it's the car that tried to run you down. I'll be surprised if it is still around; it has most likely been broken up for parts. Hope to see you soon, Sarge.*

Tommy texted back: *Thanks, Sarge. I hope someone can say if it looks like the car. I'm on a case right now but I will get over to see you as soon as I can. TT*

Then, as he pocketed his phone again, he yawned and thought, 'I better get some sleep. I'll have to stay awake all night tonight.'

He went upstairs to his bedroom, took the phone out of his pocket, set the alarm for two thirty that afternoon and put it on charge again. He placed it on his bedside cabinet and got into bed. He had another nightmare about the car and, when the alarm woke him, he was covered in sweat. He knew he had dreamt about the car, but he couldn't remember exactly what had happened in the dream. He was still thinking about the car while he got dressed.

THE BOATHOUSE

Before he left the house, Tommy got a large, fibreglass carrier that fit onto the back of his bike out of a cupboard. He packed it with some warm clothes, a large thermos flask of soup and a smaller flask of coffee. Once outside, he put the carrier in the boot of his car and drove to work.

When he got to the office car park, he put the gear lever into neutral, turned the engine off and freewheeled to his bike, to park. He didn't go into the office because he didn't want Val to go on at him to use his car. He looked up at the office window to see if she was looking out. Then he took the small carrier off his bike, exchanging it for the larger one in the boot of his car; quietly fitting the carrier onto the bike. Then he took his helmet out and put it on. He pushed the bike out of the car park and, when he reached the road, he got on and rode the bike to the bend in the river.

Once there, Tommy stopped, got his phone out and opened the app that allowed him to trace Mac's phone. Then he drove his bike for another mile towards the boathouse, stopped again and looked at his phone. He could see Mac's phone was in the bushes, just in front of the clearing facing the front door of the boathouse. Tommy pushed his bike over to where Mac was and, when he was about a hundred metres from Mac, he hid his bike in some other bushes and looked at his watch. It was now four forty pm. He quickly texted Mac: *I'm here, where are you? TT*

Mac texted back: *I'm in line with the door, with his car parked on my right.*

Tommy knew where the door and car were and headed straight through the bushes to them. Within a few minutes, he was with Mac.

Mac said, 'Nothing happening here. Or at least, you can't see a thing. We'll just have to watch and get some photos when he comes out with his lady friend. I've set up some movement monitors around the clearing and one will go off if the door opens. So, in case you fall asleep,' he said, as he handed Tommy a small, plastic device, 'put this in your ear. I have given it a good cleaning. If you do fall asleep and the door opens, it will wake you. If you get a fright, try to remember where you are and be quiet.'

Tommy asked, 'How come we've only got one earpiece between us?'

Mac replied, 'I've got all this new gear on a trial period before I buy it.'

As he was talking, he moved through the bushes; Tommy followed.

Mac came to a large tree, put a hand on it and reached up into the foliage, where he touched a camera and said, 'This will take photos when the door is opened. They won't be as good as the camera with the telescopic lens, but this camera has night vision. It will send pictures to the computer in the office.'

Tommy nodded and asked, 'Where's the tent?'

Mac took three steps back, towards a bunch of bushes. He parted them and in the middle was a small one-man tent. In front of it was a large camera with a telescopic lens, mounted on a tripod pointing at the front door.

Mac said, 'The camera can swing round to cover the whole front of the house.' Then he asked, 'Did you bring some food and coffee? Oh, and I hope you have got some warm clothes with you?'

Tommy replied, 'Yes, I've brought some supplies. I was here last night, remember, and it was bloody cold. So I've got all my warmest clothes for tonight. Well, now we're at this boathouse, what time did his wife say he gets home?'

'She said he usually gets in about two, or around that time,' replied Mac, 'but don't look so worried, I'll relieve you at five am, if he doesn't make a move till then.'

Tommy asked, 'If she knows he's here with his women, why doesn't she just take the photo of him and his fancy woman herself?'

Mac answered, 'She needs us because he said, 'he would never let her go.' She also said he's a bully and she's terrified of him. In an argument they had, he said he would kill her before he would let her go. She believes him. So can you imagine her standing out here with a camera? If he saw her, he most likely would kill her.

Anyway, if everyone did it themselves, we wouldn't be needed and you like your job, don't you?'

Tommy's face went red, as he answered, 'You know I do. I guess I wasn't thinking how dangerous it would be for her.'

Mac said, 'Your mind is on the car that you texted me about. Listen, I understand how you feel about it but you have to put it out of your mind while you are out on a job. You could put yourself in danger if you're not concentrating on what you are doing.'

Then Mac pointed to a tree with a large bunch of bushes round it, just behind the tent, and said, 'Go and get your bike, you can hide it in there.'

Tommy touched the app on his phone as he started walking in the direction of his bike. When he reached it, he moved some bushes to make a path, so he could pull the bike out. He pushed it to where Mac had suggested. When he got there, he put his bike in the bushes and lent it against the tree. Then he unclipped the carrier box off his bike and went back to the tent with it.

Mac was ready to go. He had a haversack on his back and was looking at his phone, as he said to Tommy, 'I hope I can find my car with this app, I'm completely lost in this forest.'

Tommy replied, 'They say it's a wood, not a forest, but I'm with you. I think it's a forest as well, so you'd better be careful where you walk while you are looking at your phone, there are some large holes about.'

Mac answered, 'You needn't tell me. I know - I nearly drove down one, when I was parking my car in the bushes!'

As Mac turned to go, he said, 'I hope he'll come out soon, and I don't have to come back here. I'm not a country person. Anyway, I'm off. See you tomorrow morning at five… if I have to.'

Tommy nodded and said, 'Okay. I'll still be here, unless he makes a move. If he does, I'll text you, to save you coming back here.'

Mac nodded his thanks and then headed away through the bushes.

Tommy put his carrier box by the side of the camp seat and took a large, hooded over-jacket out of it. He put the jacket on and settled down to watch the house. He sat on the small, folding camp-seat, which was placed just behind the camera and in front of the tent. As the time went by, and nothing more happened than the birds chirping in the trees, he'd stand up and stretch as he yawned. Every now and then, he would walk up and down for a few minutes in between the camera and his folding seat, all the time keeping an eye on the house.

After several hours of surveillance, he put his earphones on, but with only one of the earpieces in his ear to listen to his music. He put the earpiece for the movement monitors in the other ear. Looking at his watch, he saw it was one-fifty am. He sighed, reached down into his carrier box and took out the large flask to pour himself some soup into the cup from the flask.

He held the cup up to his nose to smell it, as he said to himself, 'I love the smell of oxtail soup.'

After he finished drinking the soup, he sat where he was for quite a while but then he wanted to lean back, so he moved his seat and the camera to a tree where he could still see the house and he would be hidden from view. Then he sat down and rested his back against the tree.

It was about ten past three in the morning, as he was starting to get sleepy, that the earpiece went off and startled him into life. He leaned forward and looked through the eyepiece of the camera. The door wasn't open and no-one was in sight. He angled the camera to check the house and then the clearing with the car in it. As the camera moved onto the car, he saw a fox running from it into the bushes.

He muttered to himself, in frustration, 'A bloody fox.'

He sat back, took his phone out of his pocket and spent a while looking at the photo of the red car with a frown on his face.

He said to the photo, 'The first chance I get, I'm going to London to check you out. I'll even go to Spain if I have to.'

Then he put the phone back in his pocket and settled down to wait for Mac to take over from him.

Mac turned up at four forty-five am, as Tommy was packing his carrier.

Mac asked, 'Any sign of life from the house?'

Tommy replied, 'No, not unless you count a fox. It's hard to believe that he, or anyone, is here.'

Mac smiled and said, 'He would have to have two cars with the same number plates to not be here.'

Tommy finished off packing while Mac unpacked his haversack into the tent.

Tommy handed him back the earpiece, as he said, 'I've cleaned it and I can confirm it works.'

Mac said. 'Keep hold of that earpiece, I've got another one. I paid for all the gear today.'

When Tommy was ready to leave, he bent down to pick up his carrier and Mac sarcastically said, 'Well, I'll just sit on the grass and draw pictures of them if they come out then.'

Tommy stood there with a puzzled look on his face for a moment; then it dawned on him, and he said, 'Oh, sorry, Mac, I'm half asleep...'

Mac grinned, as he interrupted, 'Well, you're awake now, Tommy-boy, so where are the camera and seat?'

Tommy pointed to the tree where he had been sitting and said, 'They're just behind those bushes, in front of the tree. I put them there, so I had some support for my back.'

Mac smiled, patted Tommy on his back and said, 'A broad back like this and you need support?'

Then he looked serious and continued, 'Tommy, I know you have been thinking about the red car in that photo - try to put it out of your mind. As soon as this job is over, I'll give you some time off to look into it... and you know we will help you when you need us. So, like I said, try to put it out of your mind for now and get some sleep. I'll text you if you need to come back tonight.'

Tommy, as he lifted his carrier, said, 'It's been with me ten years now, but I'll do my best to put it out of my mind. Of course I know you'll be there if I need any help. See you at five, if he doesn't go home as usual.'

Mac went to the camera and Tommy walked to his bike. Once there, he attached the carrier to it, then he pushed it through the undergrowth, back the way he had come. Now and then it was really rough going, and he and his bike nearly fell a couple of times. When he got about three hundred metres from the boathouse, he pushed the bike towards the road and, when he got to the road and thought his bike wouldn't be heard, he got on it and rode it home.

After Tommy pulled up outside his house, he took the chain out of the toolbox on the side of the bike and chained the bike to the tree. Then he unclipped the carrier off the back of it, took it into the house with him and put it in the cupboard. He took his helmet off, placed it on top of the carrier and closed the cupboard door. Then he took his phone out of his pocket and looked, again, at the photo of the car.

He started to dial Val at the office but then he remembered that she wouldn't be there because it was Sunday. So he had some breakfast and went upstairs, putting his phone on charge while still looking at the photo of the red car.

Then he said out loud to himself, 'I've got to put it out of my mind for now.'

He threw the bedclothes to one side as he got into bed. He was so tired that, even though he was still thinking about the car, he went into a deep sleep right away and slept through till the alarm woke him at two thirty in the afternoon. He got up and checked his phone to see if Mac had texted him. He had; it read: *Clark left at twelve, but no one was with him. If he's got a woman in there, he must be letting her stay. I've packed everything up. I've told Mrs Clark. She said she will let us know if he says he is going out before the weekend. This will let us concentrate on some of our other jobs till next weekend. See you in the office tomorrow.*

CHECKING UP ON CLANCY

Tommy texted Ann: *Do you fancy meeting in the Red Lion tonight, about six? xx*

Almost immediately Ann answered. Her text read: *I can make four thirty at the Red Lion if you can. I can't wait to see you, love you. xxx*

Tommy had a big grin on his face as he read the last part. Then he went through his usual routine to wake himself up. Once he was feeling more alert, he suddenly thought of Ginger and the pimp Clancy. So he quickly changed into his bike clothes, drove over to the red light district and rode slowly round the area where Ginger worked, hoping he would see her, even though he thought she might not be out at this time of day.

After a short while driving around, he was surprised to see her coming out of a shop with a bag full of groceries. At first, he wasn't sure it was her. She was in a smart, plain dress, flat shoes and she had her hair tied back and no makeup on, which was why he nearly didn't recognize her.

He stopped his bike and shouted, 'Ginger!'

She stopped, looking towards him with a frown on her face, then, when she saw who had shouted her name, she smiled and walked over to him. As she did so, some of the other women got together, and started talking and looking at them.

Tommy took his helmet off as she approached. He was blushing. Ginger pointed at his face and burst out laughing.

Tommy said, 'I didn't think you would be out this time of day.'

Ginger, still laughing, managed to say, 'I have a life, you know? And I have to eat, like everyone else.'

Tommy replied, 'Okay' as he took his wallet out.

That made her laugh even louder, and she said, 'You don't need that now. Put it away - we are the best of friends! What do you want to know now? I told you, Clancy comes about ten thirty.'

Tommy replied, 'Yes, I know you have told me, but I just wanted to know if it is every night, because I don't want to keep turning up all the time, looking for him. I'll look like a pervert.'

Ginger said, 'He's here every night. Even last night, though he didn't come near me and my two friends. It's gone round all the girls how Ricco beat him up. He's not a pretty sight, thanks to you. You've done me a big favour.'

Ginger's face took on a serious look, as she continued, 'So I asked around the girls about the car you were following. A couple of them said they saw him pick up a young blond-haired girl, two streets away from where you saw me on Friday when you were following him. She hasn't been seen since.'

Then Ginger smiled, leaned forward and kissed him full on the lips. She laughed, walking away, as all the women started to catcall at them.

His face went blood red and he quickly put his helmet on.

He thought, 'I hope Ann doesn't hear about this, I'd better get a move on.'

He checked the time and went home, changed quickly and got a taxi to meet Ann at the Red Lion. On the way there, he worried about the girl that Ginger had told him about.

When he walked into the pub and saw Ann, his face changed to a smile. She was sitting at their favourite table, watching the door and, when she saw him, she couldn't help but smile. There was a glass of lemonade in front of her and a pint of beer for Tommy.

He sat down facing Ann and said, 'I'm on the coke. I've got to go on my bike tonight. I've got a job to do.'

Ann said, 'I'm the same. That is why I wanted to meet you now. I've got to be in the local restaurant at nine tonight to help the chef. What time can you stay till?'

Tommy replied, 'I can drop you off at the restaurant, if you like?'

Ann said, 'I've just had my hair done, you're not on your bike, are you?'

Tommy laughed and said, 'I wouldn't ride my bike in these clothes! We can get a taxi together at eight and you will be with the chef by nine.'

They spent the afternoon talking. Every now and then Tommy would think of the photo of the red car and go quiet.

Ann asked, 'Have you got something on your mind?'

Tommy didn't want to tell Ann about the car, so he said, 'I'm worried about a young girl who is missing. I was told about her on this job we're working. I'm hoping she will turn up.'

Then Tommy smiled and changed the conversation, asking Ann about the restaurant.

They chatted till about eight, when Ann looked at her watch and said, 'It's been great being here with you, but I'm sorry to say it's time to call the taxi, darling.'

They held hands as they left the pub and got into the taxi.

Once there, Ann cuddled up to Tommy and whispered, 'I wish we were going to your house.'

He smiled and put his arm round her, pulling her as close as possible, as he kissed her and whispered back to her, 'Me too. I hope we find time soon.'

She gave him a long, lingering kiss as the taxi stopped at the restaurant. She got out and, as she was about to enter the restaurant, they both threw each other a kiss. He watched her as she turned and went inside.

The taxi carried on to Tommy's home. As soon as he entered the house, he changed into his bike gear, then he got on his bike and rode to where Ginger and the rest of the girls did their trade. There were quite a few women around and, about a hundred yards up the road from Ginger, there was a man with a large plaster on his forehead and two black eyes. As soon as Tommy saw him, he knew it was Clancy.

He drove past Ginger and straight up to the pimp. At the sight of the bike, Clancy backed away behind some women he was with and could hardly be seen. Tommy stopped his bike and took his helmet off. When Clancy saw Tommy's face, he pushed one of the women forward.

She said, 'Do you want to have a good time, mate?'

Tommy replied, 'No thanks, love. I'm just lost. I'm looking for...'

Clancy stepped forward from behind the women, snarling, 'Don't waste the girl's time. Now, fuck off, before I kick your fucking teeth in.'

Tommy just smiled, put his helmet back on and rode home.

PAUL PHONES TOMMY

On Monday, Tommy passed onto Mac and Val what Ginger had told him about the young girl. They wondered if she was still in the boathouse or if Clark had dropped her off somewhere. They did a few small jobs that week but, on Friday Tommy was back following Clark's car again. He was hoping to see if Clark would pick up the young blonde-haired girl, but Clark didn't. In fact, Tommy was surprised that he didn't go round the redlight district as he had the previous week.

Tommy hung back, so he wouldn't be seen as he followed Clark. Seeing the direction he was driving in, Tommy thought, 'He's heading straight to the boathouse.'

He was right. Clark did go to the boathouse. Tommy let his car pull out of sight when it got near the track that led to the boathouse. He waited for thirty minutes, then he rode along the track and got off his bike when he saw the four stones he had placed by the side of the road the previous Friday. He pushed his bike to the same hiding place Mac had suggested last Saturday.

Mac was already at the boathouse to set up the equipment and tent. Even though Tommy was trying to be quiet while he was making his way through the bushes, now and then a branch would catch on his carrier and make a rustling sound.

Mac heard him and said, before Tommy came out of the bushes, 'You're early. It's only four thirty.'

Tommy said as he got nearer Mac, 'How did you know it was me?'

Mac answered, 'I heard you and, also, you're a big lad, so I could see your blonde head just above some of the bushes. So be a bit more careful he doesn't see you.'

Tommy put the carrier down by the tent and asked, 'Any sign of life from the invisible man?'

Mac nodded and replied, 'He got here a little while before you, and he hasn't been outside the house since.'

Mac showed Tommy where he had set up all the equipment and said, 'See you at five tomorrow. So long.'

Tommy went to the tree and sat on the small seat. With the camera in front of him and his back against the tree, he placed the earpiece for the equipment in his ear and one of his earphones from his phone in the other. He spent all evening watching the house and listening to his music. Then, at ten past nine, the music on his phone stopped as the phone vibrated and rang in his one earphone.

He answered, 'Hello, Tommy here.'

'Hi, Tommy, it's me, Paul,' came the reply.

Tommy said, 'Hi, Paul, is it about our holiday? I'm on a job and haven't been able to look into it just yet.'

Paul replied, 'I'm in the same position. I've got to go to a funeral on Thursday, and I have a lot of schoolwork to sort out. I told the lads, and they said to check with you about the holidays as they can book their holidays anytime it suits us.'

Tommy was a bit worried about the tone in Paul's voice and asked, 'Who's funeral are you going to?'

Paul sounded upset as he answered, 'Well, you know how over the years you've heard me talk about my star student, Kevin? He was amazing on the computers. As you know, he left three years ago.'

Tommy was surprised and interrupted, 'It's not him? The lad who got that apprenticeship, is it? He's only nineteen!'

Paul replied, angrily, 'Yes, it's Kevin - because of those bastard, fuckin' drug dealers. Kevin's dad had a small logistics service and when Kevin left school, he was mad about old things, the likes of antiques, so he got his dad to ask one of the antique exporters that he did business with for an apprenticeship for him. His dad was proud of him and got him the interview for that trainee manager's job there. I know all this because Kevin asked me for a reference to help get the position.

He had to start as a packer and work his way around the different jobs in the warehouse before starting the training properly; he also had to go to college one day a week for the theory part of the course.

When he'd been there two months, I saw Kevin just outside the warehouse, talking to the owner. I stopped and asked him how he was getting on.

The owner patted him on the back and said he was the hardest working young man in the business and that the college reported he was doing great in his training for the office as well. I gave Kevin a lift home and he told me he loved the job and the people there, but most of all he spoke about how grateful he was to his dad. He said his dad had got him the job and he was going to do his best to make him proud.

It was about six months after that I bumped into his dad and he asked me to have a word with Kevin, as he'd been staying out late and finding it hard to get up for work. So, I left school as soon as lessons finished the next day and I met him as he came out of the warehouse. He looked like he hadn't had a wash for a week and he talked a load of rubbish most of the time. I will tell you the parts I could understand.

He was looking back as he came out of the building. I was shocked when he shouted, 'You can fuck off, the lot of you.'

Then I heard some of the other employees shouting something back at him, something like, 'Why don't you do us a favour, you lazy little fucker, and don't come in tomorrow.'

I offered him a lift home, but he just looked at me and snarled, 'I'm not going home, so you can fuck off as well.'

I was even more shocked by that. He just wasn't the Kevin I knew, but I managed to talk him into getting into the car by saying I would take him to where he did want to go.

Once he was in there, I said, 'You loved that job, what happened?'

When he replied he talked through the side of his mouth, as if his mouth was stuck like that. He told me how, a while back - he couldn't remember exactly when - he was with his mates at a club. He was knackered and had to be up for, what he called, 'that fuckin' shitty job'. Then he said that his mate, who's great, gave him two blue tablets. His mate called them uppers and said he gets them off a friend of his for nothing. Because Kevin was still knackered, his 'friend' gave him two more.

Kevin said how great it was - that he had stayed in the nightclub till four, then just walked round till it was time to go to the business. The other employees didn't think he was lazy that day, they were telling him to slow down and take it easy.

By nighttime, though, he was shattered again and got some more uppers off his 'mate'. He was working hard and playing hard, but then his mate's friend wouldn't give them anymore - they had to buy them off him.

Kevin's friend stopped taking them, at that point, so Kevin started buying them himself, just to keep working hard enough for the owner. As the weeks passed, he took more and more. He said how he had to keep taking the tablets, just to get himself out of bed to go into work.

He was making excuses for himself, saying that it wasn't his fault the tablets he'd started with didn't give him the right rush anymore, and because his tiredness made him late sometimes and he needed to rest during the workday, the other workers started moaning at him. He said he didn't care, though, because he knew the owner liked him, so the other workers could just fuck off. Then he started going on about the owner being on a month's holiday, asking why he should work his guts out for someone who was taking four weeks off.

Unbelievably, he ended his ranting by asking for a loan. He said 'The shit I take now is great stuff - way better than those pills - but it takes all my money. If you lend me thirty quid, I'll give you it back next week.'

Paul's tone became even more sombre as he continued, 'I couldn't get through to him, Tommy. I dropped him off and watched him go into an old, disused house that had an awful smell of cannabis and was full of teenagers that were definitely doing harder drugs than that. I met him a couple of times, and tried to help him but, after a while, he just kept telling me to 'fuck off'. In the end, he went on to the real hard drugs. I went by the warehouse, and he didn't come out. I didn't like to go in and ask about him, so I got in touch with his dad, and he told me the owner sacked Kevin, because he was taking drugs, breaking things and throwing antique items around. I tried to talk to Kevin again, but each time I saw him he looked like a homeless person, and all he would say was 'If you gave a fuck, you would give me some money. I need it."

Paul's voice broke, so Tommy interrupted, 'Paul, are you alright? I know you thought the world of Kevin, but you sound like you're getting really upset. Do you want to leave it now, and I will see you in person tomorrow to talk about it?'

When Paul replied, Tommy could almost hear the tears in his voice, 'Sorry, Tommy, I shouldn't be bothering you. I know you're busy.'

Tommy butted in as quickly as he could, 'No, Paul, it's not that I'm busy - at the moment I'm just sitting here. It's just I could hear you getting upset and I'm sorry I can't be there with you. If you want to carry on over the phone, please do. You said Kevin asked you for some money. Please, will you carry on?'

Paul replied, 'Thanks, Tommy. I just have to talk about it to someone, it's making me sick inside. Yes, he wanted money for drugs. I didn't give him any and, as I drove away, he threw a brick and smashed the rear window of my car. I thought he couldn't do anything worse, but I met his dad a few months later. He was standing at a bus stop, which was unusual as he was always in the latest Jaguar. I offered him a lift, and he got in. Closer up, he looked ill. I asked him how he was, and how Kevin was doing.

He started crying and said that Kevin was killing himself with drugs, and he'd bankrupted the family business by stealing things from it. He'd also broken into the warehouse he'd used to work at and stolen some really valuable antiques from there - paying off the owner to stop Kevin going to prison had used up all his dad's life savings. In the end it broke his dad's spirit, as well as his bank accounts. I didn't know what to say. I offered to drop him off at their home; I was surprised when he said they didn't live there anymore; that he and his wife had had to move into a flat.

It was in a horrible area. When I stopped outside, a woman came out to meet him. It was his wife, I didn't recognise her as Kevin's mum. She looked twenty years older than her age, and so frail. She asked him if he'd got any money off the social security. He looked afraid to say at first and then he said they'd told him that he would have to wait for a week.

She just broke down crying; I helped him get her into the flat. It was just one room, with two chairs and a mattress for a bed on the floor. They told me they shared the kitchen and toilet with the rest of the house. I gave him all the money I had on me. It was only forty pounds, and he refused at first but he and I both knew he had to take it, because they were starving. When I left there, they were holding one another and crying. I was crying myself as I got in my car. Fortunately, I managed to get a person I knew from the social security offices to help them.

I called in on them the next day. Their door was broken and when I pushed on it, Kevin's mother in a weak voice called out at me.

She said, 'Go away, Kevin. You're killing us. But get an ambulance for your dad. You've nearly killed him.'

When I entered the room, she was sitting on the floor by the mattress, crying and bathing her husband's head, which was bleeding badly. When she saw me, she tried to tell me to get an ambulance, but I was already on the phone - I got on it the minute I saw him lying there, bleeding.

While we were waiting for the ambulance, she managed to tell me what had happened through her sobs. Kevin's dad had gone out and got twenty pounds worth of food. They had just started to eat and there was a knock on the door. They asked who was there and heard Kevin say it was him. He asked them to let him in. They both refused, telling Kevin they had nothing left to give him and begging him to go away. He had started to shout terrible things at them and kick the door.

His mum was crying but his dad had pressed against the door, trying to hold it shut. They had thought he'd gone away, but he came back a few minutes later and said that he had a brick, and he'd break the door with it if they didn't open it to him. His dad had still refused - really frightened by that time - and had tried to keep the door shut, but Kevin broke the door and pushed his dad back, threatening him with the brick. He was shouting that he needed some money, ranting about him being in agony and his parents not caring.

He was trying to go in his dad's pockets as he was shouting this, so his dad had pushed him away. At that point, Kevin had hit him on the side of his head with the brick, causing his dad to fall down, with blood pouring from his head. Even then Kevin hadn't stopped. He had knelt over his dad and threw him round like a rag doll, searching his dad's pockets for any money he might have. All the while he was doing it he had been muttering, 'I love you, Dad. This isn't me, it's the thing inside of me.'

He finally found the twenty-pound note that they had left and, as she was trying to help his dad, he pushed his mother out of his way as he left the flat.'

Paul paused for a moment in telling the story. Tommy could hear that going back over what had happened with Kevin and his family was difficult for him.

After composing himself, Paul continued, 'The next day I went to see Kevin's dad in hospital. His wife was with him; I was only there a few minutes when the doctor came and said he could go home. I gave them a lift back to the flat. When we got there, a police officer was at the door. We all went inside, and the officer asked them to sit down. Then he told them that he was sorry to have to tell them that their son had overdosed on drugs. The police thought it was a suicide because he had left a note.

Kevin's mum and dad were holding each other crying. They were too distressed to look at the note, so - with their permission - I took the note from the officer and, at their request, he left us alone.

Still holding his wife, Kevin's dad asked me to read the letter to them. I still have the note. They said they couldn't bear to look at it

- that it was too upsetting - but I thought they might feel differently one day, so I've kept hold of it for them. I'll read it to you.'

It says: *I have taken just a small amount of this drug so I can think right and tell you what I really think of you both. Mum and Dad, I love you both and it's killing me what I'm doing to you through the drugs I'm taking. I'm no good and you're better off without a horrible bastard like me.*'

Paul stopped reading.

Tommy asked, in a worried tone, 'Are you alright, Paul?'

Paul's voice was low and tearful when he replied, 'In the note he's written in large capitals '*I love you both.*' The rest of the note says: *I'm thinking of when I was young and how you were wonderful parents to me. I want you to know, Mum and Dad, that I LOVE YOU BOTH. Now, I'm going to go to sleep happy, knowing that I won't be able to hurt you ever again. Please don't cry over me, I'm not worth it. I'm happy now, knowing I can't ever hurt the ones I love again, Kevin.*

Paul stopped again and, straight away, Tommy asked, 'Are you alright, Paul? I wish I could be there with you.'

Paul carefully put the note away and, as he wiped his eyes, replied, 'Yes, Tommy, I'm alright - just a bit sad. But it's helped just to talk to you about Kevin. Thanks for listening.'

Paul's voice started to sound a lot better as he asked, 'How are you getting on? You texted me and the lads a photo of a vintage car?'

Tommy thought about what to say before he answered, because he didn't want to influence Paul, so he just replied, 'I wanted to know if you've seen a car like it before?'

Paul said, 'Sorry, I don't recognise it. Is it about the car in Spain?'

Tommy replied, 'Yes, but I know you lads only got a glance of the back of it and paid no attention to it, because you didn't know what had happened.'

Then Tommy told Paul what he thought and what he was going to do about it. They talked for quite a while, and then Tommy saw something move near the house.

He whispered, 'I've got to go, Paul, something's happening. Bye.'

Paul said, 'Bye' and they ended the call.

Tommy trained the camera on the movement just in time to see a badger leaving the clearing and entering the bushes.

He said to himself, 'Well, there is *some* life around here.'

Paul was still on his mind, so he texted the other lads: *Keep an eye on Paul. He's upset because he's got to go to Kevin's funeral on Thursday, and we all know he thought the world of Kevin. TT*

He sat there, holding his phone and thinking about Paul for quite a while. He was about to put the phone in his pocket but, before he did so, his mind drifted back to the red car in the photo. He couldn't help himself; he started studying the photo of the red car again.

He said to himself, sternly, 'Put it away or it will drive you mad.'

He tried to stop thinking about it again and spent the rest of the time there listening to his music through one ear, but every now and then the red car would come into his mind.

THE MACHINE

When Mac got there at five am, Tommy had nothing to report.

As he was going, he said, 'I'll see you at five tonight. It is bloody boring trying to watch this feller, the only movements around here are from foxes and badgers. There's not been a sound from the house, it's only that his car is here - otherwise I wouldn't believe he is in there!'

Mac laughed and said, 'I haven't seen any foxes and badgers. Are you sure you weren't dreaming on the job? Off home with you, get some sleep.'

Tommy was shattered when he got home. He made a drink, then went straight to bed. It was three thirty in the afternoon when he woke. He thought he had slept through his alarm; then he remembered he hadn't put it on. He did a few light exercises to liven himself up, then he looked at his phone and found he had a text. It read: *Sorry about this, but could you come at one in the morning and stay till Clark comes out? I've an important meeting tomorrow, Mac.*

So Tommy spent the day relaxing. He spent a few hours reading and meditating, then, at twelve am, he made his way to the boathouse. He rode along the track till he came to his pile of stones, stopped his bike as usual and pushed it to where Mac was camped.

When he got near, Mac said, 'I can hear you, Tommy, you're like a bull in a China shop.'

As Tommy put his bike in the bushes, he laughed quietly and called back to Mac, in a stage whisper, 'But you didn't see my head this time, did you?' As he came out of the bushes, he added, 'No movement? Still boring, I guess?'

Mac replied, 'No movement outside but, about four hours ago, he had what I think is the machine he's working on going off and on, for about half hour on and half hour off.

It sounds louder than your bike, but I think that's just because it's so quiet round here. Still, the noise... it got on my nerves after a while.' He gestured with one thumb over his shoulder, as he continued, 'I've left the camera and seat by the tree where you put them.'

Just as Mac stopped speaking, a loud motor sound came from the boathouse. They both stood looking at the house for a few minutes.

Then Mac bent down, picked up his haversack to put it over his shoulder and said, 'He has been sticking to the times his wife said, so he should leave here about twelve thirty tomorrow afternoon.'

Tommy replied, as he took his leather jacket off and started to put his big over-jacket on, 'I hope you are right. I don't fancy spending another cold night here listening to that noise after tonight.'

Mac held out his earpiece to Tommy, saying, 'I've left you the tent in case it rains. Will you be able to fit it in your carrier when you take it down? If you can't, I'll come and get it tomorrow.'

Tommy answered, with a grin on his face, 'I've got the earpiece you gave me. That one is yours. You're not going senile, are you? No worries, though, everything will fit in the carrier, and the folding seat can just strap to the top of it.'

Mac adjusted his haversack, saying, as he turned to go, 'I'll show you how senile I am when I forget to pay you this month's wages.' Then he asked, 'Will you text me and let me know if anything happens in the next three hours? I'll be awake for a while. I've got some expenses to sort out and put the paperwork in for, so Val can understand it before she puts it in Mrs Clark's file.

Oh, and, of course, I've got that meeting at nine.'

Tommy said, 'I'll text you if anything happens. Otherwise, I'll just text you when I pack up to go.'

While he was talking the sounds from the house suddenly stopped; Tommy carried on, interrupting himself by saying, 'Thank goodness that noise has stopped.'

Mac started to walk away, looking back at Tommy as he said, 'I think the noise is going to be on and off for quite a while. See you in the office tomorrow, Tommy-boy.'

Then he disappeared into the bushes.

Tommy picked his carrier up from by the tent, took it to where the camp seat was and placed it to one side. Then he took his phone and earphones out of his pocket, and put one of them in one ear, while in the other he put the earpiece. He sat down and listened to his music, with the noise from the house drowning it out every half hour or so. He would turn it on when the noise stopped and then off when it started again. After he had been sitting there for about three hours trying to listen to his music in the breaks, the noise stopped for good. Tommy sat there for an hour and a half before he stopped waiting for it to start again.

Once he realised it probably was not going to, he stood up, stretched and walked back and forward to keep himself from getting bored and falling asleep. When he sat down again, he opened his carrier, took out the large flask, unscrewed it and poured out some soup into the cup that acted as a lid.

As usual, he breathed in the scent of it and smiled as he thought to himself, 'My mum would say, 'oxtail soup again, Tommy, you'll turn into a cup of it one of these days!" As he drank his soup, he felt a text come through on his phone. When he checked it, he saw it was off Ann. He smiled as he read it. It said: *I'm just getting up. If you're awake on that job, I just want to say I love you.*

After he read the text, he put the empty cup back on the flask and his smile turned to a frown as his thoughts of Ann led onto thinking of the photo of the red car. He just couldn't get the car out of his mind and, while he was sitting alone in the woods, he kept looking at the photo of the car over and over. Each time he did, he'd remember what had happened in Spain and he would go sick inside. So, eventually he put the phone back in his pocket and just sat there till the sickly feeling left him, listening to his music.

CLARK CAME OUT OF THE BOATHOUSE

Tommy started feeling sleepy, so, at ten forty-five am, he poured himself a cup of coffee to liven himself up, because he thought Clark and the woman would be coming out soon. He drank the coffee and, just as he was putting the cup back on the flask, the earpiece buzzed in his ear, causing him to almost drop the flask as he put it on the ground.

He leaned forward to look through the lens of the camera. The door was nearly open, and Clark came out looking like he was going to the office, even though it was Sunday. He was smartly dressed; he even had a briefcase.

He shut the door behind him. It had three door locks on it, which he used three different keys to lock; then he rattled the door handle and tried to force the door with his shoulder, checking it was secure. Tommy was surprised at the way Clark was acting, and he was flabbergasted that he didn't come out with a woman, but he kept the camera clicking the whole time Mr Clark was in its viewfinder.

Clark went to his car and put the briefcase in the boot, then he went back to the house and checked all the shutters again and, just before he went back to his car, he checked the door again. When he was sure the house was secure, he got in his car and drove out of the clearing, to the narrow track. As he did so, he passed within three metres of Tommy in the bushes. Tommy got a good, clear photo of him in the car as it passed but, obviously, he was by himself.

Tommy sent the photos to the office and then he started to pack up to go. He took the camera off the tree, but he left the sensors in place because he thought they would have to come back, given they still had not got the pictures they were after. He stopped packing a couple of times and looked over at the boathouse. He had the urge to go over, to see if he could see or hear any movement inside it, but he remembered that Val had said Mrs Clark had told her that the security round the house sent pictures to her husband's laptop, so he thought better of it. While he was standing there, looking at the house, he got his phone out and texted Mac: *He's come out, but he was by himself again. I'll see you tomorrow about 10. TT*

Tommy looked at the photo of the red car on his phone one last time, shivering as he put it away. Then he took out a small telescope from his carrier, put it on the seat of his bike and finished packing. He waited for half an hour after Clark left. Then he took the telescope, went the shortest way through the bushes to the road and used the telescope to check that Clark was nowhere in sight. When he was sure, he got his bike out the bushes and rode home. He was shattered and felt sweaty, so he had a shower and made himself something to eat. He spent the rest of the day relaxing. He even fell asleep for two hours. Still, every now and then, the red car would come to mind. He would get angry with himself for thinking of it and tried to forget about it. He even tried meditation, and after that he read a book and had an early night, thinking he would at least forget about it while he was unconscious.

VAL AND MAC'S ADVICE

The next morning, he woke at eight o clock, when his alarm went off. He was feeling good, it was Monday, and he was meeting Ann in the afternoon. Then he thought of the red car and his heart sank a bit. He didn't know whether to tell Ann or not. If he told her about it, he knew she would be upset but, if he didn't and she found out he was looking into it and hadn't told her about it, she might stop speaking to him. So he tried to put the car out of his mind and just think of Ann.

He got out of bed, did his usual routine and then went to the office on his bike. Tommy arrived at nine-fifty. Val was there, sitting at her desk and talking on the phone.

When Tommy entered, she put her hand over the mouthpiece and said, 'There's coffee in the pot. Pour three mugs out. I'll have one; then take the other two with you and go in to see Mac. He's not a happy bunny today.'

Tommy, as he was filling the mugs, said in a defensive voice, 'Well, it can't be anything I've done. Have you been winding him up again? I've never seen him with a real paddy on.'

As Val put the phone back on the receiver, she laughed and said, 'It's not you or me he's upset with. It's about a couple of jobs we've missed out on. Anyway, take the coffee into his cupboard, it might make him feel a bit better.'

She gave a little laugh and carried on, 'He'll tell you all about it and most likely bore you to death.'

Val got up as she was talking and took her mug of coffee off Tommy to put it on her desk. Tommy, with a mug in each hand, walked to Mac's door and started to lean against it.

Val smiled at Tommy, coming over to the door to help and saying, as she pushed it as far as it would go, 'With those mugs in your hands, you won't be able to get in like that'.

Tommy squeezed through but he still spilt some of the coffee. Once he made it through, he used his bottom to shove the door shut. The small room was cluttered, with papers piled up on the chair in front of Mac's small desk, so he had to stand. He reached across the small desk and placed the mug in front of Mac.

Mac looked up at Tommy, as he shook his head, and said, 'I heard what Val said; one of these days I'll sack her.'

They were both taken by surprise when they heard a loud laugh and Val shouted through, 'I dare you!'

Mac, once he got over his surprise, acted as if it hadn't happened and just said, 'Look, Tommy, you two have got to stop calling my office a cupboard. It won't go down well with the clients if they hear you.'

Tommy replied, 'Okay, Mac, it was just a joke. Now what's this about jobs we've lost?'

Mac answered, 'Well, we didn't lose them, as such... It's just that we are committed to Mrs Clark. She is paying for us to be available when or where she wants us and she said she will pay a month in advance at the end of each month, with a year's bonus if we get her the proof she needs to get her divorce within a three-month window. Anyway, there are a couple of regular jobs I've been after for a while, and we would have got them this week, if we weren't already committed to Mrs Clark... But it's no good crying over spilt milk. With a bit of luck, they may come up again - who knows? And take no notice of Val. I didn't have what you call a 'paddy on', it's just that I would have liked to have got those jobs.'

Tommy frowned, as he asked, 'How long do you think this job will take?'

Mac, with a big grin on his face, answered, 'Your guess is as good as mine, Tommy-boy, but I hope it's a long time. Jobs that pay as good as this one are few and far between. Mind you it would be even better if we could wrap it up within the three months.'

Tommy was now the one feeling upset, as he told Mac, 'I was hoping to get a few weeks holiday in.'

Mac butted in, 'Tommy, I know you want to follow up on the car in the photo but, like I said, we are committed to this job and, while we're on it, I can't afford to lose you or,' he pointed to the door, 'big mouth Val in there.'

Val's voice came back, 'I heard that! If you can't afford to lose me, I want a rise.'

Mac just continued, as if he hadn't heard her, 'I'll tell you what, if you like, you can go to London tomorrow and interview the chap who owns the car and come back Wednesday.

Val and I can manage for a couple of days. If Mrs Clark needs us, I'll do the leg work and if he goes to the boathouse before the weekend, which I doubt, I'll set up the cameras for Val to monitor them during the day, and she can keep an eye on it from here in the office. I'll do the night, and you've still got your chance to get down to London. Is that okay with you?'

Tommy was more relaxed and said, 'Thanks, Mac, I'll take you up on that offer.'

As he managed to lever open the door and started to leave Mac's office, he said 'I'm meeting Ann this afternoon, so is there anything you want me to do right now?'

Mac replied, 'No, there's nothing specific I need till Thursday afternoon.'

Val looked up as Tommy appeared. She was about to say something, but it turned into a laugh as she saw Mac squeezing through the door and the handle getting caught in the pocket of his jacket. Tommy was looking at Val and wondered what she was laughing at. He turned round when he heard the commotion behind him, and, when he saw Mac struggling, he started laughing.

Mac managed to get free without tearing his pocket off, and said, 'It's not that funny,' but he did see the funny side of it, so he had a smile on his face as he said. 'I'm the boss, you know? I've a good mind to sack the both of you.'

Val, smiling back at him, just said, 'There you go again, making promises we know you won't keep.'

There was a moment of quiet, then Mac and Val said, at the same time, 'Tommy...'

They both stopped and looked at one another, then Mac said, 'I think I know what you're going to say, Val, so I'll leave it to you.'

Tommy just stood, looking puzzled, while Val got up from behind her desk and came round to face Tommy and Mac sat himself down on a chair by the door they had just come through.

Val nodded to Mac and said, 'Tommy, you said you've got a date with Ann this afternoon? When you meet her, just forget about the red car because it might turn out that it isn't the car you're looking for and, even if it is, and you bring it up with her when you meet her... Well, you know how upset she gets about the death of her mother. It will just spoil the rest of the day for the both of you.'

Mac interrupted, 'That's just what I was going to say and I'll add this: if you do, by some miracle, find it is the car you are looking for, then do what we do here - make notes and keep everything quiet until you have everything worked out. Please, Tommy, for your own sake, don't say anything till then, especially to Ann.'

Tommy said, 'I went sick when you both went quiet. I thought you had some really bad news for me. I know I've been going on about the car quite a bit and you are both right, I was in two minds about telling Ann about it, but don't worry, with your advice I will be able to bite my tongue and keep it to myself. Thanks for talking to me about it.'

THE RED LION

Tommy walked into the Red Lion at three fifteen that afternoon and was surprised to see that Ann was already sitting at their favourite table with a pint of lager on it. She had a glass of red wine in her hand and a big smile on her face. When she saw him enter the lounge, her brown eyes seemed to widen and light up.

She waved for him to come over and, as he sat down, said, 'I can't believe it's been nearly a week since I last saw you! What have you been up to in your detective work?'

When she asked him that, Tommy couldn't help the photo of the red car coming into his thoughts and, for a moment, he just sat there.

Ann grinned and said, 'If you're working for the government and have signed the Official Secrets Act, just nod your head. I will understand.'

Tommy put the car out of his mind the best he could, smiled and said, 'Very funny. I'm just pleased to see you.'

Ann replied, 'In that case, are you looking at me, looking at you or is it me looking at you, looking at me, looking at you?'

Tommy started laughing and said, 'Ann, what the hell are you going on about?'

Ann laughed and answered, 'I'm just saying I'm happy to see you, as you are to see me.'

Tommy, still smiling, asked, 'What time did you get here? And how many have you had? I hope you're not turning to drink because you miss me.'

Ann laughed and replied, 'You've driven me to it. I've drunk half a glass of wine and I've already forgotten all about you.'

Tommy picked up the pint of lager and said, 'Here's to us, may we always love one another.'

Ann said, 'I'll drink to that.'

They clinked their glasses together and put the drinks up to their mouths, but they both burst out laughing and their drinks splattered out, everywhere. They were in a giggly mood. Tommy had some drink on him and some was on the table; Ann had some of Tommy's drink on her but none of her wine was on her. It had landed on the table.

Tommy did his best to stop but he was still laughing when he handed Ann his handkerchief and managed to say, 'Here you are, wipe yourself with that I'll get a cloth off the barman to wipe the table.'

When Tommy got up, a young man about twenty-five approached the table with a cloth in his hand and, as he wiped the table, he said, 'I can see you two are in a good mood. We like our customers to enjoy themselves.'

Ann smiled and responded, 'Sorry about the mess - Tommy was just going to get something to clean it up. Thank you for taking care of it.'

'It's no trouble at all, Miss Kenwright,' the young man said, smiling in return.

Ann was slightly surprised and asked, 'We haven't seen you here before, and everyone just calls me Ann here anyway. How do you know I'm "Miss Kenwright"?'

The young man replied, as he finished wiping the table clean, 'I learnt my trade in one of your restaurants. I loved it there and would still be there, but I knew that no one leaves and that is the reason why I left. I wanted to work my way up to management, but openings come up so infrequently in your restaurants that I took a position here as a trainee manager. Like I said, do enjoy yourselves. I'll send you a drink over on the house,'

As he was about to turn to leave, Ann took a gift voucher out of her handbag and handed it to him, saying, 'If you take a guest to one of my restaurants, you won't need any money - the night is on me.'

He thanked her as he accepted the card, adding, 'I'll enjoy going to the restaurant and seeing friends I used to work with and having one of your fabulous meals with my wife.'

Ann said, 'We wish you all the luck. Hopefully I'll see you applying for a job managing one of our new restaurants in a few years' time.'

He said, 'Thank you, I'd love to do that. Now, I'll leave you to enjoy your drinks.'

Ann looked at Tommy and asked, 'Are you working tonight?'

Tommy answered, with a smile on his face, 'As they used to say in that old comedy show 'I'm free'. I'm hoping you are too.'

Just then the barman came over to their table, and said, 'The management would like to get you some drinks, what would you like?'

Ann replied, before Tommy had a chance, 'Tell him we're sorry, but we have an appointment and have to go.'

As the waiter walked away, Tommy asked, 'You have an appointment?'

She said, 'Yes.' She stopped for a moment, watching Tommy's disappointed look, then she laughed and pointed at his face as she continued, 'It's with you!'

Tommy's frown turned to a grin.

Ann carried on, laughing, 'You've only had half a pint and I've had a whole mouthful of this glass of wine, seeing as the table had most of it, so how about you and I have a drive in the country? Then we can stop at a little café I know.'

Tommy butted in, 'You always know a little café in the country. You're not working, are you?'

Ann laughed and said, 'No, I do like to go to a nice cafe and eat without Emma buying it occasionally! And, anyway, we never buy *nice* cafes, we buy poorly run cafes, in good locations. Now, are you coming? It's no fun going by myself.'

Tommy stood up as he drank the last drop of his lager. As they walked out they waved to the trainee manager, who smiled and waved back.

While they were walking to Ann's car, she got hold of Tommy's hand, squeezed it, and said, 'After we've had a meal and driven back to town, I'll let you take me dancing.'

Tommy almost felt like he had been drinking, he was in such a happy mood. Just as they got to Ann's car, Tommy pulled her to him and hugged her. She looked up at him and he gave her a passionate kiss on the lips, which Ann happily returned. They were in one another's embrace for a while and a few cars drove past and pressed their horns. They let go of each other, laughing.

Tommy, as he opened the door of the car, bowed his head and said, 'Step this way, madam, and, may I say, I'm yours to do what you want with.'

Ann smiled as she got in the driving seat. Tommy closed the door, went round the car and got in the passenger side, preparing for a nice night together. After a lovely drive together and a good meal at the cafe, they headed to town and spent the rest of the evening in a nightclub.

It was just on midnight when they left the club and, as they walked along the road holding hands, Tommy started singing.

'We could have danced all night, I feel so bright and right - we've hardly drank, but we'll have to get a taxi from the rank.'

Ann was laughing and said, 'That doesn't scan.' Then she saw a policeman and squeezed Tommy's hand.

She reached up to his ear and whispered, 'Shut up, Tommy, you'll get us locked up for being drunk and disorderly.'

Tommy laughed, and turned his head and kissed her, saying, 'Like I said, my body is yours and what madam wants, this body will do. Any chance I can have a kiss right now?'

Ann gave a laugh, as she let go of his hand and looked at him, replying nervously, 'No chance. Not with that policeman looking at us, are you drunk?'

Tommy had a grin on his face but put his hand on his forehead and slowly wiped it down, changing his grin into a serious look as he did so.

While he was doing it Ann, with a smile, said, 'Not now, Tommy.'

He claimed, 'I'm not drunk. You know I've only had two and half pints all night,' his face changed back to a smile again and he continued, 'but being with you makes me feel great.'

Then he put his arm round her, pulled her in close to him and said, 'I'm sorry I didn't mean to embarrass you.'

Ann smiled and answered, 'I wasn't embarrassed. I was just afraid you might get booked and we wouldn't get to spend the night together.'

Tommy's face lit up and he asked, 'My place or yours? Oh, never mind about that right now, let's make sure I don't get locked up.'

As they walked past the policeman, Ann just smiled at him, but Tommy smiled and said, 'I wouldn't like your job, officer, goodnight.'

The policeman laughed and said, 'I'll put the way you have been acting down to you being happy, not drunk. Have a good night, but take care, there's a lot of trouble in town tonight and we're out in force, so, like I said, be careful.'

They walked on and Ann said, 'I think he's telling us to act sober or we could end up being one of their customers tonight.'

Tommy laughed and said, 'It's easy to act drunk when you're sober, but how do you act sober when you are sober?'

Ann laughed and replied, 'It's my turn to say what the hell are you on about, Tommy?'

He replied, 'I haven't a clue. I think I might be drunk.'

Ann asked, 'Do you think someone put something in your drink?'

Tommy smiled at her, shook his head and said, 'No, we both kept our eyes on our drinks. It's just that I feel in a great mood, being with you.'

Ann grinned and said, 'I must admit, I'm feeling the same way.'

Just then a taxi for hire came into view. Tommy whistled it and put his arm out to flag it down.

As it pulled up beside them, Ann asked Tommy, 'My home or yours?'

He opened the door for Ann to get in, suddenly remembering both the fact he was going to London about the car and the favour John had asked him to do. He went a bit sick as he held the door open for her, staying quiet.

Ann said as she got in, 'I'll give you a starter for ten and I think the driver would like to know as well, your place or mine?'

Tommy replied, 'My place, I'm out early in the morning. You don't mind, do you?'

He thought, 'I'll tell her about the wedding when I get up in the morning. Why spoil a perfect day?'

He got in, and Ann told the driver where to go, then she moved in closer to cuddle into Tommy's side.

Ann said, 'Are you out in the morning for this case? You still didn't tell me about the job you're on. Is it about the young girl who went missing?'

Tommy thought and said, 'No, she turned up. She was at a man-friend's house.'

Ann replied, 'Then the job must be the usual, a divorce? I bet it is.'

Tommy thought up a story with a bit of truth in it and replied, 'You're bang on the money. We follow him when his wife phones us. It's mainly at the weekends, but she retains us by the month, and she wants us to keep an eye on him tomorrow as well. Like I said, it's mainly at weekends and he is usually in the Fallen Eagle, drinking with a few friends, or playing cards in one of his friend's houses but there is something strange about him. On the last weekend in the month, he always goes to their boathouse and stays from Friday night to Sunday morning.'

Ann said, 'Well, there's nothing wrong with that. I suppose there must be another woman involved somewhere and you haven't spotted her yet.' Ann gave a little giggle and continued, 'I thought you were good at your job?'

Tommy pulled a horrible, angry face, leaning towards her and showing his gritted teeth, as he put his hands round her neck and asked, 'Are you the other woman I'm looking for?'

Ann laughed and answered in a whisper, 'No, but I'm the woman you want... but only if you take me to bed.'

Just then the taxi stopped by the tree where Tommy usually chained his bike.

Ann got out and Tommy paid the taxi driver, saying, 'Keep the change.'

He closed the door of the taxi and, as it pulled away, Ann asked, 'Where's your bike? I was hoping to get a lift on it in the morning.'

Tommy felt a bit embarrassed when he answered, 'I've left it at the office, doll. I was hoping that you would get a taxi home in the morning. That's if you don't mind? I will take you home in the car if you want, but I've got to be out early and, if you're asleep, I wouldn't want to wake you.'

Ann could see he was uneasy about it and said, 'No problem, you know I like a sleep in any chance I get... and I don't get many chances in my job!' She carried on, 'Anyway, where *is* your car?'

Tommy, as he opened his front door pointed across the road to the house facing, where his car stood in the driveway, and said, 'The other day, Mr Stuart suggested that I might as well park in his front, as he hasn't got a car anymore. It keeps it a bit safer.'

Ann looked at it and nodded. As she waltzed through the opened door, she got hold of his hand, pulled him inside and, with the other hand, she closed the door behind them.

Then she led Tommy up the stairs to his bedroom and said, 'Well, you said I can do anything I want to with your body, so get your clothes off now and I'll race you, the winner gets to be on top.'

Ann won, so Tommy lay on the bed and, as she climbed on top of him, she grinned and said, 'I know you didn't even try to win.'

He just laughed and said, 'It was hard work making sure you won, now you know you can do anything you want.'

She grinned again, saying, 'I'm going to,' and, with that, she leaned forward and kissed him.

Tommy woke when the alarm went off. The first thing he thought of was Ann, and then his heart sank as he remembered the car and the wedding. He didn't want to tell Ann right then, so he said to himself, 'I'll tell her when I get back from London.'

She had heard the alarm and turned over in the bed, putting her arm across his chest as he tried to get up, and asking sleepily, 'What time is it?'

Tommy, yawning, managed to put her arm gently back under the duvet as he moved from under it and said, 'It's five thirty, go back to sleep. The alarm is now set for seven, you know where everything is and I'll see you when I get back from London.'

When he bent over and went to kiss her goodbye, she put her arms round his neck and pulled him into her and they kissed.

While she was still holding on, he said, 'I've got to go, doll, you know I love you.'

She asked, 'Can't you stay a little bit longer?'

Tommy replied, 'I would love to but we can't live on love alone.'

Ann sleepily replied, 'We could give it a try.'

Tommy said, 'If only!'

Ann squeezed him close and kissed him again.

Then she sighed, as she let go of him and sleepily said, 'It would be great if we could spend the week in bed like John and Yoko Ono.'

He blew her a kiss as he left the bedroom, quietly shutting the door behind him. He went to his bathroom to get ready for his journey to London. He did a few stretch exercises and then, for breakfast, he made himself four rounds of toast, with two fried eggs and a mug of tea. He packed some clothes and a flask of coffee in a small case and went out to his car in his neighbour's drive.

He opened the gates quietly, so as not to wake Mr Stuart. Then he backed out of the driveway and parked the car in the road. He got out and closed the gates.

As he was getting back in his car, he started to yawn and thought, 'I didn't get much sleep last night. I'm knackered, next time I tell Ann to do what she wants with my body... No, come to think of it, it was great, and I can't wait till next time.'

He was looking forward to seeing Ann again when he got back from London. After he turned the key to start the motor, he sat there a little while with the engine ticking over as he put the address that Val had given him for Sam Blake into the satnav.

While he was doing so, he thought of the promise he had given to John about the photo of the red car and said to himself, 'Well, here goes.'

As he started his journey, the satnav said, 'Take the next turn on your right.'

After Tommy had been driving for two hours, he was feeling tired, so he pulled into a motorway café car park. The first thing he did was to head for the toilets. Once there, he stripped to the waist and washed himself down in cold water to liven himself up. Then he walked around the car park for a while to make sure he was wide awake to drive the rest of the way to London. After a little while he went for something to eat, and then he was back in his car and on the motorway again.

When he got to London, he struggled to follow the instructions on the satnav a couple of times because of the complicated and unfamiliar roads. On his misguided route he spotted a sign saying 'bed and breakfast with parking facilities at the back'. It was nearly twelve o clock, so he stopped and booked in to stay the night there.

While he was booking in, he asked the landlady, 'Is Station Road near here?'

She replied, 'It's not far from here, love. Stay on this road till you come to the second set of traffic lights, turn right at them and that's Station Road, you can't miss it. It has a large train station on it.'

Tommy said, 'Thanks, I'll be back about six, if that's alright with you?'

She smiled and said, 'That's fine, love. If you're getting back here for six, for another tenner you can get your tea here. It's Spaghetti Bolognese.'

Tommy said, as he paid, 'That's great, I was wondering where I would get something to eat.'

He got back in his car and drove to Sam Blake's road.

He drove slowly up it till he came to the house number 102 and the satnav said, 'You have arrived at your destination.'

He stopped a little further up the road, got out of his car and looked in the boot. He took out a large, expensive camera, a small recorder and a photographic identity badge that said 'T. Kent, press reporter'. He put the badge in his pocket, closed the boot and walked back to the house. He stopped at the gate for a few moments and took a deep breath, then he opened the gate and walked up to the front door, taking another deep breath as he knocked on it. He noticed there was a doorbell, so he pressed that as well and, a few moments later, the door was opened.

SAM'S RED CAR

Tommy showed his badge and said, 'I'm a reporter, are you Mr Blake?'

The man who answered the door said, 'Yes, I'm Sam Blake, why do you want to know?'

Tommy asked, 'Are you the father of Lilly Blake, the lady who is going to marry Mr S. Thomson, the billionaire? We're covering that wedding for our society pages.'

Sam frowned and said, 'Look, I don't know if I should talk to you. If you want an interview, you would be better off talking to Lilly and her fiancé. I don't know anything about the wedding arrangements yet.'

Tommy said, 'I was talking to one of your neighbours and they said you have a beautiful vintage car, surely you are taking her to the church in it for her wedding?'

Sam looked worried and said, 'Please don't write anything about my car.'

Tommy asked, 'Why not? We thought you'd know about this part of the wedding at least. Your neighbour says your car is in mint condition. He thought you would be taking her to the wedding in it, because she should be proud to be seen in her dad's vintage car.'

Sam was now starting to get angry, and it showed on his face as he said, through gritted teeth, 'Who is this know-it-all neighbour you have been talking to? They want to mind their own bloody business...'

Tommy cut him off, swiftly saying, 'I can't tell you who it was, but he had no malice toward you, he only had praise for you and your daughter, Mr Blake.'

Sam calmed down but still had a worried look on his face as he said, 'I don't want you to write about my car because my daughter has always said, ever since she was a little girl, that she wanted to go to her wedding in a Rolls Royce, and I don't want her to feel pressurised to use my car...'

Tommy, seeing that Sam was getting angry again, stepped back a little as he interrupted, asking, 'Well, I've come all this way and I've got to write about something... Would you mind me just doing a feature about your car and how you've done it up?'

Sam went red in the face, raising his voice as he said, 'I've told you, no. I don't want you to put anything about my car in print.'

Tommy was getting a bit nervous. He felt his mouth going dry, but he couldn't stop now, it felt like this might really be the car he'd been looking for, so he kept pushing.

'Surely there's no harm in me writing about your vintage car?' he asked. 'Could I get a photo of it? I've got to get something for my editor or I'll lose my job. I'm on my last warning, he's been shouting at me that I don't try hard enough.'

Sam seemed to calm down a bit and said, 'I wouldn't like you or anyone to lose their job because of my actions. So, I will let you in my house and I will tell you all about my car...'

Tommy was really nervous now and was worried about going into the house. Sam was getting on a bit, but he looked fit, so Tommy butted in again.

'Thanks,' he said, 'it was the editor who gave me your address, so I have to go back with something.'

Sam looked at Tommy and said, 'Do you always butt in when people are talking to you? It's a bad habit you seem to have, and it's very annoying.' Then he continued with what he had been saying, 'I will even let you take photos of my baby - by which I mean my car.'

While Sam was talking, Tommy had doubts, thinking, 'Maybe it's not the car then or why has he changed his mind and is now willing to let me see it?'

It was as if Sam knew what Tommy was thinking about his about-face; he seemed to answer Tommy's private musings, as he said, 'I don't want you to print anything about my car in case Lilly's fiancé sees it. If he insisted on her going to the wedding in it, then I would feel it was my fault she didn't get her wish and to let my Lilly down would kill me.

You've got to promise, if I give you an interview, you won't put it in print till after the wedding. Do you promise?'

Tommy nodded, gesturing with his hands for emphasis as he said. 'I promise I won't print a word.'

Sam asked, with a pleading look on his face, 'Can I trust you?'

Tommy remembered that John had said something similar to him and started to feel a little bit guilty. Sam seemed to be a genuine person and Tommy was beginning to think he was on a wild goose chase.

Then he thought, 'If I see the car, it might help me to remember something that will help with investigating Ann's mum's murder.'

So, he was determined to see the car and said, 'You can trust me. I promise I'll tell my editor to print the story after the wedding - a story about a great dad who wanted to keep his little girl's wish alive, when she grew up and got married.'

Sam's face changed to a slight smile, and he held the door open wide as he invited Tommy into his home. Tommy stepped inside and Sam shut the door. Tommy watched Sam out of the corner of his eye as he passed him because Sam had got so angry at the beginning of the conversation, Tommy was still a bit unsure what he had in mind.

Sam turned from the door and, as he looked at Tommy, he said, 'The door on the right is to the garage. Go through and you'll see my baby, I mean, my car. I'm an old fool really, I spend most of my spare money on it and all my free time with my car, and I call her my baby.'

Tommy was now feeling very guilty and thought about whether he should tell him that he wasn't really a reporter but then he remembered how angry Sam had become just a few moments earlier, so instead he just stood looking at the door.

Sam walked in front of him and opened it, as he said, 'All the flannel you gave me about seeing my car at the front door and now you stand there looking at the door as if you're wondering whether you want to see it or not.'

Tommy said, 'Sorry, Mr Blake, for a moment there, I was in a world of my own; just thinking about my editor.'

When the door opened and Tommy saw the car, he was amazed. This car looked perfect. It was the same model as the car that tried to run them down, but he thought it couldn't possibly be the same one, as that one had been black with body work in a rough condition. He slowly stepped through the door into the garage so he could see the entire car.

Sam proudly asked, 'Well, what do you think of my baby? She's a beauty, isn't she?'

Tommy replied, 'It's perfect! How can anything that old look that good?'

Sam was now in his element, watching Tommy and listening to what he was saying. Tommy went all round the car, looking at it. He even opened and shut the doors on it, still thinking it couldn't be the car from Spain. He wanted to leave, but he thought he had better carry on with the act and do the interview.

So he asked, 'Can you bring the car out of the garage, so I can take a few photos of it?'

Sam opened up the garage and drove the car onto his driveway, so Tommy could move around it, taking photos.

As he stopped, Sam, who was now smiling fully, said, 'If you've seen enough of my baby, we can go into the living room where it's more comfortable for you to interview me.'

Sam opened the door they had come through and beckoned Tommy to follow him into the hallway.

As Tommy did so, Sam opened the door facing them and said, 'This is my living room. Do go in and sit down. Would you like a drink of tea or coffee?'

Tommy replied, 'That's good of you. I could do with a cup of coffee right now.'

Sam smiled at him and said, 'You look like you need a drink of something, but I don't drink, I'm a teetotaller. I don't have any alcohol in the house. Don't worry about your editor not being interested enough in this interview. I'll tell you a good story about how I got my baby... But when you print the story, when I say 'baby', would you print 'car'? It's a bit of a habit when I'm talking about my car because I've been saying it for so long.'

Tommy said, 'Yes, of course.'

Sam smiled and said, 'You can stop worrying. Your job should be safe. I'll just nip into the kitchen and make a pot of coffee.'

While Sam was making the coffee, Tommy sat in one of the easy chairs, looking round at the pictures on the walls.

Most of them were of Lilly, with some religious pictures mixed among them. While Sam was out of the room, Tommy quickly took out his phone and snapped a photo of one of the pictures of Lilly that Sam had hanging up. In it she looked to be in her late teens or early twenties. Tommy focused on getting a good shot of her face, knowing he could look at the photo later properly.

As he put his phone away, he got that guilty feeling again, thinking, 'If Sam knew why I looked so worried, I wouldn't blame him if he threw me out by the scruff of my neck.'

He was in two minds, wondering whether to get out before Sam came back, but knowing that if he did, he would feel even worse for leaving Sam wondering what was going on.

Then he thought, 'I'll carry on with the interview and then ring him up tomorrow to say the editor said it was a good story but not the type for his newspaper.'

Sam came into the room carrying a tray. On it were two mugs, a plate of chocolate biscuits, a pot of coffee and a small jug of milk.

As he placed it on the coffee table, he asked, 'Do you take milk and sugar?'

Tommy answered, 'I don't take sugar, just a drop of milk, please.'

Sam said, 'Now you're in my home and you know my name, may I request what your first name is?'

Tommy touched the press badge and, thinking that John might well have mentioned his sister's fiancé's name, he replied, 'the T stands for Terence but my friends call me Terry.'

Sam, as he poured the coffee into the mugs, said, 'Well, Terry, help yourself to some biscuits. You can put your own milk in, you know how much you like.'

Tommy felt too guilty to eat Sam's biscuits but his mouth was so dry he was glad of the coffee. He put a little drop of milk in it and drank it right off.

Sam watched Tommy drink the coffee in one go and, as Tommy put the mug back on the table, Sam filled it up again, saying, 'I guess you have to wet your whistle before you start the interview.

I'm ready when you are, but I have to tell you it all in the way I talk, and you will have to turn it into proper English.'

Tommy took a small recorder out of his jacket pocket, turned it on and placed it on the table between them. Then he took out a small notepad with a pencil attached.

Sam asked, 'If you're recording, why do you need a notepad?'

Tommy was taken aback. He had thought it looked more professional, but he realised now that it didn't make a lot of practical sense, so he had to think quickly.

He replied, 'I write a few words now and then to help me with ideas I might have while you're telling me the story. If you're ready to begin, I'll start with: when did you get the car?'

Sam answered, 'I got it on my birthday nine years ago. She's a lot older than me. She was made in 1939, I think. She has been registered a few times and I don't think some of her owners looked after her well.'

Tommy asked, 'Well, the last owner must have looked after it. The car must have been in quite good condition when you got it, for you to get it looking so new?'

Sam wasn't pleased with the indication that the car had been in good condition when he got it.

He said, 'You're wrong. I admit the body had had work done on it and it had also had a good respray. But there were quite a few bad scratches on her, and I had to clean the rust off her and weld some of the floor, as well as doing quite a lot of other work on her.'

Tommy was intrigued by this and asked for more detail, saying, 'Well, what was it like when you got it?'

Sam answered, 'I got the body and two wheels with rusted spokes. Like I said, there had been quite a good respray done, but there were some bad scratches to the paintwork that showed the different colours the car has been over the years. And the two wheels I got weren't just rusty, they also had some spokes that were bent or missing.'

Tommy was starting to think it could be the car he was looking for, after all, if it had ever been black. However, Sam was in the clear as the driver, if he'd only had it for nine years and he'd got it in pieces. He couldn't have been the one driving it.

Trying to stay calm, he asked as nonchalantly as he could, 'Was it ever black?'

Sam nodded, 'Yes, I'd say she's been black at some time or other. Like I said, she's been about four colours. I had to work bloody hard on her; when I sanded the rusty scratches out, it showed she had been red, black and even green. The last person who had her, resprayed her red. I touched the scratches up and that's the reason she looks so good now.'

Tommy answered, 'Well, you've done a great job on it. Where did you get the other parts for it?'

Sam said, 'I got most of the parts from a scrapyard. Don't laugh, it's called *Honest Joe's*. I didn't get all the parts of the car at the same time; I've put them together over six years.'

'How did he manage to collect all the different parts for you? It must have cost a lot of money?' Tommy asked.

Sam answered, 'He didn't collect the parts. The owner of the scrapyard is an official debt collector; the car was part of a debt he collected from a man who was rebuilding the car. He still had parts from it after I bought the body and the first two wheels. I suppose the man who was restoring her must have gone bankrupt, for it to end up there.'

Tommy, thinking that maybe this man was the driver he was looking for, asked, 'Do you know the man that the scrapyard got the car off?'

Sam said, 'No. I don't. But what has that got to do with me rebuilding my car?'

Tommy acknowledged, 'Nothing, I just thought you might have got some of the parts off him directly, with you saying it took you six years. Why *did* it take you six years to rebuild it?'

Sam looked a bit annoyed as he answered, 'Do I live in a big fancy house? Is my name Rockefeller? The answer is 'no'. I could only afford to buy parts when I had the money and, even then, I needed more money to get the parts sandblasted and chromed. The parts that were damaged and which I couldn't repair myself, had to be sent away to specialists, which all cost money. Lilly helped pay for it. So that, and the fact I also have to work, is why it's taken me six years!'

Tommy said, a little shamefacedly, 'Sorry, Sam, I didn't mean to upset you. I am just confused about why *Honest Joe's* would sell a car in pieces, over such a long time. Can you see what I mean?'

Sam nodded and said, 'Well, it does sound strange... but they got the car in pieces; they wanted to be sure that they could sell it and they knew I was looking for an old car that I could rebuild. So they sold it to me and, like I said, I couldn't afford to buy the car outright, so I got it on the never-never. They let me have the car the same way I paid for it and I can see now why the trader is called *Honest Joe's*, because he said he would keep all the parts for me and he did.'

Tommy asked, 'How did they know you were looking for a car to rebuild?'

'Lilly knows the owner of *Honest Joe's*,' Sam replied, adding, 'She worked for him in the office when she first left school. So, she asked him about it. I'm not an enthusiast about MG's. I just wanted a car I could work on as a hobby and he promised her, years ago, that he would look out for one for me. So, that's how I got my car.'

Tommy clarified, 'You said you got it as a birthday present, who did such a nice thing for you?'

Sam answered, a little surprised, 'Surely you have the brains to work that one out for yourself. It was my Lilly - that's what I meant when I said she's helped pay for a lot of it. It was a surprise when a wagon pulled up outside, with the body and the two wheels on it. It was a hell of a job getting the car off the wagon without damaging her.'

Tommy agreed, 'Yes, Sam, I did think your Lilly had got it for you, but I just wanted to be sure... because it wouldn't be right if I got it wrong and printed the story without giving her credit. Can you think of anything else about your car, and would you mind telling me a bit more about Lilly?'

As he looked around at the photos on the walls, Tommy was wondering if Lilly was involved with what had happened in Spain, but then he thought that she couldn't be, because she wouldn't give her dad the car that was used in a murder if she had known about it. There was still a chance that she might know the driver, though.

Sam got a photo album out of a cupboard by the chimney breast, giving it to Tommy to look at. Tommy opened the album and Sam stood alongside Tommy, looking over his shoulder at the photos, saying things about them as Tommy turned the pages.

Tommy wasn't really listening, he heard the odd comments about the photos, like when Sam said, 'That's my wife, Lilly, and the baby. She was called after her, and that's me with them both - my wife died when Lilly was just turned seven.'

When Tommy heard this, he felt even worse about being there and looked up at Sam, saying, 'I'm sorry, it must have been hard for you, bringing up a young daughter on your own, without the support of a wife.'

Sam responded, 'Not really, she was a loving child who didn't get into any real trouble. Mind you, she got into a lot of mischief, she was a bit of a tomboy, and she played football and climbed trees.'

Tommy could see Sam was proud of Lilly. He smiled as he leaned backwards and took a frame that had four photos in it off a small, occasional table just behind him. They showed Lilly at different ages in her school life.

Sam put it down on the album, which was open on Tommy's lap, gestured towards the frame and said, 'Terry, here's my little angel. Look at the top picture on the right. When she came in looking like that, well, I'm smiling now, but back then I nearly collapsed with fright. One of her friends took that photo before she came home.'

While Sam was talking, Tommy looked at the photos. He was taken back by the photo Sam had pointed at. It was a young girl about twelve, her blond hair was covered in blood from a large cut on her forehead; her eye was closed with the blood, which was all down her face and on her dress.

As Tommy stared at it, Sam continued talking, 'I was in the kitchen washing some dishes. She came into the living room and, in a jolly voice, shouted, 'Dad, you won't believe what has happened to me.' I stopped doing the dishes and thinking something nice had happened to her, I called back, 'Well, tell me about it.' She shouted through, 'You know that big tree by the railway station?' I said, 'Yes,' and she just replied, 'Well, I fell out of it.'

I walked into the living room with a few plasters for her, saying, 'Serves you right,' but when I saw her standing there, with a grin on her blood-covered face, I went sick, and rushed her to hospital. She got four stitches in her forehead and had two black eyes.'

Tommy said, 'I would have thought that would leave a large scar, but she hasn't got one in these more recent photos, just a small mark on her forehead?'

Sam said, as he picked up the photo frame and placed it carefully back on the table, before turning a few pages in the album, 'Look at these ones, you can see as Lilly got older the scar faded. By the time she was twenty-one, you could hardly see it... but she was so self-conscious about it.'

Tommy looked at Sam and said, 'While prepping for the interview, I've seen some recent photos of Lilly and I couldn't see a mark on her face.'

Sam answered, 'She had the scar - well, it wasn't even a scar, it was just a small mark - removed, and she's always been a beautiful young lady, as anyone can see.'

Tommy said, 'I'll second that.'

Just then, a jingling sound came from Tommy's pocket. He took his phone out and looked at it. It was a text from Sergeant Torres.

He pretended to read it, saying, 'Sorry about this, Sam, it's my editor. He wants me to do another job while I'm down this way. Is there anything more you'd like to add to the interview before I head off?'

Sam replied, 'Only that I can't give you a photo of Lilly without her permission. When you do the print up after the wedding, I don't mind you saying she was a tomboy but please don't mention her scar - and remember your promise, because if you print it before the wedding, I'll come looking for you, and that's a promise that *I* will keep.'

Tommy felt bad about lying to Sam and said, 'It's alright, don't worry, I'll lose my job before I'll let it get printed early, and I know the editor will honour any promise a reporter makes.'

Sam showed Tommy out and, as they shook hands by the front door, Sam asked, 'Where is your car?'

Tommy replied, 'I've parked it up the road a bit. I wasn't sure which was your house. Thank you for the interview.'

As he turned to go, Sam reminded him in an earnest tone, 'Keep your promise, Terry.'

When Tommy got into his car, he looked at the text from Sarge. It said: *Sorry, Tommy, got home later than I thought. Will do the rounds tomorrow, Sarge.*

Tommy drove a little way from Sam's and stopped near a park. He went for a walk there, stopping for a coffee and spending a little while in the cafe, thinking about what he'd heard at Sam's. He arrived back at the bed and breakfast at six fifteen and went straight to the dining room. It had six tables in it, with flowered tablecloths, and there were four people in there already, having their evening meal.

As he entered, the landlady greeted him with a smile, saying, 'You're just in time, love, I was about to put your tea on the hot plate to keep warm.' She pulled a chair out for him and continued, 'Here you are, love, sit at this table. I'll bring your dinner out. What do you want to drink?'

'Coffee, please,' replied Tommy.

When he had finished eating, he said to the landlady, 'Thank you for the meal, the Spaghetti Bolognese was lovely. I'm off to my room now, I've got an early start in the morning. What time is breakfast?'

She replied, 'It starts at seven, do you want an alarm call, love?'

Tommy replied 'No, thanks, I'll be out for six. I'll skip breakfast, thanks.'

She said, 'I'll leave you a wrapped-up sandwich with some fruit on a tray outside your door for you to take with you when you go and, if you've got a flask, I'll fill it with coffee, if you like?'

As Tommy handed her the flask out of his haversack, he said, 'Much appreciated, thank you again.'

He went to his room and read for a bit, before getting ready for bed. He didn't sleep very well. He was feeling a bit guilty about Sam and yet he had a strong feeling that the car was involved in the death of Ann's mum. He didn't think Sam was but, surely if Lilly was the driver, she wouldn't have given her dad a car that was used in such a crime.

Tommy got up at five thirty in the morning and was on his way out at six. He found the tray the landlady had left outside his door, as promised, and picked his refilled flask and a bag up off it. The bag had the sandwich, and an apple and an orange in it. He had to pass the kitchen as he left, so he waved to the landlady who was working away in there. She smiled and waved back.

He took an hour to get through London and was glad once he was on the motorway, where he could get up to seventy sometimes. It was ten past nine when he pulled into a motorway café's car park. He went to the toilet and then washed himself down at the sinks again, to liven himself up. Then he went for a small walk around the service station's facilities to stretch his legs, finally heading back to his car, where he sat while he ate his salad sandwich and fruit and drank the coffee. Soon he was on his way again and arrived home at ten-forty.

He parked his car in Mr Stuart's driveway, and got out of the car and stretched as he thought, 'I had better have a few hours in bed before I call in to the office.'

When he got in his house, he opened the fridge, took out a can of coke and drank it as he studied the new photos of Sam's red car on his digital camera. He was feeling quite tired and climbed the stairs to his bedroom. He put his phone on charge, set his alarm to go off at three-twenty and then he got into bed. He lay there for a while, thinking about the previous day, and Sam, the car and Lilly. Then he drifted into sleep but, when the alarm woke him, the first thing he thought of was Sam, and then Lilly and the car again. He couldn't wait to talk it over with Mac and Val. He got up and made a mug of coffee, which he quickly drank, almost burning his mouth before rushing out to his car and driving to the office.

While he was driving, he used his hands-free phone to call Ann.

Her secretary answered, 'Miss Ann Kenwright's office.'

Tommy asked, 'Can I speak to Ann?'

Her secretary replied, 'I'm sorry, sir, I've been told not to disturb her at the moment. She is very busy.'

Tommy said, 'It will be alright if you just tell her it's Tommy and see if she will answer.'

There was a moment of silence, and then a voice said, 'Ann, here. It took you long enough to check if I got home in one piece.'

Tommy laughed and said, 'I knew you would be able to fight your way through all the criminals where I live, even the two five-year-olds that live on the corner - they're a handful.'

Ann replied, 'All right, you knew I'd have no problem getting home, but it would have been nice to hear from you.'

Tommy said, 'Sorry, doll, I didn't think you would miss me after just one day but I've been thinking of you all the time I was away.'

Ann laughed and answered, 'Creeping and saying things like that won't get you out of the doghouse and into my bed.'

Tommy went sick when he thought of what he had to tell her, and said in a serious voice, 'I might be in a worse doghouse. I have got to see you, can you do about eight this evening?'

Ann was concerned and asked, 'Why do you have to see me? Can't you tell me now over the phone? Are we breaking up?'

Tommy was dismayed at what she had said and almost shouted, 'No, doll, never! I'll love you always, can you meet me in the Red Lion at eight tonight? Can't talk now, I've just pulled into the office car park and there are quite a few people around.'

Ann, in a quiet, serious tone, replied, 'I'll be there on the dot.'

THE BOATHOUSE BLUEPRINTS

As Tommy entered the office, Val and Mac were standing with their backs to the door, discussing some paperwork on Val's desk, and Mac was grimacing as he drank from a mug of coffee that had gone cold.

They got a bit of a shock when Tommy shouted, with a big grin on his face, 'I'm home!'

They both swung round to see Tommy standing there, grinning, and Val said, 'You little shit.'

Mac said, 'I'll help you wipe that grin off your face!'

With that, he threw what was left of the coffee in Tommy's face. Tommy stood there for a moment, in shock, with the coffee dripping down his face and off his nose. Val started laughing, as she went into the washroom and brought back a handful of paper towels for Tommy to dry himself. Mac just stood there grinning at Tommy.

Once he was dried off, Tommy smiled and said, 'I won't try that again.'

Mac looked at Val and said, 'He's a quick learner, this kid.'

Val nodded, saying, 'I'll make another pot of coffee, and the three of us can sit down and see where we are up to.'

Mac and Tommy sat on a couple of swivel chairs that were by Val's desk. Val made the coffee on the small table by the washroom door. She put two mugs and a cup on a tray, filled all three with coffee and put some milk in them.

She placed the tray on her desk and, as she sat down on her seat behind the desk, she said, 'Well, help yourselves.'

She picked up her cup, and Mac and Tommy took a mug each.

Mac said, 'Let's get Tommy's trip out the way first. Well, how did you get on down in London?'

Tommy took his recorder out of his pocket. Before he played it back, he told them that he thought Lilly might be involved because the car was black at one time, but that he didn't think her dad knew anything about it. They listened to the recording, and Val and Mac both agreed there was a slim chance that it was the car but, like Tommy, they couldn't see Sam's daughter putting him in such a position.

Mac said, 'Right, let's sort out where we are on the Clark case.'

Val picked up some papers from a file on her desk and said, 'This is what Mrs Clark told me on the phone this morning. The engineering firm who employs her husband is doing their annual exchange placement and a manager from the states is coming to his office; so tomorrow Mr Clark's firm is sending him to their office in the US. He will be on secondment there for two weeks and she wants us to use that time to get into the boathouse.'

Tommy butted in, asking, 'Has she got the three keys to get in there?'

Val replied, 'No, but she has authorised a locksmith for when we go to help us get in.'

Mac asked, 'What about the security he tracks on his laptop?'

Val replied, in an angry tone, 'If you both stop butting in, I'll tell you what she told me.' She waited a moment to check they were both quiet and listening, and then continued, 'She said he will be taking his laptop with him. So, when we go in, we'll need to get a computer expert in, to block the wi-fi and we should make it look like it was a burglary. Another important detail to note is that she said he claims he has booby-trapped the house. So you'll have to be careful once you are in there.

She thinks the best way to *get* in is probably on the other side of the river. There's a structure there - it looks like a small house attached to the boathouse by the bridge, but it's really just a large storage room with a staircase in it up to the bridge. It's basically just a fire escape for the boathouse.'

Just then there was a knock on the door. Mac went to answer it.

The person at the door said, 'Special delivery, you'll have to sign for it, sir.'

Mac signed and gave the messenger a tip.

As he sat down with the large envelope and started to open it, Val said, 'That will be the plans for the boathouse. She said she was sending them to us, so we can study them, but the part about the house being booby-trapped really worries me.

So, Mac, do we carry on with this job, or not?'

Mac replied, 'Well, I will do this job myself, because I wouldn't be surprised if he has booby-trapped the house, the way he acts when he is leaving it.'

Tommy said, 'Sorry, Mac, but I've arranged to go camping there with my mates and, as it happens, one of them is an IT expert *and* I'm younger and fitter than you, so I think I should go.'

Mac started to argue with Tommy about it, but Val slapped both her hands down on the desk and said, 'Stop arguing. I don't like it but, if we're doing the job, well, Mac, you're too old and - let's face it - too slow nowadays to break into a house. And it makes me feel a little better to know that Tommy would have his friends with him.'

Mac wasn't pleased with what Val had said, but he knew she was right, so he just sighed and said, 'Tommy, if you see Jacko, for goodness sake don't mention this job or we will all end up in jail!

Well, that's it for today. Val, will you lock up as usual?'

Val replied, 'You wouldn't know how to, so I'll have to, won't I?'

Mac just looked at her, smiling as he shook his head, then he asked Tommy, 'Are you meeting your young lady tonight?'

Tommy grinned and replied, 'Every chance I get.'

Mac and Tommy got up to go and as they did, Mac patted Tommy on the back and said, 'You be careful next week, goodnight, son.' Then he opened the door, and called back, 'Goodnight, Val, and God bless you for locking up.'

Val smiled and stuck her tongue out at him, calling back to him, 'Night, Mac.'

As he closed the door behind him, Tommy said, 'I'll be on my way as well, Val. Can I have the plans to study this weekend?'

Val, with a worried look on her face, said, 'Wait a minute, Tommy. Are you sure you know what you are getting into next week? I can easily get Mac to cancel this job and, don't worry about it, none of us will fall out over it.'

Tommy walked over to her, hugged her and said, 'It's you who shouldn't worry, I'm dying to get a look inside that house to see what he's up to. And don't forget, I'll be with four other big lads. So, like I said, don't worry! Love you, but I'll have to go now - my other girl is waiting, I hope. Goodnight, Val.'

As she handed him the envelope, Tommy kissed her on the cheek and left.

TOMMY TELLS ANN ABOUT THE WEDDING

Tommy rushed home as he didn't want to be late to meet Ann. He had a quick shower and a shave, got changed into his best clothes and got to the Red Lion at seven thirty. He put his jacket on the chair of their usual table in the corner. He was feeling a bit nervous about what he was going to say to Ann. As he was ordering his drink, he thought about how, in films and on the TV, people always drank a whisky to fortify themselves when they were meeting their girl and had to tell her difficult news, like he had for Ann.

He said to the woman behind the bar, 'Hi, Babs, a pint of whisky, and a lager.'

The barwoman laughed and asked, 'What's up, Tommy?'

He blushed and stammered, 'I... I meant a pint of lager and a double whisky - oh, and a large red wine, please.'

While she was pouring the drinks, Babs asked, 'Are you meeting Ann tonight?'

Tommy answered, 'Yes, she will be here at eight,' as Babs placed the drinks on a tray,

She said, 'Well, while you've got Ann, everything will be alright.'

He smiled at her, took the tray to the table and sat down. Then he picked up the whisky and looked at it for a moment. He raised it towards his nose but, when he registered the smell of it, he pulled a face and put it back down on the table, picking up his pint and taking a mouthful of lager instead.

He sat looking at the whisky. He had had it once before and he didn't like it, but he kept looking at it as he was drinking his lager. Ann entered the Red Lion at seven-forty and walked to the table she knew Tommy would be sat at. He tried to smile at her as she sat down in the chair with the glass of wine in front of it, but Ann had a serious look on her face.

She was looking at the glass of whisky on the table and said, 'You don't like whisky. My God, it must be serious if you're drinking that stuff. Well, I've been worried all day, so what is it that we need to talk about?'

Tommy replied, 'Sorry I worried you. Well, it's not that bad, really...'

Ann was feeling a bit sick by this time and butted in, almost shouting, 'For goodness' sake, Tommy, just tell me what is going on!'

Tommy blurted out, 'Your dad is getting married.'

Ann sat back in her chair, surprised, and said, 'He's what?'

Tommy took a quick swig of the whisky and said, 'That's what your John's mate, Bill, told me. I didn't want to tell you, but he asked me to give you the message and I couldn't refuse. You have the right to know.'

Ann was angry. She jumped up, causing her chair to fall over behind her. Tommy went round to Ann and picked up the chair.

He said, 'Sorry, doll, but I had to give you the message.'

Ann replied, 'I'm going home, Tommy. I'm fuming to think he got away with what he did to my mum and now he's all happy and getting married... I won't be good company tonight. It's not your fault, Tommy, I love you, but I want to be by myself tonight.'

Tommy asked, 'Can I see you home? I don't like leaving you when you're so upset.'

Ann replied, 'No, please, Tommy. You know I don't have a civil tongue in my head when I think about him and it will seem like I'm taking it out on you, and that's not fair.'

Ann didn't wait for Tommy to answer; she turned and walked out.

Tommy just stood watching Ann leave. As he sat back down, he felt sick inside. He picked up his lager and as he drank it, he thought, 'I knew this would happen. Every time her bloody dad is mentioned... I'll just have to find that bloody car and the fuckin' driver. I hope we get it sorted before we're too old to start a family.'

He finished his drink and went home.

Babs looked at him as he left and said to the barman, 'I knew something was up when Tommy came in. I wonder what they were arguing about. They've been together for so long, it's a shame they've broken up.'

The barman replied, 'They mightn't have broken up. I argue with my wife all the while and we're still together. Just because they've argued doesn't mean they've split up.'

'Ah, well, let's hope that's the case then,' Babs sighed.

TOMMY DID SOME TEXTING

When Tommy got home and took his phone out of his pocket, he noticed a text from Sarge. It said: *Hi, Tommy, I've done the rounds and no luck, I'm afraid. The people who saw the car that day did think it's the same model, but they couldn't swear it was the same car. That horrible bastard who owned the garage we thought might be involved was in a crash two years ago and died at the scene. He's no great loss, but it means I obviously can't ask him about the photo. The garage is now run by his son. He's away on holiday but I'll interview him when he gets back. Hope to see you soon, Sarge.*

Tommy texted back: *Thanks, Sarge. No big rush now. I'm on a job that I can't get away from and I would like to be there when you interview his son, if that's alright with you. Hope to see you soon, TT*

Then he went to the fridge and got a Pepsi out. As he was drinking it, he thought of London, Sam and *Honest Joe's*.

He murmured to himself, 'Jacko... He'll check it out for me.'

He got his phone out again and texted: *Hi, Jacko, I was hoping you could check out a scrapyard called 'Honest Joe's' for me? I think the owner knows something about the car that tried to run us down. The scrapyard is in London. See you soon. TT*

While he had his phone to hand, he sent a text out to Jammer, Terry, and Dave that said: *Well, it's nearly time for our yearly get together. I'm hoping you can all get time off at short notice. I need help with a job I'm doing. We can go camping at the same time and I really need Terry and his I.T. gear. I know you all have camping equipment. I'll send you the GPS location on Maps later on. Let me know if you can make it or not. I don't think Paul will be with us this time, as you all know, he's been to Kevin's funeral and is behind with his schoolwork. TT*

He was just about to put his phone away, when it dinged three times. The first message he'd got back was off Jacko. The text said: *I can't do anything myself, but I will get in contact with the police in London. I know a Detective Sergeant Smith who I can ask to look into it for me and I will let you know what he says. Jacko.*

Tommy texted back, thanking him.

The other two texts were off Jammer and Dave. They both just said: *We'll be there.*

Tommy wasn't expecting the boys to answer so quickly, but now he was wondering if Terry would also be able to come. He opened the envelope that Val had given him, laid the blueprints of the boathouse on the coffee table and studied them for about an hour. When he started yawning, he left the prints on the table and went to bed.

When the alarm woke him at seven, the first thing he did was to call Ann's mobile.

She answered on his first ring, 'Hello, Tommy, I'm sorry about last night. I've been awake all night worrying you might be fed up with me because I always lose my temper when I'm talking about my dad. I've been in the Goose Green restaurant working since three-forty this morning to take my mind off the thought that you might leave me.'

Tommy replied, 'It did spoil my pint, you not being there but I understand. What else can I do? I love you and I know you love me too.'

Ann screamed, 'God, the oven's smoking. Love you - got to go!'

At hearing Ann say she loved him, Tommy smiled and said, 'Love you, see you tonight.'

Then he checked his phone for a text from Terry. There wasn't one there, so he wondered if he should send his original message again but decided that, if Terry was busy, he wouldn't be too pleased. Instead, he did his usual morning routine, had his breakfast and picked up the blueprints off the table. He went out to his car, got in it and drove to the office, where he parked alongside his bike and went into the building

THEY STUDIED THE BLUEPRINTS

Tommy could hardly get into the office because a lot of camping gear was stacked by the door.

He asked Val, 'Why is that lot there? I was going to put it in my car tomorrow.'

Val replied, 'Mac came back yesterday and checked it all, to make sure it was in good condition for you to use. He has even left two crowbars and a few other things that a burglar would use. I'll give you a hand to pack your boot.'

Tommy, as he picked up a few of the things said, 'No, thanks, Val, but you could make me a nice mug of coffee for when I've finished packing.'

Just as he was putting the last thing in his boot, Mac drove into the car park.

As he got out of his car, he said, 'Alright, Tommy, I've come to help you pack the camping stuff into your car.'

Tommy laughed and said, 'I bet you were around the corner waiting for me to put this last piece in the boot.'

Mac smiled, shrugging his shoulders as he said, 'I'm not that type of guy. You know I wouldn't do that but, well, if you've done the job....'

Tommy closed his car boot and, as they walked into the office, Mac put his arm round Tommy and said, 'I think we deserve a mug of coffee off Val, after doing such a good job.'

Val said, 'I heard that and I've made *two* coffees, for us the workers, so you will have to make your own.'

Mac asked, 'Who is the boss in this place?'

Val replied, 'You'll need a detective for that one; when we find out, we'll let you know!'

Mac pulled a face at Val and went to make himself a mug of coffee.

Then he asked Tommy, 'Have you got the blueprints there?'

Tommy took them out of the inside pocket of his jacket and laid them out on Val's desk.

As the three of them looked at the prints, Val said, 'Mrs Clark went on a bit about the bridge on the boathouse being a sun trap. They used to use it like a large veranda. It has six garden chairs on it, around a large table, as well as two benches and a three-seater lounger. They will all be covered up, so if you go on the bridge, don't be surprised by them.'

Mac said, 'Look at the second floor. The three same-sized rooms on the right-hand side at the top of the stairs are all bedrooms, each with a walk-in wardrobe. Directly opposite the main staircase, there is another small set of stairs which is a fire escape that goes up and opens onto the roof. This roof acts as a bridge to the fire escape that is in the part of the house that is on the other side of the river.

Now, look at the size of the room on the left side of the stairs - that is, on the side which runs along the river. I assume this was designed for when the original owners of the house were entertaining. It is nearly the length of the house but, unusually, can only be accessed by going through this one, small room which is next to it. You can see on the blueprints that there is another small room behind that, which we think must be a toilet, but that can only be accessed once you have gone through the small room, to get into the large room. By the way, they have toilets on the ground floor as well and I am pointing this out to you because when I've done jobs like this, I always needed to use one.'

As they were discussing the ground floor, Tommy pointed to something on the plans and asked, 'What's that just outside the house? It's underground but it can't be a cellar - it's too far away from the house.'

Mac replied, 'It looks like the house has had a septic tank in the past; now it has proper pipes going to the sewer. Tommy, are you sure you want to carry on with this job? It could be dangerous.'

Tommy answered, 'Too right, I do. I want to know what he is doing with the girls he picks up.'

Mac replied, 'Well, you be really careful in that house.' He opened the door, saying, 'Anyway, I'll have to love you and leave you both. I've got a small matter of my own to deal with.'

As he left, Mac closed the door behind him.

A BUSINESS MEETING

As the door swung shut, Tommy picked the blueprints up and said, 'I'll be on my way as well, Val. I want to see if I can have a word with Ginger.'

Val frowned, answering 'She won't be there now. It's too early, she's a night bird.'

Tommy replied, 'I know that, but I saw her last time at the shops near where she works, so she must live close to there. I think I will look round the shops again, she might be there.'

Val nodded and said, 'Well, if you want to find her, you've got to start somewhere.' She smiled as she said, 'So, like Mac, you can love me and leave me.'

Tommy winked at her as he went out the door.

Once outside, he got on his bike, looking up at the window to see if Val was watching, and then drove to where he first saw Ginger. He rode round the area for an hour, looking for her coming out of nearby shops. When he came to the road where he had seen her last time, which had a row of shops on it, he stopped his bike in about the middle of the row and took his helmet off.

After he had sat there for about a quarter of an hour, looking up and down the shops, there was a gentle slap on the back of his head. He turned round to see Ginger, standing there with a shopping bag and a grin on her face.

She said, 'You must have enjoyed me taking your forty quid to come back for more?'

Tommy answered, 'It was worth every penny, just to have a friend like you.'

She asked, 'Why do I have the feeling you're looking for me?'

Tommy said, 'Look, Ginger, were you being honest when you said the feller I was looking for picked up girls and you never saw them again?'

Ginger got angry, glaring at him as she responded, 'Fuck you.'

She started to walk away but, as she did so, Tommy got off his bike and walked beside her.

He said, 'I didn't mean to upset you. I apologise, but I want to be sure and I need your help.'

Ginger replied, 'Because I'm a working girl, you think I can't be honest, but if it was Lady Shit, you would believe any shite that came out of her mouth?'

Tommy said, 'Ar 'ey, Ginger, I do believe you. That is why I'm back here, looking for you.'

She stopped and looked him in the face, as she asked, 'How do you think I can help you?'

Tommy replied, 'Like you, I get paid for my time, so I will pay for your time. Will forty be enough for a few more questions?'

Ginger laughed and replied, 'Now you're talking my language. As we aren't meeting as friends and it's just business, that will do nicely, sir.'

Tommy felt a bit embarrassed as he handed Ginger the forty pounds, because some women nearby started talking amongst themselves, staring at Tommy and Ginger and tutting.

Ginger laughed and pointed at Tommy's face, saying, 'Your face is the colour of my name. You should be used to them talking about you by now! Anyway, what do you want to know?'

Tommy replied loudly, looking over at the women, 'Are you sure the man I was following *did* pick up a woman last Friday?'

She replied, with an angry look on her face, 'You don't have to shout. I'm not deaf, like I told you last time... Or is it that you want those women over there to know you're not a client?'

He said, 'I'm sorry, Ginger. You're right, but if my girl knows I'm hanging round here, she mightn't believe I'm working.'

Ginger grinned and said, 'So, you're not scared of Clancy, but you're afraid of your girl? You coward!' continuing, 'Like I told you, the fellow in the car did pick up the blond-haired girl and I've been thinking about it since you last asked, and I now remember another girl that a few of the girls were talking about him picking up a while back. She was a young, blond girl - about eighteen - and one of the more experienced girls said she warned her, shouting "don't go with him" when he stopped by her... but the young girl got in his car anyway. I asked around after you left, and she wasn't seen again by any of the regular girls. He doesn't come every week, but they said it's no rumour - the young girls who he picks up are going missing.'

Tommy asked, 'Have any of the girls seen his face?'

She replied, 'No, but we all know his car because we all look out for one another.'

Tommy said, 'I don't want to upset you again but, if you look out for one another, how come he can pick up these young girls?'

Ginger was annoyed and replied, 'I have told you before, we all have our own patch and the newcomers don't come near us. They usually go a couple of roads away. Even so, when we do see a newcomer, we do try to warn them... but the look on your face and the way you have been talking, it sounds like you don't believe me,'

Tommy said, 'It's not that I don't believe you. It's just that I knew where he was going but, when I got there, he didn't have a girl with him. I don't know what he did with her if he did pick her up, so I have to be sure. I'm sorry it sounded like I didn't believe you. Are we still friends?'

Ginger laughed and said, 'Of course we're friends. That was a business meeting, wasn't it?'

Tommy answered, 'That's good. Sorry, Ginger, you know I didn't mean to upset you. Thanks for your help, I'll let you get on with your shopping now.'

Ginger said, 'You're my best client, I hope to see you again soon, Lover Boy.'

Tommy said, as he put his helmet on, 'Ginger, I'm no client. I like to think we are friends.'

He got on his bike, as she answered, 'You paid me, so that makes you a client but next time we meet, I will be your friend... so don't offer me money! Bye, Lover Boy.'

She walked into the nearest shop, as Tommy called after her, 'I'll see you, Ginger!'

Then he headed home.

CAMPING

At home Tommy made something to eat, got ready and then went to meet Ann in the Red Lion.

Ann was sitting in the usual place, with a red wine and a pint of lager on the table.

When she saw him, her brown eyes widened and her face glowed with a smile. Tommy had one on his face too. She stood up and kissed him as he hugged her.

When they sat down, Ann said, 'Babs seemed surprised to see me. I think she must have thought we had split up after the last time we were here.'

With a smile, Tommy replied, 'We'll never do that.'

They talked for a while and then Tommy asked, 'Can you get away next week?'

Ann replied, 'I'm afraid I can't. We're a chef down in one of the restaurants. He's not at all well and will be off for at least the next three weeks. Why, what have you got in mind?'

Tommy replied, 'I've got to spend next week out at that boathouse, and I've asked the boys to camp there with me. If you could have come, I would have asked the boys to invite their partners.'

Ann said, 'I would have loved to see the boys again. Give them all my love.'

He said, 'I know Jammer and Dave are coming, but I haven't heard from Terry yet. I hope he can get time off, because I need an I.T. expert.'

Ann asked, 'Why do you need an I.T. expert to go camping?'

'It's all to do with the house security,' Tommy answered.

She frowned and asked, 'You're not doing something you shouldn't, are you?'

He answered, 'Of course I'm not, I have been asked by the owner to do it. So don't worry about it. Now let's forget about work, drink up and we will spend a couple of hours in town.'

Ann picked up her drink and said, 'I'm with you, but I'll have to be home by twelve. It's an early start for me in the morning.'

Tommy smiled and said, 'I'll have you home for twelve, Cinderella.'

By eleven fifty, after a wonderful evening out together, they were standing outside Ann's house.

Tommy hugged and kissed Ann, asking, 'Will I be able to see you before I go camping?'

Ann replied, 'I would love to but, with being a chef down and all the paperwork I have to do, I doubt it, Tommy.'

He lifted her off her feet, swinging her round as he said, 'I'm not letting you go then.'

Ann laughed and said, 'Come on, soft lad, let me go.'

When he put her down, he sang, 'Go now, go now, before you see me cry.'

Ann said, giggling, 'Be quiet, Tommy, you'll have the neighbours complaining about me.'

He laughed as he said loudly, 'The neighbours will be complaining? The next house is a good two hundred yards away!'

She was in a happy mood and said, 'This will shut you up,' kissing him on the lips. Then, as they embraced, she suddenly broke away and ran up the driveway laughing. When she got to the door, she opened it and went in and, as she started to close it, she blew him a kiss.

He pretended to catch it and put it in his pocket. She laughed and shut the door.

He felt so good, he was smiling all the walk home.

On Friday, Tommy got a text from Terry saying: *I got the location you sent me. I'll be there. What do you want me to do?*

He replied: *I want you to tap into some security program, so I can get into a boathouse. TT*

Terry texted back straight away: *That's against the law. We're best mates and, like the song said, I'd do anything for you... but I won't do that. Sorry, Tommy.*

Tommy responded: *I understand. I have the owner's wife's permission to be in the house. We're not breaking and entering. I know it's illegal to be hacking into the security programme - and I wouldn't even ask, but there's something very wrong going on. There's young girl going missing, Terry. You know with your skills you can get into that computer without anyone ever knowing you were there. TT*

It took a few minutes for Terry's answer to come through. Three flashing dots showed he was thinking hard about what to write. Then his text came through: *I'll have to come in my van. And, TT, you will owe me big for this.*

Tommy sighed with relief and texted back: *You're not wrong. Thanks. I really appreciate it, mate. Dave and Jammer are coming but I don't think Paul will be with us this time. See you there on Monday. TT*

Just as he put his phone in his pocket, it vibrated again. He looked at it and found a text from Paul: *I had a couple of visitors, Dave and Jammer. They said I need a break, and I think they are right, so I got the location off them, and I'll see you at the campsite.*

Tommy texted back: *As long as you can manage it, that's great. I'll see you there. TT*

Over the weekend, Tommy studied the blueprints for a couple of hours, so he would know his way round the house.

Considering the best way to enter the house, he thought, 'If Mrs Clark thinks the fire escape is the easiest way in, then Mr Clark will as well. He might have booby-trapped it, so we might be best to go in a different entrance.'

Once he had finished planning, he made sure everything was ready for Monday morning, including getting written permission to access the house from Mrs Clark, on the condition that they only use it if things went wrong and the police got involved.

Tommy was the first to arrive at the boathouse. He set up camp about fifty metres away from the house, at the GPS location he had sent to the boys. He collected some wood and set up a campfire, ready to light when they got there, and then he waited on the road for them.

Terry, in his van, was the first to arrive.

As soon as he saw Tommy, he popped his head out of his window and said, 'Hi, Tommy. You could have told me that this so-called road was a dirt track, I will be lucky if my computers still work, they've been bounced about in the back so much!'

Tommy replied, 'Terry, as usual, you exaggerate the situation.'

He guided him to a grassy piece of land that was large enough for all the motor vehicles and tents, but with lots of bushes round them to provide some cover. As Terry was setting up his tent, Tommy went back to the road and waited for the rest of the boys.

The three of them turned up at the same time, on motor bikes. He showed them where Terry was and, as soon as they got off their bikes, they were all hugging and shaking each other's hands, going on about how great it was to see one another again.

By the time they were all set up and had settled down, it was getting dark. As they sat round the campfire, eating, Tommy explained to them what he was going to do and why.

Terry said to him, 'I've brought a generator to power my computers. It will make a bit of noise. Do you think anyone might hear it?'

Tommy replied, 'We are the only ones with permission to be here, so if there is anyone round here, they'll give us a wide berth.' Then he said, 'Just remember, no one goes near the house till Terry has his computers set up.'

Terry said, 'I'll start in the morning, I'm turning in now. I'm shattered.'

Jammer asked, 'How long will it take you to set up?'

'I don't know how long it will take me,' Terry replied, 'It all depends on how complicated the security set-up is. I mightn't even be able to hack into it. 'Night all, see you in the morning.'

He went into his tent, as Jammer said to Tommy, 'If he can't hack this fellow's computer feed, you're nobbled. What will you do?'

He replied, 'Terry works for the government and he's one of their top I.T. experts... You know him, he'll do it, he just doesn't like blowing his own trumpet. Now, may I suggest, because we've had a busy day, we all turn in?'

They all agreed and, as Dave put the fire out, they said their goodnights and went to their tents.

On Tuesday morning, Terry sat in the middle of his van, surrounded by computers. Paul started the generator up for him while Dave collected some firewood.

Jammer asked him, 'What are you collecting wood for? I've got a cracking calor gas heater in my carrier.'

Dave pulled a face and said, 'We are supposed to be camping, so let's do it right.'

While Terry was working with his computers, Tommy's other friends went fishing for their tea, leaving him studying the blueprints and getting as near as he could to scope out the house.

Every now and then he would phone Terry and ask, 'How are you getting on?'

Terry's answer was the same every time, 'He knew what he was doing when he set this lot up.'

The boys got back about eight and started cooking the four fish they had caught, alongside some tinned beans they had brought with them. Terry stepped out of his van when he smelled the cooking and Tommy got back from the house just as Terry joined the others by the fire.

Terry said, 'Tommy, I cracked it, so I will set up the replacement feed tomorrow, is that okay?

Tommy replied, 'That's great. Now let's get something to eat.'

They all sat round the fire, helping themselves to the fish and the beans.

Tommy got a carton of canned beers out the boot of his car and, as he sat down and helped himself to some fish and beans, said, 'The drinks are for our afters.'

ROUND THE CAMPFIRE

When they had finished eating, they started drinking and reminiscing about when they were young boys.

Dave said, 'Paul used to come out with some good stories.'

Jammer asked, 'Do you still write short stories, Paul?'

Dave butted in, 'Yes, come on, Paul, you must have one with you?'

Paul said, 'Alright,' and went into his tent.

He came back with a writing pad, opened it, and said, 'Tommy, you're the detective, so see if you can work out "whodunnit", which is also the name of the story, by the way. So, have you all got a drink?'

They all nodded and said that they had, so Paul read them his story...

'The police were called to 12 Church Road, the home of a well-known publisher. When they got there, they were met by a young man and a teenage girl.

They looked worried and the young man said, "My stepfather has been murdered, and my mother is still in bed with him because rigor mortis has set in and he's holding her wrist, so she can't get out of the bed."

The young girl said, "For God's sake, get her out of there. She's covered in blood from my dad."

The policemen went into the bedroom and saw a man lying in the bed and a woman half sitting, half lying on the bed. She was covered in blood and was sobbing. The man was holding her wrist. There was a long knife in his chest and his hands were covered in dried blood.

The police called the station for additional help, including sending an ambulance. They asked the boy and girl why they hadn't rung for an ambulance themselves, but they both just said they didn't know. The police put it down to shock.

The paramedics helped to get the woman's wrist free from her dead husband's hand and cleaned her up. She had cuts and bruises all over her body and spent the night in hospital. The police wanted to question her but she was still in a state of shock, so they waited till she was discharged the next morning. Whilst she was in hospital, they secured the crime scene, brought forensics in and sent the knife to the lab for fingerprinting.

When the woman got home, there were two detectives there. One was tall and bald, while the other was average height and had red hair. She remembered seeing them the day before, at the hospital.

As they sat down together in the front room, the red-haired detective said, "Well, Mrs Scott, did you see who killed your husband?"

"No," she replied, "I was asleep all night and when I woke up, he was dead."

The detective was puzzled and said, "I thought you fought the killer off when I saw the cuts and bruises on you!"

Mrs Scott, who looked in shock, just started rambling, "Oh no, the bastard who did this to me is dead and, though I didn't do it, I'm glad he is dead. I thank the person who did it. Everyone thinks he was a lovely man, but he was a wicked bastard. He would beat me, just to see how long it took me to say he could do anything he wanted to me as long as he would stop, and you wouldn't believe the things he would do then. So afterwards, I would take about four sleeping pills and go to bed and that's what happened last night... and while I was asleep my prayers were answered, and someone killed the bastard."

The red-headed detective said, "Can you tell us what the fight last night was about?"

Mrs Scott started crying as she answered him, "He was carrying on with his secretary and when he had sex with her, in our bed, he would video it without telling her. So I sent her the video and hoped he wouldn't detect that it was missing, but the evil bastard did."

The red-headed detective said, "We'll leave it there for now, Megan. You don't mind if I call you Megan, do you? I know that was your name from when we were checking you into the hospital."

"No," Megan replied, "But I'm going to have a lie down - I feel faint."

She got up and walked to the door. The red-headed detective said, as she reached it, "I'm sorry we have to question you. He must have been a bully and a coward to live with."

Megan replied, without looking at him, "He was a bully, but he was too evil to be a coward. When he burnt me with his cigarette, he would laugh and then put it out on his own arm."

Then she turned, saying, "I will be in my daughter's room if you need me" as she left the living room.

The red-headed detective turned to his partner and said, "It must have been hell living with a bastard like him, but I don't think she killed him."

His partner answered in a sarcastic voice, "Hey, Red, how did you make detective? You believe anything anyone tells you. She might be a good actor."

Red replied, "Well, Cliff, I believe people till the evidence suggests they're lying, and *that's* how I made detective... before you. Now, I'll interview the young girl and you take the lad. Then we'll go and get a statement from the secretary. She might have had a key to the house."

Cliff set up in the dining room and took a statement off the young man, saying to him, "I'm sorry for your and your family's loss, but we will have to take a statement from you. Your name and age?"

"Ben Green. I'm twenty years old," he replied. He looked at the detective and said, "I don't know where to start."

Cliff answered, "Well, start with what happened last night."

"Okay," Ben said, "I went to bed about 11 o'clock. I picked up a book I was reading but I didn't even read a page before I fell asleep. The next thing I was woken by my mother screaming. At first, I just put my head under the pillow and hoped it would stop..."

Cliff interrupted, "What do you mean you put the pillow over your head when your mother was screaming?"

Ben looked ashamed and, with tears running down his face, said, "I thought he was beating her again. Three times I've tried to stop him and three times he's put me in hospital but in the end - when she didn't stop screaming - I got up and went to her bedroom anyway. Outside the door I met June. We went into the room together and saw my stepfather with a knife in his chest and my mother covered in blood. I told June to ring 999 and get the police."

Cliff said, "You didn't like your stepfather, did you?"

Ben replied, "Well, I can see why you made detective. Of course not, I hated his guts and wish I could take the credit for killing him, but I didn't do it. God bless the person who did."

Red, who had taken charge when interviewing Megan Scott also interviewed her daughter, June. When he saw her sitting in her bedroom, crying, with her stepmother's arms wrapped around her, his heart went out to her.

He introduced himself as Detective Drake and said, "I am sorry, June, but I will have to take a statement off you."

"I don't know anything, I was asleep all night," June sobbed.

"Well, just begin with when you went to bed last night - and would you say how old you are, as we have to put it in the report."

Still sobbing she said, "I'm seventeen and, as you can see, my room is next to Dad and Megan's room. He said "goodnight" to me and left my room at 12:30 and went into their room. After a while I heard him and Megan arguing and fighting, so I took some sleeping pills. When I heard her screaming, I thought I hadn't been asleep long, so I looked at the clock, but it was 7:15. So I went to their room, but I just stood outside the door till Ben came because I was too afraid to go in by myself."

She broke down, her body shaking, as she sobbed, "My dad is one wicked bastard."

Red gave her a hanky to wipe her face with and said, "I know it's hard, but we have to know what happened so we can catch the person who did this terrible thing to your dad."

June stopped crying and continued her statement, "Ben went in first, but he stepped aside as I followed him, and that's when I saw my dad, with a knife in him, and Megan covered in blood. Ben told me to ring 999 and said to send for the police. When they arrived, we turned off the alarm and let them in."

After they had finished with the family, the detectives went to the murdered man's work to interview the secretary but, when they got there, there was only one person in the office.

After explaining that the business was a publishing house, the man introduced himself as Mr Todd, the office clerk. When they told him his boss was dead, he just smiled and said, "It had to happen one day."

The two detectives looked at one another and then Red said, "You look quite pleased. Why is that?"

Mr Todd, still with a smile on his face, replied, "Well, he only employed young girls as secretaries. He'd be a real gentleman for a few months - or until he'd had sex with them, then he would turn back into the prick he really was. Even this last girl - Lucy Wright - left... and I know he had sex with her because he gave me the keys to his house a couple of days ago to give to her, and I haven't seen her since. Now I wouldn't have been surprised if you'd said *she'd* been murdered, because he's one horrible bastard."

Cliff asked, "So you've had access to the keys to your boss's house? Where were you last night?"

Todd replied, "I didn't do it, but I hope whoever did gets away with it because he's one evil bastard to work for. When I first started working for him he insisted that I go out for a drink with him, but I couldn't drink as much as he could. He took me to gambling clubs and after a few months he showed me some IOUs. I owed him hundreds of thousands of pounds. I know I borrowed a few pounds off him, but nowhere near that much, so he must have conned me into signing those IOUs while I was drunk. So, I was trapped to work for him until either I died or he did, and it looks like I won in the end."

Cliff said, "That gives you a motive to do it, so now it all depends on where you were last night. So, where were you?"

Todd answered, "I was home in bed with my wife all night - you can ask her."

Red asked, "Does she take sleeping pills? Everyone else in this town seems to!"

Todd replied, "Yes. Why?"

Cliff answered, "Then you haven't got an alibi for last night. So, we'll want to see you again. Now, can we have Miss Wright's address?"

They went to Miss Wright's home. A small girl answered the door. She looked about twelve years of age.

The tall detective looked down at her and asked, "Does Miss Lucy Wright live here?"

The girl said, "Who wants to know?"

The detective showed his warrant card, answering, "We do."

The girl stepped back and asked, "What do you want me for?"

"You're Lucy Wright?" the red-haired detective asked, incredulously.

"Yes," the girl replied, "I'm small for my age. Everyone thinks I'm younger than I am."

Red asked, "Are you the Lucy Wright who worked in Mr Scott's office?"

Lucy replied, "Yes, I worked for the depraved, dirty old bastard. If you want to put someone away, that bastard should go away for life."

Cliff said, "Someone has done better than that, they've murdered him. Now, can you tell us where you were last night?"

Lucy laughed bitterly, saying, "I was here last night - like I have been since that wicked bastard abused and raped me a few days ago. I hope whoever did it gutted the bastard."

Red said, "You should have reported him to the police. We're very helpful these days; you would have had the help of a policewoman to get you through it all."

Lucy started crying and told them why she didn't report him, saying, "He videoed me letting myself into the house, going into his den and through the door to the bedroom, where we kissed and started to make love. I had thought he was a lovely man, but he was like Jekyll and Hyde. When he started hurting me, I told him to stop and said I would go to the police, but he just laughed. Just before he threw me out, he dragged me by my hair to the T.V. and showed me the start of the video. He said that it would prove he didn't rape me. Then he kicked me and said, "no-one would believe a tramp like you." His wife sent me the video, but I destroyed it because I wouldn't like anyone to see what he did to me."

Cliff asked, "Was there anyone with you last night?"

"No." Lucy replied, through her sobs.

"It's all right, Lucy,' Red reassured her, "We'll send someone round to take a statement and help you get some counselling."

Cliff added, "Do be aware that we may have to see you again about the murder because you had keys to the house."

Lucy, still crying, said, "Mr Todd gave me the keys to the house and he hated Mr Scott. He was always saying Mr Scott was a real bad man and he would get even with him one of these days. I thought Mr Todd was a bit touched, but now I know how he feels. I wish I *had* killed him, the piece of shit."

Going over the case together later, the two detectives discussed the evidence.

Cliff said, "My money's on the lad, he's just full of hate."

"They're all full of hate," Red interrupted, "I hate the bastard myself - and I didn't do it!"

"No," Cliff said, "I just mean, I've got this feeling he did it."

"Well," Red butted in, "We'll go to see him later on. I definitely can't see Megan Scott stabbing him, then lying down next to him on the bed for hours... or putting his hand round her own wrist and waiting for the rigor mortis to set in. And the girl, June, is too timid to do it."

Cliff said, "That Todd is one to keep an eye on, though. He could easily have got a copy of the key made, so he could get into the house... and Miss Wright. She may be small but, if I did what he did to her, then I wouldn't turn my back on her... and, to be honest, Red, I wouldn't trust that Megan Scott either."

Red replied, sarcastically, "Oh, well, that's it, then. We'll arrest all of them for murder, you've solved the case! I think we'd better get out there and try a bit harder or we will be getting our arses kicked by the inspector. He said it was an open and shut case."

Cliff said, "Okay. I think we should interview the lad again."

They brought Ben into the station and advised him to get a solicitor, offering help to provide one if necessary.

He refused their offer, saying, "I don't need one, I didn't do it."

Red said, "You didn't like your stepdad, did you?"

Ben was about to answer when Cliff said, "In fact, you hated him, didn't you?"

Ben said, "Yes. I already told you that. Look, I'm glad the bastard is dead but I'm sorry to say I didn't do it."

After the detectives went over his statement for some hours with him, Cliff said, "We know it must have been you who killed him because whoever did it was still in the house in the morning, given that the alarm was still on when the first officers arrived on the scene. And you had plenty of motive - you hated him for what he did to your mother and the fact he put you in hospital a few times."

Ben answered, "Some detectives you two are! I wasn't the only one who hated him and was in the house."

Red said, "Come on, Ben, make it easy on yourself and your family."

Ben just jeered at him, saying, "Hey, you're going out of turn. It's *his* turn to be 'good cop' now... Look, I'll give you two so-called detectives a clue about who might have done it. Her loving dad wouldn't leave her alone and she hated him for it."

Cliff said, "You can go now, but we will want to talk to you again, so don't go too far."

They sent a police car for June and she and her stepmother were brought to the station to go over her statement but, as they were about to interview her, the lab report came through.

Before pressing ahead with June's interview, the detectives discussed the lab report. It said that the fingerprints on the knife were Megan Scott's and that, given the way the knife was held, her husband must have been standing up when he was stabbed. If he had been lying down, to come down with enough power to pierce his chest as it had, the knife would have had to have been held in a clenched fist, with the thumb on the end of the handle.

The detectives told June she could go home and arrested Megan Scott for the murder of her husband. Megan was taken to an interview room and questioned about exactly how she had stabbed her husband, but she just kept saying she didn't do it.

Red said, "Look, Megan, we know he beat and mistreated you, but you still can't expect to get away with murder. Tell us what happened... We know from the way you stabbed him that he must have been standing up when it happened. We can see that from the position of your fingerprints on the knife. Your thumb is near the blade, so you pushed the knife into him with you both in a standing position, which is why the blade didn't go all the way in. That's why his fingers were all cut - from trying to stop the knife. So, your story that someone stabbed him while you were both lying in bed, well, it just doesn't work."

"My fingerprints aren't on the knife, because I didn't do it," screamed Megan.

"All right," said Cliff, "We'll go over your statement again... but try to remember it's your bread knife and only you were in the bedroom with him. Now, would you start with why you were fighting with him?"

Megan said, "It may be my bread knife, but the only thing I've cut with it is bread and cake."

Red butted in, "Come on, Megan, what happened that night before the killing? Why the fight that night?"

Megan glared at the detective and said, "Manners isn't one of your strong points, is it?"

"No, and neither is murder. Now, tell us about what happened that night before the murder," he replied.

Megan cleared her throat and said, "Well, that night he was in June's room, and I could hear her crying. I knew what the dirty bastard was doing but I was too scared to go in and stop him. When he came into our room, he was carrying a bottle of whisky and a glass. He poured himself a drink and then hit me in the face with the bottle. It nearly knocked me out. He dragged me up by the hair and said, "Where is the video from the den? And don't you dare lie to me." I said I didn't know where he hid them and asked if he was sure it wasn't just with the others. Then he threw me across the room and, as I tried to get up, he started to kick me, so I told him I had sent it to Lucy Wright. He went insane. I thought he was going to kill me: he had his hand round my throat and was tightening it as he talked to me. He said something about him going to prison for life if the police got the video. I think I fainted, but I could hear him laughing, I think. I finally picked myself up, took four or five sleeping pills and prayed that one of us wouldn't wake up in the morning. I didn't really mind which one of us it was. When I woke up he was dead, but the bastard still held onto me as if he was trying to take me with him.

If my fingerprints are on the knife, I must have done it in my sleep because I know that I didn't do it while I was awake."

Red said, "I'm sorry, Megan, but you will have to stay in the station tonight."

As Megan went to the cell with the policewoman, Cliff said, "It's strange - in all the door-to-door interviews with the neighbours, they all said he seemed like a lovely family man."

The red-headed detective showed another reason why his fellow police officers called him 'Red.'

His face turned scarlet, and he said, in an annoyed voice, "So, all our key witnesses are lying? He was really a nice chap? This fellow was a self-made bastard and, if he wasn't dead already, I'd kill him myself."

His partner said, "Take it easy, Red, you'll blow a valve. I was just saying he could fool people. If you're not careful, you're going to burst a blood vessel."

Red said, "Well, whoever killed the nine-carat bastard should get a medal for it."

A police officer entered Cliff's office and said, "There's a Ben Green at the desk asking to speak to you or Red. About the murder."

Cliff took Ben to an interview room.

"Right, what can we do for you?" he asked.

Ben said, "My mother's solicitor said you're going to charge my mother for the murder. Well, I did it. I waited till they were both asleep, put on my winter gloves and then went and got the bread knife from the kitchen. I thought of those times he put me in hospital, and I brought the knife down into his chest."

The detective asked, "How come your mother's fingerprints are on the knife?"

Tommy replied, "That's because earlier on she had cut some cake for our supper."

Cliff said, "Wait here."

He went into Red's office and found that he was interviewing June.

Red said to his partner, "She arrived to give a statement just after her stepbrother did. She claims she did it."

Then he turned to June and said, "Tell him why and how you did it."

June said, "I hated my dad. From the first thing I can remember, he has abused me. When I was about six my mother said we were leaving the house and my poor excuse for a dad, but he came into the bedroom as my mother picked me up. They argued and then he started to hit me and said he would keep hitting me until my mother put me down. When she did, he dragged her out the door. I heard a scream and my mother was dead. He said she fell down the stairs and banged her head on a big, old, iron shoe-cleaner at the bottom of the stairs. But it was never kept by the bottom of the stairs, it was kept by the front door.

The night I murdered him, I asked him if he'd killed her. He laughed and said "Yes, and if you're not a good girl for your dad, I'll do the same thing to your new mummy." I went sick. Megan's taken many beatings over the last six years trying to defend me from him. When he left my room, I heard him fighting with her, so I went to the kitchen, put on the marigolds Megan keeps by the sink and got the knife she used to cut the cake we had for supper. I didn't mean for Megan to get the blame - I just took that knife because it was out on the worktop. Then I waited until they were asleep - I knew Megan wouldn't wake up because she takes sleeping tablets - and then I went to their room and stabbed him in the chest."

Red said, "Wait here, June."

He and Cliff went into another room to talk.

Cliff looked at Red and said, "We've got Ben confessing as well. Obviously at least one of them - if not both - is trying to protect Megan. Do you think either of them did it?"

Red said, "Well, if Ben did it, the knife would have gone all the way in and the fingerprints would have been smudged. The same is true for the fingerprints with June but the knife mightn't have gone all the way home."

Cliff said, "Well, let's go to Scott's office and see if we can find out some more. Maybe Mr Todd will say he did it... Almost everybody else has!"

When they got to Scott's office, Mr Todd was about to leave, carrying a box that seemed to be full.

Cliff asked, "Going somewhere? What have you got in the box?"

Mr Todd opened the box to show that the things in it were his. At the top of the box were two manuscripts in envelopes. Red picked one of the manuscripts out and looked at it. It was addressed to Miss Lucy Wright, 10 May Road.

Red asked, "Mr Todd, why is this addressed to Miss Wright?"

Mr Todd answered, in a feeble voice, "Well, I wrote it about twenty years ago and when I started to work for this piece of filth - about ten years ago - he said he would look it over and publish it for me. As you can see, he has looked it over. He's written comments all over it."

Red followed up, "Yes, but why are you sending it to Miss Wright?"

Mr Todd said, "I told her I had written a novel and said that if I ever got it back she could read it."

Cliff said to Mr Todd, "You're best leaving them where they are until the inquiry is over. In fact, we'll take these things with us to check over back at the station."

Red said, "Let's get back there. There's nothing else significant here that I can see. In my dinner hour I like to read, it helps to relax me, so I'll take a look at this novel when we get to the station."

Once there, Red said to his partner, "I can't read this. Scott wrote all over it. Put your coffee down - look at the name of Todd's story: "*Whodunnit?*" If he couldn't think of anything better than that it doesn't say much for the rest of the story! I bet Scott's remarks are more interesting. Here's one, he's written: *A shitty title, with a bad start. Then it gets worse and ends as a load of rubbish.* Yet he's written in bold: *the plot of the dead man knifed while in bed with his wife is worth looking into.*"

Red looked at Cliff, who said to him, "You better had read the story; I'll go and bring Todd and little Miss Wright in."

Cliff brought Mr Todd and Miss Wright to the station, into a large room where Megan, June and Ben sat, being watched over by a policewoman. They each looked up as Mr Todd and Lucy came in, with the detective towering over them to their rear.

Red entered the room and all eyes - including his partner's - turned towards him.

He went up to Mr Todd and said, "We know it couldn't be you who committed this crime because of the video cameras around the house. There is no way you or Lucy could get past without being caught by at least one of them and only G4 Security have access to the camera feed, so you couldn't fake that. Now, why didn't you just tell us what you knew? I've a good mind to book you for wasting police time."

Mr Todd answered, "I don't know why. I just wanted to stay out of it."

Cliff asked, "Was it Ben?"

Red shook his head and his partner said, "Well, I don't think it was June. I think Megan Scott did it."

Megan just put her head in her hands and sobbed.'

Paul stopped reading for a moment and asked, 'Tommy, do you know who did it? And if any of you three think you know, write it down on your phones.'

Tommy thought for a while. He looked at the other boys, but all three looked puzzled.

Tommy said, 'I'll write it down as well, and then you can finish the story.'

Paul took a drink of his beer, and continued:

'Red put his arm round Megan and said, "Sorry, Megan, that we've put you through all of this. The book told us how it was done. Being the evil bastard he was, your husband did it himself. He knew that if we got hold of the recording you sent to Lucy, he would have ended up in jail. It turns out he *was* a coward - because he couldn't face that. He didn't know Lucy had destroyed the tape, so he decided to take the easy way out but, being a son of a bitch, he decided to make you pay. He held the knife by the blade as he stabbed himself, so your fingerprints were still on the handle, and he held onto you as he was dying because he wanted to make sure you got the blame."

Red turned to Ben and June, saying, "It's commendable that you both wanted to help your mum so much, but you're also lucky we don't charge you with wasting police time - your statements confused an already difficult investigation. We've never had a case before where someone tried to frame somebody for their own murder!"

Having finished reading his story, Paul asked, 'Well, Tommy, what did you write?'

Tommy showed Paul what he'd jotted down on his notes app and it read '*Mr Scott*'. None of the other boys had guessed.

Paul asked them, 'Well, what do you think of the story?'

His friends all agreed that it was very good, although Dave did ask, 'Who's Mr Scott?'

The boys laughed and Terry said, 'He's the one who was killed! Were you thinking about your new girlfriend when you should have been listening?'

Dave smiled and replied, 'I guess I was now and then. You want to meet her, she's great. I was going to bring her here, but she didn't fancy it.'

Jammer butted in, 'I've written a poem, do you want to hear it?'

Tommy, Terry and Paul said 'Yes,' straight away, while Dave asked, 'It's not one of your crude ones, is it?'

Jammer laughed and said, 'Of course not. Well, judge for yourselves, it's what actually happened to me. It's called '*In the library*'.'

He narrated his poem off by heart, reciting, 'As I look for a book,
I feel like I've   been hit with a left hook
I'm nearly doubled in two and feeling blue, but I'll have to see it through
The pain, the strain, one can't complain, 'cause no one's to blame
People around, but I'm not to make a sound
I'd like to scream and shout, to get the pain out
I feel ill; I'd like to take a pill - I think the pain will kill
I hold my breath and pray the pain will go away
The pain starts to go, slow, and I say 'oh no'
A loud cheeky sound echoes all around
It trumpets in the air, people stop to stare
Oh, hell, what a smell... but I live to tell
Well, I could tell by their gaze, they were amazed, and I was in a daze
I didn't care, the pain was no longer there, but the smell lingered in the air.'

Jammer laughed at his own joke, adding, 'If Dave had been there, it would have woken him up.'

The boys, being merry with the beer they had been drinking, all laughed.

Then Terry yawned and said, 'I'm turning in, I'll be busy in the morning. 'Night all.'

As he went to his tent, Paul said, 'It is getting late, we might as well all turn in.'

The other boys agreed, so they put out the fire, stacked the dishes up for washing in the morning and headed for their tents.

GETTING READY FOR THE JOB

The next morning the first one up was Tommy. He was eating his breakfast by five-thirty and, one after another, his friends joined him.

At seven, Dave, Jammer and Paul went fishing again, and Terry started working on the security of the house. His computers had been logged into Clark's security camera for the last twenty-four hours and now he had to hack into the signal being sent to Clark's laptop in the states.

After he had been working a little while, Tommy asked him, 'How are you doing?'

Terry replied, 'It will take a few hours to create a loop so that, when he looks at his laptop, he will see the bushes moving with the wind, but you will be able to go and look round the outside of the house this morning, once that process is finished. The booby traps you told us about are listed on his laptop - he seems to be able to turn them on and off from there. I don't know what they are, but once I have full access to his computer system, I can turn them off remotely from here. By tomorrow, you will be able to go into the house.'

Tommy said, 'Great.'

He headed back out of the van and phoned the locksmith Mac had recommended, arranging for him to come in the morning.

Terry finished working about two in the afternoon. He left his computers running and went off to find the other boys, so he could join them while they were still fishing. Tommy went looking round the house, meeting up with the others for another night enjoying a meal and a chat around the campfire.

After breakfast the next morning, Terry went straight to his van to monitor his computers.

The locksmith arrived at ten thirty. Now that Terry had set up the loop, Tommy was able to wait for him by the front door of the boathouse.

The locksmith said, 'This is a bloody hard place to find.'

Tommy nodded, but before he had time to speak, the locksmith continued, 'I'm Peter. Have you got the paperwork? I need to see it now, before I can do anything, sir.'

Tommy handed him the papers as he responded, 'I'm Tommy. This is what Mrs Clark, the owner of the property, gave me to give to you.'

Peter looked at the papers, checking them against his own paperwork; then he put them in a small folder he had been carrying under his arm and placed the folder in the glove compartment in his van.

He said, 'Mac tells me that I need to keep the details of this job confidential. That's fine, Tommy, seeing as the paperwork is all correct. Now, let's have a look at the locks on this door.'

He studied the locks for a little while and then said, as he walked towards his van, 'I'll get my tools, the locks on that door could take a good few hours.'

Tommy said, 'I'll leave you to it. I don't want to get in your way. I'll come back about one-thirty, okay, Peter?'

'I should be nearly finished by then,' he answered, as he placed a large toolbox by the door.

Tommy went off to find his mates. He knew they had gone fishing again, so he headed towards the river.

When he found them, they were having a fishing contest. As Tommy got there too late to do any successful fishing himself, they made him the judge. Jammer had been the least successful - he had only caught one fish. Terry, despite getting there late, had caught two, so he still beat Jammer.

Dave and Paul were arguing about who had the best catch. Dave had caught three fish, about eight inches long each, while Paul had only caught two, but they were both about fifteen inches.

Tommy told them, 'Stop arguing - *I'm* the judge.'

He put Dave's fish in one of the plastic bags they had with them and felt the weight; then he did the same with Paul's catch. He lifted a bag in each hand and announced that Paul's fish were the heaviest.

Then he said, 'I've got to get back to the locksmith. I'll see you later.'

Terry took that as his cue to get back to the computers and hack into Clark's system to turn off the booby-traps.

Tommy got back to the house just as Peter was finishing.

Peter said, 'I've picked all the locks. You can head into the house whenever you want, so I'll be on my way.'

He packed all his tools into his van and gave Tommy his card, saying, 'If you ever need a locksmith again, just give me a call.' Then he drove off.

Tommy phoned Terry, and asked, 'Is it safe to go in now?'

Terry replied, 'Yes, I've turned everything off in the house that I can see on his system, but I'll send the boys to you because he might have other traps that aren't linked to his laptop.'

Terry phoned the boys and told them to meet Tommy at the house, saying they should swing by the van on the way, so they could pick up the crowbars he had brought with him, in case they were needed in the house.

Dave, Jammer and Paul did this and then met Tommy at the door of the boathouse.

INSIDE THE BOATHOUSE

Tommy went in first, with the boys a few yards behind him. He was very slow and careful as he moved round the house. He went into the kitchen, and it was spotless. The living room had old furniture in it, but even that looked like it had never been used. When they came to the two small cloakrooms on the ground floor, Dave and Paul both wanted to use them.

While they were waiting, Tommy and Jammer checked their surroundings for booby traps. They were just checking the stairs when the other two re-appeared. They all moved upstairs, with the other three still staying a few yards behind Tommy.

The first room he went in had a bed, with nice furnishings round it, but the second and third rooms were empty. The door to the fire escape, which sat directly opposite the top of the stairs, was bolted with a padlock on it. It was obvious from the width of the landing that there was a fourth room on the other side of the stairs, that must run nearly the length of the house. It would be large enough to be a function room, just like Mac had suggested, but there did not seem to be a way to access it.

Tommy said, 'The room on the other side of this wall should have a bathroom you can only reach from inside the big room, and another smaller room off it that provides a way in as well. That's where the door should be - at least, that's what it shows on the blueprints.'

Paul pointed to a large bookcase pushed up against the wall at the far end of the landing, saying, 'There may be a door behind that.'

Dave went over to it. He tried pushing it and then he tried pulling it, but it didn't give at all.

'It's full of books,' he said. 'The four of us couldn't move it. So I don't think just one bloke on his own would be able to move it.'

'If there's a door behind there, we should be able to move it,' Jammer replied.

With that he and Tommy started looking all over the bookcase, inspecting it carefully.

Tommy said, 'Jammer is right. Clark is an engineer. He must have made it so he could move it. It makes no sense having it here otherwise. You'd just put it further along the landing.'

He got down on all fours, looking at the bottom of the bookcase, and found small holes: one on either side of it.

He put his eye up close to one of the holes and then said, 'There's small wheels, like caster wheels, on it.'

He felt round the bottom of the bookcase, put his hand in one of the holes and said to Jammer, 'Put your foot in this hole and press down as you push it up.'

Jammer did it and it raised his side up an inch, so Tommy said, 'Dave, do the same on the other side. It's definitely on wheels.'

Dave did as he was told, and his side lifted up too. Once they had released the wheels, the bookcase moved quite freely. They pushed it out of the way to reveal a large door. They opened the door slowly and carefully. The room beyond it was pitch black.

Tommy took his torch out and looked on the walls next to the door for a light switch. Once he found it, he kept the light trained on it as he reached into the room, making sure he could quickly move out of the way if it was booby-trapped. Jammer and Paul understood why he was being so careful and held onto his belt, ready to pull him away if anything happened. When he pressed the switch, however, all that happened was that the light came on; the room they were looking into was a bathroom, but a strange one.

Tommy looked around the room and then they moved carefully into it, amazed to see how clean it was. At the far end of the room, there were two large, strange machines, with some sort of fridge in between them. Alongside them was a large freezer chest. Against another wall, there was a large bath and a wooden table, with cupboards on the third wall. Tommy moved forward nervously, with the boys, just as nervous, close behind him. Tommy opened one of the cupboards and none of them could believe what they saw: it was full of tools like those you would find in an operating theatre.

Tommy asked his friends, 'Will you all wait in the other room? I wouldn't like you to see what I think is in the freezer. I'm hoping to God that I'm wrong.'

They didn't want to leave the room without him, but he insisted and walked them to the door. Once they had gone, he went back to the freezer. He got hold of the handle, feeling a little bit sick as he did so. He took a deep breath and opened it. As soon as he saw what was inside, he slammed the freezer shut and ran out the room, past the boys, vomiting. He went to the nearest wall and put his hand on it to support himself as he vomited. The boys had an idea of what he had seen but were worried about how bad it must be - they all knew that Tommy wasn't one to sicken easily.

Jammer got his phone out and Paul said, 'What are you doing?'

Jammer replied, 'I'm calling the police.'

Dave said, 'Tommy mightn't want the police involved...?'

So Paul asked, 'Shall we call the police, Tommy?'

He nearly choked as he was wrenching so much but no more vomit was coming out, so he managed to say, 'Yes, call the police.'

Jammer called them. When they answered, he said, 'There's been a murder, so send a lot of police,' though it took him quite a while to get through to the operator exactly where they were.

They all waited outside the house till the police arrived. While they were waiting, Jammer asked Tommy, 'What did you see in the freezer?'

Tommy was still white. He was sitting on the ground with his back against the house and he said, with tears in his eyes, 'I can't speak about right now. Just leave it till we've seen the police.'

When the police got there and saw the crowbars on the floor just outside the door of the boathouse, they were going to arrest Tommy and the boys, but they all protested, with Jammer shouting, 'We were the ones who called you!'

Tommy got up and a policeman came over to him. While he was wiping his mouth with his handkerchief, he struggled to get his private investigator licence out of his wallet. Once he had, he showed it to the policeman as he explained more calmly that it was them who had called the police.

The policeman said to the other officers, 'We made a mistake. These lads are the ones who phoned us.'

Then he said to Tommy, 'Alright, we hear there's been a murder, so where's the body? And what were you doing here, with crowbars, anyway?'

Tommy showed them Mrs Clark's letter giving them permission to be in the house and advised, 'Don't go into the house. Look at the state of me. If you want to keep your breakfast, get the forensic people down here.'

Two of the police had to go in anyway. They came out looking just as shaken as Tommy and called for Forensics to come and secure the crime scene. Then they took Tommy's and the boys' statements.

While he was making his statement, Tommy told them about Terry in the van and how Clark would know the police were at the house, if Terry stopped his computers. The policeman who was taking his statement and Tommy went to the van, with Tommy leading the way. Terry was in a world of his own, staring at his monitors to make sure the loop was still working and listening to his music on his headphones. He went sick when the police opened the doors of his van.

He quickly pulled his headphones off and moved toward his keyboard, so Tommy shouted, 'Don't turn them off - the police want you to carry on.'

Terry looked confused so the policeman said, 'It's all right - we need you to keep it going for a few hours, till we get the police in the states to arrest the bastard.'

Tommy told Terry what had happened at the house, but he didn't tell him exactly what he'd seen in the freezer.

After a couple of hours, the officer who had taken charge of the operation that had been set up back at the boathouse came to the van and said to Terry, 'You can turn your computers off now. We've had word that the police in the states have arrested that evil bastard. We advise you all to head home now because, as you know, this is a murder scene.

I apologise for the misunderstanding earlier and thank you for the help you've provided with the computers. Please don't forget that we will be in touch with each of you very shortly, to ask you to come into the station and give a full written statement.'

While the boys were breaking camp, they kept asking Tommy what exactly was in the freezer.

Tommy said, 'I'm sorry but I don't feel too good. I don't want to talk about it... or even think about it.'

Dave said, 'Come on, lads. We have a good idea what was in there and we will get to know more in time, so just leave it alone, eh? You can see that it's knocked him sick.'

Jammer said, 'Sorry for going on, Tommy. Just try and put it out of your mind.'

The other boys nodded, and they all finished packing up in silence. They only spoke again when they were finally leaving. They agreed to meet up with each other soon, so they could process what had happened once Tommy felt more up to discussing things.

A BREAK FROM THE JOB

Tommy got home about three in the morning. He couldn't sleep and felt unwell. He just couldn't get what he had seen out of his mind. He made himself a mug of coffee but, when he finally managed to drink it, within seconds he had to go to the toilet and vomit it up. He lay in his bed for quite a while before he eventually drifted off to sleep at about eight a.m.

He was woken at three in the afternoon, when Val phoned him. He didn't really want to talk to anyone, so he let it ring for a little while before he picked the phone up.

He didn't say anything as he answered, so Val asked, 'Are you alright, Tommy?'

When he heard Val's voice, he felt tears coming to his eyes and he tried not to show how upset he was in his voice, replying, 'Yes, I will be in the office soon, to make my report.'

Val said, 'Jacko has been in and told us what has happened. He heard about it down at the station yesterday; he said everyone was talking about how horrible it was. So Mac said you wouldn't want to talk about it yet and that you don't need to come back to the office till you have rested.'

Tommy felt a little bit better knowing he didn't have to go over what had happened again so soon; he took the rest of the day off, distracting himself as best he could by playing video games and watching the T.V. He tried to contact Ann, but her phone kept just going to voicemail and he couldn't face ringing her PA.

The next morning, he got up and tried to get himself back into his usual routine. He did his exercises, got showered and made himself a mug of tea and a couple of rounds of toast for breakfast. While he sat down to eat it, he was thinking about whether he could bring himself to go into the office and file his report. Just then there was a knock on the front door.

He went out to open it and standing there was a policeman.

He asked, 'Are you Mr Tommy Tenant?'

Tommy nodded and said, 'Yes.'

The policeman said, 'I've been told to ask you if you will come to the station to make a full statement while everything is fresh in your mind.'

Tommy felt his stomach turn; he couldn't say anything as he pushed past the officer, who thought he was running away and grabbed Tommy's arm, just as he vomited on his garden.

The officer let go of him and asked, 'Are you alright, mate?'

Tommy wiped his mouth with his handkerchief and answered, in a muffled voice, 'Yes, just give me a minute to swill my face and brush my teeth, and I'll come with you.'

While he was in the police car, he phoned Ann again. He was flooded with relief when she picked up. He told her where he would be and why, reassuring her that he would be okay.

Val had also phoned Ann to explain to her and said, 'I tried to get in touch with you yesterday, to tell you that the job that Tommy has been on has turned into a horrible murder. I think he needs a break from the job and some counselling.'

Ann replied, 'I was out of town yesterday. I've got loads of missed calls from you both - I didn't realise the signal there was so bad. Thanks for letting me know how bad it is, Val. You know what Tommy's like - he's insisting that he's fine and I don't need to worry about him. But I'll make sure he takes a break. I'll see you when we get back, bye.'

Val said, 'Look after him. He means a lot to us. Bye.'

So, Ann was waiting outside the station when Tommy came out. He didn't look well, but he smiled when he saw her opening her car door for him as he came down the steps of the station.

She asked, 'Are you alright?'

He replied, in a weak tone, 'Yes, but can we just go for a long drive to clear my head? And it's great being with you, but I don't want to talk, if that's alright with you?'

Ann said, 'Of course, whatever you need. I just love being here for you when you need me.'

After their drive, she dropped him off at his house, as he said he needed a bit more time alone with his thoughts, but she said, 'I'm booking a holiday tomorrow for us. You need one and so do I.'

Tommy just said, 'I don't know.'

They kissed goodbye, she watched him go into the house and thought as she drove home, 'I'm definitely booking that holiday. Val is right - he needs a break.'

She took a two-week holiday from work and made Tommy go with her to California. At first, he just wasn't himself. He was quiet and looked all the time like he had something on his mind. After a couple of days, however, he started to get back to his old self. They enjoyed the rest of the holiday, but sometimes Tommy would go quiet - it was clear that what he had seen was still on his mind. Ann would do her best to take his mind off what he was thinking about;

she didn't actually know what he had seen. They never talked about it and, because he was clearly still upset, when they got home, Ann took another week off work and insisted Tommy stayed off with her.

She said to him, 'I know you like your job, but do you think it might be better if you give it up? Because that horrible job you were on, well, something like that might happen again.'

Tommy replied, 'It won't happen again. That bastard is one of a kind and I do love this job, so I don't want to give it up. Don't worry, I'll be alright, as long as I have you.'

CLARK'S STATEMENT

When he finally went back to the office, Val and Mac were made up to see him. Val hugged him, and Mac shook his hand and patted him on the back.

Mac said, 'Back so soon? You could take the year off with the bonus we got off Mrs Clark! By the way, Jacko has some news for you about your other investigation. He asked if you could give him a call, when you are up to it.'

Tommy wanted to leave it for a few days but, believing it must be something about the red car, he just couldn't wait that long. So, the next day, when he got home from the office, he phoned Jacko.

Doing his best to let on he was fine, he said, 'Hi, Jacko. I believe you have some news about the car?'

Jacko replied, 'Yes, the owner of *Honest Joe's* is an officer of the court named Gareth Davis... You would call him a bailiff. Anyway, he has a scrapyard. The red car was shipped into his storage warehouse in a container. It had been stripped down, so it was in pieces. The paperwork that came with it said it came from France and was to be stored with *Honest Joe's* for a year. He tried to trace the owner to get payment for the storage, but there weren't any details with the container and, when he checked the name of the freight transport, which was 'Cranny's', and the number plate of the truck that delivered it, they were both false. So, after the twelve months was up, when no one turned up to claim the car, he legally obtained it in lieu of payment and carried on storing the car in the scrapyard.

Handily for him, he had had a student who had worked for him part-time about sixteen years ago. While she was there, she was always on about an old car for her dad to work on as a hobby. Then, about a year after he'd been keeping this one in storage, she happened to phone, asking him to keep an eye out for an old car for her dad to rebuild. So, he saw a way to get some money back for it and let her have it, even though they couldn't afford to buy it all at once. I think that he's likely to be telling the truth about all this - his business is kosher and two of the men who work for him are retired policemen.'

Tommy said, 'Well, I think it is the car, then, if no one knows where it came from.'

Jacko replied, 'I think this time you could be right, but we've still got to prove it.'

310

Tommy said, 'So, we need to find out where that car came from and who used to own it.'

Just before Tommy had called, Jacko had been reading the report on the Clark case. He hadn't been able to stop himself thinking about the case since one of the lead detectives on the investigation had told him about what had happened in the first interview with Clark.

The detective had told Jacko, 'We were asking him about the boathouse and how he used it. The evil bastard was mad at first and was just going on about how he wanted to get his hands on his wife, that it was her fault he got caught and how he should have done her first. But when we took him to the interview room to make his statement, talking about the crimes themselves seemed to calm him down. He actually seemed to be reliving what he had done... and he enjoyed telling us about it. It knocked us sick, listening to him and seeing the pleasure on his face. We didn't even have to ask him anything beyond the initial questions - he wouldn't shut up. And that's just the first statement - the overview. There are eight more detailed statements - one for each young girl he killed.

I had to send my partner, Ken - you know Ken, yeah? Well, I had to send him out of the room during that first interview, because he wanted to kill Clark. It was when he started bragging how he did all the work himself to make the machines like a production line. That was bad enough, but then he smiled and leaned forwards across the table towards Ken, as if he was talking to a friend, and he started on about how he got this young, blond girl of about sixteen... He started going into details of what he did to the girl, and Ken went mad and jumped up and made a grab for him. As you know, we sit next to one another and I'm sorry to say I had to shoulder charge Ken to stop him. I sent him flying across the room and then I told him to leave to cool off, and get another officer in his place... I just wish it was Clark I sent flying.'

After hearing that, Jacko felt he had to read the report to understand just how bad Clark had been. In it he found Clark's initial statement about what he had done.

It read: *I had sex with the girls I took and then I would give them a drink. I would drug the wine that I gave them. It didn't knock them out though, because I wanted them semi-conscious when I hung them upside down. I'd hang them with their head hanging down into the bath and then I would cut most of their hair off, because if you left it long, it got messy with the blood when I cut the jugular vein.*

That's what I'd do to make sure that all the blood had drained away - I would slit their throats, so the blood would drain from their bodies into the bath. The bath drained straight into the old septic tank, which is buried in the grounds. It was better that way. I just can't stand messy things... ask my wife.'

Jacko felt a bit sick as he carried on reading.

'I would saw the teeth out of the top and then the bottom jawbone, again because it was messy and took too long to pull them out one by one. With the first one, I tried smashing them out but that was very messy. I kept the teeth because the fish wouldn't eat them, and they may have built up in the river under the boathouse... and that might have given me away. And I've heard it said that the police can get DNA from teeth.

The reason I drained the bodies was to make them manageable while I cut them up in the woodchipper. I'd attached it directly to the freezer, so the pieces would freeze solid again. I would leave them there for anything between a week to a couple of months. It all depended on when I found another young girl that I liked the look of, because then I would need the space. If she was still around a couple of weekends later, I would pick her up. I couldn't pick her up straight away. On the first weekend after I saw a new girl, I would empty my freezer. By then the pieces would be frozen solid, so I could feed them into my special mincing machine. I had to make sure I didn't leave it on too long because it would get warm and melt the ice, so things would get messy again. So, I would only run it for half an hour on and half an hour off.

I didn't take any chances, I only ran it when it went dark, which is why a body would take two weekends to get rid of. I also wouldn't put too much in the river at once, in case the fish didn't eat all the evidence.

The beauty of my system with the mincing machine was that I'd added an invention of my own to it, that took the mince straight from the machine down to the river. The water didn't go red because there was so little blood, and what the fish didn't eat was dispersed and washed down the river. Even the tiny bits of bone were carried away. Once that was done, and I had space for her, then I'd pick up the new girl I had chosen.'

Having read all about how Clark had murdered the victim that Tommy had found in the boathouse, Jacko was thinking while he was talking to Tommy, 'This case knocks me sick, Tommy will have to talk to someone about his feelings.'

So he said, 'I know the car is important to you, but I want to change the subject for a moment. You did a great job on the Clark case. How are you coping now? It is very important that you should talk to someone about it.'

Tommy had had a sickly feeling all the time they had been talking and, when Jacko mentioned Clark, he nearly vomited again.

He took a moment to compose himself and then said, 'Can I talk to you about it? I just can't get it out of my head.'

Jacko replied, 'Of course you can, but it's best not to do this kind of thing on the phone. Do you want me to come to your home or would you rather come to mine?'

Tommy replied, 'Have you got time now to come here?'

Jacko answered, 'I'll make time. I can be there in half an hour.'

He was as good as his word; he was knocking at the front door in no time at all.

Tommy let him in and made a pot of coffee. As they sat down in the sitting room, Tommy had tears in his eyes.

Jacko said, 'I'm not a counsellor, but I've seen the report on the case, and I had a similar situation happen to me when I was about your age. It helped me to talk about it. Just tell me what you can and how you feel about it. And, remember, it's not true that big men don't cry. I cried when it happened to me.'

Tears started running down Tommy's face and he said in a quiet tone, 'I opened the freezer. I was expecting something bad, but when I saw that young, blond girl's body, all cut up.... Her face was just a hole where her mouth should have been, and she was looking at me through her grey dead eyes, as if it was my fault because, if I hadn't lost the bastard when I was following him, she might still be alive. I just wish I hadn't lost him... Why did the bastard do that to her face? Please, Jacko, can you tell me what he was doing to those girls?'

Jacko moved next to Tommy on the couch and put his arm round him.

He said, 'It's not your fault, Tommy. Even if you saw her getting into his car, there's nothing you could have done to stop her... and if you had followed him all the way to the boathouse, you would have had to wait till he came out to see what he was up to - and by that time the poor girl would have been dead. You had no reason to think he was hurting her. Watching and waiting is what a private detective does... So, you see, there was nothing you could do about what happened. It's not your fault.'

Tommy muttered, 'But the way she was looking at me, with part of her face missing. I can't get rid of the feeling she was blaming me.'

Jacko explained, in a quiet voice, 'That wasn't her blaming you, Tommy. He cut away her teeth, just like he did with seven other young girls. He had rigged up an old woodchipper to cut them into chippings and eject them into a freezer. From there he moved the frozen parts into a powerful mincing machine which deposited the remains through a pipe into the river, at the dock where the boat house had a vacant space to moor a boat.'

Tommy went white and asked, 'Please don't tell me anymore.'

Jacko said, 'I'm sorry, Tommy, but you should know. If the young girl was trying to say anything, it would be to thank you for finding her, so her family will be able to have closure. Her parents certainly asked the police to thank you for them, and I also want to thank you on behalf of all of the young girls you have saved from going through hell with that evil bastard. The ones he would have gone on to kill if you and your friends hadn't stopped him.

So you should try to think of it that way, that she was trying to thank you. That's the only way to look at it - I know everyone that is involved in the case thinks you are a hero.'

Tommy said, 'I shouldn't have asked you about him, but I couldn't help it, I had to know.'

Jacko replied, 'That is why I told you. I was the same when I was in the similar situation that I told you about, I wanted to know too.'

Tommy stood up, saying, 'I'll just go and swill my face... And thanks, Jacko, I may look in a bad way, but I do feel a lot better about it all now I've talked to you about it.'

'That's good to hear,' Jacko replied, continuing as they made their way into the hall, 'It's still important that you get proper counselling though. I'll be on my way while you get a wash down.

Oh, by the way, I've texted Sergeant Torres about what you've been up to and he wants you to get in touch when you've got time. I'll be seeing you, Tommy.'

As Jacko went out the front door, Tommy waved and made his way up the stairs to get a wash.

When Tommy got up the next morning, he thought to himself, 'That's the best sleep I've had in a while.'

He did his usual routine and, while he was finishing his breakfast, he phoned Sarge.

A voice came from the phone, 'Hola, Torres aqui.'

Tommy said, in broken Spanish, 'Hi, Sarge, it's Tommy. Jacko said you wanted me to get in touch.'

Sarge replied, 'Yes. I'll speak in English because your Spanish isn't the best in the world... but it's coming on.

I've spoken to Mac and Val, and we all think you should take some more time off. So, if you want, you and Ann can stay with me and my wife. What do you think?'

Tommy said, 'That's great. I'll let Ann know, but she won't come with me - you know why. I'll be at your home in three days' time, if that's convenient for you?'

Sarge confirmed that it was, and they finished their conversation.

Over the next two days, Tommy spent his time between his garden and sorting things out for his trip to Spain. Now and then, he would think about the freezer and what he had learned about Clark's crime, but he would try to put it out of his mind. He spent his evenings with Ann, and he didn't want to spoil the time he spent with her by thinking about what had happened with the Clark case.

When he met up with her on the second evening after the call, he told her he had been invited to Spain by Sarge. She pulled a face.

Tommy knew the word 'Spain' wouldn't please her and said, 'You know I can't refuse. He's always asking me to visit him and I haven't been over there for quite a few years now. This was a really nice offer.'

She replied, 'I know he's a nice person. He was very understanding when we were there... I think you *should* go. You like visiting him and Maria. It will help you to recuperate; being away from here for a while may help you get the bad things you've seen out of your mind.'

He kissed her and said, 'I love you.'

She replied, 'Not as much as I love you. I'll go home with you, help you pack for tomorrow and see you off in the morning.'

He suddenly grinned and hugged her as he said, 'I've only got one bed.'

She laughed and replied, 'Yes, but you've got a large settee that you can sleep on, haven't you?'

He replied, 'The bed is a really big one... You will be lonely in there by yourself - you might even get lost in the bed clothes.'

She laughed and said, 'You could be right, but if I let you get in it with me, you've got to promise not to just lie there. You've got to make mad, passionate love to me.'

He squeezed and swung her round as he said, 'I don't know any other way to love you, but it takes two to tango... I hope you're going to do your bit.'

The evening went well but every now and then Tommy would go quiet.

After this had happened a few times, Ann asked him, 'Are you alright, Tommy?'

He replied, 'Yes, I was just thinking whether to stay at Sarge's or a hotel.'

She was worried that he was still thinking about the boathouse, and said, 'Is that all? Well, give me a smile and a kiss then.'

Tommy smiled and hugged her, seeming much more his old self throughout the rest of the night.

When the alarm woke them at five thirty the next morning, Tommy reached out to turn it off, groaning, 'Why did you put it on for this early?'

He felt Ann's feet in his back and heard her laugh as she pushed him out of the bed, onto the floor.

As he got up, she said, 'I've got to go in half an hour, so let's have a quick kiss and a cuddle.'

As he got back on the bed, he threw the bed clothes off her, grabbed her and said, 'My plane doesn't leave till two this afternoon, so let's have a long, slow kiss and a real *good* cuddle, what do you say to that?'

She kissed and hugged him, but then pushed him off her, smiling as she replied, 'Sorry, darling, I've got to go soon. I may be the boss, but I'm also one of the chefs today because we've still got a chef off.'

She was on her way by six-fifteen, leaving Tommy to do the final packing that he had meant to do the day before. He felt good, even though he hadn't told Ann the real reason he was going to Spain.

When the plane landed and he disembarked, Sergeant Torres was waiting for him.

Tommy was surprised to see him at the airport, and he said, 'Hi, Sarge, thanks for coming but you didn't have to pick me up. I know the way to your house; I've been there enough times.'

Sarge replied, 'I was down this way, so I thought 'why not?' And here I am.'

He showed Tommy to his car and, on the way to his home, he asked, 'How are you getting on after your bad experience on the Clark case?'

Tommy replied, 'I feel a lot better since I had a talk with Jacko about it.'

He didn't tell Sarge that, every now and then, he still got a sickly feeling because thoughts of the boathouse would come into his mind.

Sarge said, 'Jacko sent me a copy of the police report. How did you get on to him?'

'He killed eight young girls,' Tommy answered, 'and we didn't even know the girls were dying. If Mrs Clark hadn't wanted a divorce, we would never have found out about him. The horrible bastard even kept the girls' teeth. I think he kept them as trophies.'

He felt a bit sick and stopped talking.

Sarge was watching the road and thought Tommy had simply finished talking, so he said, 'Yes, but he might also have kept them because the police can get DNA from teeth for many years after a person has died.'

Tommy said, 'I've never believed in the death penalty, but for this bastard I think it would be right. Why should his life continue when he's taken so many young girls' lives.'

Just then Sarge pulled up outside his home and said, 'Remember, even when I was still working, I never talked about police work in front of Maria, unless she asked about some crime she had seen in the newspaper.'

Tommy was glad they could no longer talk about the Clark case and, to show he was happy not to discuss it any more, he simply replied, 'I'm on holiday.'

Sarge carried on, explaining, 'I don't mean your case about the car, of course. She's used to that! I meant the likes of the Clark case. If Maria heard anything like that it would upset her. We will be alright discussing how we are doing about the car in front of Maria, you know her English is as good as mine.'

Tommy got out of the car and stood by a six-foot wall with a gate in it, as Sarge got his case out of the boot and opened the gate. They went in, walking past a small swimming pool in the garden to get to the house. It was a nice, family-sized villa, with a veranda on the side that was catching the sun. Tommy always felt at home there.

Sarge's wife came out to meet them and said,-'I'm just about to put a meal on the table. You will join us, of course?'

Tommy answered, 'Yes, of course. Thank you.'

As they went through the living room, he thought how bright and homely it always was in the Torres' house. In the dining room, a table was set for three.

He said to Maria, 'Thank you for letting me stay in your beautiful home again.'

Maria replied, as she looked at Tommy and then at Sarge and said, 'Thank you, Tommy. It is lovely to have such a well-mannered young man staying with us, isn't it, Diego? The house can feel a bit empty at times, now that our three children are all adults and have moved away.'

The three of them sat at the table and chatted as they ate the meal, and Sarge said, 'I know you are keen to get started, Tommy, but it's a bit late now, so we'll have an easy night, a few drinks and start in the morning.'

Tommy replied, 'That sounds good to me.'

Tommy was up for seven in the morning but didn't go downstairs till he knew that Maria and Sarge were up. He headed downstairs once he could hear them talking, and he was surprised, when he got to the dining room, to see the table was already set for breakfast.

Maria placed a full English breakfast on the table, as he arrived, saying, 'You have great timing, Tommy. I was just about to give you a call for your breakfast.'

He sat down at the table as he said, 'This looks great, thank you, but please don't go to all the trouble of cooking me a breakfast, I can get something to eat when I'm out.'

Maria replied, 'It's a pleasure, I miss cooking for my children and while you are here, I can practise my English on you, if you don't mind?'

Tommy replied, 'As usual, your English is perfect but, then, you have Sarge to practise with - I'm sure he speaks English better than me!'

Maria laughed and said, 'Yes he speaks perfect English, but he prefers to speak Spanish at home, so I don't get much opportunity to practise, which is why I enjoy speaking it with you.'

Tommy said, 'Your speech is very good - any English person will understand you. I myself could listen to you speak all day.'

Maria smiled at him and said, 'Why, thank you, kind sir.'

Tommy's mind went back to how, when he first met her husband in the station, Sarge had said the same thing.

The three of them sat at the table, eating and chatting.

When they had finished their meal, Sarge stood up, kissed Maria and said, 'Time to make a move, Tommy.'

He led Tommy out to his car, which was now parked in his garage. The doors of the garage were open; they got in the car, and he drove out of it down the driveway and out of the villa. They went to a couple of vintage car clubs on their way to the garage that the now dead criminal, Alonso, used to own. When they got there, Tommy recognised the place straight away and remembered how the owner had acted last time they had visited. Even the men who had worked there had all stood round, looking at Sarge and himself in a way that wasn't at all friendly.

However, when Sarge drove into the yard and stopped the car this time, he said, 'It's safe for you to get out of the car. The bad element in this place has gone. It's run by decent people now. Although the young man who runs it is the son of the last owner, he does a lot for the community. I've never met him myself, but the boys at the station say he hated his dad and is trying to make up for the damage he did.

I spoke to him yesterday on the phone. He said he was too busy to talk then but he would get one of the men to dig up all the old paperwork they could find. He did qualify that, however, by saying his dad didn't keep much down on paper.'

Tommy asked, 'So, you don't think he can help us, Sarge?'

'You never know,' he replied, 'I'm just telling you this so you don't get your hopes up and then have them dashed.'

As they got out of the car, a large, rough-looking man came up behind Sarge, carrying a large piece of metal.

Tommy went white and shouted, 'Behind you, Sarge!'

Sarge swung round to face the man, as the man lifted the piece of metal and threw it in a heap of scrap that was near to Sarge.

He laughed, pointed to the scrap and said, in Spanish, 'I think he thought I was going to hit you with that, Diego.'

Sarge laughed and held out his hand, as he responded, also in Spanish, 'When did you start working here, Luis?'

As they shook hands, Luis replied, 'I started two weeks ago. You know I'm interested in cars and it's great to be paid to do my hobby. There's a couple of us who put in a few hours a week here now. You know, lads who have retired. This boss man, well, he's a kid really, is a better boss to work for than some of them in the force... and the pay helps with the pension.'

Sarge turned to face Tommy, who was red with embarrassment as he had understood enough words to pick up the gist of what the two of them had said.

Sarge said, speaking in English for Tommy's benefit, 'Tommy, this is an old friend of mine. He used to be on the force, and he services my car for me.' Then he turned to Luis and, switching back to Spanish, said, 'This is Tommy, the young man I've told you about.'

As he was talking, Luis and Tommy shook hands. Just then a young man, of about Tommy's age, came out of the doorway of an office at the bottom of the yard and spoke to one of the mechanics.

Luis said, 'There's the boss now. Is that who you want to see?'

Sarge replied, 'Yes.'

Luis waved to the man, shouting, 'Boss, there's a couple of people to see you.'

The man came over and as he approached them, Tommy thought, 'He's a bit younger than me.'

The man said in Spanish, 'Are you Senor Torres?'

Sarge nodded as he answered, 'Yes. We spoke about your father's paperwork on the phone?'

Alonso replied, 'I owe you an apology for the way I was with you on the phone, but I had a bit of an emergency on at the time. Will you and your friend follow me to my office?'

Sarge followed him, beckoning Tommy to come with them. They walked past some really expensive cars.

As they did so, Alonso pointed at them and said, 'See these cars? If my horrible father was alive, the owners would never see their cars again. He was a bad man. I'm ashamed to say I'm his son.'

They passed into the workshop, where a couple of cars were up on large jacks, with men working under them. There were other cars with the bonnets up.

Alonso continued talking as they passed the men working, saying, '*This* is what this garage is all about now, Sergeant Torres. Will you come this way?'

He opened a door to a small, neat office, gesturing for the two men to enter before him and then following them inside.

Sarge was surprised when his old police rank was mentioned and, once they were in the office, asked, 'You know who I am?'

Alonso replied, 'Yes, my useless father hated your guts, because as he put it - and I am just quoting him - you are a fucking bastard nuisance, always sticking your fucking nose in where it isn't wanted and fucking up his plans.

I'd like to thank you from the bottom of my heart for that, Senor Torres. You can call me Cortez, that's my given name... All he would call me was 'bastard' and I hated him even more than he hated you.'

When Alonso turned round to face them, his face was red with anger.

Sarge felt sorry for him and tried to calm him down by saying, 'I know he was no good, but he must have thought something of you to leave you the business. Don't you think so?'

Alonso replied, with a shrug, 'He didn't leave me it. He just didn't leave a will and I'm the only blood relation, so it all came to me.'

Alonso had calmed down. He picked up a small box from behind his desk and, as he placed it on the desk, he realised Sarge and Tommy were still standing by the door.

'I'm sorry,' he said, 'I've been going on, but I can't help it. My blood boils when I'm talking about that bastard. Please, have a seat.'

Tommy didn't understand most of the words as Sarge and Alonso were talking, because they were speaking too fast, but he caught the last words and sat down at the same time as Sarge.

Sarge introduced him, saying, 'This is Tommy. He's English.'

Alonso nodded and said, in English, 'Sorry, I would have spoken in English from the start if I'd have known.' He then smiled and said, 'I've only known you two for a few minutes and I've had to apologise three times! I will try to do better.'

Sarge pointed to the small box and asked, 'I didn't think there would be *much* paperwork, but is that all there is?'

Alonso answered, 'Yes, I kept on the only two decent men who worked for him when I got rid of the rest of them. They told me how, every now and then, he would burn all the paperwork and just keep the false books for the tax man.'

Tommy's face showed his disappointment, so Alonso asked, 'What are you after? It's a bit late, now that he's dead.'

Tommy blurted out, 'A car that killed a woman and nearly killed me.'

Alonso said, 'If it was a car that had killed someone, he would have had it scrapped. You know that, Senor Torres, don't you?'

Sarge replied, 'You're right - that is your father's MO, Cortez. Even so, we think he might have sold it on because Tommy has seen a car very like it. Also, the car didn't actually *hit* anyone - an English woman was killed on the mountain road through the reckless way it was driven. You're too young to remember the case, but we were hoping you might have some paperwork, if he left any about it.'

Alonso said, 'You're wrong. I do remember it. It was about ten years ago, yes? I had to stay with him at that time because my mother wasn't well. I remember it well, because he was mad, so I made sure I kept out of his way. I was staying at a small farm he had, and he was worried about you, Senor Torres - worried that you might find out about the farm and come with the police to search the place. He had a car hidden in the barn. I saw it one day through a hole in the wall... before he dragged me away by the hair and locked me in a room and called me a 'nosey, little bastard'. He didn't know I had taken a photo of the car on my phone by pressing it up to the hole. I took the photo because it was a classic black car. I liked how it looked - even then I loved cars!

Another reason I remember that time so well was because his friend, who was as horrible as him, came to the farm with a woman with black hair. I saw them from the window of the room he locked me in. Later, when the woman wasn't there, I heard the two horrible bastards saying they would scrap the car, but a week later his friend was shot. I'm glad to say my dear old dad, pardon the language, shit himself when he heard. He just left me at the farm by myself. Fortunately, one of the two decent men who still work here, came and took me to his home for a couple of weeks, till my mother was well. My mother and I didn't see the bastard for a couple of months, which was good as far as I was concerned. He would beat my mother... well, until the day I got his gun and told him I would kill him if he did it again.'

All the time Alonso was talking, Tommy was dying to interrupt, and as soon as he stopped talking, Tommy asked, 'Can we see the photo you took of the car?'

Alonso pulled a face and replied, 'You are joking, surely? It was ten years ago.'

Sarge said to Tommy, who looked a bit down, 'Show him the photo you have on your phone.'

Tommy seemed to panic as he rifled in his jacket pocket for his phone, so Sarge said, 'Tommy, slow down. Don't get so excited.'

Tommy got the phone out of his pocket and Alonso moved round the desk and stood next to Tommy as he fumbled to find the photo on his phone.

When he found it, he handed the phone to Alonso, as he said, 'Sorry, it's not like me to be so excitable, but it means a lot to me to find this car.'

Alonso took the phone and looked at the photo, saying, 'It's the same model but the car I saw wasn't in as good condition as this one, and it was black and, like I said, they were saying they were going to scrap it. I'm sorry I can't be more helpful.'

Tommy said, 'I've another photo I'd like you to look at, Cortez, if you would?'

Alonso replied, 'Of course I will, if it helps.'

Tommy took back his phone and flicked through his photos till he came to the one he wanted. He showed it to Alonso and Sarge moved round to look over his shoulder, so he could also see the photo. It was the one of Lilly Blake that he had quickly taken in Sam's living room.

Tommy asked, 'Does she look like the woman you saw with your dad?'

Alonso studied the photo for a while, taking the phone and zooming in to make Lilly's face as large as it would go.

Handing the phone back, he said, 'The woman I saw had black hair, but this could be her... I'm not sure... Was this photo taken after the death of the woman who was killed? Because the black-haired woman I saw had a plaster above her eye, just about the same place as this woman has that small scar.'

Sarge asked, 'If we can build a case that goes to court, would you be willing to have a look at a woman to see if you can recognise her?'

Alonso replied, 'I'm willing to try but, again, it was ten years ago and I only saw her for a short time.'

Sarge said, 'Of course, we understand that, but it is great news that you would be willing to try. Before we leave, is it possible to speak to the man who picked you up from the farm?'

'Certainly,' answered Alonso. He opened the door, stuck his head out and called in Spanish, 'Lucas, will you come in here for a moment?'

An older man looked up from beneath the bonnet of a car, wiped his hands and then came into the office. When he saw Sarge standing there, he went white.

His eyes shot from Alonso to Sarge, and he quickly said, 'I'm not involved in anything, Sergeant.'

Then he looked back to Alonso and, with a pleading look on his face, said, 'I wouldn't let you down, son, honest.'

Sarge stepped towards him and put his hand out, smiling as he said, 'You don't need to worry. I don't work for the police anymore, and I've always known you weren't involved in what went on here. You were the mechanic on the legal side of the business. Of course, I also know you're no saint. You knew what he did but you always kept your mouth shut when you were questioned about this place.'

Lucas said, 'He paid me well and, like you said, I knew what he was, and you need both hands and legs to be a mechanic. I wasn't going to be talking about what went on here. The one time tried to involve me, I did stand up to him and refused... and I was surprised and glad when all he did was to tell me to fuck off.'

Sarge said, 'Well, he's not here now and I would like you to tell me about the farm he used to keep.'

Lucas replied, 'I knew he had it, what it was used for and where it was. That's how I could go and get Cortez from there when he was a lad and we'd realised the bastard had just left him there with no one to look after him. Alonso senior used the barn to strip cars down or boost their engines up.'

Sarge asked, 'What about the time you picked Cortez up from there, did you see an old black vintage MG? It would have been in the barn.'

Lucas didn't answer, instead he looked over at Alonso.

Alonso said, 'It's alright. Just tell him what you know about it.'

Lucas looked at Sarge, and asked, 'if I tell you the truth about it, I don't want to be in any trouble. Do you promise me?'

Tommy was just standing there, looking puzzled. They were all talking in Spanish, speaking too fast for him to follow.

Sarge answered, 'Lucas, this off the record. Please, tell us what you know.'

'It's like you said,' Lucas replied, 'I'm no saint, but when I was a young man and I started here, as an apprentice mechanic, I didn't know that Cortez's grandad was a crook. Then he started me on stealing cars but, because I wouldn't hurt anyone to get the cars, he said I was a waste of time as a thief but that he'd keep me on anyway because I'd turned out to be such a good mechanic. So, I didn't have to steal anymore… but sometimes I had to drive the cars to the different places they needed to go to. Then one day he told me to go and pick up three men who worked for him…'

Sarge interrupted, asking, 'What has this story got to do with the car we want to know about? It's ancient history.'

Lucas replied, 'I want you to know why I stayed here and went along with everything. It's important to me.

So, I picked the men up and dropped them here, like I'd been instructed to. I was told to wait in the office and get myself a mug of coffee. The next thing I knew, it was dark and I was in my flat, with blood on my hands and clothes. There were photos scattered around me and, when I picked one up, it showed me with a gun in my hand and one of the men I'd picked up, dead on the floor, his face covered in blood. Cortez's father held onto the photos his father had faked. Now you know why I kept my mouth shut, no matter what happened here. I know I didn't kill that man, but I couldn't prove it.

As for the farm, I only learned about it shortly before I went out there to pick Cortez up and bring him back to my house. Cortez's father told me a farmer had an old car that he wanted servicing, if it was in good enough shape to bother. He said the farmer wanted to check to see if it was worth spending money on first.

I went to the farm and a man, who looked like a farmer to me, showed me into the barn. I worked on the black MG for six days, though it was in better condition than it looked. I took the engine out and serviced it. I thought it had a good engine for its age; I was able to get it running really well, and I worked on all the moving parts of the car, making sure it could get up to its top speed and drove very smoothly. I was pleased with how the job had gone… But then the scum I had to work with here turned up to reinforce the front of it. So, then I had an idea that they were up to no good, but I couldn't refuse to finish the work on the car.

On the final day that I was out at the farm, when I finished my work on it, I had been working from six in the morning. Alonso Senior was still lying to me - he said they needed it for a show, so it had to be finished that day. When I came out of the barn in the evening, I could see Cortez looking out of an upstairs window. I needed to tell his father that I'd finished with the car, so I headed for the house.

I knocked on the open door of the farmhouse kitchen and walked straight in. I was shattered and wanted to get home, so I didn't wait for an answer. I was surprised to see Cortez's father and the other bastard, Fernandez, weren't alone. They were with what seemed to be a black-haired woman… but I think she was wearing a wig: I could see bits of blond hair sticking out at the bottom. And, well, when I say woman, she was really just a girl - she looked about eighteen. She knew enough to immediately turn her back on me, though, so I couldn't see her face. Then I really knew that they were up to something…

That was the time I stood up to him. I said, 'I told you, when your old fellow died, I won't talk about your 'business' but you're not to involve me in your crooked deals. I don't care if you have got the photos.' That bastard Fernandez pointed a gun at me, but Cortez's father told him to put it away because I made a good front for the garage. Then he told me to fuck off while I could still walk.

The three of them went back to their conversation - they didn't see me as important enough to keep quiet around so, as I was leaving, I heard Fernandez say something about having a photo of some man. He told the girl that it would cost whoever he was talking about to get it back and that, with what he was getting out of their deal, he should be only too happy to pay.

Later that day I heard that a rich English woman died after being run off the mountain road by a black MG and, about four days later, some of the men at the garage were talking about how Alonso Senior made them respray the car red, and then strip it down so it could be shipped out.

About a week after that - or it might have been a bit less - someone shot Fernandez. The first we heard of it was when the big, hard, boss man came into the office shitting himself. He opened the safe and took all the money out of it. He told us that Fernandez had been shot and said he was going on holiday. He told us that if anyone was looking for him, we were to say he was never here - but he was still focused enough on the money to say he would be checking the books when he got back.

I have to admit that I was pleased when I heard Fernandez was dead. Mind you, I wasn't the only one who hated him. When the men in the garage heard he was dead, there wasn't a dry eye in there from laughing.

I always told my wife everything that went on here and when I told her about Alonso Senior leaving, she told me to check the farm to see if Cortez was alright. So, I went back there, and he was still locked in the cottage and was running out of food. The car wasn't there. I know because I did go into the garage to steal some money that I knew Cortez's dad kept there, so I could give it to Cortez's mother. I'm afraid that's all I can tell you about that car.'

Sarge patted Lucas on his shoulder and said, 'That's a lot. You've been really helpful. Don't worry about the case of the dead man in the photo with you - that's from so long ago, it won't even be a cold case. I won't mention it again; you just remember not to mention it either, when the police want to interview you about the woman you saw on the farm. Thank you for being so forthcoming about everything.'

Lucas shook Sarge's hand, then he turned and left the office as Sarge was shaking Alonso's hand and thanking him for his help.

Sarge then turned to Tommy, who didn't have a clue what Lucas had told them because he talked so fast, and said, 'I'll explain everything to you on the way home. We're leaving now.'

They said goodbye to Alonso and, on the drive back to Sarge's home, they talked over what was said in the office. They went over it again all that evening.

Tommy was excited and said, 'Where do we go from here, Sarge?'

He answered, in a serious tone, 'I'll go into the station tomorrow and explain it all to the chief inspector. I think it sounds like you have a case, but it's up to the police whether they will take it on. Remember, I'm a civilian now, so just relax about it, you will make yourself ill.'

Tommy said, 'I know you're right, but I can't help it now that I know Lilly Blake was involved in Ann's mum's death.'

That night Tommy couldn't get a decent sleep. He tossed and turned; in the few hours for which he did fall asleep, he had a nightmare. He was back on the mountain road but he was also by the boat house, watching Lilly Blake driving straight towards them, in full view, laughing, with her dad running after her shouting 'Don't do it!' Just as the car was about to hit him, the boat house turned into a big freezer, which opened under the pressure of all the body parts inside, and they all spilled out in a torrent. As the body parts crashed into him, he woke up, covered in sweat.

After a few more hours of tossing and turning, he was glad when the alarm went off and it was time to get up. He knew Sarge and Maria were up. He could hear them talking downstairs while he lay in bed, waiting for the alarm to go off. He went downstairs, just as Maria was putting his breakfast on the table.

Tommy sat down with them both and tried to eat his meal, but he was struggling, and Maria said, 'I can see you can't manage to eat your breakfast. Just leave it, I wouldn't like you to be sick and our dogs will be pleased to eat it for you.'

Sarge said, 'See, I told you not to get too excited. Now you can't get your food inside of you. Come on, I might as well get you to the police station now.'

Tommy asked Sarge, 'If you don't mind, I would like to go home after we've been there.'

Sarge smiled and said, 'Maria and I like your company, but we wouldn't keep you prisoner! Go and pack your case and I'll drop you off at the airport once we're done at the station.'

Tommy went to his room to pack and was back fifteen minutes later. Maria met him at the front door and gave him some sandwiches and a bottle of water.

She hugged him, kissed his cheek and said, 'It's been lovely having you here. You will come again soon? I would like you to meet my young adults. I think you would get on very well together.'

Tommy thanked her and gave her a hug, as he said, 'One day I will come back in better circumstances, and I hope to bring my girl Ann with me.'

Sarge was now sitting in his car and said to Tommy, 'Put your case on the back seat.'

Tommy did so and then got in the front passenger seat next to Sarge, waving to Maria as the car pulled away and they drove out the gates.

Half an hour later, they pulled into the police station's car park. When Sarge and Tommy got out of the car, a couple of police officers approached them.

They were smiling and one said, in Spanish, 'Are you going senile, Sarge? You don't work here anymore.'

He laughed and answered, 'Even if I was senile, I'd still have more sense than you two put together.'

He shook their hands and asked, 'Is the big man in?'

The two officers nodded, and one of them said, 'He's in his office, Sarge.'

'Thanks, lads,' he said, 'I'll let you buy me a drink sometime.'

Sarge and Tommy went into the building, and were waved straight past the entry desk and into the station itself. Everyone who saw them as they passed down the corridors would smile or say something to Sarge.

Tommy commented, 'Gosh, Sarge, you have a lot of friends.'

He smiled and replied, 'Everyone has a lot of friends. I bet you have a lot of friends too... but you find out who your real friends are when you are in trouble.'

Tommy nodded and said, 'I guess you're right. I class you as a real friend, Sarge.' Sarge smiled and nodded at him, stopping in front of a door and knocking on it.

The door was opened by the chief Inspector's PA who said, in Spanish, 'Yes? Oh! It's you, Sergeant Torres, how are you?'

He replied, 'Well, I'm not a Sergeant anymore, but I'm fine. How are you doing?'

The PA said, 'I'm great. I take it you want to see the boss?'

Sarge replied, 'That's the plan, love.'

She said, 'I'll go and tell him, step into my office while you're waiting.'

As they did so, she went to the door on the other side of the room, with a nameplate that had *Chief Inspector Costa* written on it.

She knocked on the door and a voice said, 'Come.'

She opened the door, popped her head in and said, 'Sergeant Torres would like a word with you.'

A voice said, 'Well, don't keep him out there, tell him to come in.'

She opened the door wide and beckoned them to go in. As Sarge and Tommy entered the office, Chief Inspector Costa stood and leaned over his desk, offering his hand to Sarge and then to Tommy.

As Tommy shook his hand, he awkwardly said 'Nice to meet you,' in broken Spanish.

Smiling, the chief inspector said, 'It's quite a while since we've seen you, Sergeant Torres. What can I do for you?'

Sarge said, in English, 'This is Tommy Tenant. As you can gather, he's English.'

The inspector smiled and said, 'I would be a lousy detective if I didn't get that as soon as he opened his mouth. So, what can I do for you, Mr Tenant?'

Tommy looked at Sarge, and then back to the chief inspector and said, 'I need help with what you would call a 'cold case' from ten years ago. Sarge was on it when he was here; I think he can explain it better than me.'

They were in the office for two hours discussing the case.

At the end of the meeting, the chief inspector said, 'I will put some officers on to investigate it.'

They shook hands with each other, then Tommy and Sarge left the station and got in Sarge's car to drive straight to the airport. Tommy was excited but he was also worried that the men the chief inspector put on the case mightn't try too hard because it all happened ten years ago.

He asked Sarge, 'Will he really bother about a cold case?'

Sarge kept his eyes on the road, as he smiled at Tommy and said, 'Stop worrying - you're going to make yourself ill with the way you're up and excited one minute and then you're down and worrying the next.

In answer to your question, he would be mad not to follow it up. It would be more than a feather in his cap to find the evidence and clear a ten-year-old murder case in this country and to give the English police the evidence to help them arrest a murderer in your country. So will you please stop worrying.'

Sarge stopped in the airport's car park and, as Tommy got his large packet of sandwiches and bottle of water out of the car, Sarge grabbed his case from the back seat.

He smiled as he said, 'I'd better carry this for you, you won't be able to carry it without crushing your sandwiches.'

Tommy said, 'It's alright, I'll manage. You and Maria have been great - I don't know how I can thank you enough,' as he tried to take the case.

Sarge kept hold of it and said, 'Enough of the small talk, let's get you on your plane.'

He went with Tommy to see him off, accompanying him as he bought a ticket and checked in. At the departure gate they shook hands, then Sarge gave Tommy a hug.

He said, 'You've done a great job, now stop worrying, the police won't let you down. I hope you'll come back soon?'

Tommy smiled at Sarge and said, 'You're crushing my sandwiches!'

They both laughed, waving to each other as Tommy went through the departure gate.

Later, as he was boarding the plane, he texted Ann: *I've missed you. I will be arriving in England about ten pm, so I'll give you a call tonight, love, Tommy xxx*

TOMMY GETS SOME COUNSELLING

While he was sitting on the plane, he wanted to tell Ann what he had been doing and what he thought, but he knew it would send her over the top again, and he couldn't stand to see her so upset. So, while he was on the plane, he thought carefully about the things he would tell her.

When he got off the plane, he picked up his case at the carousel and, as he walked through the customs gate, he was surprised to see a large sign saying 'Taxi for Mr T. Tenant' among the signs held up by the waiting drivers and chauffeurs. As it was slowly lowered, it revealed Ann, with a big grin on her face. He was made up to see her, but he felt guilty about lying.

When he reached her, he put his case down and they hugged and kissed each other, then walked to the short stay car park.

As they got in her car, Ann asked, 'Is that a present for me you are holding?'

Tommy laughed and answered, 'Sorry, doll, I've only got some sandwiches that Maria made for me... but you can have some of the ones I've got left. They taste lovely, and I just didn't know what to get for a wonderful girl who has everything, including me.'

She said, 'You're such a man, aren't you? You must know a girl can never have too many earrings. Now I want *two* pairs next time you go on holiday without me.'

He replied, 'That's a deal because from now on I intend to be joined at the hip to you, so I won't be going anywhere without you anyway.'

As Ann drove, she asked about his holiday. He described Sarge and Maria's villa, and how he spent time in their pool and sunbathing at the side of it. All the time he was talking, he felt guilty. He would have loved to tell her the truth, but he was worried what it would do to her.

She said, 'I hope you're not that boring next time we go on holiday together. Surely you did more than that, didn't you?'

He replied, 'Well, we did have a drink with some of Sarge's old friends, who were also retired.'

She stopped the car outside Tommy's house. As he got out, she just sat there and didn't make a move.

Tommy frowned, as he looked at her and asked, 'Aren't you coming in?'

Ann had a serious look on her face and said, 'You didn't give me a present, so why should I give you one of mine?'

Tommy said, 'Oh, you are joking, aren't you?'

She just looked blankly at him and said, 'Shut the car door, you're causing a draft.'

He slowly closed the door, feeling bad about not getting her a present - it hadn't occurred to him, because he hadn't really been on holiday, but he wouldn't have thought she would be so upset about it.

Just as he closed the door, she burst out laughing and jumped out of her car, saying, 'Of course I'm joking! If you could see your face...'

She closed her car door and walked round to him.

He grabbed her, swung her round, and said, 'I hate you... but I really love you, just wait till I get you inside, I'll show you how much.'

They went into the house and Tommy was surprised to see the table all set up for a romantic evening, with candles and dishes set out for two. There was even a hostess trolley with hot food on it and an ice bucket standing to one side of the table, with a bottle of champagne chilling in it.

When Tommy got over his surprise, he kissed Ann and said, 'I knew giving you that key was a good idea. I suppose you don't want any of my sandwiches. They are lovely, you know?'

Ann laughed and replied, 'Well, if they are that nice, you can eat them and I'll eat the warm meal off the heated trolley.'

They sat down and chatted while they ate the meal and drank the champagne.

At the end of the meal, Tommy said, 'That was lovely. You're a real master chef, and I'd marry you just for the meals, if I didn't love you.'

Ann replied, with a serious look on her face, 'I thought you didn't like the meal because you're quieter than usual. As for marriage, you know, I want that one day but not right now.'

He answered, 'I can live in hope that it will be soon... but, for now, let's forget it. Give me a kiss.'

She kissed him, as he hugged her, and she said, 'I was up early this morning and it's been a long day. I'm tired, let's go to bed.'

He asked, 'Are you really tired or are you having me on again?'

She replied, 'Of course I'm tired, after the romantic meal I slaved over for you! Well, I expect you to slave over this body of mine just as much!'

He stood up but she pushed him back down on the chair and said, 'I'll race you to the bed.'

Laughing, she ran out the room, closing the door behind her. Tommy caught her just as she reached the bed.

He said, 'It's a draw and you cheated, so I'm on top.'

She said, 'I dispute that and, anyway, you've got to slave over me, remember?'

He laughed and answered, 'That's what I said, didn't I? I'm over you.'

The next morning, the alarm went off at five fifteen. Tommy turned it off and yawned.

He knew he hadn't set it, so he asked, 'Are you in early?'

Ann leaned over and kissed him, getting out of the bed as she replied, 'I'll let you work that answer out for yourself.'

He said, 'I'll drive you to the restaurant.'

As he started to get up, she pushed him back down, smiled and said, 'You're too knackered after last night. While you were asleep, you were tossing and turning, and muttering something about a red car.'

He was a bit shocked and said, 'That's the car one of Sarge's friends was working on. I don't know why I'd dream of that. I'm awake now, I'll drop you off.'

'You're not awake properly,' she replied, continuing, 'You can't even remember my car is outside and that I need it to do some running around today. I told you when we were eating yesterday. Anyway, I've got to go home and change before work.'

He levered himself off the bed once more, and said, 'Well, I'll make you some breakfast then.'

She pushed him down again, and said, 'Will you give over and just stay there? You're slowing me down and I'm running late as it is… and you know I don't eat this early in the morning.'

She picked her clothes off the floor and went into the bathroom. Half an hour later, she came out and went up to Tommy to kiss him goodbye. As she tried to leave he held on to her.

'You need a beef steak for that black eye,' she said.

He answered, 'I haven't got a black eye.'

She replied, 'You will have, if you don't let go of me.'

He kissed her again, letting her go as he said, 'Alright, you win.'

She kissed him back, then ran down the stairs and out to her car.

Tommy couldn't go back to sleep. He was hoping Ann wouldn't find out about the work he had been doing on the red car - at least until it led to a break in her mother's case. He lay there for a little over an hour, going over in his mind what had happened in Spain. Sometimes what he'd seen in the boathouse would come to mind, but he tried to concentrate on Spain.

At seven a.m. he knew Jacko would be up, so he texted him: *Jacko, I know I'm right that Lilly Blake had something to do with the car. I've been in Spain, and Sarge and I found out a few things. When the police in Spain get in touch with the police here, will you let me know, please? TT*

He was sitting eating his breakfast when his phone rang. He took it out of his pocket and looked at the caller ID.

He answered the call, saying, 'Hi, Jacko, you got my text?'

'Hello,' Jacko replied. 'Yes, Tommy. I got it, and Diego called me yesterday, when he put you on the plane. He told me what had happened and what you suspect; if you are right, it will take some time to look into things. He also said he was a bit worried about the way you are taking it; that you need to calm down.

You know I will make sure I'm assigned the case when the Spanish police hand it over to us and I will let you know everything I find... on the condition that you forget about it for now. I think the case that's really behind the way you're feeling at the moment is the Clark case. I think you should see a counsellor to help you.

As for the car, please just wait till I let you know what I can find out about it when the case comes over here.'

His voice going high with excitement, Tommy said, 'But I was the one to find the car, with the help of Sarge... I would like to think I could still be involved?'

Jacko replied, 'Calm down, we'll involve you when you are needed but, like I said, forget about it for now. Once it comes through to us, it will be an official police investigation. If you start coming round the police station, making noise, you will draw attention to yourself and then I won't be able to let you know what is going on. I shouldn't be telling you anything about an ongoing investigation, so I'll be putting my job on the line just by talking to you about it. I know it's you who found most of the clues, but now it's up to us, *the police*, to put it all together and make a solid case to take to the court. Do you understand the situation we are in?'

Tommy replied, 'I know you're right Jacko. I remember when I was nearly locked up when I first kept going to the station and asking about it. I'll do my best to forget it for now. Thanks, Jacko. See you soon.'

Jacko said, 'You know it makes sense, son. Bye for now.'

Tommy felt a bit down as he put the phone back in his pocket, and said out loud to himself, 'Well, I'll call into the office and see what work they have for me to do. It might take my mind off it.'

He went out to his bike, took the chain off it and wrapped the chain around the tree and locked it, so nobody could take it. Then he got on his bike and rode to the office.

When he entered, Val was made up to see him. She wasn't very surprised when he turned up, because she knew he was back in England. Jacko had rang and told her and Mac that Diego and himself were worried about Tommy because they thought the Clark case, and what he had seen in the freezer, had been so horrifying that he was traumatised by it.

Val called into the other room, 'Mac? Tommy's here,' as she hugged him, continuing, 'I thought you were staying in Spain for a couple of weeks.'

While Val was talking, Mac squeezed out of his office door and shook Tommy's hand.

He said, 'I'm sorry, Tommy.'

Tommy frowned and was about to ask him why, but Mac continued, 'I should have sent you for counselling after the Clark case.'

Tommy butted in, saying, 'I'm alright, I don't need counselling.'

Val shook her head and said, 'Look, Tommy, you do need it. Mac's insurance won't cover you if you don't have it. It's in the contract with the insurance that you need to be fit in mind and body. After an experience like you've had, they could say that, if something happened to you or a client, it was because you were traumatised - they could claim that you're not covered.

So, we have arranged for you to see a counsellor who deals with the police when they have similar experiences.'

Tommy insisted, 'There's nothing wrong with me. I'm alright, like I said, I don't need it.'

Mac patted Tommy on the back and said, 'Tommy, you're not listening to us. You just can't work without insurance... and we are like a little family, we don't want to break up the team.'

Tommy said, 'Okay, you win, I know when I'm beaten. What's the address?'

Val handed him a card and said, 'I've been on the phone to her as soon as I got in this morning and told her you were on the Clark case, and she said that if you were on the Clark case, she wants you to ring *right* away for an appointment.'

Tommy asked, 'Why does she want me to call her so soon? What does she know about the Clark case?'

Mac replied, 'Like Val said, she does a lot of work as a police counsellor. She is working with some of the police officers that were in the boathouse and saw what you saw on that case - that's why she wants to see you so soon.'

Tommy took his phone out of his pocket, saying, 'Okay, I'll call her now.'

He looked at the card and pressed out the phone number.

A voice said, 'Mrs Winfield's clinic. How can I help?'

Tommy answered, 'I'm Tommy Tenant and I'd like to make an appointment with Mrs Winfield, please.'

The secretary replied, 'Certainly, Mr Tenant, we've been expecting a call from you. Can you be here at ten a.m. tomorrow?'

He was a bit worried and asked, 'Why were you expecting me?'

The secretary replied, 'We had a call from a lady named Val. She booked you in as a client and Mrs Winfield wants to see you as soon as possible because you were involved in the boathouse case.'

Tommy said, 'I'll be there. What time is the appointment again?'

The secretary replied, 'I have booked you in for ten a.m. tomorrow.'

He said, 'Okay, I'll be there at ten tomorrow. Thank you, bye.'

The secretary said, 'Goodbye.'

Tommy put the phone back in his pocket, then he asked, 'How did you know I was home?'

Val answered, 'Jacko rang yesterday afternoon and told us you came home yesterday. He's worried about you. He told us that all the police on the Clark case were in counselling, and he reminded us about the insurance.'

Tommy said, 'I thank you all for worrying about me. I suppose it's nice to think so many people I love are looking out for me.'

Mac said, 'I haven't accepted any new jobs, so you still have at least two more weeks of holidays.' While he was talking, he offered Tommy his hand.

Tommy shook it and then he went to Val, hugged her and kissed her on the cheek, asking, 'I take it Jacko told you what went on in Spain?'

Mac and Val answered 'Yes,' at the same time.

Mac continued, 'We know, but don't dwell on it for now. Just wait till you hear from Jacko.'

Tommy nodded, gave Val another hug and said, 'I'll be off now to do some gardening and give my other girl a ring. You know where I am if you need me.'

Tommy spent the afternoon in his back garden. It was a lovely day but every now and then he felt the sickly feeling come back. So, when he finished the weeding, he got a drink of orangeade and sat down on his garden lounger to phone Ann.

A voice said, 'Hello, Miss Kenwright's PA speaking.'

Tommy asked, 'Can I speak to Ann?'

The PA said, 'I'm sorry, sir, but Miss Kenwright is very busy at the moment and can't be disturbed.'

He said, 'Can you tell Ann it's Tommy? If she's too busy, that's fine.'

There was a slight pause and then the PA said, in a warmer voice, 'I'm sorry, sir, I didn't realise it was you. Miss Kenwright said I should always put you through, unless she is in a meeting.'

There were a few minutes of silence and then Ann said, 'Hi, Tommy, are you alright?'

He replied, 'Yes, why are you asking? Everyone is asking me that. Mac and Val have booked me in to see a counsellor.'

She replied, 'It's a good idea.'

He butted in, 'You too? I'm alright when I'm with you, aren't I?'

Ann answered, 'Yes, but since the boathouse you sometimes go off into a world of your own and last night, well, I told you that you were muttering about a car while you were asleep; I didn't want to have to tell you this but you also called out a few times. You were saying things like 'what's wrong with her face?' and you were sweating.'

Tommy said, 'I guess you and the others are right. I do get a sickly feeling for no reason at all.'

Ann said, 'So you are going to see the counsellor?'

Tommy said, 'Yes, at ten tomorrow.'

She replied, 'Good, I'll be at yours about nine tonight. I've got to get back now, bye, love you.'

He said, 'Not as much as I love you, bye.'

He went into his house and lay on his bed, meditating to help him relax, so he would feel good when he saw Ann that night.

After his first appointment with the counsellor was helpful, Tommy saw her for two hours a day for two weeks. In that time he never heard from Jacko, though he would have liked to know how the police were getting on. If he tried to mention what had happened on the mountain road to the counsellor, she just wanted to focus on the Clark case.

THE CASE PROGRESSES

Three days after Tommy had flown home, Jacko got a phone call from Spain.

He answered, 'Hello, Detective Sergeant Jackson here. How can I help?'

A voice said, 'Hi, Jacko, it's me, Diego. I'm just enquiring about how Tommy is doing? I don't want to talk to him till he's finished his counselling, but I've got some news about the car.'

Jacko said, 'Tommy will be alright. The counsellor he's with is the best around. Thanks for looking out for him when he stopped at your home.'

Diego replied, 'It was a pleasure. The news is about Alonso - the fellow who used to own the garage at the time of the incident. The police have traced a couple of his old boys in prison and offered a deal to shorten their sentence. The first one they found, Martinez, said they received the car at the farm two months before it was used. They gave it a black respray to make it look in poor condition.

His boss' clients were a man and a girl. Only the girl visited them at the farm where they had the car and Martinez said he didn't get a good look at her, but she had black hair and a plaster just above her eye. He never saw the man, so all he could tell us was Fernandez had been laughing about him after they met because he was wearing a large moustache and beard that were clearly false. He added that he remembered hearing Alonso say the man was a lot older than her and that he thought he was her 'old feller', but he said he didn't know if Alonso meant it was her father or sugar daddy.

He gave them another inmate, named Gonzales, to talk to. When Gonzales was questioned, he said he saw the paperwork that his uncle used to ship the car - in pieces - to England. His uncle also worked for Alonso and often dealt with shipping stolen cars. Gonzales couldn't remember the name of the storage firm it was sent to, but he knew it was near London. The police contacted the shipping firm he said they used. They told the police that the paperwork said it was shipped to London where it was picked up by Cranny's transport.

My sources on the force tell me you will get the report tomorrow; I just thought you would like to know it first-hand.'

Jacko replied, 'I'll look out for that report tomorrow.'

Diego said, 'You know, we have never met in person. You and your wife must come and stay with us one of these days.'

'Yes, we will do that next time I'm on holiday,' Jacko replied, 'but I'll have to go now. Hope to see you soon.'

Diego answered, 'When Tommy's case is over, I'll expect to see you both over here. My wife Maria has heard me talking about you and she said she would love to meet you and your wife. Our house is big enough, now the kids have left home.'

Jacko answered, 'So have my kids and the house seems quiet without them. Bye for now, Diego.'

Diego said, 'Goodbye' too and they ended the call.

The next morning, Jacko was in early but there was no report from Spain. After a couple of hours, he started pacing up and down in his office. One of the other police officers saw his shadow through the blinds of his office.

He knocked on the door, opened it and asked, 'What's on your mind? You're going to wear a hole in the carpet!'

Jacko replied, 'Do you remember Tommy, the boy who used to come here and badger us about an accidental death that happened in Spain? It was a good few years ago.'

The officer answered, 'I don't even remember what happened last week. I'm not like you, Jacko. When I go home, I forget about the job.'

Jacko said, 'I just thought you might remember because you were so sick of him calling in every week that you threatened to lock him up.'

The officer frowned, searching his memory, and then he said, 'Yes! I remember him now - he was a bloody nuisance.'

Jacko said, 'He's the one who solved the boathouse murders.'

The officer butted in, astonished, 'You're kidding, aren't you?'

'No,' Jacko replied, 'and he is still working on that Spanish case he was bugging you about, well, it must be just on ten years ago.'

The officer seemed embarrassed as he said, 'I guess I owe him a big apology.'

Jacko said, 'Anyway, I kept in touch with him and a report is supposed to be coming from Spain about that case he was on. It was supposed to come this morning.'

The officer suggested, 'If it's coming from Spain, it may have gone to Scotland Yard.'

Jacko said, 'You're right, of course. Thanks.'

With that Jacko picked up his phone and said to the operator, 'Put me through to Scotland Yard.' The police officer took this as his cue to leave.

Jacko waited for a few minutes and then a voice said, 'This is Scotland Yard. How can we help you?'

Jacko replied, 'I'm Detective Sergeant Jackson. Can you put me through to Detective Sergeant Smith, please?'

While he was waiting, he heard someone shouting, 'Is Smithy in the building?'

Another voice shouted, 'Smithy, are you deaf?'

Then came a reply, 'No, I'm not, so why are you shouting? I'm sitting at my desk - just put the call through to my phone.'

Finally, Jacko heard, 'Detective Smith speaking. Who is it? What can I do for you?'

He replied, 'It's me, Jacko. Smithy, do you remember I was asking you about a vintage car? Well, I believe Spain has sent you a report on it. Would you check it out and send me a copy of it? The family of the lady who was killed when it ran her off the road live up here.'

Smithy said, 'We got the report late last night. I recalled you asking about a car like this, so this morning I went to see Mr Davis to get a few more details about the car. I asked him about it and Lilly Blake, the woman he sold it to. He said that it was strange because, about twelve months after he had it in storage, she rang him, looking for a car for her dad. He said it was almost as if she knew he had a vintage car because, before that, he'd only heard from her about twice since she stopped working in the office. He asked what all the questions were about, as he couldn't see her doing anything wrong. He said she was a hard-working girl. But he did say that when she left his office, she had a boyfriend who was a nasty piece of work. His name was Eric Lang, he was nineteen - a couple of years older than Lilly - and he was always in trouble. When he was twenty, he went to jail for a couple of years.

So, I looked up his record. He was out on parole, but he's done a vanishing act and hasn't been seen in the last eight years. I'm adding my report to the Spanish one. It will be with you as soon as I've finished typing it up.'

Jacko said, 'Thanks, Smithy. I'll let you buy me a pint next time I'm up there.'

Smithy replied, 'I'm helping you, it's you who owes me a pint. In fact, you owe me two! I've got to go, see you.'

LILLY HELPS THE POLICE WITH THEIR ENQUIRIES

An hour later Jacko received the report. After reading through it, he dug out the original police report on Joan's death and took both to the chief inspector's office.

He knocked on the door and a voice said, 'Come in.'

Jacko opened the door and entered, as the chief looked up from the paperwork on his desk and asked, 'What can I do for you, Jacko?'

He replied, 'Boss, I've got some reports here from Spain about a cold case from ten years ago. One is the original case report and the other came through to me this morning - there's been a break in the case. It's a murder investigation that involves Tommy Tenant, the man who put us onto the Clark case.'

The chief asked, 'You mean he's not the hero we all thought he was?'

Jacko laughed and replied, 'As far as I'm concerned, he's twice the hero we thought he was. He's been looking into this case by himself for the last ten years, when everyone here and in Spain forgot about it. He carried on because Mrs Thomson, the woman who was killed, was his girlfriend's mother and he only survived what happened by the skin of his teeth.'

The chief took the reports off Jacko and studied them.

When he'd finished reading, he said, 'You better pick this Lilly Blake up. The older man, do you think it's her father? In your additions to the newer report, you say this Lilly is now the girlfriend of the man whose wife died. Is that right?'

Jacko said, 'In answer to your first question, it looks that way. Lilly's dad is the one with the car... but then why keep the evidence that could hang them? Tommy doesn't think the father is involved. Still, we will obviously interview him to be sure.

As you can see from the original report, the Spanish police thought the person driving the car was after the whole family, not just the mother. They reckoned Tommy's motorbike saved the rest of the family because it was in front of them as they were walking down the road.'

The chief asked, 'So this Lilly should be twenty-eight now? If she was eighteen then. '

Jacko said, 'From the photos I've seen I thought she was a little bit older than that.'

The chief said, 'If she did aim that car at this Joan Thomson on purpose, so that she could go after the woman's husband, she's one sick, money-grabbing woman.'

Jacko said, 'I'll bring her in today for questioning, but we could have a bit of trouble because I don't think Mr Thomson will believe us that she was involved. A man with his money has some clout.'

The chief replied, 'I'll back you up all the way, and I'll get the Detective Smith who wrote up this new report to interview this Sam Blake fellow down in London. He seems to be nice and thorough in his approach. We'll set it up so the father is brought in for questioning at the same time as you interview Lilly Blake, so they won't be able to communicate with each other.

What do you think about this Eric Lang who was mentioned? That's another potentially interesting angle to investigate.'

Jacko nodded his agreement and said, 'We'll look into him too and see if he has been around these parts.'

As he left the chief's office, Jacko took his phone out and texted Tommy, saying: *My colleagues are taking Sam Blake in for questioning in London and at the same time we are interviewing Lilly Blake today. We've learned one of her friends, Eric Lang, is a criminal and we will have men looking for him too. I will keep you informed.*

Tommy texted back: *Thanks, Jacko. So, you think Sam is involved? I'll tell Ann myself - it's better if it comes from me. I don't know how she will take it. I'd better get round there before the news gets out. Thanks again. TT*

He went and got his helmet from the cupboard and left his house in a hurry. He unchained his bike from the tree but, as he was about to get on it, he thought about how he couldn't expect Ann to get on his bike if she got upset. With that he chained his bike back to the tree and went over to his neighbour's driveway. He opened the gates and, as he got in his car, he threw his helmet in the back seat.

He drove out the driveway, stopped and ran back to close the gates. Half an hour later, he arrived at the restaurant where Ann was working that day. He stayed in his car and phoned her. She answered after a few rings.

As soon as he heard the phones connect, he said, 'It's me, Ann.'

Ann laughed, reply, 'I know it's you, soft lad. Your name comes up on the phone. If you're checking in with me, I haven't forgotten I'm meeting you tonight... or are you cancelling?'

Tommy said, 'No, but I need to see you now. It's important.'

She replied, 'I'll take a ten-minute break. I'll be outside within five - it will be okay, I'm due a break.'

'No,' he said, 'I need you to finish for the day.'

She was worried and said, 'You sound so serious. What is wrong, Tommy?'

He replied, 'I can't tell you over the phone. Please come now, I'm in my car in your car park.'

She said, 'I'll be with you in a minute.'

He heard her talking to the other chefs, saying in an urgent tone, 'I've got to go.' They reassured her that they would be able to manage without her, and she said her goodbyes and ran out to the carpark.

Tommy had moved to stand just outside the exit door. When she came running out, he hugged her and went to kiss her, but Ann pulled away, asking again, 'What is wrong?'

He explained what he had been doing in Spain and that the police had arrested Lilly and her father on suspicion of having been involved in her mother's death.

Ann just went white and mumbled, 'Take me home.'

He helped her to his car because he thought she might faint. Once she was seated in the car, he put the seatbelt on her and took her to his home.

Once he had finished texting his update to Tommy, Jacko put his phone in his pocket, alerted some officers they were needed and then went to the station car park, where he got in his own car to drive to the Kenwright building. He was accompanied by a police car containing two police officers. They arrived at two pm and went straight into the offices.

At the reception desk, Jacko showed his warrant card to the lady there and asked her, 'Can you ask Miss Lilly Blake to come down here, please?'

The receptionist frowned as she picked up the phone and said into it, 'Miss Blake, there's three policemen to see you.' She nodded, listening to the response on the other end of the line, and then looked at Jacko and said, 'Miss Blake said she's very busy and asked that you go up to her office. It's on the top floor, next to Mr Thomson's office and has her name on the door, so you should be able to find it easily.'

She pointed towards the lift and the policemen walked over and entered it. Jacko pressed the button for the top floor and the elevator ascended smoothly. When the lift doors opened, the police officers found themselves on a landing with five doors. Each had its own nameplate and presumably opened into an office for an important member of the business.

They went to the door with the nameplate that read: *Miss Lilly Blake - PA to Mr Thomson* and knocked, hearing a woman's voice say from within, 'Come in, please.'

Jacko opened the door and entered, with the two officers following. Lilly was at an expensive-looking desk, typing on a laptop. Behind her was a large window that looked out over the city and around the walls were filing cabinets, with lovely paintings above them.

She looked up, smiled and said, 'I'm afraid Mr Thomson is out of the country. Can I help you gentlemen?'

Jacko said, 'I'm Detective Sergeant Jackson. We are not here to see Mr Thomson. I would like you to accompany us to the police station.'

Lilly looked shocked and asked, 'Why do you want me to go with you? I haven't broken any laws.'

Jacko replied, 'We will discuss that at the station, so please get your coat, Miss Blake.'

Lilly was even more shocked at this reply, asking, 'Why have I got to come with you? What's this all about?'

The two officers stepped forward, moving in front of Jacko, but he stopped them by touching them on their shoulders.

He said, 'I don't want to have to arrest you. It wouldn't look nice if you walk out of here in handcuffs so, please, Miss Blake, get your coat. It's much better if you help us with our enquiries voluntarily. We're also talking to your father. You can call your solicitor from the station.'

Lilly, as she came around the desk to get her coat from a small closet just to the right of the door of the office, asked, 'My dad?' She had gone red in the face and had started to cry, as she continued, 'My dad wouldn't hurt a fly. Why are you talking to him?'

One of the officers helped her put her coat on and they all left the office. As they came out of the lift on the ground floor, Lilly kept her head looking downwards, with her hanky up to her eyes. The receptionist, and the few other people around, stopped and stared in surprise as the group left the building.

One officer opened the door of the police car and told Lilly to mind her head as he directed her to sit in the back of the car.

As they drove away, the receptionist rang one of the directors and told him what had happened.

The director said, 'Put me through to Mr Thomson's phone. He's in France. I'll inform him about what's happened with the police.'

Steve was in a meeting when his phone rang.

He apologised to the people in the meeting, saying, 'Sorry about this but I will have to answer as I told them no calls unless it's urgent.'

Steve walked out of the room as he answered the call. 'Mr Thomson here. This better be important.'

The director cleared his throat and said, 'Three police officers have escorted Miss Blake to the police station. Obviously, I'll send the firm's lawyer to represent her as soon as I'm off the phone, but I wanted to let you know immediately'.

Steve said, 'I'm coming back to the UK. Get someone to inform the airport to have my jet ready in three quarters of an hour.'

Steve phoned his chauffeur before he quickly stuck his head back into the room he'd just left, telling them they would have to postpone the meeting for another time due to a family emergency. Then he rushed out of the building, to find his limousine already waiting.

He shouted to the chauffeur as he got in the car, 'The airport. As quick as you can.'

SAM IS ASKED TO HELP THE POLICE WITH THEIR ENQUIRIES

Smithy and his partner, Detective Maurice, knocked on Sam Blake's door. Sam opened it and was surprised to see two big men standing there, with serious looks on their faces and two police cars parked behind them.

He said, with a puzzled look on his face, 'Yes, what do you want?'

Smithy and Maurice both reached into the inside pockets of their coats and showed him their warrant cards. At that moment two police officers got out of each of the cars.

Smithy said, 'We have a warrant to search your house, and we would like you to help us with our enquiries at the station.'

Sam went white and his legs buckled beneath him. Maurice and Smithy both reached out and held on to him, looking at each other as they did so.

'I'm alright, let go of me,' Sam said. 'What are you looking for? And what do you want me for? I haven't done anything against the law!'

Smithy replied, 'I'll explain it all at the station.'

While Smithy was talking, the four police officers walked up the path to the house and, as they reached the front door, Smithy continued, 'Now, come with us, please. These officers will respect your home while they search it.'

Sam looked at him and nodded, too shocked to disagree. The three of them walked past the two police cars and stopped next to the unmarked vehicle which the detectives had driven to the house. Maurice held open the back door of the car. As Sam got in, the detective placed his hand on Sam's head so he wouldn't bang it on the doorframe.

Once Sam was safely in the car, Maurice closed the door and said, 'Smithy, you take him in. I'll have a nose round the house with the boys.'

Smithy got in the driving seat and replied, 'Okay, I'll see you later at the station.' With that he drove off, with Sam sitting in the back, as his partner went into the house.

On the way to the station, Smithy looked at Sam every now and then in his rear mirror. He was a bit worried because his passenger looked pale.

He asked, 'Are you alright?'

Sam replied, still in a shaky voice but now feeling more like himself, 'What do you think? I've been dragged out of my home and arrested, and I don't know why.'

Smithy replied, 'You haven't been arrested yet - and we'll let you know what's going on once we get to the station.'

By the time they got to the station, Smithy was really worried about how Sam looked. He was no spring chicken and he didn't look at all well, so before he got Sam out the car, Smithy got on the car's radio.

'I've got a Mr Sam Blake with me. I'm bringing him into the station for questioning, but I don't think he's well. Can we request the on-call doctor to come out and have a look at him?'

Sam heard him and said, 'I'm alright - it was just the shock of you turning up like this. Just let me sit here for a few minutes... I want this mess you've got me mixed up in sorted out.'

Smithy gave Sam a close look in his rearview mirror and saw he looked a lot better than he had a few minutes earlier, so he said, 'Okay, but I'll get the doctor to see you in the station.'

They waited in the car for about five more minutes and then Sam indicated he was ready to move into the station. Smithy carefully helped him out of the car and tried to keep hold of his arm to steady him, but Sam shook his hand off. They very slowly walked towards the station door, with Smithy keeping a nervous eye on Sam, who was clearly finding the short walk a challenge.

At the same time as Smithy was driving Sam to the station, back at the house Detective Maurice and the uniformed officers were conducting a thorough search of Sam's property.

Maurice went into the living room where an officer was going through Sam's cupboards.

The officer stopped when he saw him and said, 'This Sam fellow seemed baffled when he saw us. To me it looks like he doesn't have a clue what's going on.'

Maurice answered, 'He could just be a good actor.'

Just then the officer picked something out of the cupboard and showed it to the detective, saying, 'It's a heart spray. Mr Blake must have a weak heart.'

Maurice took the spray off him and said, 'He didn't look too good when we took him in. I'll take this to him; he mightn't have one on him. I'll be back later.'

With that he rushed out to the police cars.

As he passed one of the officers, he said, 'You're the driver of that car, aren't you? Get in it and get me to the station as fast as you can without speeding.'

They both jumped in the car and sped off. When they got to their destination, Smithy was still helping Sam into the station.

SAM IS QUESTIONED

Detective Maurice was out of the car before it had properly stopped and he rushed over to where Smithy and Sam were now standing, near the entrance to the station and gave Sam the spray, saying, 'I thought you might need this.'

Sam took it and sprayed it into his mouth; he stood still for a moment, while it took effect, then he said, 'You're right, I do need it, thanks to you lot of idiots.'

Maurice said to Smithy, 'I'll get back to the house now.'

He got back into the car and the driver drove out of the station car park.

By the time Smithy and Sam reached the interviewing room, Sam was over the shock of the police bringing him into the station.

Smithy pointed to a seat that was between the wall and a table and said, 'Sit down on this chair, Sam. Are you sure you don't want a doctor?'

Sam replied, 'Do you mean do I want a solicitor? No, I don't need a doctor or a solicitor, unless it's about the time I was twelve and I robbed some apples off a tree.'

Smithy said, 'I wish it was about that, but it's real serious trouble we think you're in. Wait here. I'll be back in a few minutes.'

Sam replied, 'I can't go anywhere, so I'll be here when you get back, you can be sure of that.'

Once outside of the room, Smithy phoned the front desk and asked if they could notify the on-call doctor, saying, 'I want him to be on standby because, as you know I've got Sam Blake in for an interview, and he's got a weak heart.'

The custody officer asked, 'What interview room are you in? You're lucky, the doctor is already on-site today. I'll ask him to wait outside the room in case you need him.'

Smithy replied, 'Room six. Thanks.'

Smithy went back into the room and found Sam had stood up and was walking up and down the room.

He asked Sam, 'Would you like a cup of tea or coffee to drink?'

Sam replied, 'Yes, a tea, thanks. Are you 'good cop' then? When does 'bad cop' come in?'

Smithy wanted to smile at Sam's remarks, but then he reminded himself that a woman had died, and the situation was far from funny.

So he said, 'I'm afraid I've got to be 'bad cop' now. Please sit down.'

Sam said, with an angry look on his face, 'What is this all about? You still haven't told me. It's not right.'

As Sam returned to his seat, Smithy sat down on the chair on the other side of the table, so he was facing Sam. At that moment a young policeman came in and sat next to Smithy.

There was a digital recorder on the table, Smithy turned it on and said, 'Mr Samuel Blake's interview. Present are Detective Sergeant Smith and Constable Morgan. Would you say your name, Sam?'

Sam shouted at the recorder, 'I'm Samuel Blake and haven't done anything fucking wrong, pardon the language.'

Smithy said, 'Do you want a solicitor? If you cannot afford a solicitor, one can be provided for you.'

Sam said, 'What would I need a solicitor for? I've told you, I haven't *done* anything. Aren't you listening?'

Smithy said, 'At this moment your daughter is being interviewed for the murder of Joan Thomson.'

Sam went red and jumped up, causing his chair to fly back and hit the wall behind him.

'Leave my daughter alone - you're all fuckin' bastards!'

Then he put his hand on the top part of his left arm, by his chest, as he slumped back onto the chair.

As he ran around the table to Sam, Smithy said to the officer, 'Get the doc!'

The doctor was watching through the two-way mirror and entered the room as soon as he saw what was happening but, when he approached Sam, Sam put his hand up to let the doctor know he didn't want him. Instead, he took out his heart spray and sprayed it into his mouth.

The doctor stood looking at Sam for a few minutes until Sam bucked up and said, 'I don't need a doctor. It's just an angina attack, I'll be alright in a couple more minutes.'

The doctor replied, 'Well, I will still have to examine you, Mr Blake, to check you are recovered.'

Sam said, 'I don't want you to and that's my right, isn't it? We're not a police state yet.'

Smithy said, 'You're right, we're not a police state... so we can't continue with the interview while you don't look fit enough to carry on. So, the longer we have to wait before we know you're well, the longer you'll be here.'

Sam looked at Smithy as if he wanted to kill him, then he unbuttoned his shirt and said, 'Okay, doctor, go ahead.'

The doctor pushed aside the small religious medal on a gold chain around Sam's neck and examined him, saying, 'Normally I would say for you to rest after an angina attack, but the position you are in isn't normal and it might be bad for you to worry about things, so it could be better to get this interview over with.'

Sam said, 'I don't need a doctor to tell me that.'

The doctor left the room and Sam just sat there as Smithy checked the recorder was still working and started the interview again.

Smithy said, 'Sam Blake, you are being questioned about the death of Joan Thomson. How long have you had your MG?'

Sam didn't look so weak now and answered in a strong voice, 'I've had it for about a little under nine years. Why do you want to know?'

The officer said, 'Just answer the questions.'

Sam looked at him and said, 'Are you sure it's not a police state?'

Smithy said, 'These young people have no manners, but he is right, you do need to please just answer what is asked. I think you should get a solicitor, and he can speak for you.'

Sam gave a fake laugh and said, 'Oh, so *he's* bad cop, you're good cop now? I don't need someone to speak for me.'

Smithy said, 'Alright, just answer and you will get to know what we're on about as we progress. Now, we know you had the car at least eighteen months before that didn't you?'

Sam replied, 'Have you lot gone fucking mad? I got it in bits over at least two years and I only got the body nine years ago. I can show you the receipts.'

Just then there was a knock on the door, so Smithy said, 'Come in.'

A detective entered, went up to Smithy and whispered in his ear, then he left the room.

Smithy said, 'I've just been told that the front of the car, where the engine is, has been reinforced. Why did you do that to it?'

Sam said, 'I didn't reinforce it, it was like that when I got it - nine years ago. Why don't you question the man I got it from?'

Smithy asked, 'If you didn't put it in storage, how did you know the car was for sale?'

'I didn't,' Sam replied, 'Davis told my daughter about it. He knew I was looking for an old car to keep me busy. Why don't you see him about it? Oh, yes, I forgot - he does a lot of work for you lot... He's just one of the boys, hey?'

Smithy replied, 'He's nothing to do with the police and we have questioned him. He told us about your daughter somehow knowing he had the car...'

Sam butted in, 'Oh, so you believed him, but you don't believe me? Very convenient. I'm clearly being framed, so actually, I *do* want a solicitor.'

Smithy asked, 'Have you got your own or do you want the duty solicitor?'

'Yes, all of us ordinary, working people retain a solicitor... Of course I'll have the duty solicitor!' Sam said in an angry tone.

Smithy replied, 'Well, it's getting late, we'll leave it there and the solicitor can have a word in private with you in your cell.'

Sam said, 'You can't keep me here. I haven't done anything.'

Smithy turned the recorder off and the police officer with him stood up from the desk, saying, 'Come with me, Mr Blake. We will put you in holding and call the duty solicitor for you.'

Sam didn't move, so Smithy said, 'Go with the officer, Sam. If you don't, they will make you. When your solicitor gets here, you can complain to him.'

Sam got up off the chair and went with the officer out the room.

LILLY IS QUESTIONED

In the police station, Lilly, still holding her handkerchief to her face, followed Jacko down a long corridor. A police officer walked just behind her. Jacko stopped outside interview room two and opened the door.

He stepped aside and gestured towards a single chair on the far side of the only table in the room, saying, 'Sit in that seat, Miss Blake. I think you should get a solicitor.'

She replied, 'I don't need one,' as she took her seat.

Jacko and the officer sat facing Lilly and Jacko said, 'We have a warrant to search your apartment and your office, so if you're hiding any evidence anywhere, you need to understand that we are experts at finding hiding places - we know them all.' Then he asked again, 'Do you want a solicitor?'

Lilly replied, in a voice muffled by her handkerchief, 'No, I don't need one… but the firm will send one along soon anyway. What is this all about?'

'Don't you want to wait till your solicitor gets here?' Jacko asked.

'No. I want to know what I'm here for,' Lilly said.

Jacko replied, 'Okay, if you want to get started,' turning on the tape recorder and continuing, 'This is Elizabeth Blake's interview. Present are DS Jackson and Officer Knox. Will you say your name for the tape, Lilly?'

She still had the handkerchief on her face as she answered in a low voice, 'Lilly Blake. I shouldn't be here.'

Jacko said, 'Lilly, please take the handkerchief away from your face and say your full name, louder for the tape.'

She did as she was told and said, 'Elizabeth Blake. Why am I here?'

He replied, 'We have evidence to suggest you were involved in the death of Mrs Joan Thomson and that is why you are here now.'

Lilly replied, 'That's daft. She died ten years ago… and it was in Spain. I was at home with my dad in London. Ask him.'

Jacko said, 'I told you, we are talking to your dad at this moment… and how can you remember where you were so easily after ten years? My officer here can't remember what happened last week.'

Lilly answered, 'It's obvious why I can remember! The woman who owned the place where I work died while she was on holiday.

I'm sure if you died in such circumstances your officer would remember where he was.'

'Be that as may, Miss Blake,' Jacko replied, watching closely for her reaction, 'that doesn't explain why your father currently owns the car that was driven in the incident that caused Joan Thomson's death.'

Lilly looked shocked but, before she could respond, there was a knock on the door.

Frustrated, Smithy said, 'Come in.'

A police officer entered with a well-dressed man, who looked about sixty years old, and announced, 'This is Miss Blake's solicitor.'

The solicitor said, 'Miss Blake, don't say another word until we have spoken. I'm Mr Douglas Thomas.' Then he asked Jacko, 'Can I have somewhere private to speak to my client?'

Jacko said, 'We'll leave you in here,' switching the tape recorder off and gesturing to Officer Knox to follow him as he exited the room.

Once they had left, Mr Thomas sat down facing Lilly and said, 'The duty officer handed me a summary of the details of the crime in which you are implicated.'

He took a manila envelope from his briefcase, opened it and looked at the piece of paper laying out the details of the potential charge.

Then he looked at Lilly and said, under his breath, 'I don't believe it.'

Lilly didn't catch what he said and said, 'Pardon?'

Mr Thomas said, 'I'm sorry. I was just taken aback. They want to…'

She interrupted, 'I know what they want, it's to blame me for Joan Thomson's death. They're claiming some nonsense about my dad owning the car that was involved. What are you going to do about it?'

He asked, 'What have they asked you and what have you told them?'

'They asked where I was when Joan died,' Lilly replied, 'and I told them I was at home with my dad. That's all I could say. Then they asked how I could remember after ten years. Can you remember where you were when it happened?'

Mr Thomas answered, 'Yes, it was such a shock at the time, it's not surprising that you remember where you were when it happened. It would be a terrible coincidence if your father's car does turn out to be the one that was involved in Joan's death. Have you any idea how that might have happened?'

Lilly looked shocked and said, 'No! It's ridiculous, he got that car off a storage firm; it must have been about fourteen months after Joan's death and, when he got it, half of it was missing. He got parts from all over the country, and he had to put it together like a Lego toy. It took him about four or five years. So how could that be the car they're looking for?'

Mr Thomas said, 'They have a warrant to search the firm's offices. Steve is on his way back. Once we're done here, I will get him a visiting order to see you in the morning. Are you ready to finish answering their questions now?'

Lilly nodded that she was and, after telling her to simply answer any questions that she was unhappy about with 'no comment', he opened the door and let the police know that the interview could continue.

Jacko and his attending officer questioned Lilly for several hours about her whereabouts on the days around Joan's death, and when and how her dad had taken possession of the MG. If they were hoping to catch her out, they were disappointed. Lilly's answers remained the same: she had been at her dad's on the day Joan died, she couldn't remember many specifics about what they had been doing on exact days because of the decade since the incident had happened, and her dad got his MG well after one had aimed itself at the Thomson family in Spain. Eventually, Jacko called the interview to a close and left Lilly alone with her solicitor for a few moments.

They spoke about how well the interview had gone and then Mr Thomas started putting the notes he had taken away in his briefcase.

Lilly asked, 'Are you going now? But I want you to get me out of here.'

Mr Thomas said, 'I'm afraid I can't do anything about that. They have the right to hold you for twenty-four hours without pressing charges, Miss Blake.'

Just then an officer knocked on the door.

Mr Thomas said, 'Come.'

The officer entered and said, 'Will you come with me, please, Miss Blake.'

As she was escorted from the room, Mr Thomas said, 'Don't worry, we will get this all sorted out tomorrow when Steve comes to visit you.'

As Mr Thomas left the station, he got a phone call.

He answered, 'Mr Thomas speaking.'

A voice replied, 'It's me, Steve. I want you to meet me at the airport. I will be landing in half an hour.'

Mr Thomas said, 'I've just left Miss Blake and I'm already getting into my car; I'll be there when you land.'

Steve replied, 'Okay, I'll see you then.'

Mr Thomas put his phone away and got into his car, heading towards the airport.

While Lilly was being questioned, the police had requisitioned all the firm's old personnel paperwork from ten years ago.

At first the people in the offices stopped and stared in amazement at the line of officers carting boxes of paperwork through the building and out the door, but then one of the managers came round shouting, 'Get back to your jobs now.'

The police looked over all the offices that had anything to do with the personnel files, but they searched every inch of Lilly's office with particular focus; nothing was missed.

ANN IS SHAKEN

While Sam and Lilly were being questioned by the police and Steve was travelling home, Tommy had driven Ann home.

Keen to get her inside as quickly as possible, after the shock he had given her at the restaurant, Tommy parked his car outside his own house, but Ann said, 'Please go in, Tommy. I just want to sit here for a little while.'

Tommy replied, 'Okay, love, I understand. I'll make you a cup of tea.'

He left her sitting there and went into the house. He watched Ann through his front window, and he could see she was crying.

After twenty minutes with no sign that she was coming in, he went out to her, opened the passenger door and said, 'Come on in, love. You can't sit there all day; I've made a pot of tea.'

He bent down and got hold of her hand, and she looked up at him with tears in her eyes as he helped her out of the car.

As they walked up the small path, she asked, 'Tell me again what is going on, Tommy.'

He replied, as they went into the house, 'Just sit down, I'll get you a drink and we can go over it all.'

He led her to the settee, and she sat down, wiping her eyes. In no time at all Tommy was back with two cups of tea. He handed one to Ann as he sat down beside her.

She said, 'Put it on the coffee table. I'll drink it later.

The way you told me about this... My mother is dead and it's all because of that cow, Lilly, and her dad. So, I was right that it was a woman driving the car, but I'm beginning to think I was wrong about my dad.

Lilly stood in sometimes for his PA back then. He would have got her to arrange everything about the holiday - even the stuff for my birthday picnic - and everyone in our offices knew Mum was terrified of heights, so she would have known my mum would be on the road rather than the pavement overlooking that cliff. Her plan must have really been to run my mum down... but even though Dad pulled her out of the way, that bitch still got what she wanted: my mum's death and a free run at my dad.

For all these years, I have been blaming my dad... but everybody who said he couldn't keep hold of Mum was right and I was wrong.'

She started crying, and mumbled, 'I can't face him to say I'm sorry. What can I do Tommy?'

He put his arm round her and hugged her to him, saying, 'It's best if we wait till it's all sorted out. Your dad will be made up to have you back in his life but, right now, he will be angry and upset about it all. This is his fiancée we're talking about.

Anyway, John will be only too happy to help you with your dad. I'll phone him up when I think your dad and John have had time to take it all in, but right now you need to get some rest. Why don't you go up to bed?'

Ann replied, 'I have this sickly feeling in my stomach, and I don't want to be by myself. Will you come with me, Tommy?'

He helped her up and as he walked with her into his bedroom, he said, 'I'll stay with you as long as you want me to.'

The next morning Tommy didn't wake Ann because she hadn't slept well. He rang her PA and asked her to tell Emma that Ann wasn't well and would be in touch later, and that they would need someone to take over helping out at the understaffed restaurant. He realised they really needed to get in touch with Emma themselves, once Ann was awake, to let her know what had happened with her sister's case.

Then he texted Jacko: *How is the case going? TT*

Jacko's reply came almost instantly: *London branch thinks you're wrong about Sam. They think he is involved and they will find more evidence in his house and the garage. They are continuing to question him. I think Lilly hasn't the willpower to stand up to our questioning and will break soon. Here's hoping. Bye, Jacko.*

He texted back: *Thanks, Jacko. I hope you're right, see you soon, TT*

STEVE ARRIVES HOME

Not long after Steve landed, Mr Thomas drove into the hanger where the jet was parked. Steve came out of the jet and down the steps as a man moved over towards the car and opened the door for him to get in.

He sat in the back of the car and, as they drove out of the hangar, Steve said, 'What the hell is going on, Doug? No one has been able to tell me anything.'

Doug cleared his throat and said, 'Steve, I don't know how to tell you this...'

Steve butted in, saying loudly, 'Fuckin' hell, don't you start. What's happening and why have the police arrested Lilly?'

Doug took a deep breath and said, 'They want to charge Lilly with being involved in Joan's death.'

Steve didn't make a sound. As the silence continued, Doug started to get a bit worried. He looked at Steve in his rear-view mirror. Steve just sat there, looking pale.

After a while he said, 'I don't believe it, Lilly didn't even know Joan... She would have seen Joan around the office, but the only time Joan would have spoken to Lilly would be to ask for me. Did the police tell you why they are saying Lilly is involved?'

Doug could tell, by the tone in Steve's voice, that he was getting angry. He didn't want to get distracted by too complicated a discussion while he was driving, so he didn't answer the question.

He said instead, 'On the way to pick you up, I phoned DS Jackson and requested a visiting order for you in the morning, but he said he wanted to see you before you see Lilly.'

Steve asked, 'What would he want to see me for?'

Doug replied, 'They are most likely worried about how you will react when you see Lilly.'

Steve said, 'Right now, I don't know how I feel about it all. At this moment, I feel sick. Drop me off at home.'

Doug continued to worry as he drove Steve home. Steve had gone quiet in the back of the car and, from over the years when Doug had seen the few times Steve had lost his temper, he knew Steve went quiet first and then he turned into a nasty bastard, and God help anyone near him. So Doug just wanted him out of his car before he lost his temper.

He knew the code for the security gates at Steve's home, and speedily entered it into the system, heading over the bridge and up the driveway as soon as the gates opened far enough to let the car through.

As he slowed to a stop, Steve asked in a nasty tone, 'What time am I meeting this copper?'

Doug replied, 'I'll pick you up at ten in the morning.'

The car stopped by the door and Steve got out, saying angrily, 'You make sure this gets straightened out tomorrow.'

He slammed the car door and went into his house. Doug drove away only too glad that Steve was out of his car, though he felt sorry for the horrible situation Steve was in.

When Steve got inside the house, the first thing he did was to shout, 'John? Are you in?'

Then he saw a note, on the small table by the phone, that said, 'Out for the night. Will stop at Billy's, love, John.'

Steve put the note in a small waste bin at the side of the table. He picked up the phone and called Lilly's dad. He rang the number about six times during the evening. Eventually, he went to bed at two a.m. but, wondering why he didn't get an answer, he couldn't sleep.

Steve couldn't wait for morning. After tossing and turning for two hours, he gave up on sleeping. He got up at four a.m. and went into his gym. He trained for two and a half hours, and, after that, he spent half an hour in the swimming pool. Then he went into the sauna before heading back to his room to shower and change.

While he was getting dressed, he heard the maid come in. By the time he went into the dining room, his breakfast was on the table. He couldn't eat it, he just drank four mugs of coffee and walked up and down the dining room.

At eight a.m. he tried phoning Lilly's dad again.

When he didn't get an answer, he smashed the phone down on the receiver, saying out loud, 'Where the fuck are you?'

Then he picked up the cracked phone and called Doug at home.

The phone rang a few times and then a woman's voice said, 'Hello, Mrs Thomas here.'

Steve replied in an angry tone, 'I want to speak to Doug.'

Steve heard her put the phone down and say, 'Doug, it's some abrupt man who wants to speak to you.'

He heard the phone being picked up and Doug said, 'Doug here. Who is it, please?'

Steve replied, 'It's me. I want to go to the station now, what time will you be here? I'm ready to go.'

Doug answered, 'I'll be at yours in about an hour. We will have plenty of time. The meeting isn't till ten.'

Steve said, 'Well, I want to get there as soon as possible, so get your arse in gear. I want you here.' Then he ended the call by slamming the phone down.

Doug was angry and, as he put the phone down on the receiver, he said to his wife, 'That was Steve, the hard-faced bastard.'

His wife asked, 'Is there any need for that language?'

'Sorry, love,' he replied, 'but if it wasn't for the mess he's in, I would tell him to get another solicitor. He's never spoken to me like that before... and he better not talk to me like that again.'

His wife said, 'Steve is usually so well-mannered, it must be the pressure of the situation getting to him. You'll just have to cut him some slack. I'll suppose I'll see you tonight - you'd best be off now!'

Doug said 'Goodbye,' and his wife blew him a kiss as he went out the door.

Twenty-five minutes later, he was outside the big iron gates at Steve's house. He pressed the buzzer on the intercom and said, 'Doug here.'

The gates opened before he had finished speaking. He drove over the bridge and up the driveway, only to see Steve walking down to meet him. He stopped the car and Steve got in.

Doug said, 'You should have stayed at the house, I'll have to drive up there anyway to turn around.'

Steve answered, in a sharp voice, 'Just bloody well turn round here on the grass, I've got things to do, and I want you to get this lot sorted.'

Doug replied in an angry voice, as he turned the car round where it was, 'Steve, I understand you are upset with everything that is going on, but you need to talk to me in a civil voice or I will take your firm off my books.'

Steve went red with anger, but he knew Doug was right.

He said, 'I'm sorry, Doug. I'm out of line - it's just because we're friends that I let my feelings take over.'

Doug said, 'Okay, let's just forget it and go sort this mess out.'

He drove back down the driveway and over the bridge. The gates opened just as they approached them. On the way to the police station, the two men didn't say another word.

SAM IS BACK IN THE INTERVIEW ROOM

The morning after Sam had been brought in for questioning, Smithy was in early and held a meeting with the officers who searched Sam's house.

One of the officers who had searched the garage said, 'He'd done a hell of a job on reinforcing the engine compartment. The way it's reinforced, if it hit something, like a person, it wouldn't buckle. The car could just keep going.

We also found some old holiday brochures and all of them were about Spain, and in an old bin full of all sorts of rubbish,' the officer started laughing, pointed to another officer and said, 'he thought there was a rat and shit himself. But when I 'killed' it, it was just what looked like might have been a fake beard at one time, so we put it in an evidence bag.'

Then a young officer said, 'I found a family tree he was working on. It was in a cupboard full of dust and went about eight generations back. It showed that a Kenwright woman married a man named George Blake a few generations ago. So, they may be distant relations - maybe they thought if something happened to the family they might get some of the money.'

All the other policemen laughed, and Smithy said, 'They would have to get rid of about ten families for the money to go to them, but I'll bring it up along with the brochures for Spain, it might help to mess with his head a bit and he might slip up. Did anyone find his passport? That would really help us, if he used it to go to Spain.'

There was a general murmuring of 'no'.

Then another officer said, 'If he did it, he is a hypocrite. He has a Bible and rosary beads next to his bed, and holy pictures hanging around the house. I've put The Bible on your desk.'

Smithy said, pointing towards the officer in question, 'Officer Morgan, I like the way you think about the big picture while you're investigating. Can you go to the house and spend a few hours looking for his passport? If you find it, let me know right away. Jones, you're with me in the interviewing room.'

He left the room to ask the duty sergeant to get Sam Blake and bring him to interview room two. Smithy and Officer Jones were already sitting at the table when Sam was brought in.

Smithy pointed to a chair on the other side of the table and said, 'Sit there, please, Sam.'

At the same time, Sam's solicitor came in and said, 'I'm Mr Blake's solicitor, my name is William Phillips.' With that, he sat down beside Sam and said, 'Morning, Sam, how are you doing today?'

Sam replied, 'I'm doing as well as I can be in the situation they have put me in.'

Smithy turned on the recorder and said, 'This is the second interview of Sam Blake. Present are Detective Sergeant Smith, Officer Jones, Sam Blake and his solicitor, William Phillips.

Sam, my officer here found your family tree in your house. It shows that you're a very distant relation of the Kenwright's and he believes you thought that, if you got rid of the family, some of the money would come to you. Is he right?'

Sam gave a false laugh and replied, 'It's not mine, it's my daughter's. She did it years ago, when she was in school. It mightn't even be the same Kenwrights and, even if it is, I would have to bump off quite a lot of families for the money to come to me. This must be some kind of sick joke! Are you sure you lot are in the right job?'

Smithy smiled and replied, 'It does sound silly, but the question had to be asked.'

Sam turned and looked at his solicitor saying, 'Aren't you supposed to help me? Don't just sit there - say something and earn the money the tax man is paying you.'

The solicitor said, 'Sam, like I told you last night, if you don't want to answer, just say 'no comment'. I'm here to see that you are treated fairly and to stop the police putting words into your mouth. Do you understand this, Sam?'

'Okay,' he replied, but then he shook his head and said, 'I'm innocent of whatever they say I've done. So, I don't want to say, 'no comment'. You only say that when you have something to hide.'

With that he turned back to face Smithy, who said, 'We also found the Spanish brochures that you used to help plan your crime ten years ago. Well, what do you have to say to that?'

'What brochures?' Sam answered, 'I've never been to Spain in my life... In fact, I've only ever been out of the country once, and that was when I was in the army, and I was shipped to Northern Ireland.'

Officer Jones said, 'A man involved in this case was shot ten years ago and our research into your background has shown that when you were in the army, you were a top marksman. Did you shoot this man?'

Sam replied, 'The only things I shot and killed were cardboard cutouts. I don't know who you're talking about, but I can tell you that I didn't shoot that man, and I didn't shoot John F. Kennedy either. Unless you want to blame that on me as well? I haven't touched a gun since I was in the army.'

Smithy said, 'We'll see about that when we get your passport and the gun.'

Sam looked angry at first, but then he grinned and exclaimed, 'Of course! You haven't found it yet, have you? But why not? If I was this horrible person that you say I am, I would have two passports! *I* know why you can't find either a gun or a passport.'

Smithy thought Sam was getting overconfident and said, 'Have you got rid of the passports then?'

Sam now seemed more relaxed, answered with a smile, 'No, I can swear on The Holy Bible, I haven't got rid of anything.'

Officer Jones said, 'We have your Bible here, in the box by DS Smith's feet, will you swear on it now?'

Sam looked and sounded annoyed as he said, 'I wouldn't really swear on The Bible for the likes of this nonsense. You won't find my passport because I've never had one.'

Smithy said, 'This change in your attitude... You think you're going to get away with it. You won't because we have the evidence, we have the fake beard you were seen using ten years ago.'

Sam said, 'You're making this up as you go along. I've never had a fake beard.'

Smithy replied, 'Yes, you did, and, like all criminals, you made a mistake. You left it in that old bin in the corner of your garage.'

Smithy took the beard out of the evidence box next to his seat, placed it on the table in front of Sam and asked him, 'Don't you recognise this beard?'

Sam frowned as looked at it, saying, 'That's a beard? It looks like a dead rat to me.'

Smithy answered, 'It's not a rat, Sam. It's your fake beard - look at these photos of where it was found.'

Sam looked at the images of the bin sitting in the corner of his garage. He went quiet and looked deep in thought, then he smiled.

'Yes, I recognise it now,' he answered. 'It was jammed under the one seat that came with my car. All of that stuff in the bin came in the car. I put it all in one place because some of the smaller things were parts of the car. I never got round to sorting it out.'

Sam's solicitor said, 'I think Mr Blake should have a break from your questions and be given a meal.'

Officer Jones said into the recorder, 'We're stopping for lunch at one o'clock.'

Smithy pressed a bell on the wall.

After a few minutes, the duty sergeant entered and said, 'Come with me, Mr Blake. We have a meal waiting for you in your cell.'

Sam followed the sergeant out.

As he left, his solicitor said, 'I'll see you in ninety minutes, Sam.'

Back in his cell, Sam ate the meal and tried to rest but he was worried about Lilly and had to take his heart spray a couple of times. The officer in charge of his cell put a request for the on-call doctor to check Sam over. When the doctor arrived, Sam let him examine him.

The doctor said, 'I don't think you should go on with the interview. It's too stressful with your condition. I can let the officer in charge know continuing today is against my medical opinion.'

Sam replied, 'It's the worrying about what is going on that's killing me. I need to know what they are on about and why they have arrested my Lilly. So, I want to carry on with the interview. Please don't ask them to stop.'

The doctor gave in and said, 'Well, if you want to carry on, there's nothing I can do about it.'

STEVE IS TOLD LILLY'S DAD HAS AN OLD MG

While Sam was in London being questioned, Steve was meeting with Jacko. Doug parked his car in the police station's car park. The two of them went round the front of the building and into the main entrance of the police station. They went up to the counter.

As they approached, the duty sergeant asked, 'How can I help you, gentlemen?'

Doug answered, 'We have an appointment with DS Jackson. Could you tell him Mr Steve Thomson and his solicitor are here?'

The duty sergeant nodded. He picked up the handset of the phone in front of him, pressed a number and said, 'DS Jackson, you're wanted out here. A Mr Steve Thomson and his solicitor are here.'

He put the phone back on the receiver, and said, 'He'll be out in a few minutes.'

A door on their right, at the end of the counter, opened and Jacko stood in the doorway, waving for them to enter as he said, 'This way, gentlemen, please.'

They followed Jacko along a corridor. When Jacko got to interview room five, he opened the door and stepped aside, gesturing for them to go in.

As they passed him, he shook their hands and said, 'I take it you're Mr Steve Thomson. Please, take a seat.'

Steve and Doug sat on one side of the table and Jacko took a chair on the other side, so he was facing them.

Jacko said, 'I'll introduce myself. I'm DS Jackson and I'm heading up this case.'

Steve butted in, 'I just want to know what is going on? I'm going to marry Lilly in five weeks.'

Jacko replied, 'I'm sure Mr Thomas has told you that your fiancée is being questioned about the death of your wife.'

Steve looked angry as he said, 'I don't believe you. Lilly wouldn't hurt a fly; she didn't really know my Joan then.'

Jacko replied, 'Well, we believe that her father has the MG that was driven at your family that day.'

Steve went white, looking sick as he just sat there.

Doug put his hand on Steve's shoulder and asked, 'Are you alright, Steve?'

Steve's face suddenly changed, going red with anger as he spluttered out, 'It's not true is it, Doug?'

Doug replied, 'They are saying the MG that Lilly's dad has is the car that nearly ran your family down, Steve, but there are still a few of those old cars about and up to now they haven't offered any proof that it is the car used that day.'

Jacko said, 'We have paperwork going back ten years that shows Lilly worked sometimes as your PA, and she was doing so at the time your wife was killed...'

Steve broke in, 'So what if she was working for me? You're wrong. I don't believe you. The police in Spain said it was a professional hit... and that whoever did it was after my whole family. They also said a man who was involved was shot by a professional killer because he was shot twice, once in the heart and once in the head. Lilly wouldn't know people like that, would she, Doug?'

Doug would have liked to back Steve up but he didn't know Lilly very well, so he just replied, 'I can't imagine she would.'

Jacko said, 'Well, as I was about to say, the diary entries for the trip to Spain are in her handwriting. It seems you left her to arrange everything: the holiday and the picnic trip up the mountain. So, she knew all your plans and we think she added a few plans of her own.'

Steve said, 'I still can't believe it. How would the driver know when we were coming down, and where would she get the money to pay all these people involved with it?'

Jacko answered, 'We know two people were involved: a woman with blond hair under a black wig and a man with a fake beard. As her father has the car now, we think he was the man.'

'It's hard for me to believe... but you make it sound possible.' Steve said. He looked at Doug and continued, 'I need your advice. What do I do? It's my firm's solicitors defending her - which it can't be if she's guilty of killing Joan, but if I take the firm's help away and she didn't do it, it will break her. And there'll be no going back for Lilly and me. That'll be the end of our relationship. Help me, Doug. What do you think I should do?'

Doug replied, 'I'm sorry, Steve, but there's no going back now. You can either leave it with the firm's solicitors or you can pay for her defence through another law firm and then, if she is innocent, you might be able to get back together.'

'Okay,' Steve replied, 'Yes. I'll do that. Will you explain it to her: that the firm can't be seen to be defending her, but I love her, so I will pay for her defence myself?'

Doug answered, 'I will inform her today,' before turning to Jacko and adding, 'You will have to leave Lilly's interview today because she hasn't got a solicitor, and it could take the rest of the day to get one.'

Jacko said, 'We have an extension on how long we can keep Miss Blake, so we can do the interview tomorrow. If you wait here, I'll get an officer to bring her to you.'

Steve was now wiping his eyes and, with tears in them, said, 'I just can't face her. I love her but, if she is guilty, it's best she goes to prison because Joan was my soulmate, and I still love her... If Lilly did it, I will kill her myself.'

With that, he stood up, wiped his eyes and left. Jacko and Doug were taken by surprise and the both of them also stood up, looking at each other and then at the door as it shut behind Steve.

Jacko said to Doug, 'I would hate to be in his situation. He looks confused and upset.'

Doug replied, 'That's not surprising given he is supposed to marry the woman accused of his wife's death in a few weeks. The wife and I have even got an invite.'

Jacko shook his head and said, 'It's sad. I'll go and send Miss Blake to you. Good luck.'

Doug frowned and said, 'With what I have to tell her, I think I'll need more than luck. It's a job I didn't ask for.'

As Jacko left the room, Doug sat back down, saying to himself, 'I know now where they get the saying "don't shoot the messenger".'

He didn't like the idea of telling her what Steve had decided, as he knew she wouldn't be pleased.

After ten minutes, an officer opened the door and Doug stood up and held his hand out to Lilly as she entered. She didn't look like the sophisticated woman he had seen in the past: the stress of the night in the cell showed on her face and in the way she held herself.

She shook his hand as she asked, 'Where is Steve?'

Doug said, 'You'd best sit down, Lilly.'

'No, where's Steve? I want Steve,' she replied, starting to sob.

Doug put his arm round her and led her to a chair.

She sat down and looked up at Doug with sad, begging eyes and shrieked, 'You promised me Steve would be here. Why isn't he?'

He didn't know what to say to calm her down, so he just came out with it, saying, 'Steve knows you didn't do it, and he loves you but, because you're being accused of his wife's death - and he's the firm's owner now - he can't come and see you until you are proven innocent.'

Lilly sobbed even louder, and he found it hard to understand her as she asked, 'What do you mean, he can't come to see me?'

He replied, 'Steve owns the firm, so he has to think about its reputation which means the firm's solicitors - including me - can't represent you. But he loves you, so he is going to pay for your defence himself.'

Lilly went hysterical and started shouting, 'I don't understand. Where is Steve? I want Steve.'

Doug put his arm back around Lilly's shoulders and was trying to calm her down; then the door opened, revealing two police officers about to come into the room.

Doug held his hand up and said, 'It's okay, gentleman. There's no trouble here - we are just a bit upset. I'll let you know when I'm finished with my client.'

Doug was with Lilly for another hour before she calmed down. By that point she was angry with Steve.

'He said he loves me,' she spat out, 'but he's leaving me to rot in here? Well, tell him he better get me and my dad a good defence team... And if he loves me like he is always telling me, well, tell him he needs to come and see me.'

Doug said, 'I'm sorry, Lilly, I won't be seeing you again, but I will make sure you get the best legal team that deals with this kind of case.'

As he was talking, he pressed the bell on the wall and the door opened.

The two police officers came in and one of them said, 'Come with us, Miss Blake.'

Lilly got up from her seat and one officer stepped aside for Lilly to pass him. The other then went out the room, with Lilly following him, and the officer who had stepped aside moved behind her as they left the room.

Doug got on his phone to Steve as he left the police station.

A voice answered, 'Steve Thomson here.'

Doug said, in an angry tone, 'You had no right to leave me in that mess. You should have stayed and explained your plans to Lilly yourself.'

Steve said, 'Sorry, Doug, I was so upset and confused, I couldn't handle the situation. I had to get out of there, you understand?'

Doug replied, still angry, 'If you try to use me like that again, it will be the last time; I don't care if you are upset or confused. Now, do *you* understand that?'

Having made his position clear, Doug began to calm down, and he told Steve how Lilly had taken the news and what she had said.

Then he said, 'I told Lilly you would get her the best legal team around and she wants the same for her father. Also, she wants to see you.'

Steve replied, 'I think you would be the best one to sort the defence out, but just for Lilly. Her dad can get his own. Will you do that for me, Doug? I'll be in your debt forever.'

'I'll do it for Lilly,' Doug said, 'because I've always thought she was a nice woman and I think, if she was involved, it was the man the police were talking about who put her up to it. If her dad really has got the car, it seems he must have been in on it... but I don't know why he would keep it! Now, when are you going to see Lilly? She's desperate to see you.'

Steve answered, 'I don't know what to do for the best. I love her but, if she was involved, I would feel like I was letting the love of my life, Joan, down... So, no, I won't go and see her.'

Doug said, 'Well, at least write her a letter explaining how you feel. I've told Lilly why the firm can't defend her, but I think you should let her know what you're doing to help in the letter. I'll engage the firm *Shannon and Shannon* for her defence. They are a good team.'

Steve replied, 'Thanks, Doug. I'm busy at the moment, so I've got to go, bye.'

Doug didn't answer. As the line went dead, he just shook his head and thought back to when he read Joan's will and the way Steve had reacted then.

He phoned his wife, who answered, 'The Thomas home.'

Doug said, 'It's me.'

His wife asked, 'Are you alright? It's not like you to phone during office hours without a good reason - what is wrong?'

Doug replied, 'Sorry I worried you, love. I wanted to hear a voice I know is not selfish and thinks everyone is at their beck and call! I'm just sick of Steve Thomson, I'll tell you all about it when I get home. Bye, love you.'

His wife said, 'Try to relax and I'll see you when you get home. Bye, love you.'

Doug then phoned *Shannon and Shannon* and explained the case and that they were being retained by Steve Thomson to defend his fiancée, Lilly, on a potential murder charge, saying, 'I'll send you all the paperwork my firm has on it.'

Once he was done, he put his phone away and drove to his office.

JOHN LOOKS FOR HIS DAD

John had been getting ready to go and meet his mate Billy when he had got a text off his dad that read: *I'll be home tonight, I'll see you then.* He thought his dad must be in the closing stages of the business deal he was doing, so he didn't text him back. Instead, he left his dad the note Steve had found when he got home, saying, 'Out for the night. Will stop at Billy's, love, John.'

The next morning, John overslept, so he didn't go home; he went straight to the office instead. John was shocked when he got there. As he entered the building, the people who usually said 'hello' or smiled at him, looked away or down at their feet while the people who usually didn't pay him any attention stopped work and looked at him as he passed.

As he moved through the building, he tried to phone his dad, but his calls kept going to voicemail. He started to worry that something bad had happened. He felt sick when he got to his dad's office and his dad wasn't there. He immediately went next door to Lilly's office and, when he opened the door, he was surprised to see a woman he didn't know sitting at Lilly's desk.

He asked, 'Where's my dad and Lilly? And who are you?'

She replied, 'Just call me Eliza. I'm a PA from Accounts. Please come in and sit down, Mr Thomson.'

She waited while John moved to sit in one of the big executive chairs, then she said, 'One of the directors told me to temporarily take over Miss Lilly Blake's workload because she was taken away for questioning by the police yesterday afternoon. I believe your father is with the firm's solicitor at the police station.'

John was really worried and asked, 'Which police station is my dad at?'

She replied, 'I'm afraid I don't know for sure, but I could check with the firm's solicitors and get back to you.'

John waited a moment while she did so and took down the address of the police station when she gave it to him.

John said, 'You said they searched Lilly's office - why? Do they think she has been doctoring the books? She wouldn't do anything like that.'

Eliza replied, 'I'm from Accounts and I can tell you it's nothing to do with the firm's books. They are in great shape; Lilly's expenses are all in order.'

John suddenly got up and ran out of the office. Everyone stopped what they were doing as he ran past them. When he got to the lift, he pressed the button, but the lift was too slow for him, so he didn't wait for it. Instead, he ran down the stairs, out of the building and across the carpark, where he quickly got in his car and drove to the police station.

When he arrived, however, and asked after his dad, the duty sergeant at the counter told him Steve had just left.

John asked him, 'Why was my dad here and where is Lilly?'

The officer said, 'I don't know anything about your dad or the Lilly person you're on about, all I know is your dad has left the station. You should go home and check if he's there. If he is, then you should ask him these questions.'

John got back in his car and headed home. On the way, he kept using his hands-free phone to try and get in touch with his dad, but it still just kept going to voicemail. By the time he got back home it was nearly afternoon and he was worried sick.

He went swiftly into the house, shouting, as soon as he entered, 'Dad? Where are you?'

The housekeeper came into the lobby, approached him and said, 'Your father is in the gym working out. I'm worried - he didn't look well when he came in, but don't tell him I told you.'

John said, 'Thanks, Mary. I won't.'

With that, he went into the gym and saw his dad, stripped to the waist and covered in sweat. He was pummelling the punch bag with all his might and didn't look at all well.

John called to his dad but, at first, his dad didn't seem to hear him, as he was in a world of his own. So John shouted again as he walked up to him. His dad stopped, a bit startled, and turned to see John. When the punch bag swung back, it nearly knocked Steve off his feet.

John said, 'Sorry, Dad, I did shout a couple of times. Are you alright? And what is going on with Lilly?'

His dad got a towel and started to wipe himself down, replying as he did so, 'I'm alright. I will tell you what has happened after I've had a shower. Have you had anything to eat today?'

John answered, 'No, I've been running around trying to find you. Why was Lilly arrested?'

His dad said, 'Well, go and get something to eat - I will jump in the shower and when I come out, I will explain what is happening.'

John was frustrated his dad wouldn't just tell him what had happened, but didn't want to make Steve's day even more stressful, so he answered, 'Okay, Dad. Come to think about it, I am hungry. I'll be in the dining room.'

His dad nodded and went into the shower room. John moved through to the dining room and sat down at the table. The housekeeper placed a plate with his usual favourite, a BLT sandwich, on it in front of him. However, although he was hungry, he found it hard to eat.

His dad came into the dining room half an hour later. He was now smartly dressed and looked every bit the part of a well-groomed businessman, but his face had a worried look on it. As he walked toward John, he could see that most of the food was still on John's plate.

He said, 'I'm sorry I didn't answer my phone when you called, but you can stop worrying now and eat your dinner.'

John stood up and said, 'I can stop worrying about *what*? I don't know what's going on! Will you please, Dad, tell me why Lilly has been arrested and you don't look your usual confident self?'

Steve replied, 'Lilly was arrested because, according to the police, her father has the car that tried to run us down and caused the death of your mother.'

John went white and sat back down, saying, 'I have driven that car. I feel sick.'

His dad shouted at him, 'What do you mean, you've driven that car? Why didn't you tell me about it? It's the car that caused your mother's death!'

John said, 'I thought there was something about it that made me think I'd seen it before, but I didn't know why.'

His dad said again, in an angry voice, 'Why didn't you tell me about it? We could have sorted this lot out long ago, if I'd known about it.'

John could see his dad was upset and angry, so he explained, 'I didn't know it was that car, Dad. Sam said he didn't want you to know about his car in case you wanted to use it for the wedding. He said it was because Lilly wanted to go to the church in the rolls.'

His dad went red and was quiet for a moment, and when he did reply, he roared, 'That fuckin' Sam Blake said that because he didn't want me to see it; because I'd know it was the car. It makes me sick to think I was to marry that cow, Lilly, when she killed my Joan.'

John asked, 'Are you sure it is really the car? Her dad is very religious.'

Steve calmed down a bit, but said, 'So was Rasputin.'

John said, a bit sheepishly, 'He said Lilly used to go out with a man named Eric Lang and he went to jail...'

His dad went red in the face again, and butted in, 'That cow! I saw her talking to some man a few years ago and she seemed very friendly with him, so I asked her who he was. She said he was Eric Lang, just an 'old friend' from her younger days.

I can't talk about this anymore right now, but I need you and Ann to help me get over this. I'm going out to get drunk.'

John said, 'You're best staying in. When the newspapers get hold of the news, the reporters will be looking for you and they won't give you any peace. Please, Dad, stay home?'

His dad replied, 'Well, they aren't going to make me a prisoner in my own house. I'll try to stay out of their way but, don't worry, John, I can take care of myself. I feel like punching someone, and I hate them fuckin' blood-seeking reporters anyway. I'll be in late tonight.'

John watched his dad slam the door behind him as he left.

SAM IS CHARGED

Smithy said to the duty sergeant, 'Bring Sam Blake to interview room one.'

When Sam came in with the duty sergeant, Officer Jones was sitting by the table while Smithy met Sam at the door.

Smithy pointed to a chair on the opposite side of the table to the officer and said, 'Will you sit there, please, Sam? How was your meal?'

Sam replied, as he sat down, 'It looked nice but - I can't think why - I couldn't enjoy it. Could it be because you lot are messing me about?'

Smithy said, 'We are just waiting for your solicitor to return.'

At that moment Sam's solicitor walked into the room and sat down next to him.

Smithy sat down, went through the routine with the recorder and then he said, 'We'll start again, Sam. This is your chance to tell the truth.'

Sam went red and banged his two fists down on the table, roaring, 'I've been telling you the fucking truth, but you just don't want to hear it.'

The other three around the table sat back in their chairs with shock, as none of them were expecting Sam's reaction.

Just then the door opened and two officers, who must have been passing, started to come into the room.

Smithy said, 'It's alright, lads. Close the door on your way out.'

The officers nodded and backed out, closing the door as they went.

Then Smithy said to Sam, 'You will get twenty-five years for this. That means, at your age, you might never see the outside of prison again... but, if you come clean and tell us if Eric Lang was involved with you and your daughter, the judge at your trial will go a lot easier on you.'

Sam's face was blood-red with anger as he shouted, 'Eric Lang? I haven't seen that waste of space in years. And I know Lilly hasn't either because, when he went to jail, she promised me on The Holy Bible that she wouldn't have any more to do with him.'

Smithy ignored Sam's outburst, asking, 'Was killing Joan Kenwright his idea or was it your idea? We've been looking for him and we will find him, no matter how long it takes.'

Sam rolled his eyes and said, 'What's the use? I did it and I also shot Kennedy in Dallas. Is there anything else you want me to admit to? What about the gunpowder plot?'

His solicitor looked at him in surprise, causing Sam to say to him, 'Well, they might as well blame me for everything else as well. To say that you're supposed to be my mouthpiece, you seem to have left your tongue at home!'

His solicitor touched Sam's arm and said, 'Calm down, Sam, they want you to get upset. Just stay calm and say 'no comment' like I told you to before. They can threaten all they like but, in the end, they have to prove what they are charging you with.'

Sam looked at Smithy and said, 'Well then, to everything you asked the answer is 'no comment'. Okay?'

Smithy asked, 'Where were you and your daughter when Joan Thomson was on holiday with her family?'

Despite his solicitor's advice, Sam couldn't just say 'no comment'; instead, he replied, 'I was at home. My daughter was on holiday and was staying with me for a couple of days.'

Smithy responded, 'How can you remember so easily where you were ten years ago, when a woman you apparently didn't even know was killed?'

Sam replied, 'It's easy because my daughter was staying out at her friends for a couple of nights and, when she came back, she was upset. She'd brought in a newspaper with the headline 'Joan Thomson plummets to her death' and she said, 'Dad, that's my boss's wife. Do you think I should go back to the office?' I told her to stay with me till it was time to go back to work, because she couldn't do anything to help. I'm sorry now, because she would have been able to prove where she was if she had.'

Smithy asked, 'So, now you're saying you don't know *where* your daughter was when Joan Thomson died?'

Sam said, in an angry voice, 'I've told you she was with me. Are you deaf? Play the tape back if you can't remember.'

Smithy just replied, 'If she was with you, then we know she was in Spain. Was it friends of Eric Lang that helped you to plan Joan's death? You have the car that was used...'

Sam butted in angrily, almost shouting, 'I've told you I've never been to Spain in my life *and*, I've just told you, my Lilly was with me, in my house in London, not Spain. I don't know where Eric Lang was or is!'

Smithy responded, 'You said that she wasn't with you until she brought the newspaper with the headlines in - that was *after* Joan's death. You can't get your story right and, as I was saying, you have the car. We have traced it from the garage in Spain that helped you set the whole thing up and shipped it into storage. From there, we've traced it to you. With that, and the other little details like the false beard and the old Spain brochures, the evidence is mounting up.

We also have two witnesses who saw you, with that false beard on, and who swear you were with your daughter. We know it was you because they said the person they saw was an older man, and Eric Lang is only three years older than Lilly.

Not only that, but we know that Lilly arranged the family's holiday and would know every move they would make on the day that Joan Thomson was killed. But it turned out she still couldn't mount the pavement to run them down, because there was a boy with them who had a motorbike and, even with the reinforced body parts, the car couldn't keep going if it hit the bike. We also know from the Spanish police that your daughter was driving that day....

So, Mr Samuel Blake, I'm charging you with the murder of Joan Thomas for now, with another charge of murder to follow, as soon as we can definitively connect you to the death of Mr Isaac Fernandez.'

Sam went red in the face and said, to his solicitor, 'Well? Say something. You said you were here to stop them putting words into my mouth. I said my daughter was with me in London and he changed it to me saying she wasn't with me and now, apparently, I've committed two murders! Well, will you say something, for God's sake? I know I'm not paying you, but my taxes are!'

His solicitor replied, 'Calm down, Sam. We will discuss it when we are alone in the cell.'

Once Sam and his solicitor were finished talking, Smithy said the time they had completed the interview into the recorder and then he stopped the tape. After that, he pressed the bell on the wall by the table.

A few minutes later, the duty sergeant entered the room and said, 'Come with me, Mr Blake.'

Sam stood up and said, 'I'm glad that I *don't* live in a police state. Well, that's what you lot tell me.'

He walked out the room with the duty sergeant and the solicitor following behind them.

LILLY'S NEW SOLICITOR

The next morning a grey-haired, smartly dressed and distinguished looking man holding a large attaché case walked into the police station.

He strode up to the counter and said to the policeman there, 'I'm Patrick Shannon, Miss Lilly Blake's solicitor. I'd like to see her, please. Could you bring her to one of your interview rooms for me?'

The policeman got on the phone and made the arrangements.

After a short while, he said, 'Miss Blake will be brought to interview room one. Do you know the way?'

The solicitor replied, 'Yes. I've been here quite a few times over the years. I take it you're new in this station?'

The policeman said, 'Yes, I just started here this week.'

The solicitor said, 'Well, you'll see a lot of me from now on. This is a busy nick.'

The police officer buzzed him through the door at the side of the counter and he walked down to interview room one. He went in, put his case on the table, opened it and started reading the file he took out of it. After a little while, a police officer opened the door and stepped aside for Lilly to enter. She looked worn out and quite small, standing next to the large police officer.

The officer said, 'Miss Blake will be interviewed this morning. DS Jackson said he will be with you in an hour,' then he closed the door, leaving the two of them alone.

The solicitor said, 'Sit down, Miss Blake,' and, as Lilly did so, he introduced himself, 'I'm your new solicitor. My name is Patrick Shannon, but all my clients call me Rick. I'm a friendly chap. And you are Miss Lilly Blake, may I address you with your first name?'

She replied, 'Why not? I guess I will be seeing you for quite some time.'

Rick asked, 'Is there anything you want to ask me before we get started?'

Lilly said, 'Besides being a 'friendly chap', are you any good at your job?'

Rick replied, 'The only cases I've lost were all cases that Our Lord couldn't win himself. They were all obviously guilty and they were all pleased with the deals I got for them.'

Rick sat down next to Lilly and spread some of the papers from the file in front of the two of them. The papers were photocopies of the documents about the shipping and storage of the car. Amongst them were photos of a false beard, some of the old brochures of Spain, Eric Lang and her dad's car.

Rick said, 'Shall we get started? If you are guilty, don't tell me. All the clients I defend are innocent till the court says differently.'

Lilly looked at the photo of Eric Lang and asked, 'Why is Eric Lang there? He was an old boyfriend of mine. I haven't seen him in years.'

Rick replied, 'I haven't read up on him yet, they must think he is involved.'

Lilly asked, 'Are you defending my dad as well, Rick?'

He replied, 'No, I take it that a firm in London is defending your father, but I don't know who. I'm waiting to hear. Now, this is important, can you tell me how you see the situation you are in?'

Lilly said, 'They are trying to blame me for the death of Joan Thomson. When she died ten years ago, she was my boss' wife. My boss is now my fiancé... and we were due to be married in five weeks' time...'

The tears were running down Lilly's face and her nose was streaming before she had finished talking.

Rick handed her his handkerchief and said, 'I know this is hard for you, but it's best if you can hold back your emotions and stay calm. I've read all the paperwork that I got from Mr Thomas's firm. I understand he's your fiancé's firm's solicitor, and that your fiancé's wife was killed while they were on holiday in Spain.'

Lilly and Rick went over all that had happened to her in the last few days. While they were still talking, there was a knock on the door. Lilly and Rick looked toward it as it opened. Jacko walked in, with a police officer just behind him.

Jacko looked at Rick and said, 'You've got your hands full this time, Rick.'

As Jacko and the officer sat down facing the two of them, Rick replied, 'Anyone can see that this young lady is innocent.'

Jacko smiled and replied, 'You say that about all your clients. Are you ready for the interview to start or would you like a little more time?'

Rick said, 'You will be asking my client a lot of questions so could you get a fresh jug of water placed on the table, please? And can we register at the start that we will be expecting to receive one of the master copies of this interview recording, so that we can go over your questions later in Lilly's cell and make sure there are no mistakes.'

Jacko got on the phone and asked for a jug of water. The four of them sat in silence for the few minutes it took for an officer to bring the water.

When he left the room, Jacko said, 'Are we ready to start now?'

Rick looked at Lilly, touched her arm and, when she nodded her agreement, said, 'Yes.'

Jacko turned on the tape recorder and said the date into it, continuing 'This is the second interview with Miss Lilly Blake, present is DS Jackson...'

In the space Jacko left, the officer said, 'Officer Porter.'

Then Lilly's solicitor said, 'Solicitor P. Shannon.'

At that point, Jacko prompted, 'Say your full name for the tape, Lilly.'

She looked at Rick, who nodded, and then she said, 'Elizabeth Blake.'

The young officer looked a little puzzled, turning towards Jacko, who smiled and said, 'It's alright, Lilly is the nickname for Elizabeth,' before asking, 'Lilly, where did you get the car that caused Joan to fall to her death in Spain?'

Rick said, 'My client wants to make a statement to tell you what she knows. After *that* you can ask your questions, but she will be saying 'no comment' to them. Following that, she and I will have a talk about your questions separately, in her cell, and this afternoon she will try and answer the ones she can.'

Jacko said, 'Okay, then. Let's hear your version of events.'

Lilly replied, 'Like I told you before, when Joan Thomson died in Spain, I was in London at my dad's house. I was upset when I read about it in the papers. I was out with some friends when I found out, but when I saw the papers, I went straight home and said to my dad that my boss's wife had been killed in Spain and that I was going to go back to the office because, at the time, I was acting as Steve's PA. I did that sometimes. He didn't used to like having someone else in control of his diary, but when he particularly needed help - at busy times - they would send me.

So, I was going to go back, but my dad told me to stay in London. He said there wasn't anything I could do... and he was right, I was just a number in the firm in those days, so I stayed with him instead, until my leave was over.

When it comes to my dad's car, I told you the truth before, but I will go over it again. When I was in my last few years at school, I worked part-time in the office of an old scrap yard. The owner's name is Gareth Davis. He is an official bailiff as well as owning the scrap yard, so I asked him, if he came across an old motor car, would he let me know. That was because my dad loves fixing old things up and I knew I would be moving away from home when I left school, so I wanted something that would help to keep him busy.

So, a few times over the years, I would call to see if he had anything in his scrap yard that might do. About nine years ago, I phoned him again and he said he had an old car, that was in pieces, that he would sell to my dad. The price was too much for me to pay but he said, seeing how he knew me, he would let me have it over a couple of years and pay for it in instalments. He said he thought that would work okay because it would take my dad a few years to rebuild it as a hobby anyway.

I'm sure my dad has told the police in London all this about the car. He always tells the truth because, unlike me, he's very religious.

I got to know Steve properly over the three years after Joan's death, when I became his permanent PA. He needed one then, because he had taken over running the company. During that time, it was strictly a working relationship. I only saw him during the working day and at work events, like Christmas parties. After a while, I would go on business trips with him and then, one Christmas, he asked me out on a date. Once we started dating, I fell in love with Steve quite quickly. I was to marry him in five weeks' time.'

Lilly wiped tears away from her cheeks as she sat up straight and said, 'I don't think that will be happening now, do you?'

Jacko didn't bother to respond to her question, instead saying, 'You tell a good story, Lilly, but you left out the part about you and Eric Lang.'

Lilly went to interrupt but Rick squeezed her arm and shook his head.

Jacko continued, 'Now, you said you asked Mr Davis about a car for your dad every few years, but he said you asked him when you worked for him and then he never heard from you till he put the car from the storage warehouse into a container in the scrap yard. He even said you seemed to know it was there. What do you say to that?'

Lilly wiped her eyes and her running nose, looking over at Rick, who nodded his head for her to answer, mouthing, 'No comment.'

Lilly looked back at Jacko and from then on followed Rick's advice, simply saying, 'No comment.'

Jacko continued regardless, asking, 'Why has your father got a false beard hidden in his garage?'

'No comment.'

Jacko nodded, but continued, saying, 'If you say the car wasn't yours and you knew nothing about it, how could you know it was there? Did Eric Lang arrange it for you?'

'No comment.'

'Come on,' said Jacko, 'We know about your boyfriend Eric Lang. He's one bad man and we'll find out where he is anyway, so don't you want to help yourself by telling us where he is?'

'No comment.'

Jacko persisted, 'Why were the old brochures of Spain in the bin with the false beard? Was it your father's or Eric's? It was your dad's, wasn't it?'

'No comment.'

'Why did your dad hide the false beard and the Spanish brochures in the bin?' Jacko repeated, 'Did he just forget to get rid of them or did Eric Lang put them there to get rid of your dad, so he would have you to himself?'

'No comment.'

'Who bought the car, Lilly? You or your dad?' Jacko asked, his patience wearing thin.

'No comment.'

'You're not helping yourself,' Jacko tried to explain to her. 'It will go a lot better for you if you tell the truth. When did you go to Spain?'

'No comment.'

'Well, when did your dad go to Spain?'

'No comment.'

'Can you at least tell me when you and your dad met Eric Lang's friend, the garage owner Alonso? He was the one who supplied the car, wasn't he?'

'No comment.'

'We *know* you used Alonso's garage to reinforce the engine compartment. Whose idea was that? Yours or your dad's?'

'No comment.'

'Where is Eric Lang? Do you know where he is or what has happened to him since then?'

'No comment.'

Jacko spent a couple of hours asking Lilly questions, but it was always the same answer, 'no comment.'

Finally, Rick said, 'I think my client needs a break for now, and a meal.'

Jacko replied, as he turned the recorder off, 'Okay, we'll break for dinner.'

He pressed the bell on the wall and a few minutes later an officer opened the door and stepped inside.

He nodded to Jacko and said, 'Come with me, Miss Blake.'

Jacko asked him, 'Please make sure Miss Blake gets something to eat whilst we break.'

Rick said, 'Go with the officer, Lilly. I will give you time to eat your dinner. I'll be with you in three quarters of an hour, to discuss what we are going to do afterwards.'

She nodded, got up and walked out of the room, with the officer walking behind her.

Jacko stood up, gathered his papers together and put them back in his folder, as Rick did the same with his paperwork.

Jacko looked at Rick and said, 'Doesn't your act ever change? It's the same routine every time.'

Rick smiled, winking at Jacko as he said, 'Why change a winning formula? And, let's face it, you're scratching about in the dark.' As he walked out the room, he added, 'Enjoy your lunch, Jacko. I'll see you after it, with Miss Blake.'

Jacko replied, 'Will do, Rick. Enjoy yours too.'

When he had left the room, Officer Porter, who was straightening the chairs around the table, said, 'We'll get some answers this afternoon.'

Jacko gave a sarcastic laugh, and said, 'Don't believe what Rick Shannon said, he'll have her saying 'no comment' right up to the trial... But, with a bit of luck, we might get some help from London. I'll get on to Smithy, while I'm eating my sandwiches.'

Officer Porter said, 'I didn't know Lilly was a nickname for Elizabeth. All the girls I know who are called Lilly, it's their first name.'

Jacko laughed and said, 'The name Elizabeth is like me, old-fashioned. Now go and get your dinner while you can.'

Jacko went back to his office and sat down at his desk. He opened the bottom drawer and took out a flask and some sandwiches wrapped in tinfoil. He took the top off the flask and poured himself a cup of tea. Then he opened the tinfoil and looked at the inside of one of the sandwiches, nodding happily to himself when he saw the filling was cheese spread and crisps.

Then he thought, 'I better phone Smithy before I start eating.'

He picked up the phone and said, 'Put me through to Scotland Yard, please.'

While he was waiting, he couldn't resist taking a bite of a sandwich and, as he chewed it, a receptionist asked, 'Scotland Yard, how can we help?'

He took a quick mouthful of tea to wash the food down and said, 'Hello, you were quick to answer, I nearly choked on my sandwich.'

The receptionist asked, 'Is that you, Jacko?'

He answered, 'Yes, can you...?'

The receptionist interrupted, 'I know. You want your mate, Smithy, right?'

He said, 'You're bang on the button, put me through, please.'

A few moments went by and then a voice said, 'Detective Smith here. How can I help?'

Jacko said, 'It's me, Jacko. I'm just checking how you are getting on there with my case. I haven't seen a report from you about what happened yesterday.'

Smithy said, 'I don't understand that. We charged Sam Blake yesterday and wrote a full report for you, late afternoon. I put it in the out tray, just hang on - I'll check if it's still there.'

Jacko could hear a muffled Smithy shouting, 'Why wasn't this report sent to Jacko?' Then he came back on the phone, saying, 'Sorry, Jacko, some idiot didn't do his job. You just can't get any good staff nowadays. I've just sent it to you - sorry, it won't happen again.'

Jacko said, 'Well, I think you owe me a pint for that, don't you?'

Smithy said, 'Well, you can take it out of all the pints you owe me.'

Jacko replied, 'Alright, Smithy, fair-dos. I owe you a lot more than you owe me! Don't worry, I'll pay you one of these days - and I hope it's soon! I've got to go now - busy, busy. Bye.'

Smithy said, 'I will hold you to that. I'll be seeing you, bye.'

Jacko was just finishing his sandwiches when there was a knock on his door.

He drank the last drop of tea and said, 'Come in.'

The door opened and the chief inspector came into the office, carrying a file.

Jacko went to stand up, but the chief waved his hand for Jacko to stay where he was, saying, 'Don't get up, I know you're having your dinner.'

He placed the file on Jacko's desk in front of him and said, 'It's from Scotland Yard, about the Spanish case. Were you expecting it?'

Jacko smiled and said, 'Yes, Smithy has charged Samuel Blake with attempted murder.'

The chief asked, 'Are you going to charge this Lilly Blake today?'

Jacko's smile faded, as he said, 'Sorry, Boss, we've no real evidence. It's all circumstantial. But the Spanish report makes her father the brains behind it all - although they don't know about Eric Lang - and I think she was just doing what they told her to do. So, I'm hoping that, once she hears her father has been charged, she might lose her confidence and break down and make a statement.'

The chief said, 'Surely if you tell her that her father has been charged, she will keep her mouth shut, because she will think her father won't give her away? You and I both know many men have tried to take the blame for their child.

Well, that's what I think... but it's your case, so you call it the way you see it. I'll leave it all in your capable hands. We've had no reports back about this Eric Lang. Do you think he's left the country?'

Jacko pulled a face and said, 'I don't know, it's strange that no one has seen or heard from him in the last seven years.'

The chief patted Jacko on the shoulder and left. Before heading back to the interview, Jacko took a quick moment to text Tommy: *Scotland Yard has charged Sam Blake with attempted murder. We are hoping to get a confession from Lilly Blake soon, but it could take a while because she has a bloody good solicitor. I'll keep you in the picture. Remember, mum's the word. See you soon, Jacko.*

TOMMY TELLS ANN ABOUT SAM AND LILLY

When Tommy received the text, he was at home. He hadn't been to the office because Ann wanted to stay with him for a while and he could see she was worried sick about what she had been saying about her dad over the years. He was worried too, because sometimes she was clingy and, at other times, she was testy and wanted to just be by herself. He didn't know what to do for the best.

Ann was in the back garden, keeping herself busy by weeding the small plot of flowers Tommy had grown and he was in the kitchen, making a pot of tea, when Jacko's text came through.

Tommy took the phone out of his pocket and read the message, texting back: *That's good news. It looks like I was wrong about Sam Blake, if he was in on it. Thanks, Jacko. TT*

He put the phone back in his pocket, poured out two mugs of tea and took them to the garden.

He placed them on the small garden table and called, 'Ann, here's a mug of tea. Get it before it goes cold,' as he sat on one of the two chairs that were either side of the table. Ann got up from where she was working, put some weeds in the compost bin and came over and sat on the other chair, facing Tommy across the table. They picked up their mugs while looking at each other but, for a few moments, neither of them took a drink. Tommy was deep in thought about what to tell Ann.

She said, 'What's on your mind, Tommy? Just say it. Is it something to do with my mum?'

He put the mug back down on the table and said, 'I've had a text off Jacko, but he said I'm not to tell anyone, so if I tell you, you've got to promise that - no matter how hard it is or how upset you get - you will keep it to yourself. I could lose a good friend otherwise and he's always been there when I've needed him.'

She could see he was serious and said, 'I promise, no matter how upset I get, I will never talk to anyone about it. On the lives of the two men I love. That's you and John.'

Tommy asked, 'Shouldn't it be three, with your dad as well?'

Ann replied, with tears in her eyes, 'I don't know. In my mind, I still can see him - letting go of my mum. I've tried to get it out of my mind, I feel bad about it and now and then I want to be close to him... Tommy, I just don't know what I feel about my dad anymore.'

He replied, 'Well, this might help you. Jacko said in his text that the London police have charged Lilly Blake's dad with attempted murder and the police up here are hoping to charge Lilly Blake soon, but he said she has a good solicitor, so it might take a while.

So, all the police in Spain, London *and* here think your dad did his best to save your mum. And I was there, and I thought so too.'

Ann started crying, and put her hanky to her face, as she mumbled, 'Tommy, I hope everyone is right, because it's broken my heart all these years, thinking my dad deliberately let my mum fall.'

As she was talking, he got up and went round the table, bending down to put his arms around her shoulders and kissing her on the head. He just didn't know what else to do, he'd never felt so awkward in his life.

Ann stood up and said from behind her hanky, 'Tommy, I'm sorry but I'm going to the bedroom for a lie down.'

He said as she went into the house, 'If there is anything you want, just give me a shout. I'll be in the house in a minute, so I'll hear you.'

As he started to tidy up the cups, Tommy's phone rang.

He took it out of his pocket and said, 'Hello?'

An upset voice said, 'Hi, Tommy. This is John. I thought I'd better let you know, so you can break it to Ann... The police have arrested Lilly Blake because they say she was involved in the death of our mum - they say that she was driving that car I showed you the photo of.'

The phone went quiet for a moment but, as Tommy went to speak, John's crackly voice came back on, 'I can't believe I drove it, Tommy. Dad is torn up - I think he hates Lilly now. He wants Ann and me to be by his side and help him through this. Can you ask Ann for me?'

Tommy replied, 'Ann knows about it and is very upset right now, but I will do my best to break it to her that her dad needs her. It will take time, though.'

John said, 'Thanks, Tommy. See you, bye.'

His phone went dead before Tommy had time to answer.

That afternoon there was a knock on Tommy's door. He opened it and was shocked to see John standing there.

John looked upset as he said, 'I have to see Ann, Tommy. Will you tell her I'm here?'

Tommy said, 'Come in. Ann is lying down at the moment, and I am hoping she has fallen asleep.'

Tommy closed the front door as he was talking. They heard the bedroom door open and then Ann was standing at the top of the stairs, looking at John through watery eyes. She swiftly came down into the hall, and John walked to her, and they hugged.

John said, 'God, I've missed you, Ann, and now the police have arrested Lilly. Her dad has the car that tried to run us down. Dad hates her and he said he needs us now. He is in a terrible state. Will you come home with me and see him?'

Ann stepped back and, with tears running down her cheeks, she looked John in the eyes and said, 'I can't just yet. I'm going to get some counselling to try and get it out of my mind that I saw Dad letting Mum fall.'

John had tears in his eyes as he said, 'I'm worried about Dad. I haven't seen him eat anything since yesterday… and he's crying all the time and saying Mum's name, and yours. Last night he went out and came back blind drunk - I found him on the floor this morning, and when he woke up things got even worse. So, can I tell Dad you will be coming home soon?'

She replied, 'I will try; that is all I can promise. What worries me is that I was right about it being a woman driver, so it's not just that my memory of the whole thing is faulty… So, it's still hard to get it out of my mind that he let go of Mum.'

After a little while they both calmed down and then they talked about the holiday and how things were before it.

After a couple of hours, John said, 'I'll have to go. When I left home, Dad was already drinking the whisky.'

As John opened the living room door to leave, he didn't look too good.

Ann was worried about him, so she said, 'I will go home with you, but I want Tommy to come with me… And I don't know what to say to Dad.'

As they moved towards the front door, John replied, 'You won't have to say anything. Dad loves you. You were always his favourite between the two of us and that hasn't changed - Dad will do anything for you. If it feels a little bit strange, Tommy and I will help, won't we, Tommy?'

ANN GOES TO SEE HER DAD

Tommy put his arm round Ann and pulled her to him, saying, 'Of course we will, but even I know your dad loves you, and he needs your love back at this moment.'

With that, Tommy kissed her on the cheek.

Ann said to him, as she held his hand and walked toward the door, 'You will stay with me, Tommy, won't you?'

John opened the door and said, 'My car is parked just outside of your gate, Tommy. I'll go and open the back door for you and Ann to get in.'

An hour later they were at the gates to John and Steve's home. John pressed a button on a remote in his car and the gates opened. He drove onto the drive, over the small bridge and up to the house.

John got out of the car as quickly as he could and opened the back door where Ann was sitting, but she didn't move. Tommy got out of his side of the car and went round to Ann. She was wiping her eyes and just sat there. John didn't know what to do, so he looked at Tommy.

Tommy bent into the car and said, 'Come on, doll, you've come this far.'

Ann nodded, resolutely, and climbed out of the car. John got on one side of her and Tommy was on the other side. John opened the front door and the three of them entered the hallway. John took hold of Ann's hand as he went into the living room. She was nervous as she followed him through the door.

Their dad was sitting in an armchair with a glass in one hand and half a bottle of whiskey in the other. He looked like he hadn't washed for a week and, when she saw him, Ann's nervousness turned to sorrow for her dad.

When he saw her, he dropped the glass and the bottle of whiskey, and tried to stand but fell back down onto the chair, muttering, 'Ann? Is that really you?' as he struggled to get back up.

She went over to him, sat him down again and said, 'I'm sorry, Dad. I love you, please forgive me.'

Her dad hugged her and kissed her on the forehead. They sat like that for a little while, and then Steve said, 'I'll have to go and straighten myself up for my lovely daughter.'

She offered to help him to the shower room, but he seemed to sober up as he kissed her on the forehead again and said, 'I've missed you, Ann. Please stay here while I clean myself up.'

With that he left the living room and John started to clean up the mess his dad had made.

Ann said, 'You're doing the cleaning woman out of her job, where is she?'

John replied, 'We haven't got any staff.'

She was puzzled and asked, 'Why haven't you got any staff?'

He replied, 'This morning, when the housekeeper tried to help him, after we found him on the floor, he told her to 'fuck off'. She said she didn't appreciate being spoken to that way and then he told her that she could fuck off permanently and the same went for the rest of the parasites hanging round his house.'

Shaking their heads sadly, Ann, Tommy and John spent an hour starting to clean the mess Steve had made over the last day.

When their dad walked back into the living room, he was back to being a smart-looking businessman but for his eyes, which were red and watery. He walked straight to Ann, picking her up and kissing her on both cheeks as he hugged her.

When he put her down, she wiped her eyes as she said, 'I'm sorry, Dad, can you forgive me?'

Her dad hugged her again and said, 'I love you and as far as I'm concerned it's all forgotten.' Then he kissed her on the forehead.

John said, 'Dad, you have some apologies to make to the staff, you were out of order the way you dismissed them.'

Ann said, 'We will sort that out later. I'll make Dad something to eat.'

She went into the kitchen and her dad followed her in.

He took a chair from the table, turned it so he could watch her while she was at the cooker and said, 'Please, Ann, don't ever leave me again. I've lost your mum and, like a fool, I tried to get the feeling that I had with your mum back with Lilly... and that cow caused it all. She must have known that I would miss being with your mum and she wormed her way into my life.'

Ann put a plate of food on the table and, as her dad turned the chair back to face the table where the food was, she kissed him on the cheek.

She said, with tears in her eyes, 'I miss my mum, and I've blamed you, when it was all Lilly's fault. I'm so sorry, Dad. I love you, please forgive me.'

Steve had become teary too and, as he wiped his eyes, he said, 'I've told you, Ann, it's all forgotten. I'm sorry, I don't want to upset you, but I have to explain it to you - I did my best to save your mum.

I thought I had saved her when I pulled her out of the way of the car, then when I hit the wall, it knocked the wind out of me.' He stopped and wiped his eyes again, hugging Ann because now she was silently crying. He continued, 'I did my best, but I couldn't hold on to your mum and she fell.'

He stopped, and wiped Ann's tears and then his own tears. John and Tommy were watching from the doorway. John went in and hugged his dad and Ann. Tommy went to Ann and stood with his hand gently rubbing her back.

Their dad said, as he put his arms round the both of them and squeezed them to him, 'I'll go and wash my face and then I will finish this lovely meal Ann has made for me. After that, we can all move into the living room, and I'll try to explain what a fool I've been. I hope you will forgive me.'

With that he let go of them and Tommy put his arm round Ann, who was still holding on to John, as Steve went to the kitchen sink and swilled his face.

Ann said to Tommy in a shaky voice, 'I'll go to the bathroom and freshen up.'

Tommy was so focused on Ann, he didn't notice that John was heading for his bedroom to take a moment to compose himself.

Thinking Tommy might be uncomfortable being left alone with her dad after all this time, Ann said, 'Come with me, Tommy, you can freshen up too.'

Tommy agreed and followed her to the bathroom.

Half an hour later, all three of them were in the living room, with Tommy and Ann sitting on one Chesterfield sofa and John on the other.

Tommy said to Ann, 'If you get too upset, ask your dad...'

Ann butted in and said, 'Tommy, no matter how upset I get, I want to understand what happened. So, please, just be there for me.'

John said, 'It's better if we hear Dad's explanation, it might clear the air.'

Steve walked into the living room and pulled over a big easy chair so that it was facing the three of them. He sat down, placing a box of tissues on a small table that was in the middle of them as he did so.

He cleared his throat, and said, 'I've been a fool. I was too proud to realise that I could be manipulated, and it cost your mum her life.'

He stopped and wiped his eyes. Ann started crying again and Tommy put his arm around her. John took his hanky out of his pocket and wiped his eyes.

Their dad said, 'I met Lilly about two years before we lost your mum. Whenever I needed a PA, she was sent to my office. She had worked for me a lot and she was very efficient, so I asked...' He paused for a moment and wiped his eyes. When he saw how upset they were all getting, with even Tommy becoming teary, he leaned towards Ann and asked, 'Ann, we're all getting upset. Shall I stop?'

She managed to reply from behind a handful of tissues, 'Please, don't stop.'

Steve reached out and patted her on the knee, then he sat back in the chair, and continued, 'I asked Lilly to arrange the holiday. I said that I wanted my lovely Ann to have a surprise picnic on the beach on her birthday. She said her family never had picnics on the beach, because food and sand don't go well together; that the sand gets everywhere and spoils the picnic, so I was worried the day might not go very well. But then she said she had been to that resort and there was a beautiful well-kept picnic area on the mountain road near the beach. I agreed with her, saying I knew it too and that having the picnic there was a great idea. Then she suggested that it would be lovely to stroll down to the beach after the picnic, to make sure you got to spend some time there.

When I think about it now, she did go on a bit about exactly how we should organise the events... and she knew your mum was afraid of heights, because she heard me on the phone trying to get a councillor to help your mum get over her fears. She even asked me about it, saying she wanted to make sure that Joan would be okay with the venue for the picnic...

I thought I could read people, but she manipulated me. Now it sounds like a friend of hers, a bloke named Eric Lang, was involved. He's been to jail.

She went on about the sand and the food, seeming so helpful, and it was all just so I would get your mum to walk on the mountain road and her and her father could run your mum, my Joan, down. '

In a trembling voice he continued, 'I'm as strong as an ox, I should have been able to hold Joan but the force of hitting that wall just seemed to take all my strength away.'

As he was talking John got up and went round to Ann, whose whole body was now shaking with the force of her sobs and tried to hug her. She looked up from Tommy's arms, and reached up and pulled John down to her, so all three of them were hugging and crying, as even Tommy's eyes had tears in them.

Steve said, 'I'm sorry I let that cow and her father kill my Joan. When the police told me, I couldn't believe it. I thought I could love Lilly; now I know I was just trying to get back what I had with your mum and I'm sorry I let her worm her way into our lives. So, Ann, in a way you were right to be angry at me.'

Tommy and John let go of Ann as they felt her turning to face her dad.

She said, 'No, Dad. I had no right to take it out on you. I see that now. Will you forgive me, please?'

Their dad, with tears running down his face, replied, 'You were just a child. I've told you, I don't blame you… Emma helped put the bad things about me in your mind.'

Ann was still crying but had to shake her head, saying, 'No, Dad. I know Emma hates you, but she didn't say anything to me about the holiday all the time I lived with her. In fact, she said she couldn't believe you would deliberately let my mum die.'

Steve asked, 'Will you stay the night? Because I'm afraid you mightn't come back if you leave again. I love you and you look a lot like your mother, and, when I look at you, I feel like I have a little bit of your mum back with me.'

Ann said, 'I'm sorry, Dad. I can't stop tonight. I have a meeting with Emma. We are bidding for a restaurant that I want and talked Emma into going for. So, I can't let her down… and I've got to let her know about the fact that bitch Lilly and her dad were behind Mum's murder. No-one has told her anything yet.' She wiped her eyes and said, 'I hope you understand, Dad?'

His face didn't agree with what he said, as he answered, 'I understand, Ann. You can't let Emma down. I hope you and Emma secure the restaurant.'

While Ann and her dad were talking about the restaurants, John and Tommy sorted out the mess in the kitchen. Then John made a pot of coffee. They all sat for a little while drinking the coffee, and the family told Tommy about when Ann and John were kids and went to interesting places with their mother.

John said, 'We'll have to go back to that hotel Mum was going to buy.'

Ann replied, 'Yes, I'd love that. We might feel close to Mum there.'

LILLY AND HER DAD ARE INTERVIEWED AGAIN

That afternoon, at the same time as the family were talking in Steve's home, Lilly picked at the meal she was given. Then she paced up and down in her cell as she drank the plastic cup of coffee; she didn't stop pacing till a policewoman opened the door and Rick walked in, with his attaché case.

The door wasn't even properly closed when Lilly asked Rick, 'What is happening to my dad?'

Rick said, 'I texted Doug Thomas and asked him who he has got for your father's defence, but I haven't had an answer yet, so we are in the dark till he gets back to me.'

Lilly started crying, and said, 'I'm worried about him. He has a weak heart and, if he's having the same experience as me, I don't think he could take much of the way they're treating us. Can you find out how he's managing, please?'

Rick replied, 'I will do my best, but I can't do much till I know who his solicitor is.'

Rick took a little while to help Lilly calm down and then they discussed how they were going to proceed with her case.

A little later, Jacko went back to the interview room. Officer Porter was already there.

As Jacko sorted out his paperwork, the officer picked up the phone and said, 'Would you bring Miss Lilly Blake to interview room one, please?'

A few minutes later, there was a knock on the door, and it opened. A police officer stepped into the room, moving aside for Lilly and Rick to enter. As they sat down at the table, the officer left the room, closing the door behind him.

Jacko and Officer Porter sat down on the other side of the table. As Rick was sorting out his notes, he took a box of tissues out of his attaché case and placed them on the table.

Jacko waited a couple of minutes till Rick had his papers in order, then he asked, 'Are you ready, Rick?'

'Lilly and I, we're ready,' Rick replied.

Jacko turned on the recorder and went through the opening routine with them, listing everyone present at the interview.

Jacko asked, 'Do you want to make a statement, Lilly?'

Lilly looked at Rick and then back at Jacko, and said, 'Yes, I shouldn't be here, I'm innocent. Can I go home, please?'

Jacko and the officer looked at each other; Jacko's look was to say, 'I told you so.'

Jacko shook his head and asked, 'Can you answer any of the questions I asked you before your dinner?'

Lilly returned to simply saying, 'No comment.'

'Did you or your father shoot the man, Fernandez, in Spain or was it Eric Lang who shot him?'

'No comment.'

'What did you or your father do with the gun? Or was it Eric Lang who got rid of it?'

'No comment.'

'We know your father is a top marksman with a gun. So was he the one who shot Fernandez?'

Lilly now had tears running down her face but, even as Rick handed her a handful of tissues from his supply, still just answered, 'No comment.'

'You're getting upset, Lilly,' said Jacko, in a sympathetic tone, 'so why not just tell the truth and get it over with?'

As she wiped the tears from her face, she shouted, 'You don't know the truth when you hear it!'

Rick touched Lilly's arm and shook his head.

Jacko ignored her outburst and carried on, 'None of Eric Lang's criminal associates have seen or heard from him for at least seven years, do you know why?'

Lilly looked at Jacko and was about to say something, but Rick touched her arm and, instead, she said in an angry tone, 'No comment.'

'We know your father has the car and you were driving it that day, weren't you?'

Before Lilly had time to answer, Rick touched Lilly's arm again and mouthed, 'No comment.'

Lilly did as Rick said and just repeated his words, 'No comment.'

'We have two witnesses who saw you by the barn where the work to reinforce the engine compartment was carried out. What do you have to say to that?'

Lilly looked at Rick and repeated, 'No comment.'

'At the time of Joan Thomson's death, who were the friends you say you were out with? Was one of them Eric Lang? It's a simple question to answer, Lilly.'

Lilly said, 'The answer is the same as before: no comment.'

'Come on now, Lilly,' Jacko responded, 'you must remember who you were with, because you were so upset about your boss's wife's death. At least, that's what you told us when we spoke last time - so you must have told your friends about what had happened to her. Was Eric Lang one of the people you were with?'

'No comment.'

'Are you willing to be in a line up, for our witnesses to identify you?'

Rick said, 'My client is willing to be in a line up. When will you want it?'

'We're bringing the witnesses in from Spain as soon as we can,' smiled Jacko.

'Well, you can only hold my client for a little while longer... or you have to charge her. And, from what I've heard, so far you only have circumstantial evidence which won't stand up in court.'

Jacko said, in an annoyed tone, 'Don't let your solicitor give you false hope, Lilly. We have the beard, the brochures and the car you drove, as well as our eyewitnesses to you being present in Spain at the site where the car was deliberately tailored to withstand cutting a person down in the street... So, is there anything you have to say?'

Lilly shook her head and said, 'No comment.'

'Fine,' said Jacko, continuing with his questioning. 'When did you get the small scar removed from your forehead?'

'No comment.'

'Did your father shoot Fernandez because he'd seen him without his makeup and wig on? Or was Eric Lang the one who did the shooting?'

'No comment.'

'Was the plaster on your forehead to hide the scar you got when you were a child? When did you get it removed?'

'No comment.'

'We know you had a scar ten years ago, didn't you?'

'No comment.'

'Look, Lilly,' Jacko said, trying the sympathetic angle again, 'if you want the courts to go easy on you, just make a statement and the court will understand your father and Eric Lang made you do it.'

Rick squeezed Lilly's arm, doing his best to keep her quiet, but she took no notice of him, screaming at Jacko, 'My dad didn't do anything wrong! You leave him alone.'

'Oh, did we hit a nerve?' asked Jacko, pleased to have shaken Lilly out of just saying 'no comment'. 'So, your father was the one behind it all, was he? Well, come on, spit it out. You know you want to.'

Rick squeezed Lilly's arm hard, shook his head, and said, 'My client is getting tired. She needs a break and a drink.'

'Alright,' nodded Jacko. 'We will give you a half hour break. What do you want to drink, Lilly?'

Lilly, as she wiped the tears off her face and wiped her nose, said angrily, 'Coffee.'

Rick said, 'I would like a drink too, please.'

Jacko turned the recorder off and, as he and the officer got up to go, he replied sarcastically, 'I know what you want, Rick.'

'What's that?' Rick asked.

'A coffee,' Jacko replied, 'You always want four coffees.'

Rick smiled and said, 'No, Jacko, you can have the four coffees. Just one will do me.'

When Jacko and the officer had left, Rick said to Lilly, 'You're doing fine, we have Jacko worried. I can tell, because he told me to have four coffees.'

Lilly looked at Rick with a frown on her face and asked, 'Was he telling you to eff off?'

Rick replied, 'He would like to but I've never heard him swear, so it's his way of swearing, I guess.'

'I'm worn out,' said Lilly. 'I can't take much more of all these questions... and Eric Lang? I haven't seen him in years - he was just a boy I went out with when I was a teenager. Why do they keep bringing him up?'

Rick answered, 'Lilly, I've just told you, you're doing fine. They are clutching at straws. Just keep saying 'no comment', like I told you, and don't let them get under your skin again.'

Lilly started crying just as there was a knock on the door.

Rick said, 'Come in.'

The door opened and a policewoman, carrying a tray with two mugs of coffee on it, came in. She placed the cups on the table and left.

Rick said, 'Come on, Lilly, pull yourself together and try to stop crying. We don't want Jacko to think he's wearing us down.'

During the questioning, Lilly had gone through half of Rick's box of tissues; now she took another out of the box, sitting up straight and saying, 'You're right. I won't let him get under my skin again. I'll do what you told me and just say 'no comment'.'

Rick said, 'Good. If we hold our nerve, it's up to them to find proof and, as far as I can see, they have no real evidence to go on.'

Rick carried on talking to Lilly to boost her confidence, while they were drinking their coffee, saying, 'This Eric Lang they keep going on about, don't worry about him. They can't even find him; all they know is that he was an old friend of yours. So, they just are using that connection to him to confuse you, hoping you will say something they want to hear.'

After a quick mug of coffee, Jacko left Officer Porter at the canteen. He was on his way back to his office when he met the chief inspector.

The chief asked, 'How are you getting on with this Lilly Blake?'

Jacko shook his head and said, 'It's hard going. She's got Rick Shannon with her and you know what he's like, he only lets his client say 'no comment'.'

The chief said, 'Buck up, Jacko. You've beaten him before, and I've no doubt you will win this one.'

Jacko said, 'Well, the only thing I've got left to help break her story is to tell her that her father has been charged. She gets really upset when he is mentioned. So I'm going to my office to see if Scotland Yard has sent any more information about her father.'

'Well, carry on,' the chief said, as he stepped aside to let Jacko pass.

Back in the interview room with the remains of their coffee growing cold, Rick looked at his watch and said to Lilly, 'It's not like Jacko to be back late, we must have him worried. He'll be going back over his paperwork now so, no matter what he says he can do, he'll be just bluffing. So, remember, don't let him get under your skin with questions you don't like; just stick to our plan and say no comment.'

Lilly asked him, 'Will you tell them that I want to go to the toilet?'

Rick said, 'Let's show Jacko he's got a job on his hands. Wipe your face over and, when he comes in, stand up straight, look him in the face and say, 'I want a toilet break.''

Lilly took a couple of tissues out of the box, dipped the tissues into the jug of water standing on the table and wiped her face with them.

As she did, she said, 'While I'm in the toilets I'll have a wash to freshen myself up.'

There was a knock on the door, it opened, and Officer Porter walked in with Jacko following.

As soon as he shut the door, Lilly stood up and said, 'I want someone to show me where the toilets are, please.'

Jacko walked over to the table, picked up the phone and said, 'Could you send a woman police officer to interview room one, please?' As he put the phone down, he said, 'An officer will be with you in a few minutes, Lilly.'

Officer Porter sat down in his chair as Jacko placed his folder, with all his papers in it, onto the table. Lilly stood glaring at Jacko, but he didn't seem to notice. He was looking down at his notes.

There was a knock on the door and Jacko said, 'Come in.'

A policewoman entered and, as she shut the door, asked, 'I was told to report here?'

Jacko replied, 'Please show Miss Blake to the toilets and wait outside for her.'

The policewoman looked at Lilly who stood there with a running nose, holding a tissue to her eyes and looking in a sad state and said, 'Come with me, Miss.'

She opened the door and went out, waiting for Lilly to follow. When they were in the corridor, the policewoman walked beside Lilly as she showed her the way to the toilets.

While they were waiting for Lilly to return, Rick smiled at Jacko and said, 'Sit down, Jacko, and relax. It could be a while; you know what women are like when they get near a mirror.'

Jacko said, 'It's all a game to you, you don't seem to care about your clients. This girl, I know she did it but I still feel sorry for what I've got to put her through. And she will go down for what she and her father did, I'll see to that.'

Rick's smile turned to anger as he said, 'If I didn't care, I wouldn't fight so hard to keep her out of prison. You think I don't care? Well, wait till she comes back. You'll see a different girl and I *will* keep her out of prison. I'll make sure of that.'

After that the three men sat in silence, with Jacko looking at his watch now and then. Lilly was away for a good half hour and, when the policewoman opened the door and stepped aside for Lilly to enter, Jacko and Officer Porter were surprised as she walked in. Even Rick hadn't thought she could change her appearance so much. She didn't look like the stooped over, little, crying girl with messy hair that had left just over half an hour ago. Now she stood up straight, with her hair all tied back and no tears on her face. The only tell-tale sign that she was upset was that her eyes were still red. She even walked to her chair and sat down with an air of confidence. Rick gave Jacko a knowing look and smiled at Lilly.

Jacko said, 'I take it you are ready to start?'

'We are,' Rick replied.

As Jacko got over his surprise of how confident Lilly looked, he thought, 'I better keep going on about her dad and hope she will break down under the pressure.'

He turned the recorder on and restarted the interview.

'Why did you - or your father - shoot Fernandez?' Jacko asked.

Lilly looked Jacko directly in the eyes and said, 'No comment.'

'Why was there a false beard in your dad's house?'

Lilly just sat there, wiping her eyes and didn't answer. Rick and Jacko both looked at her, waiting for her to say 'no comment' but she didn't speak.

'Well, if you don't want to answer that question,' said Jacko after the silence had dragged on for more than a minute, 'Can you tell us what your father hoped to gain by you driving the car at the family… Or were you just aiming for Joan Thomson, so you could get together with her husband?'

Getting no response to this new tack, Jacko asked again, 'Why did your dad have a false beard and Spanish brochures concealed in his garage?'

'No comment.'

'We know your father used the beard in Spain because the witnesses said you were with an older man. Were you supposed to get rid of it for him? Because he was really surprised when we found it in his garage. He nearly had a heart attack.'

'No comment.'

'Were you supposed to destroy your father's brochures for him too? And, like his false beard, you forgot?'

'No comment.'

'Your father kept the car. Why did your father think no one would find out that it was the car they made you drive at the family?'

Lilly still replied, 'No comment' but it was clear that she was getting angry, so Rick looked at her and shook his head, squeezing her arm again to remind her to stay calm.

'Why didn't your father or Eric Lang drive the car?' Jacko persisted, feeling he was getting somewhere.

This time Lilly couldn't hold back tears as she answered, 'No comment.'

'Your father mustn't be a very nice man to leave you in this mess,' Jacko said. 'You were just a kid when all this happened. Just tell us what you did, and how your father and Eric Lang were behind it all, and the courts will take that into account when you and your father go on trial. Your father won't see the outside of prison because he will get twenty-five years for this, but you've still got a chance of having a decent life after you get out. Isn't that what your dad would want?"

Lilly picked some tissues out of the box in front of her and wiped her eyes.

Rick could see Lilly was about to say something and so he said, 'My client is getting a bit upset, so I will request a small break.'

He poured Lilly a glass from the beaker of water and handed it to her. They sat in silence and all you could hear was a slight sniffing noise from Lilly, as she drank the water.

As soon as she put the glass down on the table, Jacko started up again with his questioning.

'Who were the friends you were out on the town with the night that Joan Thomson died? How many of them were there, and what are their names?'

Lilly wiped her nose and replied, 'No comment.'

'Look, Lilly,' Jacko said, 'We have enough evidence to charge you and your dad. What do you have to say to that? We haven't found your boyfriend Eric Lang yet, but we will in time. We're like the Mounties, we always get our man and, when he testifies against you both, your father will spend the rest of his life in prison.'

Lilly went red with anger but, before she could say anything, Rick squeezed her arm really hard and said, 'Well, are you going to charge Lilly or let her go?'

Jacko replied, 'I want Lilly to answer a few more questions before I charge her. Tell me, Lilly, who shot the man in Spain? Was it your father or was it Eric Lang?'

Lilly, with Rick still squeezing her arm because he could see Jacko was getting to her by going on about her dad, managed to control herself enough to say, 'No comment.'

'We know it *was* your father who shot Fernandez, because in the army he was an expert with a gun. That's right, isn't it?'

'No comment.'

'Did you tell your father that Mrs Thomson was afraid of heights, and she would be on the road when they were walking down to the beach, and your father and Eric Lang came up with the idea from there, Lilly, or was it your idea all along?'

Lilly took another handful of tissues out of the box, wiped the tears from her face and replied, 'No comment.'

'I can see you don't like me focusing on your father's involvement; you must be worried about what is happening with him, so I will tell you now: Scotland Yard has charged your father with one count of murder, with other potential murder charges to follow.'

Lilly jumped up and shouted, 'They can't do that! He hasn't done anything wrong. It will kill him. It's that bastard's fault, he lied to me and now my poor dad is getting the blame.'

Leaning back, whilst trying not to let his relief show on his face, Jacko said, 'Sit down, Lilly. So, it was Eric Lang who's behind this.'

Lilly turned to Rick and said, 'I need to know who's defending my dad.'

Rick said, 'Sit down. Lilly, I strongly advise you not to say anymore. No comment should be the only statement out of your mouth going forward.'

Lilly slowly sat down, looking at Rick with tears running down her cheeks, but she repeated, in a determined tone, 'I need to know who is defending my dad.'

Rick nodded and said, 'My client needs a break now.'

'Lilly can have a ten-minute break,' Jacko answered, 'but we are all staying in this room.'

Lilly said, wiping her nose and eyes, 'I don't want a break, I want to know who Steve has got to help my dad.'

Rick replied, 'I've had a text from Doug Thomas. I didn't want to tell you until after the interview was over, because I knew you would get upset...'

Lilly butted in, 'What do you mean, I'd get upset? You shouldn't have been keeping anything about my dad from me. I would rather go to prison than put him in this mess. What did the text say?'

'He said Steve Thomson hasn't done anything about getting representation for your father,' Rick replied.

'Well, who's helping my dad then?' Lilly asked. 'He can't afford a solicitor.'

Rick answered, 'It will be a legal aid solicitor.'

Lilly banged her two fists down on the table as hard as she could, saying through gritted teeth, 'The bastard. I hate him. This is all his fucking fault.'

Jacko said, 'Cut out the tantrums, Lilly. Who do you hate? Is it your partner, Eric Lang?'

Lilly was red in the face and replied, 'Eric Lang? Why do you keep going on about Eric Lang? I haven't seen him for years. I'm talking about that bastard Steve Thomson. He tricked me. He said he loved me and he let me think he would get us the best solicitors money could buy but he's just leaving my dad in this mess.'

Jacko said, 'Well, what do you expect? He still loves his wife. Even now, ten years later he still puts flowers on her grave every week... Did you really think he loved you enough to forgive you for killing the love of his life.'

Lilly looked confused for a moment, then said, 'What? No, he doesn't do that. *I* send the bouquet of flowers from *Rose's Florist* each week, because *I'm* sorry. I didn't want Joan to die. I just put his name on them because it wouldn't look right with my name on them.'

Jacko hid his surprise at what Lilly had claimed, asking, 'Really, what have you got to be sorry about?'

Rick said, 'Lilly, be quiet and calm down. They're taking note of everything you're saying. They want you to talk.'

Lilly went quiet for a moment. Then she wiped her face and looked over at Jacko, who was surprised when she said, 'Rick's client wants a half hour break... and if you give it to her, you *will* be told the truth.'

Rick was in shock and said, 'What are you doing, Lilly?'

Before she had the chance to answer, Jacko said, 'You can have the half hour.'

He turned the recorder off, and he and the officer got up to go, as Rick said, 'Lilly, I'm sure if you do what I tell you to you could walk away from this without a blemish on your character. They haven't got any real evidence.'

Jacko and the officer closed the door behind them as Lilly watched them go; then she said, 'Rick, I love my dad, and he is innocent... but I'm not. Will you still be my solicitor? Steve Thomson won't pay you once I tell the truth.'

Rick said, 'I did tell you not to tell me if you're guilty, but that is up to you. Now that you have, I have no other option but to advise you to plead guilty, in which case the retaining fee will more than cover my wages - the whole process is going to be much shorter... So, let's get what happened sorted out before they come back.'

Lilly told Rick what had happened ten years ago.

Then Rick phoned the front desk and asked, 'Can I speak to Jacko.'

After a few moments he heard a voice say, 'Hello? Jacko here.'

Rick said, 'This is Rick Shannon. Lilly has changed her mind and wants to make a full statement.'

Jacko said, 'Well, why am I not surprised? I'm on my way back now.'

Rick said, 'Jacko, keep your hair on. She is going to tell you the truth, but it's messy and I need more time with her to sort it all out. Can you leave seeing her till the morning?'

Jacko asked, 'Is she really going to tell the truth or are you up to something?'

Rick replied, 'I promise, I wouldn't ask for this delay just to mess with you. We just need time to get her statement completely clear.'

Jacko said, 'Okay, I'll see you in the morning, at nine.'

Rick replied, 'Okay, thank you. We'll see you then.'

SAM HAS A HEART ATTACK

On the morning of the same day as Lilly was being interviewed by Jacko and the Thomson family were reuniting, Smithy said to the duty officer, 'Will you send Sam Blake to interview room two?'

Smithy and an officer were already sitting in the interview room by the time an officer opened the door and walked in with Sam.

As the officer left and closed the door, Smithy said, 'Take a seat, Sam.'

Sam asked, in a weak voice, 'Where is my useless solicitor?'

He sat down, facing Smithy, who replied, 'Your solicitor has been informed.'

Just then, there was a knock on the door, it opened, and the solicitor walked in and sat next to Sam.

He asked Smithy, 'What have you got my client in here for now?'

Smithy said, 'It's about the shooting of Isaac Fernandez in Spain.'

Then he turned the recorder on, and went through the routine of getting everyone's names down for the record before asking, 'Sam, why did you kill Fernandez? Was it because he could recognise you? And where's Eric Lang? We know he's a big mouth, did you get rid of him as well?'

Sam just sat there looking at Smithy, so his solicitor said, 'Sam, if you don't want to answer, say 'no comment'.'

Sam, in a low voice, said 'What's the use? I did it.'

The solicitor asked, 'Sam, do you know what you're saying?'

Smithy said, 'Will you repeat that, Sam? You shot Fernandez? Why did you do it?'

Sam just sat there. He seemed to be in a world of his own. The solicitor looked at him and then, with a worried look on his face, looked over to Smithy. He went to say something, but Smithy had already leaned forward, noting with concern that Sam's face had turned white and had little beads of sweat all over it.

Smithy got up and left the room. In just a few minutes he was back with the on-call doctor. The solicitor left the room to give the doctor space to examine Sam. As the doctor came towards him, he weakly waved her away, but the doctor took no notice.

She carried on and examined him, saying, as she did, 'This man is having a heart attack. Get an ambulance here now.'

Sam said, in a weak voice, 'I'm not worth saving. Ask them.'

The doctor said, 'I don't care what they think. To me you are a patient, and all my patients are worth looking after. I see you have a medal of the Holy Mother, so you must believe, so pray to her and I will also pray for you.'

He tried to smile and muttered, 'You're right. I'll pray for you too, if I get to heaven.'

Some paramedics came rushing in with a wheelchair; with the doctor's help they put Sam on the chair and took him out to the ambulance. The doctor went with Sam to the hospital while Smithy picked up all his papers, put them in the folder and went to make a phone call.

Jacko was sitting at his desk when his external line rang; he picked the phone up and said, 'DS Jackson speaking.'

The voice at the other end replied, 'It's me, Smithy. It's about Sam Blake. He's in a bad way - he's had a heart attack. The doctor has taken him to hospital. I'm afraid you will have to tell his daughter. I hope this doesn't put a spanner in the works for you.'

Jacko said, 'It could do that. She said she will come clean when I next interview her, because I've been going on about her father and, to save him, I think she wants a deal and will take the blame with Eric Lang.

My thinking was to let her tell us how it was done and, if what she tells us when she pleads guilty to prove her father wasn't involved helps us with the investigation, she could have a deal... but if she hears that he's a sick man and she gets it into her head that it's our fault, she might change her mind and go back to just saying 'no comment'. Of course, she's said enough to incriminate herself now, but it'll still be a lot easier to put this case to bed if she tells us exactly what happened all those years ago.'

Smithy said, 'Sorry, Jacko. Myself, I was beginning to think the two of them had done away with Eric Lang. It's strange how he's gone missing. I'll let you know how her dad's getting on as soon as I hear. Well, good luck. Bye.'

Jacko replied, 'I'll need it. She's got a real smart-arse solicitor. I'll see you, Smithy.'

He put the phone down and shook his head, muttering to himself, 'I thought I had it all wrapped up. Now we might have to start all over again.'

Although he knew he should really pass on the information about Sam's heart attack to Lilly straight away, instead he decided to hedge his bets and let her write her statement first. That way she would have less time to change what she was intending to tell them, if she blamed the police once she found out her father was ill. He decided he would definitely wait until the interview to tell her.

LILLY'S STATEMENT

The next morning, shortly before eight o'clock, Rick walked into the police station and up to the front counter, where an officer stood, facing the opposite direction as he dealt with something out of sight.

Rick said to him, 'Good morning, Officer.'

The officer turned around and replied, 'Good morning, sir. How can I help you?'

Rick said, 'I'm the solicitor for Miss Lilly Blake. Can you inform Sergeant Jackson that I would like to see my client, to finish sorting out her statement.'

The officer picked up the phone and relayed the message to Jacko, nodding in response to what was said in return.

After a short while, he put the phone down and said, 'Sergeant Jackson said for you to go to interview room three. Do you know the way?'

Rick smiled and said, 'Yes, only too well, thank you.'

With that, he made his way to the interview room. When he arrived, he went in, opened his attaché case and put some papers on the table. There was a knock on the door, and it opened. An officer stepped into the room, moving aside to let Lilly walk in. Her hair was tied back, but it wasn't as neat as the day before, and her eyes looked red and sore.

As the officer left, Rick pulled a chair out from the table and said, 'Sit here, Lilly.'

She sat down on the chair, and he sat on the one next to her, saying, 'I told Jacko we would be finishing your statement, so we won't see him for about an hour or more.'

Lilly asked, 'What happens now?'

He replied, 'Well, I've had everything you told me typed out. I want you to go over it and point out if there's anything I've got wrong, okay?'

Lilly nodded, almost crying and started rambling, 'I didn't want Joan to die. He told me the idea was to scare her and I believed him, the lying bastard. It was a shock when I read it in the papers the next day... and, even then, I believed him when he told me it was an accident. He said he didn't realise the wall was so near and so small. I guess I wanted to believe him, but later on I knew it wasn't an accident... but I didn't say anything then because I loved him and, also, I was afraid of him.'

All the time she was talking, Rick was holding her statement, impatiently waiting for her to stop talking and read it.

When Lilly did stop, Rick said, 'You've told me all this in your statement already, Lilly. Now it's important that you read the statement of yours that I've had typed up. They will be here soon, and it is vital that we have everything in place. Please read it.'

She said, 'I'm sorry, Rick. I'm that frightened... I know I'm going on...'

Seeing she was about to start rehashing it all again, he had to interrupt, saying in a sympathetic voice as he put the statement in her hands, 'I know, now read your statement, before they come in.'

She got hold of the document and put it on the table while she wiped her eyes and blew her nose.

Rick picked it up, put it in her hands again, and said in a firm tone, 'Read it now.'

She read it and, when she had finished, she looked at Rick and said, 'Yes, you have it written down correctly and it all is true. I'm sorry I've been so useless this morning.'

Rick replied, 'No, it's I who should apologise, I should have tried to help you calm down earlier, rather than forcing you to go at my pace. Now we can go over it again together, before Jacko comes in.'

Rick and Lilly were still discussing what Lilly was to say when there was a knock on the door, and it opened. Jacko walked in, with Officer Porter following. Rick and Lilly looked up as Jacko and the officer sat down facing them.

Jacko asked, 'Am I going to get the truth this time, Rick?'

Rick put one hand on the table and the other in the air, as if he was swearing on a Bible and said, 'Nothing but the truth, the whole truth.'

Jacko turned the recorder on and went through the routine of clarifying who was present at the interview.

Then he asked, 'Lilly, where were you when Mrs Joan Thomson was killed?'

Lilly started crying again and said, 'In Spain.'

Rick said, 'Jacko, Lilly will give you the murderer, but she wants to make a deal. Do you agree?'

Jacko said, 'I promise to do my best for her, but I can't make any deals till I hear what she has to say. I also have some bad news for Lilly.'

Still crying, she muttered, 'It's my dad, isn't it?'

Jacko replied, 'Yes, your father has been taken to hospital. He's had a heart attack. I'm sorry.'

He was expecting Lilly to blame the police and start screaming it was all his fault, but instead Lilly put her head in her hands and bent forward so her forehead was touching the table, crying even louder.

In between her sobs she muttered, 'It's all my fault. Please God, help my dad.'

Jacko said, 'We are in touch with the hospital, and we will let you know how your father is doing.'

Rick said, 'Lilly needs a break. She is too upset to carry on.'

Jacko nodded, saying, 'Yes.'

As he turned the recorder off, Jacko asked, 'Do you want to leave the interview till this afternoon?'

Before Rick could answer, Lilly sobbed, 'No, it's my fault and that bastard's fault. I want to tell you everything, so he gets what he deserves.'

Rick said, 'Lilly, you at least need time to calm down. Sorry, Lilly, but I must insist.'

Jacko agreed and said, 'We can't interview you while you are so upset because you might get things wrong. Rick can call us when you're ready.'

With that Jacko and the officer left the room. After a few minutes there was a knock on the door.

Rick said, 'Come in.'

A smart, older-looking man entered, and Rick asked, 'Who are you and what do you want?'

The man replied, 'I'm Doctor Saunders and I've been asked to check that Miss Blake is fit enough to continue when she is ready to.'

Lilly had stopped sobbing whilst the doctor checked her breathing and pulse.

He asked her, 'Lilly, do you feel you can carry on with this interview? If you don't feel up to it, just say so and I'll stop it.'

Lilly replied, 'I want to do this now more than ever.'

The doctor said, 'Well, I can see no reason why you can't carry on.'

As Doctor Saunders left the room, Lilly asked, 'Rick, do you think my dad will be alright?'

Rick replied, 'I honestly don't know, but you pray for him.'

Lilly wanted to talk about her dad for nearly an hour, telling Rick all about how he had brought her up single-handed, after her mum had died, and how he had always been a good father to her.

When Rick got her back to talking about the interview, he picked up the phone and said, 'Put me through to Jacko.'

Jacko answered almost right away, saying, 'Is that you, Rick?'

He replied, 'Yes, Lilly is still upset but she wants to carry on, so we'll see you in a few minutes.'

Jacko said, 'I'm on my way.'

A few minutes later Jacko and Officer Porter entered. They sat facing Lilly and Rick. Jacko turned the recorder on and restarted the interview.

Then he said, 'Lilly, do you feel fit enough to carry on?'

She said from behind a handful of tissues, 'Yes.'

Jacko asked, 'Did you drive the car at the Thomson family?'

Rick said, 'Sergeant Jackson, Lilly is willing to tell you everything she knows. I have a statement here that she has asked me to read for her. Can I read it now, and then she will sign it and answer any questions you have afterwards. '

Jacko said, 'Well, let's hear it, Rick.'

Rick cleared his throat and read from the papers in front of him; all the time he was reading, Lilly was crying.

'I, Elizabeth Blake, swear that my dad, Samuel Blake, knows nothing about Mrs Joan Thomson's death, and that is the truth. When I was sixteen, I had a part time job with a man named Gareth Davis. He is an officer of the court and also owns a scrapyard, so when I worked for him, I asked him, if he got an old car in, would he sell it to me for my dad. He said he would, so from that day any spare money I had I saved, so I could buy the car. I didn't save enough to buy all of the car, so my dad bought the rest of the parts over the years and that's where I got the car for my dad.'

Jacko said, 'Rick, I thought you were an honest man. This is the same story that Lilly was telling us before, so what's the difference?'

Rick replied, in an angry tone, 'She's telling you the truth about this, don't be so impatient. Now, if it's okay with you, I'll continue.'

Jacko went red in the face but didn't say anything, he just nodded that Rick should continue.

Rick picked the statement up and started reading again, 'When I was in Spain ten years ago and I saw the old motor car, I thought of my dad. So, I paid Alonso and that madman Fernandez to ship it to England without letting anyone else know I was buying it. They were keen to make even more money from the car, so they agreed. Even after Joan Thomson died, they sent the car, but they must have stripped it down because of her death. I didn't think it would cause my dad to get mixed up in this mess when I asked them to send the car, because I was told no one was supposed to die. I flew home the same day I drove it on the mountain road, and I didn't know Joan had died till I picked a newspaper up back in England. I went sick when I read it. I didn't know how to stop the shipping of the car because I had only met Alonso and Fernandez once. They picked me up at the airport and took me to a farm. While I was in the car with them, every now and then Fernandez would point a gun at me. I was terrified the whole time I was being driven to the farm.

After I had driven the car that day on the mountain road, they took me to a bank because I wanted to get the money to pay for the car for my dad. Then, from there, I was taken straight back to the airport.

So, I couldn't stop the car from being shipped here - I didn't know how to. When they wanted to get in touch with me about the arrangements, I would pick up messages from a PO Box at the bank they gave me the details for. Although I thought it would be better to forget about the car when I read about Joan's death and so I just left it at Davis' scrap yard, about eighteen months later my dad was talking about getting an old banger to work on. Seeing as there hadn't been any trouble after Joan's death and everyone thought it was an accident, I thought I'd see if Davis would sell the car to me for my dad to work on if he did still have it. I also thought that if I left it there Mr Davis, being an officer of the court, might look into it and trace it back to me. So, that is how my dad ended up with the car. He knew nothing about what happened in Spain. He is innocent, I swear it.

This is what did happen with Joan Thomson in Spain, from when it all started. I was eighteen and went for a job at Kenwright's. I started working there as a trainee PA. I did paperwork and admin in a large, well-staffed office. After I had been there a year, I became one of the girls who would be sent as a stand-in when someone needed a temporary PA. Then, one day I was told to go to Mr Thomson's office, and, after that, I was told to go there quite often. After six months I was working there a lot of the time. I was very happy as he was so nice to work for. At first, he would take me to business dinners to take any notes that were needed. Then, after a while, he started to take me to dinner and it was just him and I, and it built up from there. We became lovers.

Then he seemed to change. He seemed to be angry whenever he was alone with me. I asked him if he wanted to break up but he said it wasn't me he was angry with - it was his wife. He said she was always letting on that she built the firm up to what it was but when they got married the firm was on its knees and really *he* was the one who had built it up to what it had become. I thought it wasn't right that she had taken all the credit and told him I wished I could help him.

He went on about how he wasn't given enough credit or responsibility in the firm for months. Then, one day, he said that if he made managing director, we would be able to see one another a lot more. He asked me if I would like that and, of course, I said that it would be great.

So then he said he had a plan to make his wife want to please him by giving him the promotion, but he needed my help. He told me what he wanted me to do. He wanted me to drive a car at her in Spain. At first, I said 'no'. I thought I could kill her if I drove a car at her - it was too dangerous to risk. But over the next couple of months, he kept going on about how it was safe and that I wouldn't kill her because it would all be perfectly arranged for him to be the hero and pull her to safety. He said that he would drop hints about wanting to be the managing director in the weeks before and after the 'accident' and that he knew she would agree because she would be so grateful to him for 'saving her life', as she would have seen it.

I was still unconvinced, but he went on about how, if I loved him, I would help him. He carried on about it for weeks and I felt bad because I wouldn't help him, when he made it seem so simple. Then, one day he said he was determined to do it and that, if I didn't help him, he would leave me. So, like a fool, I agreed. Even then I said I was afraid I might hit her, but he dismissed it, saying that I wouldn't. He said that he needed me to be a hundred percent with him on the plan and to stop worrying, because that was the only way to make sure we could do it safely - if I was calm and focused.

He told me how it was all supposed to work. He said he'd seen a vintage MG we could use, so people would definitely notice it on the road. He said it belonged to a man who would do anything for money, so there would be no chance of it being traced back to us. He'd already been out to Spain and timed the run.

I told him that I still didn't like it but he said it would all be alright. He told me it was going to be arranged to happen on Ann's birthday. I trusted him when he said he loved Ann. He'd always seemed such a good father, so when he told me that Anne was his world and he wouldn't dream of doing anything that would upset her or spoil her birthday, I started to think we must be able to make his plan work without Joan ever being in real danger.

He went on about how Ann would think her dad was a hero and how the whole idea was just to make his wife actually appreciate him for all the things he did for her. He said he would use his strength to pull her out of the way of the car - that he didn't want me to run her down as then the car could break down and be stuck there. That would get the police involved and we would both be in real trouble. He insisted he didn't want Joan to actually get hurt and said that was why the timings of the plan mattered so much. He told me his idea was that he would get the family to walk down to the beach, while I parked the MG just round the bend, where there was a small car park. He said that I needed to put my foot down at three-thirty precisely and drift to the wrong side of the road as I went round the bend. He was going to arrange for Joan to be standing there and, he said, he would pull Joan out of the way as I got near. The plan was that I would drive on for a couple of miles until I reached a small side road that led into some woods, and he would arrange for a large van, with a ramp into the back of it, to be waiting, so the MG could drive into it. I was to leave the car with the van and go with Alonso and Fernandez back to the airport. He said he'd get me a disguise - a black wig and dark glasses - and a false passport, as well as tickets for the plane, there and back.

Of course, that's not what happened at all. I drove the car like he told me to, but I got a fright as I came round the bend. The wind moved the wig and it blew across my eyes, and when I moved it out of the way Ann and the boy, Tommy, were there - not Joan. I started to brake but, thank God, Tommy pulled Ann out the way and I went past them.

The car was heading right towards Joan, but then I saw Steve pull her out of the way. In my rearview mirror, I saw her go over the wall, but I could see Steve did have hold of her. I knew he was very strong, so I thought he would definitely save her. I couldn't believe it when I got back to London and saw what had happened in the paper. I thought our plan had gone tragically wrong. I knew we'd killed Joan, but at first I genuinely thought it was just because the plan had gone wrong.

Then, once Steve was made managing director, I became his permanent PA and I realised, from watching him work and talking to the other PAs, that he wasn't the one who built the firm up. He's not a bad businessman but he's not as good as his wife was. I started to wonder then - did he do what Ann said and let Joan fall on purpose? Because, if she were alive, there would have been no way his wife would have let him take over the running of the firm as managing director. And I know for a fact that he shot the madman Fernandez. So, I always wondered about Joan and whether it had been an accident she died or if that was his plan from the very start.'

Rick stopped reading, and Lilly looked at Jacko and said, 'Now you know. So leave my dad alone.'

Rick put the statement down on the table and put his arm around Lilly as she wiped her eyes, saying, 'It's up to you now, Jacko.'

Jacko was shocked by what Lilly had claimed, but kept it from showing, asking, 'Lilly, is this the truth? Not you trying to get revenge on Steve Thomson because he didn't get a good solicitor for your father?'

Lilly replied, from behind a handful of tissues, 'I swear it.'

Jacko said, 'Alright, Lilly. Please will you sign your statement.'

Lilly did as she said, as Jacko noted it for the recording, then he turned the recorder off.

Rick asked, 'Now what are you going to do for Lilly?'

Jacko replied, 'Bearing in mind she's just confessed to her role in a high-profile murder case, I can't make any promises - and particularly not till we have checked whether what she has said is true. I'll take the statement to the Crown Prosecutor to see where we go from here.'

With that Jacko and the officer got up and left.

Rick said, 'Lilly, I know Jacko will do his best for you, but it would be better if we can offer them some evidence that will help them prove the truth of your statement. Have a think about whether you do have access to anything like that.'

As he put the paperwork in his case, there was a knock on the door and Rick said, 'Come in.'

A policewoman entered and said, 'Will you come with me, Miss Blake. We'll take you back to your cell.'

Lilly stood up and looked at Rick.

He said, 'Go with them, Lilly. Don't worry, I'll be back to see you at about two o'clock this afternoon, to see if we can come up with any proof for your statement.'

Jacko took the statement to the chief inspector's office. He knocked on the door and waited. Then he opened the door and went in when a voice said, 'Come.'

The chief looked up from some papers and said, 'Take a seat, Jacko. I'll be with you as soon as I've read this.'

Jacko sat on an easy chair and, after five minutes, the chief looked up and said, 'Well, I hope you've got some good news for me. I need it.'

Jacko replied, 'Yes and no. I've got a statement from Lilly Blake, but I'd like to discuss it with you.'

He took the statement over to the desk and held it out to the chief, who reached over his desk and took it.

Jacko reclaimed his seat, saying, 'You read it and see what you think of it.'

The chief sat back in his chair as he read the statement.

When he had finished, he said, 'It sounds like she is blaming this Thomson fellow for everything, and it is just her word. According to the reports from Spain, he was a broken man when it happened... and we had the head of the security firm he hired interviewed. He said Thomson hired them to follow his children around and keep them safe as soon as he got back in England, just after his wife's death. Surely if he was involved, he would know he didn't need the security.

Do you think she's accusing him because he didn't stand by her father? I heard she was upset yesterday when she found out Thomson wouldn't help him get a solicitor. I think she might just be a bitter woman who is trying to save her dad. It's also strange that she hasn't even mentioned her boyfriend Eric Lang in her statement given that he disappeared not long after the woman's death. That seems too much to be a coincidence. If she is lying about Thomson's role, then it could be possible that she and her father got rid of Lang, because he could incriminate them.

After all, if Tomson was behind a plot to kill his wife, surely he would've provided solicitors for both of them, because he would know Miss Blake would involve him if he pinned it on her father. What do you think?'

Jacko replied, 'It's hard to believe that Thomson could do such a wicked thing, as to plan his children be there to see their mother die, particularly on his daughter's birthday. We know that a large bunch of flowers is sent to his wife's grave every week. To all outward appearances, it looks like he loved her very much, but this Lilly Blake claims she sends the bouquet of flowers. I don't know, there's something about her - she's got me believing that what she's said is the truth. And I think her solicitor, you know him, it's Rick Shannon, believes her too. In fact, I know he believes her, otherwise he would have had her saying 'no comment' up until the day she went to jail! He's got pretty good instincts, so that's another reason making me think there might be something to it.'

The chief said, 'I'll go with you on this one. Thomson is a rich man with a lot of powerful friends, so we'll have to go carefully. Get in touch with the Crown Prosecutor and see what she thinks. If she says to get Thomson in for questioning, you can do it this afternoon. Keep me informed.'

Jacko stood up and said, 'Okay, I'll send a car to bring him in,' thinking to himself, 'after I've made sure I've had my lunch.'

With that he left and went to his own office.

STEVE IS ASKED TO COME TO THE STATION

That same afternoon, Steve was in his office with John, who had decided to work there rather than in his own office over the coming days, so that he could support his father through a difficult time.

John was asking, 'What are you going to do about Lilly?'

His dad said, 'I don't know, John. I'm worried she might get away with what she's done. You wouldn't believe it by looking at her, but she's a very clever, conniving bitch. I only realise it now. I hope they throw the key away, for her and that bastard father of hers. It's just a pity we don't have the death penalty anymore.'

Just then there was a knock on the door, so Steve called, 'Come in.'

His temporary PA came into the office but, before she could speak, Steve snapped, 'What have you come in here for? We do have phones in these offices.'

She replied, 'Mr Thomson, there's two police officers in the reception area downstairs who wish to speak to you.'

Steve said, 'Well, you know I'm here in this office, so just tell them to come up.'

'I did suggest I would inform you and said that they should come up to your office,' she replied, 'but they said they would like a word with you in *their* office.'

Steve said, 'Okay, Eliza, tell them I'll be down in a moment.'

She nodded and closed the door as she left the room.

John said, 'I'm coming with you, Dad, alright?'

His dad answered in an angry tone, 'No, John, stay here and get on with the work you were doing.'

John replied, 'I have the right to know what is going on. She was my mum.'

His dad cut him off, saying in the same angry tone, 'For goodness' sake, John, just do the job you get paid to do. I'll tell you what the police have to say when I get back, if that's okay with you?'

John realised his dad was getting upset and felt sorry for the situation he was in, so he said, 'Sorry, Dad. You will let me know, won't you?'

His dad looked at him, with a sort of smile on his face, and said, 'Of course I will.'

Steve left the office, walked through the reception area and went into the lift. When it got to the ground floor, he walked out of it and up to the two police officers.

As he drew level with them, he asked, 'Why couldn't you tell me what is going on here, in my office?'

One of the officers said, 'We're sorry, sir. We don't know what this is all about. We were just asked to come here and take you to the station. So, if you will come with us, Mr Thomson, we have a car outside waiting.'

They showed Steve to the car, where one of the officers opened the back door and, as Steve got in, said, 'Mind your head, sir.'

During the drive, Steve just sat there in silence but when they got to the police station, he asked, 'Was it Detective Sergeant Jackson that sent you to pick me up?'

The driver, as he put the hand brake on, said, 'Yes, we will take you to him.'

Steve tried to get out of the car but found the doors were locked. Then the officer in the passenger seat got out and opened the back door for him, and Steve paced up the stairs ahead of him. Once they were in the station, however, he didn't know where to go, so he let the officer lead him to interview room three.

Once there, they knocked on the door and Jacko's voice said, 'Come in.'

One officer opened the door and then stepped back so Steve could enter.

He walked in and, when he saw Jacko and the other officer sitting at the table with papers on it, Steve said, 'I thought I was coming to get a report on how you are getting on, but where we are... this looks more like you are going to question me, am I right?'

Jacko began to explain, 'We have reason to believe Lilly Blake...'

Steve butted in and said, 'So, that bitch did do it. I hope she gets life.'

Jacko shook his head at the interruption and said, 'Mr Thomson, I suggest you call your solicitor, because she has said you were involved in the death of your wife.'

Steve said nothing - he just stood there, looking shocked.

Jacko continued, 'You can use this phone on the table.'

As the news sunk in, Steve went white and said, 'That vindictive cow. She's done this because I wouldn't stand by her and her fucking dad, but she's mad to think I would help her after what she did to my family.

I had nothing to do with her back then and I want nothing more to do with her now.'

While Steve was going on, Jacko had picked the phone up and held it out towards him, but Steve didn't seem to notice. He put his hand into the inside pocket of his jacket, took out his mobile phone and put in a number.

A woman's voice said, 'This is Mr Thomas' solicitor's office, how can I help you?'

Steve said, 'I'm Mr Steve Thomson and I need my legal representation down at the station.'

The secretary said, 'Would you like me to put you through to Mr Thomas?'

'No, just tell him who I am,' Steve said, 'and ask him to come to the police station as soon as possible.'

The secretary asked, 'Which police station are you being held at, Mr Thomson?'

Steve said, 'He knows which one, thank you' and put the phone back in his pocket.

Jacko said, 'Sit down, Mr Thomson, while we wait for your solicitor, he probably won't be long.'

Steve sat down, facing Jacko, and said, 'Why are you calling me 'Mr Thomson'? You were calling me by my first name before.'

Jacko replied, 'I'm afraid you are now a suspect, and I just wanted to let you know that I'm not your friend, I'm a police officer who has to interview you in relation to a murder. Now that's established, I will call you Steve during the interview, if you are still fine with that.'

Jacko left Steve in the room for half an hour, while they waited for Doug Thomas to arrive. When the duty sergeant notified him that the solicitor had reached the front desk and was being shown to the interview room, Jacko headed back there.

He arrived at the same time as the solicitor, who said 'What is this all about? Why are you interviewing my client?'

Before Jacko could answer, Steve shouted, 'They are trying to say I killed Joan. That cow Lilly said I did it, and they obviously believe her.'

Doug sat there, in silence, for a moment, regaining his composure.

Then he turned to look at Steve and said, 'Calm down, Steve, and let them tell me why they have brought you in and if you are seriously a person of interest in the investigation. If you are, they're going to need to provide some evidence that could prove it, if that is the case.'

Steve went red in the face and said, through gritted teeth, 'Of course they don't have any evidence to prove it, because I loved Joan and tried my best to save her. You believe me, don't you?'

Doug replied, 'For goodness' sake, Steve, calm down. I have to ask these types of questions, so I can defend you. The sooner we get started the sooner you get out of here.'

Jacko said, 'We have a search warrant for your office and home; it will be getting carried out about now.'

Steve looked at Jacko in anger and was about to say something, but Doug put his hand on Steve's shoulder and shook his head.

Doug asked, 'Well, what have you got on my client? I would like to see it.'

Jacko handed him a copy of Lilly Blake's statement.

He sat for a while studying it, then he said, 'Reading this, all you've got is a story she made up to get her dad off a murder charge. I see she's been careful to make it sound like she thought what happened to Joan was a prank, so it's not her fault either. We all know she's angry at my client because he didn't pay for her father's defence. Surely all that must tell you that my client isn't involved at all, and this statement is just a load of nonsense. It's just her word, there's no proof here. Lilly knows what Steve's daughter has been saying these last ten years and she has built her entire story on it.'

Jacko said, 'Well, regardless of all that, this is only an interview, and your client is just helping with our enquiries; we won't need anything more definite unless we decide to charge him. So, let's get started.'

Jacko turned the recorder on and said, 'This is the interview of Mr Stephen Thomson. Present is DS Jackson…'

He waited for his officer to add, 'Officer Porter,' and then Jacko asked, 'Will you say your full name for the record, Steve?'

Steve said, 'Stephen Thomson.'

Doug said, 'Solicitor Douglas Thomas.'

Then Jacko went straight into asking, 'Why did you let your wife fall?'

Steve replied, 'I didn't let Joan fall, I just couldn't hold on. I loved Joan.'

'If you loved Joan, why did you stop going to her grave?'

'I hated the thought of Joan being down there in the ground, so I just remembered Joan in my own way, and I still love her.'

'Well, if you still love Joan, you could have still sent flowers to her grave. Why didn't you?'

'I used to, but I think keeping Joan in my mind is better than sending flowers.'

Doug broke into the back-and-forth, asking, 'What kind of questions are these? You should be asking my client if he loved Joan when she was alive. We can produce hundreds of witnesses to tell you Steve loved his wife, and I'll go as far as to say you'd struggle if you want to find one who will say he didn't.'

Jacko just looked at Doug, then he turned his attention back towards Steve and said, 'If you loved her, why did you let go of her and let her fall to her death?'

Steve went red in the face and shouted, 'I told you - I couldn't hold her.'

Doug touched Steve's arm and said, 'Stay calm, Steve. If you have answered a question and you don't want to answer again, or, even if you don't want to answer anything for any other reason, just say 'no comment.'

Jacko started his questions again, asking, 'Do you have, or have you ever owned, a gun, Steve?'

'No, I don't own one now and I've never had one. I wouldn't have one in the house. I have top security, so I know my family is safe.'

'Did you know a man in Spain, called Fernandez?'

'No. I know a lot of people in Spain but none of that name.'

'Did you shoot a man named Fernandez in Spain?'

'How could I? I just told you - I don't have a gun, and I don't know this Fernandez you're talking about.'

'So, you say you haven't met the Spanish man named Fernandez who was killed?'

'I've told you I know lots of people in Spain, but I can't recall anyone named Fernandez.'

'Well, do you recall anyone named Alonso?'

'Yes, I know a Mr Alonso.'

'If you know Alonso, you must know Fernandez.'

'I'm telling you - I don't know anyone named Fernandez.'

'You know Alonso… Well, before he was killed, Fernandez was his partner in the garage they ran together. So, you must know him?'

At this point Steve frowned in confusion, and said, 'What are you on about? Alonso is a top surgeon in his field.'

Jacko was a bit embarrassed and said, 'We are talking about Alonso the garage owner, not a surgeon. Now, where did you get the MG from? It was from Alonso and Fernandez's garage in Spain, wasn't it?'

'You're not listening, I don't know anyone named Fernandez.'

Doug interrupted and said, 'If you just keep on going over the same thing, I'll advise my client to say, 'no comment'. This is a waste of time for all of us.'

Jacko nodded, though it was obvious he was irritated by the solicitor's threat, and changed tack with his questions, asking 'Did you get a false passport for Lilly Blake?'

'I wouldn't know where to go to get such a thing. I don't know those types of people.'

'Would you know where to get a black wig from?'

'I'm not sure, but if I needed one, I imagine I could find one. It wouldn't be hard to do.'

'Did you shoot Fernandez because he could recognise you?'

'No comment,' said Steve, catching Doug's eye and shaking his head.

'How did you get Lilly Blake to drive the car at your wife?'

At that, Steve went red in the face and was almost shouting as he leaned towards Jacko, 'I didn't tell that bitch to drive at Joan. I loved my wife. I'm not putting up with this - if I'm not under arrest, I'm going home.'

Doug put his hand on Steve's shoulder to stop him as he went to get up to go, but he said, 'You heard my client. Charge him or we are leaving.'

Jacko said, 'You can go at this point, Mr Thomson, but don't leave the country… we may want to speak to you again.'

With that Steve and Doug got up and left the room.

As they walked out the station, Steve said to Doug, in an angry tone, 'You didn't say much to help me, why?'

Doug replied, 'They have nothing on you, so why say anything? It's up to them to prove a person committed a crime and - as we know - you didn't, so let them bang their heads against a brick wall if they want to. Still, it's best to answer their questions, so they can rule you out quickly and get on with the case against Lilly.'

Back in the interview room, Jacko picked up his paperwork and, as he put it in the folder, he said to Officer Porter, 'Go to the canteen and have a break. I'm going to put this folder in my office and then go for a walk and a think in the park. I might need you later.'

The officer replied, 'I'll be here. I've quite a bit of my own paperwork to finish.'

JOHN FINDS OUT HIS DAD IS IMPLICATED IN HIS MUM'S DEATH

John was in his dad's office when three plain clothes police officers opened the door and walked in.

John said, in an angry tone, 'Don't you know how to knock? Who are you and what do you want?'

One of the officers handed him a piece of paper and said, 'We are police officers, and we have a warrant to search this office.'

John said, 'Why? Where's my dad?'

The officer said, 'I believe he is helping us with our enquiries, that is all I know.'

Just then John's mobile rang; he took it out of his pocket, and said, 'Hello?'

A voice replied, 'It's Joe, your gardener. I can't get in touch with your dad, so I thought I'd better let you know... the police are searching your house and the grounds around it.'

John just stood there, flummoxed for a while, so the gardener asked, 'Are you still there? Did you hear what I said?'

John said, 'Sorry, yes, I'm still here and I heard what you said. Thank you. I'll come home soon, bye.'

He put the mobile back in his pocket, left the office and went to the police station. He parked right outside the main door and, as he got out of his car, two police officers standing on the steps, talking, stopped their conversation and looked at him.

One of them said, 'Don't be hard-faced, son, move the car.'

John got back in, drove round the corner and parked there. He walked back to the station.

As he walked up the steps, and past the two officers, he said, 'Sorry about parking there, lads. I'm in a hurry and wasn't thinking.'

The officers smiled and nodded to him.

He went into the station and up to the counter, saying to the officer in a nervous tone, 'Is my father here?'

The officer replied, 'I've just come on duty, so I wouldn't know, son. What's your father's name and I'll find out for you?'

John answered, 'Steve Thomson. He left our offices with some policemen this afternoon.'

The officer picked up the phone and chatted to someone at the other end of the line.

After a short time, he put the phone down and said, 'You've just missed him. He left a little while ago, with his solicitor.'

John frowned and asked, 'Why did he have his solicitor with him?'

The officer replied, 'I don't know, son, and I'm afraid I couldn't tell you even if I did. He's most likely to be home now.'

John rushed out of the station, and, on the steps, he saw Jacko, returning from his walk.

He stopped and said, 'Excuse me, Detective, aren't you the person dealing with my mother's death? Her name is Joan Thomson. Why are you searching our office and home?'

Jacko replied, 'I'm sorry, you're John, aren't you?'

He said, 'Yes, what is going on with my dad? And why are you searching all our properties?'

Jacko said, 'I'm sorry, John. You will have to ask your father, because that's a question I'm not allowed to answer. Your father will be home now.'

John looked at Jacko and said angrily, as he walked down the steps, 'It's a waste of time asking you crowd anything.'

He went to his car and drove home as quickly as he could, with a sickly feeling in his stomach.

When John got home the police were all getting ready to go, so John just strode past them without stopping and, as soon as he entered the house, shouted, 'Dad, are you in? Where are you?'

Steve came out of his bedroom, smartly dressed and looking ready to go out.

He said to John, 'You were lucky to catch me. I'm just going to the clubhouse for a drink and some relaxation.'

John said angrily, 'What do you mean you're going to the golf club? I need to know what is going on. Why did the police escort you to the police station? I want to know now.'

His dad replied, 'You know how over the past ten years Ann has been going on, saying that I let your mum die? Now that cow Lilly has made up a story using what Ann has been saying to give it credibility. She's claiming that her dad wasn't involved, and it was all my idea to run your mum down...

But, John, you were there. You saw how I pulled your mum out of the way of the car. You know I tried my best to save your mum and that I loved her with all my heart, so you know she's just saying anything to try and get herself out from under the charges.

Even so, I know I could lose Ann again now, because of what that cow is saying. So, as Doug said, seeing as I didn't do it, I thought I'd buck myself up and think of some way to prove to Ann and the police I'm innocent, but it's all getting on top of me just sitting round here, where the police have been poking around. That's why I'm going to the club to get away from it all, so I can think and clear my head.'

John was flabbergasted and just stood there staring at his dad.

His dad said, 'I know it's a shock, John. It was to me too… but you do believe in me, don't you, John?'

John replied, in a dazed voice, 'Yes, but what do we tell Ann?'

Steve answered firmly, 'We won't tell Ann anything until I get it all sorted out, and that cow Lilly and her dad are charged with what they did.'

John nodded and said, 'Don't drive to the club, Dad… and make sure you get a taxi home. Don't drink and drive; please, Dad, don't get drunk again.'

His dad said, 'I have no intention of getting drunk, I just want some thinking time to work out how to prove Lilly is lying and that she's the one that killed your mum, with her fucking father.'

John replied, 'I hope you can come up with something, Dad.'

Then he phoned for one of their chauffeurs to take his dad to the club.

JACKO LET'S TOMMY KNOW HOW THE INVESTIGATION IS GOING

Ann had decided to stay over at Emma's house the previous night, because after their meeting with the investors she had told Emma that Lilly had been arrested in connection with her mum's murder and that her dad wasn't implicated at all. As Emma was distressed to hear Joan's death had been on purpose, Ann thought she could use some emotional support, so she went home with Emma, rather than coming back to Tommy's.

As he had been left to his own devices, Tommy had spent that morning in his back garden, pottering about. In the afternoon he decided to text Jacko: *I know I'm a nuisance, but I can't wait. How are you getting on with Lilly and Sam Blake? Can you tell me anything at all? TT*

Jacko was having lunch in his office when the text came through on his mobile. He picked it up off his desk, read it and was just about to answer it when the landline rang.

He put his mobile back on the desk and picked up the other phone, saying, 'DS Jackson here.'

The voice at the other end of the line said, 'Hello, Jacko, it's me, Smithy. I'm just wanting to know how you are getting on with the case at your end.'

Jacko replied, 'You and everyone else. I thought I'd cracked it, but Lilly threw a spanner in the works. I was going to let you know about it this afternoon, just as soon as I'd finished my lunch.'

Smithy asked, 'What do you mean? Down here we've got Sam Blake banged up and no way will he be getting out.'

Jacko replied, 'Well, it was a bloody big spanner, Smithy. It may well knacker your case against Sam Blake.'

Smithy asked, 'What are you on about?'

Jacko told Smithy what Lilly had said in her statement and Smithy said, 'Well, you've been a copper long enough to have an idea... Is she telling the truth?'

Jacko said, 'I don't know. Yes, I've been a copper for a long time but, like you, in that time, I've got it right sometimes and I've got it wrong sometimes. Still, I can tell her solicitor, Rick Shannon, believes her - and he's a good judge of character. So, it is possible that she could be telling us the truth.'

Smithy said, 'I had a feeling Sam Blake was innocent, but he had all the evidence stacked against him and that beats a gut feeling every time, particularly as, like you said, that gut feeling can be wrong.'

Jacko replied, 'Let's wait and see where we go with Steve Thomson before we make any decisions about what to do with Lilly and Sam Blake. How is he? It's certain Lilly will want to know how he's doing.'

Smithy replied, 'He's okay now. The officer outside his room said he's sitting in a chair by the side of his bed and chatting the nurses up. He even had two of the nurses praying with him, and they all had rosary beads in their hands.

So, if he's innocent, it looks like it might be back to the drawing board for both of us.'

Jacko said, 'I asked Steve Thomson if he shot Fernandez and, the way he answered, I got the impression he didn't like guns and hasn't even touched one. When I question him again, I'll ask him again if he has ever owned a gun to see whether that reaction stays consistent.'

Smithy said, 'Well, let me know how you are getting on.'

Jacko replied, 'I'll send you a full report. See you, Smithy, I've got to go.'

Smithy said, 'Bye,' and hung up the phone.

Jacko picked up his mug of coffee and took a mouthful, thinking, as he swallowed it, 'Another cold mug of coffee!'

Then he remembered Tommy's message and picked up his mobile from his desk to text him: *Hi, Tommy, this case is getting a bit complicated. Lilly Blake has made a statement, but she claims her father wasn't involved and it was all down to Steve Thomson. She could just be trying to help her father, as she knows what Ann has been saying for years about Steve Thomson, so it's possible Lilly has built a story around what Ann has been saying. This information is for your eyes only. I would be in a lot of trouble if it gets out that I've told you this so, for goodness' sake, don't you tell Ann. Let her brother say something about it to her because he knows his dad was questioned. Jacko.*

Tommy's heart dropped when he saw the text. He was shocked to hear that Steve might have been involved in Joan's murder after all and dreaded to think how this might affect his and Ann's relationship now. He was relieved that his promise to Jacko meant he couldn't tell Ann what was happening and that, if Steve was shown to be involved, the police would have to be the ones to inform her. Not knowing what else to do, he went and immersed himself in a shoot 'em up game on his PlayStation.

The next morning Tommy got a phone call just as he was getting out of bed. Still half asleep, he picked his phone up off the bedside cabinet and got a shock when it pulled out of his hand. It was still attached to the charger.

He disconnected it and said, 'Tommy here.'

He heard Val's voice ask, 'Are you awake yet, sleepy head?'

Tommy answered, 'I've been up for hours, have we got a job on today?'

Val replied, 'Yes, call in to the office and I'll give you all the information.'

Tommy didn't bother with his morning exercises, instead he just grabbed a can of coke to wake him up. He left his house in record time, got on his motorbike and rode to the office.

When he got in, looking a bit flustered, Val said, 'There's no rush. It's just a divorce case. Mr Phillips wants his wife followed.'

Tommy replied, 'Oh, just a bread-and-butter case?'

Val smiled and said, 'Ah, I suppose these cases aren't good enough for a great detective like you?'

He was a bit embarrassed and slightly red in the face, said, 'No, I'm just saying what you called them the other day.'

Val laughed and said, 'I know, I'm just joking.'

He looked at her and grinned, as he put the kettle on to make a coffee.

While he was sorting their drinks, he said, 'I think Ann might want me to go with her to her dad's tonight, but I've got to put her off going there.'

Val frowned and said, 'You've been trying for years to get Ann and her dad together. What are you up to now?'

He handed Val a cup of coffee, took a mouthful from his own mug and said, 'Things are happening with her mum's case. I can't tell you what, because Jacko asked me to keep it to myself, but I think that Lilly Blake is guilty of Ann's mum's murder and is trying to cause trouble for the family.'

Val said, 'I'll mind my own business and won't ask you anything about the case because I know Jacko means a lot to you. If you work on this divorce case, it will take over a week, which will give you a good reason not to go with Ann to her dad's. From everything you've said in the past, I've got the impression she won't go without you.'

He replied, 'You're right. I don't think she will. I'll phone her now.'

He took his mobile out of his pocket and called her.

Ann answered, 'Hello, Tommy what can I do for you, darling?'

He cleared his throat and said, 'I hope you still want to call me that after the news I've got for you. I'm afraid I'm on a case for a week or two. It involves tailing someone, so we'll only be able to snatch a little while with each other of an evening, and I'm sorry, but I won't be able to get over to your dad's with you.'

He could hear the disappointment in Ann's voice when she answered, 'I was hoping you would come with me to my dad's. I don't think I can go without you, but I'll send Dad a text saying I'm short-staffed at the moment. What's one little white lie? I still think you're my darling. Got to get back to work now, bye.'

He answered, 'Bye, love you.'

As he put his mobile back in his pocket, he thought guiltily, 'That's actually two *large* white lies and they are both down to me.'

Val handed Tommy some papers and said, 'Here's all the information you need for this job. You won't have to start till tonight, so you can take the day off.'

Tommy smiled and said, 'I can take the day off? You're too good to me.'

Then he kissed Val on the forehead and rushed out laughing, before she could give him a playful slap. Just as he was about to get on his motorbike, his mobile rang.

He answered it, saying 'Hello, Tommy here.'

It was Jacko, who replied, 'Tommy, it's me. I'm going to interview Steve Thomson this morning and Lilly Blake this afternoon. I shouldn't do this but you've been involved from the beginning, so I will tell you what is going on after each interview… But you mustn't tell Ann anything till it is all over.'

He answered, 'I won't tell Ann anything till you say I can. I now believe Lilly Blake and her dad did do it; she just made up a story to cover herself. That seems the most likely option. Her and her dad have the car, and you said Sam Blake has other evidence against him in his house.'

Jacko said, 'That's very possible, but we're keeping an open mind right now and investigating all possibilities - that's why we're interviewing both Lilly Blake and Steve Thomson again. So, be careful, Tommy, Ann's dad is still very much a person of interest.'

Tommy felt his heart sink as he nodded and said, 'Bye Jacko,' before heading away on his bike.

STEVE'S SECOND INTERVIEW

That same morning, Steve was drinking a mug of coffee while he was waiting for the limousine he had ordered. Standing by one of the windows in the front room, he watched the car drive up to the house. He quickly finished his coffee and opened the front door just as the driver was about to knock.

The driver went to the back door of the limousine and opened it for Steve to get in.

Once the driver took his own seat, Steve asked, 'Do you know Doug Thomas' office?'

The driver replied, 'Yes, sir. I've taken people from the business there a few times.'

Steve said, 'Take me there. I've told him we'll pick him up on the way to the police station.'

As the limousine pulled up outside Doug's office, he came out to the car and the driver got out and opened the door for him to get in.

Steve said, as Doug sat down, 'I hope this is the last time I have to go to this police station. Do you think that's possible?'

Doug replied, 'Well I haven't heard news of anything else they're working with other than what Lilly is claiming, so it might be possible. I'm glad to see and hear you sound calm.'

Steve said, 'Well, I took a good look at myself last night and I didn't like the state I was in. Like you said, I didn't do anything wrong, so they can't prove I did.'

Doug said, 'It's important that you stay calm today. Don't let them upset you, because if you start getting angry from what they say, they will think you have something to hide.'

Steve replied, 'I know, you're right.'

They rode for a while in silence and then the limousine stopped outside the station.

An officer who was passing stopped and opened the back door for them to get out, saying as they did so, 'The driver can't park here.'

The driver said, 'Yes, officer, I know. I'm just dropping them off.'

The officer nodded and went on his way. Doug closed the door of the limousine behind him and the two of them went up the steps into the station.

They walked up to the counter and Doug said to the duty officer, 'This is Steve Thomson and I'm his solicitor. We have an appointment with DS Jackson. Will you inform him we are here, please?'

The officer nodded and picked up the phone, he spoke on it for a little while, then called another officer over and said, 'Take Mr Thomson and his solicitor to interview room one.'

'Follow me, gentlemen, please,' said the officer, opening the door near the counter and gesturing to indicate they should follow him through it.

Jacko and Officer Porter were already in the interview room when the door opened and the officer announced, 'Mr Thomson, and his solicitor are here.'

Jacko said, 'Ask them to come in.'

With that Steve and Doug walked in and sat down, facing Jacko and Officer Porter. The officer who had shown them in closed the door as he left.

Doug said, as he sat down, 'I know you have no credible reason to question my client, so why are we here?'

Jacko said, 'I want to be sure Steve is telling us the truth, so shall we get started?'

With that Jacko turned the recorder on and logged who was present at the interview, before asking, 'Do you know the man Fernandez who was killed in Spain?'

Steve answered, 'I've never met the man, as I have told you before.'

'Do you still say you don't know Alonso as well?'

'As I've said previously, I know a Mr Alonso who is a surgeon. Does that count?'

'Did you shoot Fernandez?'

'How could I? I don't know him.'

'Do you have a gun?'

'No, I don't - and I've never owned one.'

'We've been told you bought the MG that tried to run your family down, did you?'

'You know I didn't. You've already got the person who did.'

'Where did you get the gun from?'

'I didn't get a gun; I've never had a gun and I've never used a gun. Does that finally answer your questions about a gun?'

'Well, when did you start going out with Lilly Blake?'

'About eight years ago, the evil, conniving, head-working bitch.'

'I'll ask you again, when did you start going out with Lilly Blake?'

'I've just told you - about eight years ago.'

'Lilly Blake claims you have been going out together for eleven years. What do you say to that?'

Steve frowned for a moment, then he answered, 'I know what she's on about. Up to about eighteen months before she was my permanent PA, when she was still a temp, she would sometimes come away with me on business. When I did start going out with the cow, even though it was two years after my Joan died, Lilly said to me that she'd felt like we had been together from the first time I took her away on a business trip. I thought it was a bit strange, but the relationship was going well at that point, so I didn't make a big deal out of it. It feels a lot more sinister now.'

Before Jacko could ask another question, there was a knock on the door and Jacko said, 'Come in.'

An officer entered and as he did so, Jacko said into the recorder, 'Officer Brown has entered the room.'

The officer leaned over and whispered into his ear, 'A Detective Smith is on the phone, and he wants a word with you right away.'

Jacko got up and said, 'I'll be back in a few minutes.'

As Jacko left the room, Officer Porter said into the recorder, 'DS Jackson and Officer Brown are leaving the room. Interview paused at 11:15 am,' and then he turned it off.

Jacko rushed to his office and, as soon as he entered, picked up the phone and said, 'Jacko here, Smithy. This better be good. I told you I'd be interviewing Steve Thomson this morning.'

Smithy said, 'Let him sweat a bit. I thought you should know a detective called Fred Saunders has just been transferred to this station and I was talking about the Thomson case to him. When I told him about the shooting of Fernandez being a professional killing, he smiled and said, 'You couldn't know if it was professional killing or not.' Then he went on to say he used to work with Steve Thomson as a car salesman about thirty years ago. Anyway, he took Steve out to a shooting range and, apparently, after about the fifth shot with a handgun, Steve never missed. By the fourth time they were going, just for fun, they used cardboard men with guns as targets. Steve Thomson would put a bullet in the bull on the target, one through each eye and then the rest in the mouth. Fred said to me 'It makes you think, doesn't it?' I had to agree, which is why I thought you'd want to know this for your interview.'

Jacko said, 'Are you sure it's the same Steve Thomson? In the last interview with him I got two people with the same name mixed up. So, can you find out if your mate Fred is talking about the right Steve Thomson? I don't want any more embarrassments.'

Smithy replied, 'Oh, it's the right fellow, all right, because he said the Steve he knew married a Joan Kenwright, who had a sister Emma. In fact, Steve told Fred back then he couldn't stand the sister; she just got under his skin and Fred said, from the look on his face when he was talking, he wouldn't have been surprised if he'd heard Steve had shot *her.*'

Jacko said in a ruminative tone, 'He goes on as if he wouldn't touch a gun if you paid him. Thanks, Smithy, this is really useful information.'

Smithy answered, 'Well, Sheriff, go and get that high-shooting cowboy. See you soon, Jacko.'

Jacko put the phone down and went back to the interview room,

When Jacko had left the room Steve's face had changed into a frown.

Doug looked at him and, seeing his expression, asked, 'Are you alright? Don't you feel well?'

Steve replied, 'Oh, I'm alright. I'm just wondering what he is up to now. Innocent people do go to prison sometimes, don't they?'

Doug said, 'Yes, unfortunately, but it won't happen to you because you have expert counsel. They are going on what they call hearsay evidence and the fact that evidence is coming from someone who is already implicated of being guilty of the crime themselves means it won't stand up in court, okay?'

Steve seemed to get back his confidence and said, 'Thanks, Doug, I feel a lot better about it now. Of course, they can't prove anything against me because I didn't do what that bitch is saying. I just have to keep reminding myself of that.' Then he asked Officer Porter, 'Can I have a glass of water, please?'

The officer got up and went out of the room, to a drinking fountain in the corridor. Once there, he filled a small plastic beaker, came back into the room and gave it to Steve. He drank the water and a few more minutes went by before Jacko re-entered the room.

As Jacko sat down, Officer Porter turned the recorder back on, and said into it, 'DS Jackson has just come back in. Interview resumed at 11:25 am.'

Jacko sat down and said, 'Where were we? Oh yes, I know... Did you shoot Fernandez? You were there at the time he was shot.'

Steve replied, 'You know I didn't. My answer is the same as before.'

'Have you ever shot anyone?'

'That's a daft question. Of course I haven't.'

'Do you know how to shoot a gun?'

'Yes, I think I could work it out.'

'So, you are saying definitively that you have *never* handled a gun.'

'No, I've never handled a gun.'

Jacko was getting ready to ask another question and Doug was getting ready to complain if that question was just more badgering of Steve over the same fact of whether he had ever used a gun.

However, neither had the chance to speak before Steve suddenly said, 'Sorry - I tell a lie... I actually have handled a gun. I forgot; it was just after I left university. I used to go to a gun range with a friend of mine.'

Doug looked surprised, as Jacko asked, 'How could you forget you were a top marksman with a handgun?'

'I wasn't a 'top marksman',' Steve said, shaking his head, 'Yes, I could aim the gun, and I would hit the target nine times out of ten but, when I pulled the trigger, I'd have to close my eyes, so I just stopped going.'

Jacko looked Steve in the eyes and said, a little incredulously, 'You're telling us you actually shut your eyes when you pulled the trigger and somehow still reliably hit the target?'

Steve replied, 'Yes. I've got a very steady hand but, if I kept my eyes open when I pulled the trigger, well, I don't know why but my hand would jerk. So, I stopped going before someone noticed it, because they were talking about me joining the gun team. I'm sorry I gave you the run around about the gun, but I honestly forgot, it was about thirty years ago, and I only went for a few weeks.'

'I'll ask you again, now we know you can hit a target with your eyes shut, do you still say you didn't shoot Fernandez?'

'You know I didn't. You have got the man that I think did the shooting...Sam Blake. And, if you don't think it was him, then what about Lilly's friend? The jailbird, Eric Lang. Do you know about him? I met him once, years ago, and I remember she was very friendly with him because, at the time, I was a bit jealous of him and asked who he was. She said he was just an old friend. I only found out the other day that he was a criminal.'

'It's very convenient you are remembering all this just when we find out you do know how to use a gun.'

Doug interrupted the detective to ask, 'What are you accusing my client of now? How is he to know what information you get and when? He's not psychic. I think this interview has come to the end of the road. So, charge my client now or we are leaving.' He then turned to Steve and said, 'Let's go.'

Jacko noted the termination of the interview and then turned off the recorder as Doug put his paperwork away in his attaché case.

Steve stood up and said, 'Well, DS Jackson, the only time I hope to see you again is in court, when the people who really caused the death of my Joan are on trial.'

'Don't worry,' smiled Jacko, 'Now we know a crime has been committed, we'll be like a dog with a bone; we won't let go till we have it all. And one day you will see me in court, with the guilty parties in the dock. I promise you that.'

Neither Steve nor Doug answered - they just walked out of the room.

Once outside the station, Steve asked, as they got into the waiting limousine, 'Doug, do you think they will leave me alone now and concentrate on Lilly and her fucking dad? I know they did it.'

Doug replied, 'It looks that way to me. I think they believe you and assume Lilly is lying.'

Steve said, 'That's good. I'm going to the golf club for a drink, do you fancy coming, Doug?'

'No thanks, Steve,' he replied. 'I've got a lot of work to do back at the office. Can you drop me off there, please?'

After the two men had left the interview room, Jacko said to Officer Porter, 'Well, we've found nothing to show Lilly Blake wasn't lying. We've been through everything he has and found nothing. I think his solicitor is right, with him we've come to the end of the road unless we turn something else up. But it does seem suspicious that he would 'forget' he used to go to a gun club.'

Officer Porter said, 'I agree with you that his whole story about hitting the target with his eyes shut was strange but, you're right, we really don't have anything on him. Why don't we really go to town on Lilly Blake's story and see if we can shake something loose there that incriminates either one.'

Yes,' agreed Jacko. 'She's definitely got the evidence stacked up against her at the moment: she knew where to get the car, and those brochures and that false wig were found at her dad's place.

Admittedly, she was clearly telling the truth about sending the flowers to Joan's grave, because Steve knew nothing about them... but she could have been doing that just because of a guilty conscience over plotting the woman's death. Still, it's important to remember that Steve Thomson has made millions from his wife's death - and money is a motive as old as time, so we can't just discount Lilly's statement in the light of that.'

With that Jacko picked up his paperwork, put it in a folder and said to Officer Porter, 'Get your lunch now. We will interview Lilly Blake again this afternoon.'

Then he went to his office and picked up the phone, put in a number and was met by a voice that said, 'Tommy here.'

Jacko said, 'Hi, Tommy, I'm calling just to let you know about how the interview with Steve Thomson went, but you can't tell anyone, and that includes Ann. My job is on the line if anything comes out before it's official, okay?'

He replied, 'I promise I won't tell a soul.'

Jacko said, 'Good lad. We've been through the last fifteen years of his records in his offices, and we've also searched his house and grounds, and we didn't find anything to connect him to the story that Lilly Blake told us. I'm going to send a full report to Smithy in London, so he can interview Sam Blake again when he comes out of hospital.'

Tommy said, 'Great. Ann and her dad have just got back together, I don't know how she would take it if he looked like he really was involved. Still, I know it's wrong, but I feel sorry for Sam. I took a liking to him when I met him.

Oh, and I think I ought to tell you this: John, Ann's brother, phoned me this morning and said that Lilly was the woman Ann saw driving the car in Spain. He also passed on that the police told his dad that she is trying to say he is involved. His dad told him this morning he had to go for another interview with the police, but that John shouldn't worry because she is only saying it because he wouldn't get a solicitor for her dad. So, this morning Steve was saying that the police won't do anything to him because he had nothing to do with the murder, apart from trying to save their mum. Then he told John he would see him when he got home in the afternoon. So apparently Steve didn't sound worried at all."

Jacko said, 'Well, don't rush into reassuring Ann about anything just yet. Like I said, we haven't found anything solid to incriminate Steve and we're going to interview the Blakes again this afternoon.

We hope, if she is lying, which seems the most likely option, we can get her to admit that her dad or Eric Lang was the one behind it all. But the investigation is still open, and Steve is still a person of interest, particularly as there's been a couple of inconsistencies in his story, so don't jump the gun and assume it's all rosy just yet. Are you back at your job now?'

Tommy replied, 'Yes, it's just a divorce case.'

Jacko laughed and said, 'Just a divorce case? Is that not good enough these days for you?'

Tommy got flustered and said, 'Don't you start as well! I just mean... Well, I don't know what I mean but I do know that I'm not saying I'm too good to do it. Anyway, Jacko, thanks for keeping me in the picture.'

Jacko replied, as he opened the large bottom drawer of his desk, 'You're welcome, but I need to say bye now. I'm getting my dinner - and a mug of hot coffee, I hope, before it goes cold again.'

Tommy said, 'Thanks again, bye.'

Jacko took his sandwiches from the drawer, opened them and poured out a mug of coffee. Just as he was about to drink it, his phone rang; he put the cup down with such force that some bounced out of the mug and onto his desk.

He picked up the phone and, in a sharp tone, said, 'Yes?'

A voice said, 'Oh no, someone has got their dinner interrupted again! I'll speak to you later, bye.'

Jacko said, as he put the phone on speaker, 'Alright, Smithy, what can I do for you?'

Smithy said, 'I know how you feel, Jacko. I hate a cold mug of coffee as well.'

Jacko replied, 'Just tell me what you want while I drink it.'

Smithy said, 'I'll make it quick. I got your report on Steve Thomson's interview, I just want to be clear that you haven't got any evidence that suggests he was behind things? I don't want to push Sam Blake with his dodgy ticker unless I really have to.'

Jacko replied, 'As far as we're concerned, the case is still open and the evidence against the Blakes is the most damning. Unfortunately, I think we're going to have to push them to try and get to the bottom of things.'

Smithy sighed and said, 'Well, looks like that's what I'll be doing, then. Thanks, Jacko, enjoy your coffee. Bye.'

Jacko turned the phone speaker off as he shook his head and thought, 'Why does that phone always have to ring when I'm having a drink of coffee?

MORE EVIDENCE COMES TO LIGHT

After his dinner Jacko met Officer Porter, and they went to interview room three.

On the way there, Jacko said to the duty officer, 'We are in interview three. Will you send Lilly Blake there? And tell her solicitor to come straight through when he arrives.'

Jacko was setting up his paperwork when the door opened, and an officer stepped inside. Lilly followed him.

Officer Porter said, as he pulled a chair out from the table, 'Sit here, Lilly, please.'

Lilly sat in the seat facing Jacko as the officer who had accompanied her left the room. Ten minutes later the door opened, and her solicitor entered.

Rick pulled the chair next to Lilly out of the way, so he could stand and sort his paperwork out on the table.

As he did, he smiled at Lilly and said, 'Don't worry, Lilly, you will get a good deal.' Then he pulled the chair next to him up to the table and sat down.

Jacko said, in a sharp tone, 'Yes, Lilly, you will get a good deal but *only* if you tell the truth.'

Lilly replied, 'I'm not worried about myself, how is my dad?'

Jacko said, 'Your father, I believe, is getting well. He's grown stronger over the last two days, so you've no need to worry.'

Lilly asked Rick, 'Is he telling me the truth? It's my fault he's in hospital.'

Rick replied, 'Yes, he's telling you the truth. I knew you were worried about your father, so I inquired at the hospital and your father is well. In fact the nurse I spoke to said he's chatting up all the nurses.'

Lilly said, 'Thank God for that.'

Jacko turned on the recorder, logged who was present at the interview and then asked, 'Lilly, is there anything you want to add to your statement or change in it, before we do the interview?'

Lilly replied, 'Yes, I remembered Steve said that he would get his family to put their phones in the safe at home before they went to Spain, so his wife couldn't get called back to England by the firm.'

Jacko said, 'You will have to do better than that! Steve Thomson said he's not involved at all, and that it was all planned by you and your father. He thinks Eric Lang was in it with you as well. What do you have to say to that?'

Lilly looked at Rick and then at Jacko, with anger on her face and said, 'I've told you, I haven't seen or spoken to Eric Lang in years. And what else would you expect Steve to say? He's hardly going to go to the lengths he did to stay squeaky clean and then admit everything to you just because you asked him nicely, is he?'

'Well, Lilly, we got search warrants for everything he owns; we've checked everything we could on him, and we didn't find any evidence that he did what you claimed. What are we supposed to think without anything to suggest he was involved?'

'No,' said Lilly, shaking her head, 'You searched *my* apartment, so you must have found proof of his involvement by now. So, he must be paying you lot to hide it. Was it a lot of money he offered you? God knows he has enough!'

Jacko asked, 'What are you on about? When we searched your apartment, we didn't find anything at all, nevermind something tying Steve to his wife's death.'

'Liar - you know you did. You're all in his pocket.'

At this point, Rick interrupted and said, 'Lilly? You didn't tell me you had proof of Steve's involvement.'

Lilly replied, 'I'm sorry, Rick. My mind went blank when I found out my dad had been arrested and then I was thinking even less clearly when I found out he had suffered a heart attack. I only remembered this morning.' Still looking at Rick, she pointed accusingly at Jacko and continued, 'He knows I had proof. He must have seen it.'

Jacko, in an angry tone said, 'If you think that by saying my officers and I are corrupt you will confuse the case and that will get you off the charge, it won't. If you say you've got evidence, what is it? And why would you think we know about it already?'

Rick got hold of Lilly's arm and squeezed it hard.

She went quiet and he asked, 'Lilly, will you explain to me what you are talking about?'

Lilly was crying by this point, but she pointed at Jacko, and exclaimed, through her tears, 'He told me when they searched my home and office, that they know all the places where people hide things and they would find anything I hid. Well, I had some proof hidden about Steve and now he's claiming they didn't find it...'

Jacko went red with anger and said, 'I don't believe any of the police who searched your apartment would take a bribe, and I certainly didn't. I'll look into it.'

Lilly wasn't listening to Jacko, she just continued talking over him, telling Rick, 'But they must have found my tin box with all the letters and photos in it. It was about a month after Joan's death that Steve told me to empty and cancel the PO Box he had used to communicate with the man he had worked with in Spain. He told me to destroy anything that I found there. By that time, I had heard through the grapevine at work that Ann was claiming that he had let go of her mum on purpose. So, I was worried, Rick, that if Steve had deliberately killed his wife, he might do the same to me. After all, I knew all about his schemes. So, when I went to cancel the PO Box and found two envelopes in it, I took the contents home. It was against Steve's instructions, but I opened them both. One had six photos in it, and on each one was written '*I know who you are*'. The other had the same six photos, but there was a letter with them.'

As they'd been talking at the same time, Jacko hadn't heard the first part of what she had said but he was paying close attention now.

He asked her, 'Will you tell me again how you came by these photos and letter? Who is in the photos? And what did the letter say?'

While Jacko was talking, Lilly was shaking her head and muttering, 'What's the use? If they didn't get handed over to you, they will have been destroyed by now.'

Rick said, 'Lilly, pull yourself together and tell him what he wants to know. He hasn't seen the photos, and he needs to know what they show.'

Lilly lifted her head up and, in a low voice, replied, 'Alright, the photos were of Steve Thomson shooting that madman, Fernandez. I'll tell you again, I went to cancel the PO Box and two envelopes were in it, so I took them home and opened them. One held six photos and the other had the same six photos and a letter.'

Jacko said, 'Well if these photos and letter exist, they are vitally important. I'd like to see the letter in particular rather than asking my questions in a vacuum. So we can all move forward on the same page, we will take a break now, while I ask the officers who searched your apartment to go back again. This time I'll send a sergeant I personally trust to go with them and, if they find your hiding place has been disturbed and is empty, all hell will be released in this station. But, for this to work, you're going to need to tell me where to look.'

Before she could answer, Rick touched Lilly's arm to indicate she should keep quiet and said, 'My client is cooperating and being helpful and we want our deal now, because she was simply a naive young woman duped by a charming older man - she never had any intention to cause Joan Thomson any real harm.'

Jacko replied, 'If the photos and letter are there, I'll make sure she gets a good deal with the Crown Prosecution.'

Rick said, 'Lilly, tell him where the letter and photos are.'

'I thought if you had searched my apartment, you definitely would have found where I hid them,' Lilly said. 'If you go into my bedroom and pull the bed away from the stud wall, you'll find I stuck the skirting board to the wall there with silicon. If you put a sharp knife between the stud wall and the skirting board and run it along the length of the board, it will come away from the wall. Behind it is a hole with a tin in it, and the photos and letter are in the tin.'

As Jacko left the room, Officer Porter said, 'DS Jackson is leaving the room. Interview paused at 1:15 pm.' Then he turned the recorder off.

Jacko went to the chief inspector and asked him to send the same officers who had conducted the original search on Lilly's flat back to search where Lilly had told him to - but asked if this time his good friend Sergeant Holman could be sent with them. Then the chief and Jacko phoned the Crown Prosecution Office and discussed Lilly's claims with them to find out what kind of a deal they would offer her in exchange for the evidence.

As soon as Jacko got out of the chief's office, he phoned Tommy on his mobile.

'Tommy here,' said the voice at the other end of the line.

'Hi, Tommy,' Jacko said, 'Can you do me a favour, as soon as possible?'

Tommy replied, 'Of course, what do you want me to do?'

Jacko said, 'You're friends with John, Ann's brother, right?'

Tommy replied, 'Yes, why?'

Jacko said, 'I don't want you to ask Ann, but John might handle the question I need answered without getting upset.'

Tommy said, 'You've got me curious now, what do you want me to ask him?'

Jacko replied, 'Just ask him if they took their mobiles with them when they went to Spain on the holiday where his mum died.'

Tommy said, 'I know you won't tell me why you want to know, but I'll phone John now and text the answer back to you. Bye.'

Jacko said, 'Good lad, bye.'

Tommy got on to John right away. He was back working in his dad's office again when his mobile rang.

He picked it up from under some papers on his desk, answering it so swiftly he didn't have time to check the caller ID, and said, 'John here. Hello?'

'It's me, Tommy,' he heard in response.

'Oh,' John said, a little bit disappointed. 'When I heard my phone ring, I was hoping it was my dad. Has Ann heard from him at all?'

Tommy replied, 'No, she hasn't. You sound worried, has something happened?'

Just then the landline on the desk rang and John said, 'Can you hold on, Tommy?'

As he picked up the other phone and put it to his ear, he heard his dad say, 'Is that you, John?'

John replied, 'Yes, Dad. Where are you?'

His dad said, 'I'm sorry, John, I just stopped in at the club for a quick drink and I got talking to some friends and lost track of time. I'm glad to say I believe the police now know it was Lilly and her dad who were behind the attack on your mum. I know this is a lot to take in, so feel free to take the rest of the day off and come and join me at the club if you need to. I'm going for a game of golf to try and shake off some of the tension of the last few days. If you don't fancy joining me, I'll see you tonight, when I get home. Love you.'

John replied, 'I love you too, Dad,' then put the phone back on the receiver, and put the mobile back to his ear and asked, 'Are you still there, Tommy?'

'Yes,' said Tommy. 'Was that your dad?'

'Yes,' John replied. 'With all this going on with the police, I was a bit worried he might be out getting drunk, but he's going for a round of golf instead. He even asked if I wanted to join him. Anyway, what can I do for you?'

Tommy said, 'Don't tell Ann I asked you this, but she was saying that after that trip to Spain, she couldn't remember what she had done with her mobile phone. And I just thought you might know what happened to it.'

John said, 'Yes, I actually do - her phone is probably still in the safe where dad made us put all of our mobiles, even his and mum's, when we went to Spain. I got mine back out afterwards, but Ann never came back home, so it probably just got left there. We don't use the safe very often and dad wouldn't have got rid of anything of Ann's - he always hoped she'd come back home. That phone will be no good now though. Why do you want to know?'

Tommy replied, 'Well, as you know Spain isn't a subject Ann will talk about, but she was saying how she had some photos of her mum on that phone that she wished she still had and I was thinking it would be nice if I could track it down for her. If she does mention her mobile again, I'll be able to tell her it might be in your dad's safe - particularly now she's talking to him again. Don't do anything with the phone unless she says it's okay though - you know what she can be like! Anyway, thanks, John. Got to go now, the boss man is calling me! Bye.'

Straight after their conversation, Tommy texted Jacko: *I've had a word with John and he said their dad made them all leave their mobiles in the safe at home when they went to Spain, even their mum and dad. See you soon, TT*

Jacko was on the way back to the interview room when he got Tommy's text. He read it and said to himself, 'Well, she is telling the truth about the mobiles at least.'

With this new information in mind, Jacko phoned Smithy and said, 'If Sam Blake is fit enough to question, would you hold off for now?'

Smithy replied, 'He's making good progress, but even so, I think it will be a good week before we can question him again. Why? What's going on at your end?'

Jacko said, 'Remember that spanner Lilly Blake threw in the works? Well, it just got bigger! I've got to go, I'm in the middle of her interview. Speak soon.'

Smithy just said, 'Okay,' and put the phone back down on his desk.

Then, as he passed the canteen, he popped his head in and said to one of the officers in there, 'I'm in interview room three. Would you bring four coffees to us, please?'

When Jacko entered the interviewing room, Rick said, 'Well, we've been sitting here for over an hour and a quarter. Have you got any news for us?'

Jacko, as he sat down, said, 'I've been in touch with the prosecutor and they said, if the photos and letter are real, they will only charge Lilly with aiding and abetting a murder rather than murder itself. They will also ask for her help to be taken into account during sentencing... But we are still waiting for the results of the search, so I don't know if that deal will be going ahead yet.'

Rick said, 'Lilly, that's a good deal. It's the best we can get, with you pleading guilty.'

Lilly gave Rick a weak smile as a knock sounded on the door.

Rick said, 'Well, Lilly, it looks like our wait is over.'

As Rick was talking to Lilly, Jacko said, 'Come in.'

The door opened and an officer came in, carrying a tray with four mugs of coffee on it. He placed the mugs on the table and took the tray with him when he left.

Jacko smiled and said, 'I ordered four coffees - one for each of us - because that's what you requested last time.'

Almost simultaneously, they picked their mugs up and had a drink.

Rick said, 'The job must be looking up if the police can afford mugs now. Weren't there any plastic beakers left?'

Jacko replied, 'I think it's safe that I got the drinks from the canteen. I don't think anyone in here is going to cause trouble with the mugs, do you?' Then he continued, 'I've told DS Smith not to question your father for now, and if the photos and letter are real, he won't be bothered again.'

Rick said, in a sarcastic tone, 'You did send someone to pick up the photos, didn't you?'

Jacko said in a tone to match Rick's, 'Well, what do you think?'

Rick said, 'I think we have been sitting here for a couple of hours now, that's what.'

Lilly nodded, saying, 'My legs are cramping, and I would like to go to the toilet.'

Rick said, 'I'm requesting a toilet and short break from sitting for my client.'

Jacko picked up the phone and asked, 'Will you send a female officer to interview room three, please?'

Almost immediately, a policewoman knocked and walked into the room, and Jacko said, 'Please take Miss Blake to the toilets and let her walk round the yard for up to fifteen minutes afterwards. We've been cooped up in here for quite a while.'

As the officer said, 'Follow me, Miss Blake,' Lilly stood and followed her out the room, walking in front of her down the corridor.

When Lilly got back, she sat back at the table, in the same chair she had used earlier.

Rick said, 'Well, Lilly's back. Where are your men with the photos? Lilly's apartment is only half an hour away, have they got lost?'

Jacko said, 'Maybe they can't find them because they don't exist? What do you think?'

Lilly shouted, 'I've told you what I think - you're all corrupt.'

Rick said, 'Calm down, Lilly.'

She started crying and muttering over and over, 'That bastard paid them off. I know it.'

Rick put his arm round her and said, 'Why don't you see where your men are?'

Jacko nodded, getting up to leave the room, as he said, 'I'll be back as soon as I can.'

He was on his way to the chief inspector's office to find out what was going on, when the first officer he saw said, 'Jacko, the two men and the sergeant you sent to search that apartment have been held up. There was a big crash on the motorway just in front of them, and they had to stop and help out.'

Jacko said, 'I knew there would be a good reason for the hold up. Actually, I have a job for you. Will you go to *Rose's Florist* and ask them who paid for the flowers that they send to Joan Thomson's grave every week?'

The officer nodded and left. Jacko went to see the duty officer, and asked, 'Have you any idea when the men doing the search at Lilly Blake's will be back?'

The duty officer said, 'The traffic police have taken over from them. They are on their way to the apartment now... and they know where to look, so I'd say about an hour.'

Jacko said, 'Thanks.'

Then he made his way back to interview room three. On the way there he had to pass the canteen, so he called in and got another four coffees on a tray. When he got to the interview room, he couldn't open the door. He had his hands full, holding the tray, so he tapped on the door with his foot.

Officer Porter said, 'Come in.'

Jacko tapped a bit harder. Officer Porter got up and opened the door, and they were all surprised to see Jacko standing there with the tray in his hands. Officer Porter opened the door wider, so Jacko could walk in with the tray, which he carried over to the table, placing it down in the centre.

Jacko said, 'Help yourself.'

The other three picked a mug each and, as Jacko picked up the final one, he and Officer Porter sat down in their chairs.

Rick took a drink and said, 'Well, what have you found out?'

Jacko told them about the crash on the motorway and said, 'My men will be back here with the results in about three quarters of an hour, so make yourselves comfortable and, Lilly, don't worry. None of my men would take a bribe, I can promise you that. So if the photos and letter are there, no one will bother your father again.'

Lilly wiped her face with some tissues, sitting up straight in her chair as she did so, and said, 'If you're right about no one taking a bribe, the tin will be there with the photos and the letter. The only promise I want off you is for you all to leave my dad alone.'

Rick said, 'Lilly, they will stick to their promises, so try to relax.'

Half an hour later there was a knock at the door.

Rick and Lilly looked at one another, and Rick said, 'Let's hope this is it.'

At the same time Jacko said, 'Come in.'

The officer who had told Jacko about the crash entered and whispered in Jacko's ear, '*Rose's Florist* said they have a standing order delivered directly into their accounts from an E. Blake at the beginning of every month.'

Jacko said, 'Thank you,' and the officer left.

Lilly and Rick both looked at Jacko expectantly, so he said, 'No, sorry, that's not about your tin. But it is helping me to believe you.'

Jacko said to Rick, 'I would like to ask Lilly a few more questions, while we are waiting.'

He turned the recorder back on and said, 'Lilly Blake's interview, resuming at 3:30 pm,' then he asked, 'Lilly, if Steve did what you say he did, and on his daughter's birthday, even you must think he's an evil man, surely?'

Lilly said, 'I guess I told myself he didn't really mean it - that Joan's death was an accident. Because I loved him, I wanted to believe him.'

'But you knew in your heart that he murdered his wife, didn't you?'

'Yes, I suppose I did... but I didn't want to believe it.'

'Lilly, if you knew he was a murderer, why did you stay with him?'

'I loved him and, even though I was afraid of him on some level, I couldn't leave him. I know I should have because even though I know he did actually love his wife, the money and power were more important to him. That's why I kept the photos and letter, because I knew one day he might fall out of love with me, and I might have an 'accident'. I hid a letter with all this on in my personal documents, the ones I knew my dad would go through if anything happened to me.'

Jacko replied 'If you are telling the truth, that's good. You definitely should have.'

Just then there was another knock on the door, and Jacko said, 'Come in,'

Rick looked at Lilly and said, 'Well, this must be the photos and letter.'

Sergeant Holman came in with a small white plastic bag.

Jacko said into the recorder, 'An officer has just brought a white plastic bag in from Lilly Blake's apartment.'

Sergeant Holman handed the bag to Jacko and whispered, 'This is what you're waiting for.'

As he took it, Jacko whispered back, 'You're only right. Thank you.'

The officer turned and left, as Rick said with a frown on his face, 'A plastic bag, Lilly?'

She replied, 'It's in a plastic bag in case I ever got a burst pipe and flooded - that way the photos and letter wouldn't get damaged.'

While she was talking, Jacko turned the bag upside down and emptied the contents out. A small biscuit tin wrapped in a transparent plastic bag with Sellotape round it fell onto the table.

Jacko said into the recorder, 'Inside the white plastic bag was a biscuit tin, wrapped in another, see-through, bag.'

Jacko struggled a bit to get the Sellotape and bag off the tin. Then he opened the tin and counted aloud that there were twelve photos and left the letter inside it.

He was amazed when he saw the photo of Steve Thomson with a gun in his hand, standing over a man lying on the ground. Another showed Steve shaking hands with a man by an old black MG; Jacko could see the man was Fernandez, the dead man from the previous photo. At first, he thought they had made a huge break in the case, but then he moved on to look at the next photo and saw it showed Steve Thomson, standing over Fernandez with the gun pointing down at him. The photo was from Fernandez's actual perspective, revealing what the dead man would see if he was looking up at the man who had just shot him.

Jacko thrust the picture towards Lilly and Rick, saying angrily, 'These photos must be fake. You've just set them up, to make it look like Steve Thomson has shot this man. A dead man couldn't take this picture - and nor could anyone else, without Thomson seeing them doing so!'

Lilly shouted, in a crying voice, 'Of course they're real. Do you think I made them? I couldn't make fake photos if I tried. I don't know how to use Photoshop - I don't even use filters on my phone, for God's sake. Now I know you're on his side. Is that bastard paying you as well?'

Rick interrupted, putting his hand on Lilly's arm to calm her down, as he said, 'I don't believe anyone is getting paid, but I do also believe Lilly is telling the truth. So, I suggest you get the photos checked out to see what can account for that photo being in the pile.'

The fact Jacko was still angry could be heard in his voice, as he said, 'You're right about the first thing, Rick: Steve Thomson's paying no one at this station. But fake photos can easily be made on a computer. Did your father make them?'

Lilly went red with anger and shouted, 'No, my dad doesn't even know how to use a computer. He's never had one. And you can talk all you want about not being paid off - I don't trust you. I want Rick to read the letter first. Will you read it, Rick?'

Rick replied, 'I would like to see it before they open it, but I'm afraid that's not our choice anymore, Lilly. It's in police custody now. I can't do anything without their permission.'

Jacko said, 'Lilly, you don't trust me, but I do want you to realise that the police at this station have integrity and that no-one is being paid off by anyone. We just want to see justice done. So, Rick, you take the letter out of the tin and hand it to me, so Lilly can see there's been no funny business, and I'll read it out loud, so everyone gets to know what is in it at once and Lilly can check no details are being changed.'

While Jacko was talking, Lilly calmed herself down. Once she seemed ready, Rick took the letter out of the tin, showed it to Lilly, so she could see it was the same letter she had placed in the box; then he handed it to Jacko. Jacko took it out of the envelope, so he could read it aloud but, when he unfolded the letter, it was written in Spanish.

Jacko picked up the phone, dialled the duty sergeant and said, 'Can you get me a Spanish interpreter? They'll need to be brought along to interview room three.' He put the phone back on the receiver, and said, 'We'll only have to wait a short while. One will come from the university just down the road.'

Then he looked at Lilly and asked, 'Did you read this letter, Lilly?'

She sat up straighter in her chair and replied in a sharp tone, 'I looked at it, but it's in Spanish and I can't read Spanish… and before you accuse me or my dad of writing it, neither of us can do that either.'

Lilly sat there, looking a sad mess, but when she looked at Jacko, he could see the contempt for him in her eyes.

Within twenty minutes an officer knocked on the door and Jacko said, 'Come in.'

The officer opened the door for the interpreter. She walked in, introduced herself and stood by the table they were sitting at, as the officer closed the door and headed away again.

Jacko gave her his seat, and then handed her the letter, and asked her to read it out loud in English, so they could all hear as she translated it.

She cleared her throat as she looked at the letter, and then she started to read, saying, 'I know your name is Steve Thomson and that you own the firm named '*Kenwright's*'. If anything happens to me, a friend of mine will send another copy of this letter to the cops, so don't do anything stupid. These are just some of the photos I have of you, and I also have a film of you shooting Fernandez. Presumably you thought he was the only one who knew you and who could tie you to the car that nearly ran down your wife, but you were wrong.

You might not have seen me when you first met up with Fernandez to organise buying *our* car, but I was there, with a gun and a camera - just like I was the night you were supposed to pay him for the photos we took of you buying the MG.

As you can see, I got some more photos that night, even though you picked an isolated place to do the swap. Fernandez made sure he stood under the lamp you had chosen as the place to meet. We'd even visited earlier that day and put a brighter bulb in it, to make sure you couldn't take him by surprise and so we could get some more photos of you. Fernandez wanted to have evidence of you paying him off, to add to your motivation to pay the next time he blackmailed you. He was planning on taking you for everything he could. Of course, you put an end to that.

I was supposed to shoot you if you tried anything but, really, I was only too happy when you shot Fernandez. He was getting out of hand; I knew he'd get us in trouble one day. So, I'm not complaining. Now I get to keep all of the money you paid us for the car and the job we did to reinforce it.

We knew you were going to kill your wife from the way you carried on about how she 'kept you down', but we thought you were just going to have someone run her over. It wasn't until your girl saw the car and asked to buy it for her dad, that we worked out what you were up to. She obviously didn't know what you were intending, or she wouldn't have paid us to ship the car back to England. She was overjoyed you bought it - you must have had her believing everything you said, and we were only too happy to ship the car to England, out of our way.

After we saw it on the news, we realised just how clever your plan to cause your wife's death was. I must say, it was brilliant the way you stopped by the lowest part of the wall, so you looked like a hero trying to save your wife, when really you wanted her dead... and it was a genius plan to have your own kids there as witnesses for how you tried to save her.

So, why am I writing all this to you? Well, you never saw me, but you know the car came from my garage and that *someone* took those photos Fernandez was blackmailing you with. It wouldn't take you long to work out it was probably me. I can tell from how minutely you planned your wife's death, and from what you did to Fernandez, that you don't want to leave any loose threads. I was impressed at how you even thought to pat him down for a camera after you'd shot him. You're clearly a thorough man and I don't fancy being your next target.

I want to make it clear to you that the blackmail was only Fernandez's thing. It's a dodgy and dangerous business and I'm not interested in pursuing it. I won't be asking you for any more money and I don't intend to tell anyone you planned your wife's death. So, you are alright - you're in the clear as long as you leave me alone.

But, if you come after me, then my friend will send all of the information and the pictures in this letter to the cops. Sadly, for you, even though you did find and take the pinhole camera from Fernandez's top pocket, the whole time you were with him, that camera was sending pictures to the computer in my office.

Not only that but, as I said, I was supposed to shoot you if you did anything to Fernandez, and I did shoot you - just with my own camera. So, you may have got the camera off Fernandez but, as you can see on the pictures I've sent you, I've got you killing him caught from all angles. The pinhole camera photos might be a bit blurry but you're so close to Fernandez that even a blind man could recognize you in them, and the long-shots from *my* camera are as clear as day. Fernandez always said it was best to get the top surveillance gear in our line of work.

So, remember, I don't care about what you did to Fernandez; this isn't a blackmail letter - just leave me alone and we can both get on with our lives.'

The interpreter said, 'It just ends there; there's no signature.'

Jacko said to her, 'Thank you for coming on such short notice. Don't forget to log the job with the duty officer at the counter on the way out, so that you are paid.'

With that she left the room, as Rick said, 'Well, that letter tells you how the photo was taken. Now, with all the help Lilly has given you, the additional testimony in this letter that even the criminals involved didn't think she knew it was a murder plot *and* the way you haven't believed her whilst she's been trying to assist you in your investigation, I think you should put in a good word for her regarding the charges. The worst thing she thought she was doing was to give her boss a fright.'

Jacko said, 'She has already been guaranteed a good deal and I will try to get her a better one, but it is really up to the Crown Prosecution Office. I do think they'll take this new evidence into consideration.' Then he continued, 'Lilly, has Steve seen these photos or the letter?'

Lilly replied, 'No, he would have destroyed them.'

Jacko nodded thoughtfully and brought the interview to a close; then he turned off the recorder, and said, 'Officer Porter, will you take Lilly to her cell?'

As Lilly got up to go with Officer Porter, Rick said to her, 'I'll be in to see you tomorrow, to start sorting out your defence.'

Then he put his paperwork in his attaché case and followed Officer Porter and Lilly out of the room. Lilly was taken to her cell and Rick went back to his office.

Jacko also left the interview room, heading straight to the duty sergeant and saying, 'I want two officers to go and get Steve Thomson. Tell them to be nice about it, but if he refuses to come in they should arrest him and bring him in for questioning. Tell them to be careful too - it seems he's a dangerous man. Let me know when you have him in the station.'

From there he stopped at the computer lab, took a quick scan of the letter and sent it off to his contact in Spain. Then he went to the chief inspector's office and told him how the case was going.

Jacko showed the chief the photos and said, 'I'm going to get the forensic techs to give the photos the once over, to make sure they aren't fake. I've also sent a scan of the letter to the Spanish police and asked them to check with Alonso's son for samples of his father's writing, so they can compare the two. I've requested that they let me know what they find out as soon as possible.'

The chief said, 'They are excellent quality to say they were taken in the dark and with only the lamp light to illuminate them. They are almost too good to believe.'

Jacko said, 'Yes, that's why I would like the photos checked today, Chief.'

The chief frowned and said, 'The forensic department has gone home.'

Jacko said, 'I know. Can you bring one of the analysts back in to check the photos? I want to interview Steve Thomson this evening.'

The chief said, 'Alright, but I will have to pay him overtime money and we haven't any to spare.'

'Like I said, I'm getting the letter checked as well, to make sure it's not forged, but that'll be happening over in Spain, so they'll be paying for that. Hopefully that will help us cover the expenses at this end."

The chief frowned and said, 'Well let's hope you're right about his guilt - Steve Thomson has got a lot of pull in this country. I'm putting a lot of faith in you, but I'll leave it all in your capable hands.'

Jacko replied, 'Okay, boss, I'll keep you informed.'

With that Jacko left and went to his own office. On the way there he met Officer Porter, who had dropped Lilly off at the cells and then spent a little time in the canteen.

Porter asked, 'How did you get on with the chief?'

Jacko said, 'Oh, the usual way. He's worried about paying out for overtime and he left it in my 'capable hands' as usual, that way if it goes wrong, it's my fault, and if we solve the case, he will take the credit.'

Porter said, 'Well, good luck then, sir.'

Jacko said, 'I'll see you in the interview room when they bring Steve Thomson in.'

Then he went into his office, walked round his desk, sat down on his chair, opened the bottom drawer in his desk and took out a flask. He poured himself a mug of coffee and sat there, drinking it, while he went over Lilly's statement again. Then he phoned Diego at home, in Spain.

Diego answered in Spanish, 'Hello, Diego here.'

Jacko said, 'Hi Diego, it's me, Jacko.'

Diego swapped to English, saying, 'Hi, Jacko, how can I help you?'

Jacko asked, 'Will you do me a big favour?'

Diego answered, 'No problem, what do you want me to do?'

Jacko said, 'Well, I've sent a scan of a letter to your old police station, so it can be checked to see if it was written by the gangster Alonso. I know from Tommy that you know his son and, whilst it's not quite official what I'm asking you to do, it would be a great help to me to speed things up if you would go to Alonso's old garage and persuade his son to quickly provide a writing sample for the police, so it's ready when they ask for it.'

'I know the handwriting expert the station uses,' Diego replied, 'he's a friend of mine. I'll ask him to make it a priority job, so he gets it back to the police as soon as possible, once they send it through to him. It shouldn't take long if I do that. I think you will get the report back in a couple of hours.'

Jacko said, 'Thanks, Diego. I owe you one... Actually, let's make that two - do you remember whether Steve Thomson had a phone on him when he was in Spain?'

Diego said, 'You know, I do remember because we thought it was a little strange at the time: it was brand new and didn't list any contacts - there were only numbers in the call list.'

'Thanks again, Diego' Jacko said, 'I didn't actually think you'd know, but that's really helpful information. I'll let you know how it all goes. Goodbye.'

'Thank you, Jacko. I'll be waiting to hear from you.'

Jacko kept hold of the phone and called Tommy, who answered, 'Tommy here.'

Without even saying hello, Jacko said, 'You know the rules, Tommy. You can't tell anyone what I'm about to tell you. It could ruin our entire investigation, and my job is on the line. So, when I say anyone, I mean anyone, and I'm afraid that definitely means Ann as well.'

Tommy asked, 'Is the case coming to an end then?'

Jacko replied, 'I think so. It all depends on some photos that have come into our possession, and whether they are fake or real. I don't know if it's good or bad news for you and Ann.'

Tommy asked, 'Why, what has happened?'

Jacko replied, 'Well, the evidence does now point to Steve Thomson.'

Surprised, Tommy caught his breath and said, 'That must be rubbish. He tried to save Joan. I know, I was there. You must be wrong?'

Jacko said, 'Well, we'll find out soon enough. I have sent two officers to pick him up and if he won't come, they are to arrest him. The evidence is quite damning, Tommy. I've only told you this because of the work you've put into it, so - no matter how you feel right now - keep this news to yourself, okay? Bye.'

Still shaken, Tommy replied, 'Okay, Jacko, I will do. Bye,'

As he put his phone back in his pocket, he said out loud to himself, 'When is this going to end? It just seems to get worse the longer it goes on. At this rate, it looks like I'll never get married.'

STEVE IS ASKED TO COME TO THE STATION

A police car pulled up outside of the Thomson's gates and an officer got out and pressed the button on the intercom.

John answered, 'Who is it? And what do you want?'

The officer said, 'It's the police, and we want to come in and have a word with Mr Thomson.'

John replied, 'My dad isn't home right now.'

The officer said, 'Well, let us in and we'll wait for your father.'

John said, 'I can see you and the police car through the monitor here. Will the both of you please show your warrant cards to the camera, so I can see them?'

The other officer passed his warrant card out of the driver's window, and the officer John was talking to raised them towards the camera by the top of the gatepost. Satisfied, John pressed the remote for the gates to open and, as the officers drove over the small bridge and up the long driveway, the two of them looked around in amazement.

The driver said, 'This place must have cost a pretty penny,' while the other just nodded. The police drove round the house and parked at the back of it. Then they both got out and walked round to the front, where John was standing at the door, with his mobile in his hand.

As the two policemen approached him, John asked, 'Why have you parked round the back of the house? There's lots of room here in the front of the house to park.'

The officer who had been driving the car replied, 'We like to be discreet where we can. You don't want your neighbours talking about you.'

John gave a sarcastic smile and said, 'What neighbours? There are none for miles. Anyway, I rang my dad and told him you're here. He was at the golf club, but he's on his way home now. Do you want to come in and take the weight off your feet?'

The other officer said, 'No, thank you, sir. We'll bring the car round to the front and wait for your dad there.'

It was an hour later that Steve arrived home, in a chauffeur-driven limousine which parked next to the police car.

He got out and said, 'Thank you.'

The chauffeur said, 'Will you be needing me at all tonight, sir?'

Steve replied, 'No, that will be all.'

The chauffeur nodded and drove off down the driveway.

The two police got out of their car, so Steve went over to them and asked, 'You want a word with me?'

One asked, 'Are you Steve Thomson?'

'Yes,' Steve replied.

The officer asked, 'Will you come with us, sir? DS Jackson would like a word with you at the station.'

Steve asked, 'I take it I can go and get freshened up first?'

He said, 'Certainly, sir.'

Steve said, 'Come in and take the weight off your feet.'

The two officers smiled, and Steve asked, 'Did I say something funny?'

The driver answered, 'No, sir, it's just that your son used the same words when he invited us in.'

Steve smiled and said, 'Well, you know what they say, like father like son. Please follow me.'

He showed them into the living room and the two of them stood looking round the room in amazement.

Steve said, 'Take a seat, I won't be long. Would you like something to drink?'

They both replied, 'No, thank you.'

Steve left the room, and one said, 'He said, 'take a seat'! A year's wages wouldn't buy the seat I'm sitting on.'

While they were waiting, they could hear that John and his dad were talking in the den.

John asked, 'What do you think they want to talk to you about?'

Steve replied, 'It will be about Lilly and her dad. I think they have all the evidence they need to put the both of them away. I think they're going to tell me that they're going to charge them. I've got to go now, John. I don't like to keep the police waiting.' Then he smiled at John and said, 'Go and play a game on your Xbox thing. I'll let you know what they tell me when I get back.'

John said, as he sat down in front of the television and picked up the remote control, 'Okay, Dad, but I get a funny feeling every time the police ask you to go to the station… and it's not an Xbox, it's a PS5.'

Steve was as good as his word. He went from the den up to his bedroom and was back with the two officers in less than twenty minutes; an hour later they were walking up the station steps.

They went inside and up to the counter, where one of the officers said to the duty sergeant, 'Mr Steve Thomson is here to speak to DS Jackson.'

The duty sergeant picked up the phone, spoke into it and nodded in response to what was said at the other end of the line.

Then he put the phone back on the receiver and said, 'Show Mr Thomson to interview room one. DS Jackson will be there by the time you get there.'

Jacko went into the interview room with Officer Porter and sat down saying, 'The air-conditioning isn't working in here,' just as the constable said, 'It's so hot in here!'

They both took their jackets off and Officer Porter sat down again, as Jacko stood by the table and rang through to the duty sergeant to see if there were any other interview rooms free.

'Sorry, Porter', he said when he got off the phone, 'They're all busy. Looks like we're stuck in here.'

He remained standing at the table, studying his paperwork, until Steve followed the two officers through the door, with one saying, 'Mr Steve Thomson is here.'

The officer stepped aside to let Steve enter the room properly and, as soon as he saw Jacko and Officer Porter together at the table, Steve's smile turned to a frown.

'I'm not here for good news, like I thought, am I?' he asked.

Jacko replied, as he pulled a chair that was facing Officer Porter out from the table, 'Mr Thomson, please take a seat in this chair. You could be right, so let's find out. I strongly suggest you call your solicitor before we start.'

Steve, with an angry look on his face, sat in the chair and got his mobile out of his jacket pocket, putting in the numbers to call Doug's firm.

A voice said, 'Mr Douglas Thomas' office. How can I help you?'

Steve was going red with anger, and said in a sharp tone, 'I'm Steve Thomson, and I'm in the police station *again*, being questioned *again*. Put me through to Doug. Now.'

The secretary said, 'Right away, Mr Thomson.'

A few moments later, Doug answered, 'What's going on, Steve?'

He replied angrily, 'I'm back in this station being questioned again and they said I need you here now.'

Doug said, 'I'll be there right away.'

Steve hung up the call, glared at Jacko and snarled, 'My solicitor is on his way. What have you dragged me back here for? You know Lilly and her dad did it all.'

Jacko said, in a serious voice, 'I advise you to say nothing until your solicitor gets here, though if you want to make a statement before he gets here, that's up to you.'

Steve shot up out of his chair so swiftly that it crashed backwards onto the floor, shouting, 'Why should I make a statement? *I* didn't do anything. You've got the bastards that caused Joan's death. It was that cow Lilly and her dad - why haven't you charged them yet?'

Jacko quietly got up and walked around the table to pick up Steve's chair, saying, 'Mr Thomson, sit down and calm down please.'

Steve did as he was asked, and Jacko went back to his side of the table and sat down again.

Steve said, 'It's not right, me being here like this. I think you just want to make a name for yourself. I didn't cause my wife's death, and you know it, so what are you persecuting me for?'

Jacko just looked at his paperwork, refusing to answer Steve's question or engage with him further in case speaking to him without his solicitor present might jeopardise the interview.

From then on no one spoke, till there was a knock on the door about half an hour later, and Jacko said, 'Come in.'

The door opened and Doug, carrying his attaché case, walked in and sat down next to Steve.

As he sat down, he said to Jacko, 'I would like a few minutes with my client in private to find out why he is here.'

Steve butted in and said, 'It's no good asking me why I'm here, they haven't told me. The only thing I can come up with is that they want to frame me for something I didn't do.'

Jacko said, 'Before we start, this could be a lengthy process and it's very warm in here, would you like to take your jackets off?'

Steve and Doug both stood up and took their jackets off. When they sat down, Jacko turned the recorder on and noted who was present at the interview.

Then Jacko said, 'New evidence regarding your wife's case has come to light. When you were in Spain and your wife was killed, did you have a mobile phone with you?'

Steve hesitated briefly and then answered, 'Yes, I gave it to the Spanish police to get my address when they drove me to the villa. I don't see what it has to do with my wife's death.'

'Ah,' said Jacko, 'well, it has come to light that your children thought you had left your mobile phone at home in the safe. In fact, that you personally insisted that the whole family left them at home, even those belonging to you and your wife, so how did you come to have one in Spain?'

Steve went red with anger again and shouted, 'What are you going on about a bloody phone for? I bought it in Spain, okay?'

'So, how come none of your family knew you had it?'

'I kept it on silent because I didn't want our holiday to be interrupted by business other people could take care of. That's why I got Joan to leave her mobile at home, but then I bought one, so we still had a phone in case of an emergency.'

'You've got a reputation as a man who wastes nothing, so have you still got the mobile phone that you bought in Spain? If you have, we would like to see it.'

Steve gave a sarcastic laugh and replied, 'Yes, I hold onto things that are useful, but a ten-year-old mobile is well past its sell by date. I haven't got that anymore.'

'Fine,' said Jacko. 'Did you buy the car that nearly ran your family down and caused the death of your wife?'

'No, I didn't, I never saw the car till the day it drove at my family, and I haven't seen it since.'

'Do you know the man called Fernandez who was shot and killed?'

'Not this again,' Steve groaned in frustration. 'I've told you I don't know how many times; I don't think I ever met a man named Fernandez.'

'Right. Have you ever been to a garage in Spain called *Alonso's*?'

'I might have done. I've got business links with lots of garages all over Europe and even send cars to Africa.'

'Do you own, or have you ever owned, a gun?'

'No, I've never owned a gun,' Steve snapped, then he turned to his solicitor and said, angrily, 'Why are you even here, Doug? You're just sitting there and saying nothing to help me.'

Doug replied, 'I can't answer for you, and I have told you before: for any question you've already answered, if you're asked it again, just say 'no comment'. Do the same for any other questions you don't want to answer too.'

Jacko asked again, 'Did you buy the car that nearly ran your wife down? And do you know the man Fernandez?'

This time Steve just folded his arms and snapped, 'No comment.'

At that, Jacko took a photo out of his folder and placed it on the desk in front of Steve and Doug. It showed Steve shaking hands with Fernandez as they were looking at an old, black MG, that sat just behind them.

Then Jacko said, as he handed a copy to Doug for his records, 'I'll ask you again, did you buy the car that nearly ran your wife down, and do you know the man Fernandez?'

Doug looked surprised and even a bit angry, as Steve went white with shock.

Steve sat in silence for a moment with all three men staring at him, and then he slowly said, 'Yes... I remember now, I didn't know that man's name was Fernandez, though. That picture must have been taken about... fifteen years ago? That man told me he owned the garage I was visiting and that his name was Alonso.

If you go through my financial records, you will see I was going round garages, buying luxury cars about that time, but I didn't buy *that* car. That photo must be from back then.'

Jacko said, 'He said he was called Alonso, and he owned a garage you were visiting? But when I asked you if you knew a garage owner called Alonso, you said several times that the only Alonso you knew was a doctor. So, I'll ask you again... Have you ever met anyone involved with cars named Alonso?'

Steve said, 'Alright, so I met a garage owner who called himself Alonso. Like I said, it was fifteen years ago, and I didn't remember till you showed me the photo. It's not a big deal.'

Jacko asked, 'Right. So, we know you met this man and we know you bought the car off him, so just tell the truth, you did buy the car, didn't you?'

'No,' Steve replied, 'I don't know what's going on here. I didn't buy that car, then or later.'

Jacko asked, 'Do you own a gun?'

'I don't have a gun. The last time I touched one, I was in my twenties.'

'Did you shoot Fernandez? That is, the man you say you thought was called Alonso.'

'No, but I remember now that the Spanish police told me a man had been shot. They didn't tell me that was his name.'

Jacko took another photo out of his folder and showed it to Steve and Doug, handing a copy to Doug, and saying, 'For your records,' before continuing for the benefit of the recorder, 'This photo shows Steve Thomson standing with a gun in his hand over Fernandez, who is dead on the ground.'

There was silence in the room again for a moment, while Steve and Doug took in the details of the photograph, and then Jacko said, 'Well? What's your explanation for this photo?'

'I don't know, but I do know that definitely didn't happen; that's not me in that photo. It must be a fake, most likely made by Lilly and her dad. Lilly is great on the computer - she could easily take her dad out the picture and put me in his place.

In fact, the one of me and Fernandez in that garage is most likely to be fake as well. I don't really remember meeting him in the garage and, even though it was fifteen years ago and I was in Spain going round buying cars from lots of garages, and I've only just remembered now that one was *Alonso's* garage, I just don't remember meeting that man. I don't feel like I did.'

Jacko said, 'Well, if you say so. We are just waiting to hear back on that from our analyst.'

Doug got angry at this and, as he pushed the photos back towards Jacko's folder, he exclaimed, 'You don't even know if these photos are real? So, you're on a fishing trip? This could cost you your job and the Justice department a lot of money.'

Jacko didn't seem to be listening; instead, he picked the phone up and asked, 'Have you got my reports about the photos and that letter? They should be here by now.' Then he continued, in an angry tone, 'What do you mean the reports are in my in-tray? God, you lot would make a saint swear! Well, open it and let me know what it says.'

The other three men watched him fixedly as he listened to the voice on the other end of the phone, all the time keeping his face impassive and giving nothing away.

After about a minute, Jacko said, 'And what did the report from Spain say about the handwriting?' Then he went red in the face and almost shouted, 'Well, bloody well open it now and let me know.'

Jacko listened a little while longer, then he put the phone down and said to Doug, 'You should keep those photos… and I've several more to give you, as well as a very incriminating letter.'

As Doug went white with shock, Jacko turned and looked Steve in the eyes as he said, 'Steve Thomson, I'm charging you with the murder of your wife, Joan Thomson, ten years ago on the sixteenth of August, and the murder of Isaac Fernandez, ten years ago in the week commencing the twentieth of August.'

Steve shouted at Doug, 'Well, don't just sit there. What are you going to do about this lot? They are trying to pull a fast one here. I didn't do it.'

Doug had recovered somewhat and had an angry look on his face as he said to Steve, 'Like I told Lilly when you told me to drop her case, I will get you a good solicitor, but I can't represent you anymore.

I knew Joan all her life, she was a good friend, and her father helped me to start my firm. It wouldn't be right. You need a solicitor who has no connection to Joan or the Kenwright firm... and, in all honesty, with what I know, I just couldn't represent you and do a good job. I don't even want to.'

Steve's face was twisted with hate as he roared at Doug, 'You're just a rat leaving a sinking ship.'

Doug looked at him and thought to himself, 'No, I'm a ship getting rid of a wicked, conniving rat,' but all he calmly said to Steve was, 'I'll tell John the police have arrested you.'

Jacko got up and opened the door, and two officers who had been waiting outside came into the room.

Jacko said, 'Go with the officers, Steve.'

As Steve stood up and wiped the sweat off his forehead, his hanky touched one of his eyelids and tears started running down his cheeks.

Officer Porter said, 'He's crying,' as Steve wiped the tears away.

Steve snarled, 'I'm not fuckin' crying.'

Then he went out of the room, sandwiched between the two officers, muttering over and over, all the way to his cell, 'It's not right... That fucking stupid fucking cow, bringing the car over here for her bloody stupid father. If the fucking daft cow had just told me, I could have got ten old cars for him...'

When Doug came out of the police station, he got into his car and drove straight to John's home.

He pressed the intercom for the gate and John asked, 'Who is it?'

Doug replied, 'It's me, Doug Thomas.'

'Is my dad with you?' John asked.

Doug said, 'No, John. Let me in, please, I need to talk to you.'

The gates opened and Doug drove up to the house.

John came out to meet him and, before Doug could even get out of his car, John had walked up to the car, and asked, 'Where is my dad? Wasn't he with you?'

Doug got out of the car and said, 'There's no way to make this easy for you, John. I'm so sorry, son, but your dad has been arrested for your mother's murder.'

John's legs buckled, so Doug put his arm around John and led him into the house.

John just kept saying, 'But my dad tried to save my mum. I was there. I saw him. They must be wrong.'

Doug got John back inside the house and took him through to the living room. He sat John down in an easy chair and called for a maid, asking her, 'Will you make John a warm, milky, sweet cup of tea, please?'

The maid left the room to make the cup of tea, while John sat with his head in his hands and Doug took his mobile out of his pocket.

He phoned Emma but couldn't get through, so then he called Ann's number instead.

He was surprised to hear a voice at the other end of the line say, 'This is Ann's phone, Tommy speaking. Sorry, Ann can't come to the phone right now. Can I help?'

'Hi Tommy, it's Doug, the Thomson's family solicitor. I think you should ask Ann to come and stay with John. Their dad has been arrested, and John has taken it really badly.'

Tommy said, 'Yes, we know about Steve. Jacko has just been here to deliver the news to Ann and I that he's been arrested for her mum's murder. So Ann is beside herself too. I'll get her over there as soon as possible. We need to get in touch with Emma and let her know as well, but she's away on business at the moment.'

Doug said, 'Don't worry, I'll stay with John until you can get here, and I'll get his friend Billy's number off him, to see if Billy can come over in the meantime. Bye for now.'

Tommy replied, 'Hopefully see you soon. And thank you - bye.'

Then he went over to Ann and tried to tell her as gently as he could, that John was upset and would need her to be strong. As soon Tommy got through to her, she got him to drive over to the house, so she could be with John.

As time went by, and they came to terms with the situation, Ann and John went together to the court to watch the trials of both Lilly and Steve. When Lilly got five years' probation, they would have preferred her to have been sent to prison but they did accept that she had been tricked into her part by their dad and when their dad got sentenced to twenty-five years, both of them looked at their dad, then got up, turned their backs on him and walked out. They never looked back.

Sam Blake recovered from his heart attack, but didn't want 'his baby' back once he knew how Lilly had come by her. He sold the car and gave the money to a Christian charity, but he and Lilly had dinner with each other every week.

Two years after the court case, Ann and Tommy got married. All their friends were invited, Emma gave Ann away and they held the wedding and their reception at the *Lake Hotel*.

John suggested the venue because the hotel was the last holiday they had in England with their mother. Joan had never completed the deal for the hotel, so John said he would pay for the ceremony and reception as his wedding gift to Ann and Tommy.

When John and Ann went to book the hotel, they were met outside by a very old man who said to them, 'Do you know my name? I know yours, Ann and John.'

They both said at the same time, 'It's Lawrence.'

He said, 'I've been expecting the two of you for some time. Come in.'

Ann and John followed him into the hotel and, as soon as they entered, Ann said to John 'I've got a strange, warm feeling inside of me.'

John said, 'I feel it too.'

Lawrence said, 'That feeling you have is the love of your mother. Eliza has just told me so; they knew that the both of you would be back here one day.'

Printed in Great Britain
by Amazon